KV-638-442

The Spinners' Book of Fiction

The Gregg Press Western Fiction Series
Priscilla Oaks, Editor

The Spinners' Book of Fiction

Gertrude Atherton et al.

with a new introduction by

Priscilla Oaks

Gregg Press

A division of G. K. Hall & Co., Boston, 1979

With the exception of the Introduction, this is a complete photographic reprint of a work first published in San Francisco and New York by Paul Elder and Company in 1907. The trim size of the original hardcover edition was 5¾ by 8⅜ inches.

Frontmatter designed by Designworks, Inc. of Cambridge, Massachusetts.

Printed on permanent/durable acid-free paper and bound in the United States of America.

Republished in 1979 by Gregg Press, A Division of G. K. Hall & Co., 70 Lincoln St., Boston, Massachusetts 02111

First Printing, September 1979

Library of Congress Cataloging in Publication Data

Spinners' Club.
The Spinners' book of fiction.

(The Gregg Press western fiction series)
Reprint of the ed. published by P. Elder, San Francisco.
1. American fiction—California. 2. American fiction—20th century. 3. Western stories. I. Atherton, Gertrude Franklin Horn, 1857–1948. II. Title. III. Series: Gregg Press western fiction series.
PZ1.S757 1979 [PS3571.C2] 813'.01 79-16762
ISBN 0-8398-2582-X

Introduction

THE SPINNERS' BOOK OF FICTION (1907) came into being because of a terrible natural cataclysm, the San Francisco earthquake of April 18, 1906, which crossed energy lines with The Spinners' Club, a group of young, self-styled "Bohemian" society women dedicated to literature and the arts.

Fires from the earthquake burned to the ground the home of Ina Coolbrith, California's first poet laureate, destroying everything she owned, including all of her manuscripts, and the materials for a planned history of California. Coolbrith, an Associate Spinner, along with Gertrude Atherton, and other professional writers, both women and men, was then at the height of her fame. She was much loved in the city and an integral part of the San Francisco literary scene which included Jack London, Frank Norris, Joaquin Miller, Ambrose Bierce, Mary Austin, Mary Halleck Foote, Bret Harte, and Charles Warren Stoddard.

Now homeless, sick with arthritis and unable to work as a librarian, Ina Coolbrith's plight came to the attention of the Spinners then in their tenth year as "an organization for encouragement of creative genius as found in women" (*San Francisco Examiner,* Sunday, November 3, 1907). What better encouragement could the Spinners give to their bereft poet than to raise the funds to build her a new home? What more perfect way for a literary group to raise such funds than to put together a collection of short stories and sell it?

The club's original plan for the book was to have the nonprofessional Spinner members contribute their work. But since a number of America's most famous writers were associates of the society, it was decided to ask them and others to donate short stories and illustrations for *The Spinners' Book of Fiction,* as the book was immediately named.

The group of young women who set about zealously to put together this book were as naive as they were enthusiastic. The resulting social upheavals, at least 8.5 on any literary Richter Scale, were worthy of their cataclysmic predecessor. But regardless of the complications, the Spinners did produce a beautiful volume, still meriting praise not only for its design but for the quality of the writing in it. Most unusual also were the altruistic motivations with which the professionals contributed, without charge, some of their best creative work.

Before describing the authors and the stories that they donated to this book, it is important to explain the Spinners club and the activity of the San Francisco literary groups at the turn of the century. The names on *The Spinners' Book of Fiction* title page connected the collection to every important publication in northern California. These included all the newspapers as well as such famous Western magazines as *The Golden Era,* founded in 1852, two years after California reached statehood, *The Pioneer, The Californian,* and, the most nationally well-known, *The Overland Monthly,* for which Bret Harte, as well as Sam Clemens (Mark Twain), that Easterner from Missouri, wrote.

The lists of contributors to these newspapers and magazines included many professional women writers, who created their own social and cultural clubs when they found themselves excluded from the deep leather chairs of the Union Club, and the Bohemian. Some belonged to the Pacific Coast Women's Press Association. Julia Ward Howe, on lecture tour, inspired the illustrious Century Club whose roster included such important Californian names as Hearst, Sargent, Stanford, Otis, and Bancroft, and whose dedication was to the cultivation of intellect, the arts, and "the advancement of womankind."

The Spinners were organized in 1897 by Ednah Robinson, soon married to Charles S. Aiken, publisher and founder of Southern Pacific's *Sunset Magazine.* The first meetings of the club were held in the Robinsons' barn loft, fixed up with "burlap and pretties," indications of the club's desire to be Bohemian, yet, at the same time, safe.

The original Spinners group grew too big for the barn, and meetings became more elaborate with programs, receptions, and entertainments that were open to society. Before *The Spinners' Book of Fiction* appeared, the club had collected a series of popular toasts, which they were successful in publishing as *Prosit* (1904). The funds were used as a nest egg to start the Ina Coolbrith Relief Fund.

For their second book, the Spinners negotiated a contract with Paul Elder and Company, one of the finest printers in San Francisco, and agreed to receive a 10% royalty for each $2 copy of the book sold, a price selected to bring the book "within the reach of all." When Elder heard of the stellar writers who had agreed to contribute chapters, he insisted upon using the best paper and design, colored illustrations, and an outside binding of "Spinners linen." The club book committee dreamed of raising $10,000!

Ina Donna Coolbrith (1845–1928), the central figure of inspiration for *The Spinners' Book of Fiction,* was the niece and namesake of the Mormon founder, Joseph Smith. She had been christened Josephine Donna Smith, but early a poet, chose "Ina" for herself as more romantic and "Coolbrith" after her mother's family, for her professional name. A plaque at Beckworth Pass states that she was the first white child to cross the pass in a covered wagon in 1854 en route to Los Angeles, then a small pueblo. She became an important part of the San Francisco literary scene as an assistant to editor Bret Harte on *The Overland Monthly,* where she and Charlie Stoddard made so many contributions and all were such good friends that they were nicknamed "The Golden Gate Trinity" and "The Overland Three."

Accepted among the elite because of her charm and her talents, Coolbrith still had to support herself which she did by writing reviews, editing, and serving as librarian for the Oakland Free Public Library and, later, for the Bohemian Club, an organization of newspapermen, who made her their honorary member.

As she grew older, Coolbrith was plagued by ill health. At the time of the San Francisco earthquake, several disasters further undermined her stamina. First, her home was destroyed by the fire. Then she was knocked down by a runaway horse. Finally, the situation involving the Spinners' book fund received such bad press reports that after one she wrote that she had a slight stroke with loss of eyesight for a short time. She was a proud and independent woman and chafed at being depicted as "helpless with illness, lingering and hopeless, and [with] the sort of poverty that is final." (*San Francisco Call,* Sunday Magazine, October 27, 1907.)

Needless to say, no one likes to be labelled hopeless or afflicted with terminal poverty. The Spinners created the conflict which finally broke out in the newspapers because they lacked not only tact but common sense. Carried away with enthusiasm about their grand project, they changed their original plan to help Ina Coolbrith by amending their bylaws to create a permanent fund that would help other writers and artists when they became old, infirm, or simply misfortunate. With the first $1000 they assiduously collected, they bought a railroad bond and then proceeded to pay out to Coolbrith the 5% interest in monthly payments of $4 and some cents.

Gertrude Atherton, who had already donated $200 to the original fund, became so incensed that she decided to teach those "queer cattle"—as she once labelled the Spinners in a letter to Ina—a practical lesson. She organized a gala night of readings at the Fairmont hotel and packed the big ballroom to the doors, raising $1000 that was handed over to Coolbrith in its entirety. Everyone attended including Luther Burbank who fell asleep at the back of the room on some chairs. And, reports Atherton in *My San Francisco* (1946), Joaquin Miller outshone all the other authors in his top boots, lace tie, and flowing white hair and beard. "He recited his poem 'Columbus' with such dramatic fire that when he finished the audience stood up and shouted" (p. 90).

Coolbrith, meanwhile had faced the reality that she would obtain no new home from *The Spinners' Book of Fiction.* She took matters into her own hands and decided to rent a house:

Wanted immediately—Some kind of shelter; rent less than $2000; can search no longer. Address: INA COOLBRITH, 770 Seventeenth, Oakland*

Near the narrow little house at 15 Lincoln Street on Russian Hill that she obtained from this ad is the Ina Coolbrith Park where a bronze plaque with her profile is inscribed "Loved Laurel-Crowned Poet of California."

Personal integrity is important. A newspaper article accused her of being ungrateful to the Spinners, who, themselves, had hired a lawyer to protect their permanent fund from the pressure of Coolbrith's irate friends. There is a receipt in the Bancroft Library (of the University of California at Berkeley) dated November 5, 1908, in which the proud poet put an end to the whole business as far as she was concerned. Eleanor M. Davenport, then Spinners' treasurer, acknowledged in this receipt the return of $90.80, "the sum total of all monies received by said Ina Coolbrith from the Spinners Benefit Fund."

One final communication from the Spinners to Ina Coolbrith concerned the book's royalties. In a statement dated May 24, 1912, five years after publication, Paul Elder reported the following:

Printed 372 copies
1 review copy
3 damaged
5 returned to binder
1 sold below cost
113 copies on hand
249 sold.

The club's royalties of ten percent from *The Spinners' Book of Fiction* totalled $49.80.

Regardless of the backbiting and tensions that swirled around funding the Spinners' book, production of the collection of short stories was flawless. Possibly to avoid argument, the selections donated were printed alphabetically by author. The authors chose well and the tales and narratives are lively and dramatic in presentation. With two exceptions, all take

*Josephine Rhodehamel, *Ina Coolbrith, Librarian and Laureate of California* (Provo, Utah: Brigham Young University Press, 1973), p. 264.

place in the West, with emphasis upon California or places touched by the Pacific Ocean.

Values and attitudes in several of the stories seem dated today; but they clearly reflect the radical elite group of writers that lived in San Francisco before World War I. There are tinges of racism here and there in the speech of the characters. But that is more than counterbalanced by a number of stories which feature the decency and heroism of nonwhite peoples, such as Eleanor Gates' **"A Yellow Man and a White."** The worst bigot in the book is also the villain in Herman Whitaker's **"The Tewana."** Stories by women writers show heroines that are independent and sturdy and equipped with wit, humor, and intelligence.

The dedication poem, completely out of style today because of its sentimentalism and vocabulary, was written by one of the founders of Carmel's Bohemian colony, George Sterling (1869–1926). Handsome and well-regarded, Jack London used to call him "Greek" and he, in turn, labelled Jack "Wolf." Atherton reports in *My San Francisco* that when Mary Austin's long hair became tangled in the leaves and twigs of the trees where she liked to sit and write, it was Sterling who scrambled up and helped her down. Friends were shocked when he committed suicide by swallowing poison.

Gertrude Atherton (1857–1948) had a long career both as a writer and society leader of the San Francisco scene. Generous, as always, she created an original tale for *The Spinners' Book of Fiction*. The historically valid story of the nun, Sister Dominica, was later reprinted with Atherton's biographical romance, *Rezánov* (1906), the story of the handsome count who arrived aboard the first Russian ship to sail into the Bay in 1806 and fell in love with the exquisite Concepcion Argüello, daughter of the Presidio Comandante. It is she who became **"Concha Argüello, Sister Dominica."**

Like the above, Mary Hunter Austin's (1868–1934) tale of competition and murder, **"The Ford of Crèvecoeur,"** is also a dramatic monologue, the confession of a simple French immigrant shepherd. This is not Austin's usual Indian desert account, but it is a pastorale, nonetheless, even though it shows the violence latent in Arcadia, both in the tempers of men and in the land itself, with its floods and quicksands.

Geraldine Bonner's (1870–?) "**A Californian**" is completely different in tone from the first two stories. A drama critic and novelist about California, whose best known work was a mining novel, *Hard Pan* (1900), also a pen name that she used, Bonner here shows the social pressures put upon the daughter of a newly rich San Francisco family. Genevieve has more of the rough and ready Barney Ryan in her than she has of her pretentious mother who wants her to marry a title. In the same gutsy tradition of the early California Spanish women who broke colts and lassoed cattle with their brothers, this heroine takes the initiative in solving her problem.

Recently rediscovered, Mary Halleck Foote (1847–1938) was as well known for her illustrations as for her writing about Western and Mexican life. Like her first novel, *Led Horse Claim* (1883), "**Gideon's Knock**" also uses a mining camp locale, in this case for a ghost story told before the fire.

Another writer about Western life, Eleanor Gates (1875–1951) became a newspaperwoman after her graduation from Stanford and the University of California. Her novel *The Poor Little Rich Girl* (1912) became so popular that she dramatized it for a play that had a long run.

Set in the mining camp, Whiskey town, "**A Yellow Man and a White**" contrasts the corruption of Anthony Barrett with the astute humanity of an unpretentious but exotic Chinese herb doctor and scholar, against a background of exploitive coolie labor. Cleverly, Gates exposes the racial and class values of the white couple and highlights the wife's struggles with her biases and her enlightment about her husband's addiction, assisted by the compassionate Fong Wu.

James Hopper's (1876–1956) story, "**The Judgement of Man,**" reflects his interest in athletics and adventure and comes from his collection about the Philippines, *Caybigan* (1906). Hopper, a founder of Carmel's literary colony, wrote over 500 freelance tales. In this character study of Miller, introduced as a repulsive coward and thief, Hopper uses local color in scene and dialogue and creates a fast pace of action to make the tale engrossing until the tricky sentimental end.

Jack London (1876–1916) was also an athlete and adventurer, and he, too contributed a local color story about Imber, an old Indian of the Yukon territory, on trial for his life **("The**

League of the Old Men"). Through his confession, London skillfully traces the entire history of Indian-white relationships showing how they ruined Imber's tribe and drove him to murder. The story poses the question of what justice really is.

(Frank) Bailey Millard (1859–1941), city editor of two San Francisco newspapers, has created a funny dialectic story with a Sierra lumber camp background, "**Down the Flume with the Sneath Piano.**" Jess will marry Jud if he can bring a "pianner" for her down the flume. He doesn't keep the pianner from falling over the cliff, but they marry anyway, another pianner in the offing. Similarly light and sentimental is drama critic Mirian Michelson's (1870–1942) "**The Contumacy of Sarah L. Walker.**" Here, an old lady violates the rules of the Old People's Home by feeding crumbs to birds and allowing them to flutter into her room in cold weather. Human understanding helps overcome both disobedience and loneliness.

William Chambers Morrow's (1853–1923) "**Breaking Through**" deals with the conquest over fear by an odd and disruptive 14-year-old boy. It is a disquieting, moody story involving violence as a cure-all for discipline and hostile behavior.

Frank Norris, who died after an appendicitis operation in 1902, has also created an atmosphere piece in this posthumous story, "**A Lost Story,**" which is, at times, satiric in tone. Rosella is sensitive, refined, and delicately constructed, as is her writing style. She is a publisher's reader in New York, who dreams of fame as a writer. Norris puts in passages from the manuscripts that she turns down with relish as he shows up the various writing styles of the day. Rosella's moral dilemma occurs when another writer turns in a story similar in concept to the one she is working on herself and she rejects it. But she is not tough and this act causes her to write her own story in a dispirited way that ruins it.

"**Hantu**" by Henry Milner Rideout (1877–1927) and "**A Little Savage Gentleman**" by Isabel (Field) Strong (1968–1947) are both exotic tales, one of the Orient, the other about Samoa. Rideout, a specialist in sea stories, both of the New England coast and the Pacific, recounts a ghost encounter. Isabel Strong, stepdaughter of Robert Lewis Stevenson, has written a sketch of her life at Vailima, Stevenson's Samoan estate. True or not, it reads as an anecdotal narrative.

The longest story in *The Spinners' Book of Fiction* is "**Miss Juno**" by Charles Warren Stoddard (1843–1909). Stoddard based his story on people and places that he knew well. Miss Juno was actually Constance Fletcher, a young San Franciscan, Mme. Lillian was Mrs. Lillian Clapp, and Harry English was Harry Edwards, who lived on Telegraph Hill. Stoddard wrote to Mrs. Wilson, of the Spinners:

> I'm glad you like Miss Juno! I do! She is a regular boy's girl and the young man's best companion because there is no nonsense about her. Did I tell you the sequel to Miss Juno? Robert Browning introduced her to Lord Wentworth, or vice versa, who engaged himself to her. Lord Wentworth [grandson of Lord Byron by his daughter Ada] . . . was a widower and as mad as his grandfather, but with no excuse for being anything of the sort. An enemy of Miss Juno, a lady much in vogue in the sixties, seventies, and eighties in Rome, now dead some years, told Wentworth that the mother of Miss Juno was a divorced lady. He at once wrote a brutal letter to her announcing that the engagement was off. She nearly died of brain fever and has never married. *Sic* passion. (From a review of the book in the *San Francisco Call,* October 27, 1907).

With this information, it is fascinating to see what Stoddard does to his plot.

Richard Walton Tully (1887–1945) was married to Eleanor Gates, introduced previously, and is best known for his coauthorship with David Belasco of the play, *Rose of the Rancho* (1906). His story, "**Love and Advertising,**" with its New York setting, is light and frivolous, poking fun at the advertising business, and also demonstrating how to marry your way to the top.

The last short story, "The Tewana," by Herman Whitaker (1867–1919), the novelist, Socialist leader, and friend of Jack London and Joaquin Miller, sums up many of the themes and settings of the collection. A primitive Tewanan maiden, deep-breasted and golden-hued, as in many male fantasies, is bathing in the river in Tehuantepec, innocent and naked as if it were Eden. Enter the gringo, the mining engineer Paul Steiner, a dull conventional German-American, reprsenting the colonial mentality described in "The League of the Old Men." Male foil to him is the artist Bachelder, who represents the decent moral perspective demonstrated in many of the Spinner stories, but who is cut from the same cloth, being passive in allowing the exploitation of native women to go on. His only action as an artist is to lock up his two masterpieces because they made his heart ache: one showing a woman sold in payment of debts, and Andrea and her child kneeling at a church altar. Paul is correct when he states: " 'It was a beastliness that we committed—' " (p. 356).

Steiner "marries" Andrea, fathers her child and then departs on assignments that bring him back several years later with his legitimate wife Ethel, sweet and "intellectual without loss of femininity" (p. 355). He is seeking to take his daughter away with a parental coldness similar to the father's attitudes in "Breaking Through." However, the child is already dead.

But nature intervenes in the form of a terrible flood. Ethel is trapped in her room and Andrea, tall and active as Genevieve and Miss Juno swims through the pouring waters to rescue the wife just in time. Ethel, of course, cannot swim and is in a panic, nearly drowning Andrea. But the primitive woman is strong and heroic. Almost ashore, however, she sees Paul and suddenly understands everything. Like the French shepherd, she exacts her revenge; like Concha Argüello, she buries herself from time, forever true to her original love. Acknowledging her betrayal and her grief, she dives deep into the flood, carrying down the senseless bride. Later, the jungle, equally melodramatic, wreathes over their twin graves, not with the rose and the briar, but the morning glory and the orchid.

As pure entertainment and as real and fictional social document, *The Spinners' Book of Fiction* is a fascinating study. The writers and their stories say much about the literary achievement on the West Coast at the turn of the century, and their concern for society. Threaded through many of the stories is the theme of the interrelationship between the Anglo imperialist and the native peoples with whom he came in contact. This is a subject treated in the Pacifica stories as well as in the California stories. Most interestingly, in these stories about California, in a time of great prejudice against the "yellow peril," the writers in *The Spinners' Book of Fiction* show sympathy towards the various immigrant groups and their problems in becoming Americans.

For this reason, *The Spinners' Book of Fiction* is important not just for the style and excellence of most of its stories, but also as a precursor of the concept of the melting pot which became a symbol of the United States after World War I.

Priscilla Oaks
Laguna Beach, California

SAN FRANCISCO, CALIFORNIA

Greetings:

In the holocaust that has come to San Francisco none have suffered more than the writers, artists, and musicians. Their incomes are permanently reduced or cut off, for, until the city has been reconstructed, there will be little leisure for the enjoyment of art.

Ina Coolbrith, who with Mark Twain, Bret Harte, Joaquin Miller, and Charles Warren Stoddard, was among the first Californians to achieve distinction in literature, has been made homeless by the great fire. Her treasures, her valuable correspondence with Whittier, Longfellow, Booth, Lowell, Emerson, and the more intimate friendship letters of the early Californians including William Keith and John Muir, were destroyed. Even her manuscripts were not saved. Miss Coolbrith had been ill for a month and it was with difficulty that she escaped with her companion, who carried but a few necessities.

The Spinners have therefore undertaken to raise a fund, the income of which is to go first to Miss Coolbrith as long as she shall live, and afterward to any other San Francisco writer, artist, or musician whom the trustees shall find in need of it.

They have established a loan fund of $1,000 from which the members of the club can draw to relieve temporary needs, but they have started the permanent "Coolbrith Fund" with a contribution of $200, and it is hoped the whole sum of $10,000 or more can be raised immediately. Will you, as a club or an individual, contribute toward this fund as soon as possible? The amount can be paid in installments during the year 1906-07 if it will be more convenient to do so.

Knowing that you will be glad to aid in paying this international tribute to Ina Coolbrith, whose songs of California are world famous,

Loyally yours,

The Spinners.

COMMITTEE:

MISS MARY BELL
MISS GRACE LEWELLYN JONES
MISS SARA DEAN
MISS ELEANOR DAVENPORT
TREASURER
1981 Pacific Avenue

The Spinners also announce the publication of a book, the proceeds of its sale to go toward the Ina Coolbrith Fund. It will be a collection of California stories and verse by California writers and illustrated by California artists. It is to be known as "The Spinners' Book."

TO INA D. COOLBRITH

With wilder sighing in the pine
The wind went by, and so I dreamed;
And in that dusk of sleep it seemed
A city by the sea was mine.

No statelier sprang the walls of Tyre
From seaward cliff or stable hill;
And light and music met to fill
The splendid courts of her desire—

(Extolling chords that cried her praise,
And golden reeds whose mellow moan
Was like an ocean's undertone
Dying and lost on forest ways).

But sweeter far than any sound
That rang or rippled in her halls,
Was one beyond her eastern walls,
By summer gardens girdled round.

'Twas from a nightingale, and oh!
The song it sang hath never word!
Sweeter it seemed than Love's, first-heard,
Or lutes in Aidenn murmuring low.

Faint, as when drowsy winds awake
A sisterhood of faery bells,
It won reply from hidden dells,
Loyal to Echo for its sake.

I dreamt I slept, but cannot say
How many dreamland seasons fled,
Nor what horizon of the dead
Gave back my dream's uncertain day.

But still beside the toiling sea
I lay, and saw—for walls o'ergrown—
The city that was mine had known
Time's sure and ancient treachery.

Above her ramparts, broad as Tyre's,
The grasses' mounting army broke;
The shadow of the sprawling oak
Usurpt the splendor of her fires.

But o'er the fallen marbles pale
I heard, like elfin melodies
Blown over from enchanted seas,
The music of the nightingale.

George Sterling.

THE STORIES

THE ILLUSTRATIONS

WHEREFORE?

Wherefore this book of fiction by Californian writers? And why its appeal otherwise than that of obvious esthetic and literary qualities? They who read what follows will know.

The fund, which the sale of this book is purposed to aid, was planned by The Spinners soon after the eighteenth of April, 1906, and was started with two hundred dollars from their treasury. To this, Mrs. Gertrude Atherton added another two hundred dollars. Several women's clubs and private individuals also generously responded, so that now there is a thousand dollars to the credit of the fund. A bond has been bought and the interest from it will be paid to Ina D. Coolbrith, the poet, and first chosen beneficiary of the fund. The Spinners feel assured that this book will meet with such a ready sale as to make possible the purchase of several bonds, and so render the accruing interest a steady source of aid to Miss Coolbrith.

All who have read and fallen under the charm of her "Songs from the Golden Gate," or felt the beauty and tenderness of the verses "When the Grass Shall Cover Me," will, without question, unite in making "assurance doubly sure" to such end.

From the days of the old Overland Monthly, *when she worked side by side with Bret Harte and Charles Warren Stoddard, to the present moment, Miss Coolbrith's name has formed a part of the literary history of San Francisco.*

The eighteenth of April, 1906, and the night which followed it, left her bereft of all literary, and other, treasures; but her poem bearing the refrain, "Lost city of my love and my desire," rings with the old genius, and expresses the feeling of many made desolate by the destruction of the city which held their most cherished memories.

When Miss Coolbrith shall no longer need to be a beneficiary of the fund, it is intended that it shall serve to aid some other writer, artist or musician whose fortunes are at the ebb.

To the writers, artists and publishers who have so heartily and generously made this book possible, The Spinners return unmeasured thanks.

San Francisco, June 22, 1907.

CONCHA ARGÜELLO, SISTER DOMINICA

BY

GERTRUDE ATHERTON

Dedicated to Carolina Ximéno

Written for The Spinners' Book of Fiction

CONCHA ARGÜELLO, SISTER DOMINICA

ISTER TERESA had wept bitterly for two days. The vanity for which she did penance whenever her madonna loveliness, consummated by the white robe and veil of her novitiate, tempted her to one of the little mirrors in the pupil's dormitory, was powerless to check the blighting flow. There had been moments when she had argued that her vanity had its rights, for had it not played its part in weaning her from the world?—that wicked world of San Francisco, whose very breath, accompanying her family on their monthly visits to Benicia, made her cross herself and pray that all good girls whom fate had stranded there should find the peace and shelter of Saint Catherine of Siena. It was true that before Sister Dominica toiled up Rincon Hill on that wonderful day—here her sobs became so violent that Sister María Sal, praying beside her with a face as swollen as her own, gave her a sharp poke in the ribs, and she pressed her hands to her mouth lest she be marched away. But her thoughts flowed on; she could pray no more. Sister Dominica, with her romantic history and holy life, her halo of fame in the young country, and her unconquerable beauty—she had never seen such eyelashes, never, never!—

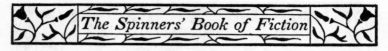

what was she thinking of at such a time? She had never believed that such divine radiance could emanate from any mortal; never had dreamed that beauty and grace could be so enhanced by a white robe and a black veil—— Oh, well! Her mind was in a rebellious mood; it had been in leash too long. And what of it for once in a way? No ball dress she had ever seen in the gay disreputable little city—where the good citizens hung the bad for want of law—was half as becoming as the habit of the Dominican nun, and if it played a part in weaning frivolous girls from the world, so much more to the credit of Rome. God knew she had never regretted her flight up the bays, and even had it not been for the perfidy of—she had forgotten his name; that at least was dead!—she would have realized her vocation the moment Sister Dominica sounded the call. When the famous nun, with that passionate humility all her own, had implored her to renounce the world, protested that her vocation was written in her face—she really looked like a juvenile mater dolorosa, particularly when she rolled up her eyes—eloquently demanded what alternative that hideous embryo of a city could give her—that rude and noisy city that looked as if it had been tossed together in a night after one of its periodical fires, where the ill-made sidewalks tripped the unwary foot, or the winter mud was like a swamp, where the alarm bell summoned the Vigilance Committee day and night to protect or avenge, where a coarse and impertinent set of adventurers stared at and followed an inoffensive nun who only left the holy calm of the convent at the command of the Bishop to rescue brands from

the burning; then had Teresa, sick with the tragedy of youth, an enchanting vision of secluded paths, where nuns—in white—walked with downcast eyes and folded hands; of the daily ecstasy of prayer in the convent chapel misty with incense.

And in some inscrutable way Sister Dominica during that long conversation, while Mrs. Grace and her other daughters dispensed egg-nog in the parlor—it was New Year's Day—had made the young girl a part of her very self, until Teresa indulged the fancy that without and within she was a replica of that Concha Arguello of California's springtime; won her heart so completely that she would have followed her not only into the comfortable and incomparably situated convent of the saint of Siena, but barefooted into that wilderness of Soledad where the Indians still prayed for their lost "Beata." It was just eight months tonight since she had taken her first vows, and she had been honestly aware that there was no very clear line of demarcation in her fervent young mind between her love of Sister Dominica and her love of God. Tonight, almost prostrate before the coffin of the dead nun, she knew that so far at least all the real passion of her youth had flowed in an undeflected tide about the feet of that remote and exquisite being whose personal charm alone had made a convent possible in the chaos that followed the discovery of gold. All the novices, many of the older nuns, the pupils invariably, worshipped Sister Dominica; whose saintliness without austerity never chilled them, but whose tragic story and the impression she made of already dwelling in a heaven of her own, notwithstanding her sweet and consistent humanity, placed her on a pinnacle where any display of affection would have been unseemly. Only once, after the beautiful ceremony of taking the white veil was over, and Teresa's senses were faint from incense and hunger, ecstasy and a new and exquisite terror, Sister Dominica had led her to her cell and kissing her lightly on the brow, exclaimed that she had never been happier in a conquest for the Church against the vileness of the world. Then she had dropped the conventional speech of her calling, and said with an expression that made her look so young, so curiously virginal, that the novice had held her breath: "Remember that here there is nothing to interrupt the life of the imagination, nothing to change its course, like the thousand conflicting currents that batter memory and character to pieces in the world. In this monotonous round of duty and prayer the mind is free, the heart remains ever young, the soul unspotted; so that when——" She had paused, hesitated a moment, then abruptly left the room, and Teresa had wept a torrent in her disappointment that this first of California's heroines—whose place in history and romance was assured—had not broken her reserve and told her all that story of many versions. She had begged Sister María Sal—the sister of Luis Argüello's first wife—to tell it her, but the old nun had reproved her sharply for sinful curiosity and upon one occasion boxed her ears. But tonight she might be in a softer mood, and Teresa resolved that when the last rites were over she would make her talk of Concha Argüello.

A few moments later she was lifted to her feet by a shaking but still powerful arm.

"Come!" whispered Sister María. "It is time to prepare. The others have gone. It is singular that the oldest and the youngest should have loved her best. Ay! Dios de mi alma! I never thought that Concha Argüello would die. Grow old she never did, in spite of the faded husk. We will look at her once more."

The dead nun in her coffin lay in the little parlor where she had turned so many wavering souls from fleeting to eternal joys. Her features, wasted during years of delicate health, seemed to regain something of their youth in the soft light of the candles. Or was it the long black eyelashes that hid the hollows beneath the eyes?—or the faint mysterious almost mocking smile? Had the spirit in its eternal youth paused in its flight to stamp a last sharp impress upon the prostrate clay? Never had she looked so virginal, and that had been one of the most arresting qualities of her always remarkable appearance; but there was something more—Teresa held her breath. Somehow, dead and in her coffin, she looked less saintly than in life; although as pure and sweet, there was less of heavenly peace on those marble features than of some impassioned human hope. Teresa excitedly whispered her unruly thoughts to Sister María, but instead of the expected reproof the old nun lifted her shoulders.

"Perhaps," she said. "Who knows?"

It was Christmas eve and all the inmates of the convent paused in their sorrow to rejoice in the happy portent of the death and burial of one whom they loyally believed to be no less entitled to beatification than Catherine herself. Her miracles may not have been of the irreducible protoplastic order, but they had been miracles to the practical Californian mind, notwithstanding, and worthy of the attention of consistory and Pope. Moreover, this was the season when all the vivacity and gaiety of her youth had revived, and she made merry, not only for the children left at the convent by their nomadic parents, but for all the children of the town, whatever the faith of their somewhat anxious elders.

An hour after sundown they carried the bier on which her coffin rested into the chapel. It was a solemn procession that none, taking part, was likely to forget, and stirred the young hearts at least with an ecstatic desire for a life as saintly as this that hardly had needed the crown of death.

Following the bier was the cross-bearer, holding the emblem so high it was half lost in the shadows. Behind her were the young scholars dressed in black, then the novices in their white robes and veils, carrying lighted tapers to symbolize the eternal radiance that awaited the pure in spirit. The nuns finished the procession that wound its way slowly through the long ill-lighted corridors, chanting the litany of the dead. From the chapel, at first almost inaudible, but waxing louder every moment, came the same solemn monotonous chant; for the Bishop and his assistants were already at the altar. . . .

Teresa, from the organ loft, looked eagerly down upon the beautiful scene, in spite of the exaltation that filled her: her artistic sense was the one individuality she possessed. The chapel was aglow with

the soft radiance of many wax candles. They stood in high candelabra against the somber drapery on the walls, and there were at least a hundred about the coffin on its high catafalque before the altar; the Argüellos were as prodigal as of old. About the catafalque was an immense mound of roses from the garden of the convent, and palms and pampas from the ranch of Santiago Argüello in the south. The black-robed scholars knelt on one side of the dead, the novices on the other, the relatives and friends behind. But art had perfected itself in the gallery above the lower end of the chapel. This also was draped with black which seemed to absorb, then shed forth again the mystic brilliance of the candles; and kneeling, well apart, were the nuns in their ivory white robes and black veils, their banded softened features as composed and peaceful as if their own reward had come.

The Bishop and the priests read the Requiem Mass, the little organ pealed the *De Profundis* as if inspired; and when the imperious triumphant music of Handel followed, Teresa's fresh young soprano seemed, to her excited imagination, to soar to the gates of heaven itself. When she looked down again the lights were dim in the incense, her senses swam in the pungent odor of spices and gum. The Bishop was walking about the catafalque casting holy water with a brush against the coffin above. He walked about a second time swinging the heavy copper censer, then pronounced the *Requiescat in pace*, "dismissing," as we find inscribed in the convent records, "a tired soul out of all the storms of life into the divine tranquillity of death."

The bier was again shouldered, the procession re-formed, and marched, still with lighted tapers and chanting softly, out into the cemetery of the convent. It was a magnificent, clear night and as mild as spring. Below the steep hill the little town of Benicia celebrated the eve of Christmas with lights and noise. Beyond, the water sparkled like running silver under the wide beams of the moon poised just above the peak of Monte Diablo, the old volcano that towered high above this romantic and beautiful country of water and tule lands, steep hillsides and canons, rocky bluffs overhanging the straits. In spite of the faint discords that rose from the town and the slow tolling of the convent bell, it was a scene of lofty and primeval grandeur, a fit setting for the last earthly scene of a woman whose lines had been cast in the wilderness, but yet had found the calm and the strength and the peace of the old mountain, with its dead and buried fires.

The grave closed, the mourners returned to the convent, but not in order. At the door Teresa felt her arm taken possession of by a strong hand with which she had had more than one disconcerting encounter.

"Let us walk," said Sister María Sal in her harsh but strong old voice. "I have permission. I must talk of Concha tonight or I should burst. It is not for nothing one keeps silent for years and years. I at least am still human. And you loved her the best and have spoiled your pretty face with weeping. You must not do that again, for the young love a pretty nun and will follow her into the one true life on earth far sooner than an ugly old phiz like mine."

Sister María, indeed, retained not an index of the beauty with which tradition accredited her youth. She was a stout unwieldy old woman with a very red face covered half over with black down, and in the bright moonlight Teresa could see the three long hairs that stood out straight from a mole above her mouth and scratched the girls when she kissed them. Tonight her nose was swollen and her eyes looked like appleseeds. Teresa hastily composed her features and registered a vow that in her old age she would look like Sister Dominica, not like that. She had heard that Concha, too, had been frivolous in her youth, and had not she herself a tragic bit of a story? True, her youthful love-tides had turned betimes from the grave beside the Mission Dolores to the lovely nun and the God of both, and she had heard that Dona Concha had proved her fidelity to a wonderful Russian throughout many years before she took the veil. Perhaps — who knew?—her more conformable pupil might have restored the worthless to her heart before he was knifed in the full light of day on Montgomery Street by one from whom he had won more than thousands the night before; perhaps have consoled herself with another less eccentric, had not Sister Dominica sought her at the right moment and removed her from the temptations of the world. Well, never mind, she could at least be a good nun and an amiable instructor of youth, and if she never looked like a living saint she would grow soberer and nobler with the years and take care that she grew not stout and red.

For a time Sister María did not speak, but walked rapidly and heavily up and down the path, dragging her companion with her and staring out at the beauty of the night. But suddenly she slackened her pace and burst into speech.

"Ay yi! Ay de mi! To think that it is nearly half a century—forty-two years to be precise—for will it not be 1858 in one more week?—since Rezánov sailed out through what Frémont has called 'The Golden Gate'! And forty-one in March since he died—not from the fall of a horse, as Sir George Simpson (who had not much regard for the truth anyway, for he gave a false picture of our Concha), and even Doctor Langsdorff, who should have known better, wrote it, but worn out, worn out, after terrible hardships, and a fever that devoured him inch by inch. And he was so handsome when he left us! Dios de mi alma! never have I seen a man like that. If I had I should not be here now, perhaps, so it is as well. But never was I even engaged, and when permission came from Madrid for the marriage of my sister Rafaella with Luis Argüello—he was an officer and could not marry without a special license from the King, and through some strange oversight he was six long years getting it—; well, I lived with them and took care of the children until Rafaella—Ay yi! what a good wife she made him, for he 'toed the mark,' as the Americans say—; well, she died, and one of those days he married another; for will not men be men? And Luis was a good man in spite of all, a fine loyal clever man, who deserves the finest monument in the cemetery of the Mission Dolores—as they call it now. The Americans have no respect for anything and will not say San Francisco de Assisi, for it is too long and they have time for nothing but the gold. Were it not a sin, how I should hate them, for they have stolen our country from us—but no, I will not; and, to be sure, if Rezánov had lived he would have had it first, so what difference? Luis, at least, was spared. He died in 1830—and was the first Governor of Alta California after Mexico threw off the yoke of Spain. He had power in full measure and went before these upstart conquerors came to humble the rest of us into the dust. Peace to his ashes—but perhaps you care nothing for this dear brother of my youth, never heard of him before—such a giddy thing you were; although at the last earthquake the point of his monument flew straight into the side of the church and struck there, so you may have heard the talk before they put it back in its place. It is of Sister Dominica you think, but I think not only of her but of those old days—Ay, Dios de mi! Who remembers that time but a few old women like myself?

"Concha's father, Don José Dario Argüello, was Commandante of the Presidio of San Francisco then; and there was nothing else to call San Francisco but the Mission. Down at Yerba Buena, where the Americans flaunt themselves, there was but a Battery that could not give even a dance. But we had dances at the Presidio; day and night the guitar tinkled and the fiddles scraped; for what did we know of care, or old age, or convents or death? I was many years younger than Rafaella and did not go to the grand balls, but to the little dances, yes, many and many. When the Russians came—it was in 1806—I saw them every day, and one night danced with Rezánov himself. He was so gay—

ay de mi! I remember he swung me quite off my feet and made as if he would throw me in the air. I was angry that he should treat me like a baby, and then he begged me so humbly to forgive him, although his eyes laughed, that of course I did. He had come down from Sitka to try and arrange for a treaty with the Spanish government that the poor men in the employ of the Russian-American Company might have breadstuffs to eat and not die of scurvy, nor toil through the long winter with no flesh on their bones. He brought a cargo with him to exchange for our corn and flour meanwhile. We had never seen any one so handsome and so grand and he turned all our heads, but he had a hard time with the Governor and Don José—there are no such Californians now or the Americans would never have got us—and it took all his diplomacy and all the help Concha and the priests could give him before he got his way, for there was a law against trading with foreigners. It was only when he and Concha became engaged that Governor Arillaga gave in—how I pick up vulgar expressions from these American pupils, I who should reform them! And did I not stand Ellen O'Reilley in the corner yesterday for calling San Francisco 'Frisco'?—*San Francisco de Assisi!* But all the saints have fled from California.

"Where was I? Forgive an old woman's rambling, but I have not told stories since Rafaella's children grew up, and that was many years ago. What do I talk here? You know. And I that used to love to talk. Ay yi! But no one can say that I am not a good nun. Bishop Alemany has said it and no one

knows better than he, the holy man. But for him I might be sitting all day on a corridor in the south sunning myself like an old crocodile, for we had no convent till he came eight years ago; and perhaps but for Concha, whom I always imitated, I might have a dozen brats of my own, for I was pretty and had my wooers and might have been persuaded. And God knows, since I must have the care of children, I prefer they should be mothered by some one else, for then I have always the hope to be rid of them the sooner. Well, well! I am not a saint yet, and when I go to heaven I suppose Concha will still shake her finger at me with a smile. Not that she was ever self-righteous, our Concha. Not a bit of it. Only after that long and terrible waiting she just naturally became a saint. Some are made that way and some are not. That is all.

"Did I tell you about the two young lieutenants that came with Baron Rezánov? Davidov and Khostov their names were. Well, well, I shall tell all tonight. I was but fourteen, but what will you? Was I not, then, Spanish? It was Davidov. He always left the older people to romp with the children, although I think there was a flame in his heart for Concha. Perhaps had I been older—who knows? Do not look at my whiskers! That was forty-two years ago. Well, I dreamed of the fair kind young Russian for many a night after he left, and when my time came to marry I would look at none of the caballeros, but nursed Rafaella's babies and thought my thoughts. And then—in 1815 I think it was—the good—and ugly—Dr. Langsdorff sent Luis a copy of his book—he had been surgeon to his excellency—and alas! it told of the terrible end of both those gay kind young men. They were always too fond of brandy; we knew that, but we never—well, hear me! One night not so many years after they sailed away from California, they met Dr. Langsdorff and another friend of their American days, Captain D'Wolf, by appointment in St. Petersburg for a grand reunion. They were all so happy! Perhaps it was that made them too much 'celebrate,' as the Americans say in their dialect. Well, alas! they celebrated until four in the morning, and then my two dear young Russians—for I loved Khostov as a sister, so devoted he was to my friend—well, they started—on foot—for home, and that was on the other side of the Neva. They had almost crossed the bridge when they suddenly took it into their heads that they wanted to see their friends again, and started back. Alas, in the middle of the bridge was a section that opened to permit the passage of boats with tall masts. The night was dark and stormy. The bridge was open. They did not see it. The river was roaring and racing like a flood. A sailor saw them fall, and then strike back for the coming boat. Then he saw them no more. That was the last of my poor friends.

"And we had all been so gay, so gay! For how could we know? All the Russians said that never had they seen a people so light-hearted and frolicking as the Californians, so hospitable, so like one great family. And we were, we were. But you know of that time. Was not your mother Conchitita Castro, if she did marry an American and has not taught you ten words of Spanish? It is of Concha you would hear, and I ramble. Well, who knows? perhaps I hesitate. Rezánov was of the Greek Church. No priest in California would have married them even had Don José—*el santo* we called him—given his consent. It was for that reason Rezanov went to obtain a dispensation from His Holiness and a license from the King of Spain. Concha knew that he could not return for two years or nearly that, nor even send her a letter; for why should ships come down from Sitka until the treaty was signed? Only Rezánov could get what he wanted, law or no law. And then too our Governor had forbidden the British and Bostonians—so we called the Americans in those days—to enter our ports. This Concha knew, and when one knows one can think in storeys, as it were, and put the last at the top. It is not so bad as the hope that makes the heart thump every morning and the eyes turn into fountains at night. Dios! To think that I should ever have shed a tear over a man. Chinchosas, all of them. However—I think Concha, who was never quite as others, knew deep down in her heart that he would not come back, that it was all too good to be true. Never was a man seen as handsome as that one, and so clever—a touch of the devil in his cleverness, but that may have been because he was a Russian. I know not. And to be a great lady in St. Petersburg, and later—who can tell?—vice-Tsarina of all this part of the world! No, it could not be. It was a fairy tale. I only wonder that the bare possibility came into the life of any woman,—and that a maiden of New Spain, in an unknown corner, that might as well have been on Venus or Mars.

"But Concha had character. She was not one to go into a decline—although I am woman enough to know that her pillow was wet many nights; and besides she lost the freshness of her beauty. She was often as gay as ever, but she cared less and less for the dance, and found more to do at home. Don José was made Commandante of the Santa Barbara Company that same year, and it was well for her to be in a place where there were no memories of Rezánov. But late in the following year as the time approached for his return, or news of him, she could not contain her impatience. We all saw it—I was visiting the Pachecos in the Presidio of Santa Barbara. She grew so thin. Her eyes were never still. We knew. And then!—how many times she climbed to the fortress—it was on that high bluff beside the channel—and stared out to sea—when 1808 and the Spring had come—for hours together: Rezánov was to return by way of Mexico. Then, when I went back to San Francisco soon after, she went with me, and again she would watch the sea from the summit of Lone Mountain, as we call it now. In spite of her reason she hoped, I suppose; for that is the way of women. Or perhaps she only longed for the word from Sitka that would tell her the worst and have done with it. Who knows? She never said, and we dared not speak of it. She was always very sweet, our Concha, but there never was a time when you could take a liberty with her.

"No ship came, but something else did—an earthquake! Ay yi, what an earthquake that was! Not a *temblor* but a *terremoto*. The whole Presidio came down. I do not know now how we saved all the

"She was always very sweet,
our Concha, but there never was a time when
you could take a liberty
with her."

From a Painting by Lillie V. O'Ryan.

babies, but we always flew to the open with a baby under each arm the moment an earthquake began, and in the first seconds even this was not so bad. The wall about the Presidio was fourteen feet high and seven feet thick and there were solid trunks of trees crossed inside the adobe. It looked like a heap of dirt, nothing more. Luis was riding up from the Battery of Yerba Buena and his horse was flung down and he saw the sand-dunes heaving toward him like waves in a storm and shiver like quicksilver. And there was a roar as if the earth had dropped and the sea gone after. Ay California! And to think that when Luis wrote a bitter letter to Governor Arillaga in Monterey, the old Mexican wrote back that he had felt earthquakes himself and sent him a box of dates for consolation! Well—we slept on the ground for two months and cooked out-of-doors, for we would not go even into the Mission—which had not suffered—until the earthquakes were over; and if the worst comes first there are plenty after—and, somehow, harder to bear. Perhaps to Concha that terrible time was a God-send, for she thought no more of Rezánov for a while. If the earthquake does not swallow your body it swallows your little self. You are a flea. Just that and nothing more.

"But after a time all was quiet again; the houses were rebuilt and Concha went back to Santa Barbara. By that time she knew that Rezánov would never come, although it was several years before she had a word. Such stories have been told that she did not know of his death for thirty years! Did not Baránhov, Chief-manager of the Russian-Alaskan Company up there at Sitka, send Koskov—that name was so like!—to Bodega Bay in 1812, and would he fail to send such news with him? Was not Dr. Langsdorff's book published in 1814? Did not Kotzbue, who was on his excellency's staff during the embassy to Japan, come to us in 1816, and did we not talk with him every day for a month? Did not Rezánov's death spoil all Russia's plans in this part of the world—perhaps, who knows? alter the course of her history? It is likely we were long without hearing the talk of the North! Such nonsense! Yes, she knew it soon enough, but as that good Padre Abella once said to us, she had the making of the saint and the martyr in her, and even when she could hope no more she did not die, nor marry some one else, nor wither up and spit at the world. Long before the news came, indeed, she carried out a plan she had conceived, so Padre Abella told us, even while Rezánov was yet here. There were no convents in California in those days—you may know what a stranded handful we were—but she joined the Tertiary or Third Order of Franciscans, and wore always the grey habit, the girdle, and the cross. She went among the Indians christianizing them, remaining a long while at Soledad, a bleak and cheerless place, where she was also a great solace to the wives of the soldiers and settlers, whose children she taught. The Indians called her 'La Beata,' and by that name she was known in all California until she took the veil, and that was more than forty years later. And she was worshipped, no less. So beautiful she was, so humble, so sweet, and at the same time so practical; she had what the Americans call 'hard sense,' and something of Rezánov's own way of managing people. When she made up her mind to bring a sinner or a savage into the Church she did it. You know.

"But do not think she had her way in other things without a struggle. Don José and Doña Ignacia—her mother—permitted her to enter upon the religious life, for they understood; and Luis and Santiago made no protest either, for they understood also, and had loved Rezánov. But the rest of her family, the relations, the friends, the young men—the caballeros! They went in a body you might say to Don José and demanded that Concha, the most beautiful and fascinating and clever girl in New Spain, should come back to the world where she belonged,—be given in marriage. But Concha had always ruled Don José, and all the protests went to the winds. And William Sturgis—the young Bostonian who lived with us for so many years? I have not told you of him, and your mother was too young to remember. Well, never mind. He would have taken Concha from California, given her just a little of what she would have had as the wife of Rezánov—not in himself; he was as ugly as my whiskers; but enough of the great world to satisfy many women, and no one could deny that he was good and very clever. But to Concha he was a brother—no more. Perhaps she did not even take the trouble to refuse him. It was a way she had. After a while he went home to Boston and died of the climate. I was very sorry. He was one of us.

"And her intellect? Concha put it to sleep forever. She never read another book of travel, of history, biography, memoirs, essays, poetry—romance she had never read, and although some novels came to California in time she never opened them. It was peace she wanted, not the growing mind and the roving imagination. She brought her conversation down to the level of the humblest, and perhaps—who knows?—her thoughts. At all events, although the time came when she smiled again, and was often gay when we were all together in the family—particularly with the children, who came very fast, of course—well, she was then another Concha, not that brilliant dissatisfied ambitious girl we had all known, who had thought the greatest gentleman from the Viceroy's court not good enough to throw gold at her feet when she danced El Son.

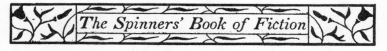

"There were changes in her life. In 1814 Don José was made Gobernador Propietario of Lower California. He took all of his unmarried children with him, and Concha thought it her duty to go. They lived in Loreto until 1821. But Concha never ceased to pray that she might return to California—we never looked upon that withered tongue of Mexico as California; and when Don José died soon after his resignation, and her mother went to live with her married daughters, Concha returned with the greatest happiness she had known, I think, since Rezánov went. Was not California all that was left her?

"She lived in Santa Barbara for many years, in the house of Don José de la Guerra—in that end room of the east wing. She had many relations, it is true, but Concha was always human and liked relations better when she was not surrounded by them. Although she never joined in any of the festivities of that gay time she was often with the Guerra family and seemed happy enough to take up her old position as Beata among the Indians and children, until they built a school for her in Monterey. How we used to wonder if she ever thought of Rezánov any more. From the day the two years were over she never mentioned his name, and everybody respected her reserve, even her parents. And she grew more and more reserved with the years, never speaking of herself at all, except just after her return from Mexico. But somehow we knew. And did not the very life she had chosen express it? Even the Church may not reach the secret places of the soul, and who knows what heaven she may have found in hers? And now? I think purgatory is not for Concha, and he was not bad as men go, and has had time to do his penance. It is true the Church tells us there is no marrying in heaven—but, well, perhaps there is a union for mated spirits of which the Church knows nothing. You saw her expression in her coffin.

"Well! The time arrived when we had a convent. Bishop Alemany came in 1850, and in the first sermon he preached in Santa Barbara—I think it was his first in California—he announced that he wished to found a convent. He was a Dominican, but one order was as another to Concha; she had never been narrow in anything. As soon as the service was over, before he had time to leave the church, she went to him and asked to be the first to join. He was glad enough, for he knew of her and that no one could fill his convent as rapidly as she. Therefore was she the first nun, the first to take holy vows, in our California. For a little, the convent was in the old Hartnell house in Monterey, but Don Manuel Ximéno had built a great hotel while believing, with all the rest, that Monterey would be the capital of the new California as of the old, and he was glad to sell it to the Bishop. We were delighted—of course I followed when Concha told me it was my vocation—that the Americans preferred Yerba Buena.

"Concha took her first vows in April, soon after the Bishop's arrival, choosing the name Sister Maria Dominica. On the 13th of April 1852 she took the black veil and perpetual vows. Of course the convent had a school at once. Concha's school had been a convent of a sort and the Bishop merely took it over. All the flower of California have been educated by Concha Argüello, including Chonita Estenega who is so great a lady in Mexico today. Two years later we came here, and here we shall stay, no doubt. I think Concha loved Benicia better than any part of California she had known, for it was still California without too piercing reminders of the past: life at the other Presidios and Missions was but the counterpart of our San Francisco, and here the priests and military had never come. In this beautiful wild spot where the elk and the antelope and the deer run about like rabbits, and you meet a bear if you go too far—Holy Mary!—where she went sometimes in a boat among the tules on the river, and where one may believe the moon lives in a silver lake in the old crater of Monte Diablo—Ay, it was different enough and might bring peace to any heart. What she must have suffered for years in those familiar scenes! But she never told. And now she lies here under her little cross and he in Krasnoiarsk—under a stone shaped like an altar, they say. Well! who knows? That is all. I go in now; my old bones ache with the night damp. But my mind is lighter, although never I shall speak of this again. And do you not think of it any more. Curiosity and the world and such nonsense as love and romance are not for us. Go to bed at once and tie a stocking round your throat that you have not a frog in it tomorrow morning when you sing 'Glory be to God on High.' *Buen Dias!*"

THE FORD OF CRÈVECŒUR

BY

MARY AUSTIN

Reprinted from *Out West* by permission.

THE FORD OF CREVECŒUR

YES. I understand; you are M'siu the Notary, M'siu the Sheriff has told me. You are come to hear how by the help of God I have killed Filon Geraud at the ford of Crèvecœur.

By the help of God, yes. Think you if the devil had a hand in it, he would not have helped Filon? For he was the devil's own, was Filon. He was big, he was beautiful, he had a way—but always there was the devil's mark. I see that the first time ever I knew him at Agua Caliente. The devil sit in Filon's eyes and laugh—laugh—some time he go away like a man at a window, but he come again. M'siu, he *live* there! And Filon, he know that I see, so he make like he not care; but I think he care a little, else why he make for torment me all the time? Ever since I see him at that shearing at Agua Caliente eight, ten year gone, he not like for let me be. I have been the best shearer in that shed, snip—snip—quick, clean. Ah, it is beautiful! All the sheepmen like for have me shear their sheep. Filon is new man at that shearing, Lebecque is just hire him then; but yes, M'siu, to see him walk about that Agua Caliente you think he own all those sheep, all that range. Ah—he had a way! Pretty soon that day Filon is hearing all sheepmen say that Raoul is the best shearer; then he come lean on the rail by my shed and laugh softly like he talk with himself, and say, "See the little man; see him shear." But me, I can no more. The shears turn in my hand so I make my sheep all bleed same like one butcher. Then I look up and see the devil in Filon Geraud's eye. It is always so after that, all those years until I kill Filon. If I make a little game of poker with other shepherds, then he walks along and say:

"Ah, you, Raoul, you is one sharp fellow. I not like for play with you." Then is my play all gone bad.

But if Filon play, then he say, "Come, you little man, and bring me the good luck."

It is so, M'siu! If I go stand by that game, Filon is win, win all the time. That is because of the devil. And if there are women—no, M'siu, there was never *one* woman. What would a shepherd, whose work is always toward the hills, do with a woman? Is it to plant a vineyard that others may drink wine? Ah, non! But me, at shearings and at Tres Piños where we pay the tax, there I like to talk to pretty girl same as other shepherds, then Filon come make like he one gran' friend. All the time he make say the compliments, he make me one mock. His eyes they laugh always, that make women like to do what he say. But me, I have no chance.

It is so, M'siu, when I go out with my sheep. This is my trail—I go out after the shearing through the Cañada de las Viñas, then across the Little Antelope, while the grass is quick. After that I go up toward the hills of Olancho, where I keep one month; there is much good feed and no man comes. Also then I wait at Tres Piños for the sheriff that I pay the tax. *Sacre!* it is a hard one, that tax! After that I am free of the Sierras, what you call *Nieve*—snowy. Well I know that country. I go about with my sheep and seek my meadows—*mine*, M'siu, that I have climbed the great mountains to spy out among the pines, that I have found by the grace of God, and my own wit: La Crevasse, Moultrie, Bighorn, Angostura. Also, I go by other meadows where other shepherds feed one month with another; but *these* are all *mine*. I go about and come again when the feed is grown.

M'siu, it is hard to believe, but it is so—Filon finds my meadows one by one. One year I come by La Crevasse—there is nothing there; I go on to Moultrie—here is the grass eaten to the roots, and the little pines have no tops; at Bighorn is the fresh litter of a flock. I think maybe my sheep go hungry that summer. So I come to Angostura. There is Filon. He laugh. Then it come into my mind that one day I goin' kill that Filon Geraud. By the help of God. Yes. For he is big that Filon, he is strong; and me, M'siu, I am as God made me.

So always, where I go on the range there is Filon; if I think to change my trail, he change also his. If I have good luck, Filon has better. If to him is the misfortune—ah—you shall hear.

One year Gabriel Lausanne tell me that Filon is lose all his lambs in the Santa Ana. You know that Santa Ana, M'siu? It is one mighty wind. It comes up small, very far away, one little dust like the clouds, creep, creep close by the land. It lies down along the sand; you think it is done? Eh, it is one liar, that Santa

Ana. It rise up again, it is pale gold, it seek the sky. That sky is all wide, clean, no speck. Ah, it knows, that sky; it will have nothing lying about when the Santa Ana comes. It is hot then, you have the smell of the earth in your nostrils. *That*, M'siu, is the Santa Ana. It is pale dust and the great push of the wind. The sand bites, there is no seeing the flock's length. They huddle, and the lambs are smothered; they scatter, and the dogs can nothing make. If it blow one day, you thank God; if it blow two days, then is sheepman goin' to lose his sheep. When Gabriel tell me that about Filon, I think he deserve all that. What you think, M'siu? That same night the water of Tinpah rise in his banks afar off by the hills where there is rain. It comes roaring down the wash where I make my camp, for you understand at that time of year there should be no water in the wash of Tinpah, but it come in the night and carry away one-half of my sheep. Eh, how you make that, M'siu; is it the devil or no?

Well, it go like this eight, ten year; then it come last summer, and I meet Filon at the ford of Crèvecœur. That is the water that comes down eastward from Mineral Mountain between Olancho and Sentinel Rock. It is what you call Mineral Creek, but the French shepherds call it Crèvecœur. For why; it is a most swift and wide water; it goes darkly between earthy banks upon which it gnaws. It has hot springs which come up in it without reason, so that there is no safe crossing at any time. Its sands are quick; what they take, they take wholly with the life in it, and after a little they spew it out again. And, look you, it makes no singing, this water of

Crèvecœur. Twenty years have I kept sheep between Red Butte and the Temblor Hills, and I say this. Make no fear of singing water, for it goes not too deeply but securely on a rocky bottom; such a one you may trust. But this silent one, that is hot or cold, deep or shallow, and has never its banks the same one season with another, this you may not trust, M'siu. And to get sheep across it—ah—it breaks the heart, this Crèvecœur.

Nevertheless, there is one place where a great rock runs slantwise of the stream, but under it, so that the wáter goes shallowly with a whisper, ah, so fast, and below it is a pool. Here on the rocks the shepherds make pine logs to lie with stones so that the sheep cross over. Every year the water carries the logs away and the shepherds build again, and there is no shepherd goes by that water but lose some sheep. Therefore, they call it the ford of Crèvecœur.*

Well, I have been about by the meadow of Angostura when it come last July, and there I see Narcisse Duplin. He is tell me the feed is good about Sentinel Rock, so I think me to go back by the way of Crèvecœur. There is pine wood all about eastward from that place. It is all shadow there at midday and has a weary sound. Me, I like it not, that pine wood, so I push the flock and am very glad when I hear toward the ford the bark of dogs and the broken sound of bells. I think there is other shepherd that make talk with me. But me, M'siu, *sacre! damn!* when I come out by the ford there is Filon Geraud. He has come up one side Crèvecœur, with his flock, as I have come up the other. He laugh.

* **Break-heart.**

"Hillo, Raoul," say Filon, "will you cross?"

"I will cross," say I.

"After me," say Filon.

"Before," say I.

M'siu does not know about sheep? Ah, non. It is so that the sheep is most scare of all beasts about water. Never so little a stream will he cross, but if the dogs compel him. It is the great trouble of shepherds to get the flock across the waters that go in and about the Sierras. For that it is the custom to have two, three goats with the flocks to go first across the water, then they will follow. But here at Crèvecœur it is bad crossing any way you go; also, that day it is already afternoon. Therefore I stand at one side that ford and make talk with Filon at the other about who goes first. Then my goat which leads my flock come push by me and I stand on that log while we talk. He is one smart goat.

"Eh, Raoul, let the goats decide," cries Filon, and to that I have agree. Filon push his goat on the log, he is one great black one that is call Diable—I ask you is that a name for a goat? I have call mine Noé. So they two walk on that log very still; for they see what they have to do. Then they push with the head, Diable and Noé, till that log it rock in the water; Filon is cry to his goat and I to mine. Then because of that water one goat slip on the log, and the other is push so hard that he cannot stop; over they go into the pool of swift water, over and over until they come to the shallows; then they find their feet and come up, each on his own side. They will not care to push with the heads again at that time. Filon he walk out on the log to me, and I walk to him.

"My goat have won the ford," says he.

"Your goat cannot keep what he wins."

"But I can," say Filon. Then he look at me with his eyes like—like I have told you, M'siu.

"Raoul," he say, "you is one little man."

With that I remember me all the wrong I have had from this one.

"Go you after your goat, Filon Geraud," say I.

With that I put my staff behind his foot, so, M'siu, and send him into the water, splash! He come to his feet presently in the pool with the water all in his hair and his eyes, and the stream run strong and dark against his middle.

"Hey, you, Raoul, what for you do that?" he say, but also he laugh. "Ah, ha, little man, you have the joke this time."

M'siu, that laugh stop on his face like it been freeze, his mouth is open, his eyes curl up. It is terrible, that dead laugh in the midst of the black water that run down from his hair.

"Raoul," he say, "*the sand is quick!*"

Then he take one step, and I hear the sand suck. I see Filon shiver like a reed in the swift water.

"*My God*," he say, "*the sand is quick!*"

M'siu, I do not know how it is with me. When I throw Filon in the pool, I have not known it is quicksand; but when I hear that, I think I am glad. I kneel down by that log in the ford and watch Filon. He speak to me very quiet:

"You must get a rope and make fast to that pine and throw the end to me. There is a rope in my pack."

"Yes," say I, "there is a rope."

M'siu, I think I would not have killed him with my hands, but if God give him over to me in the quick-sand of Crèvecœur, how then? So I hold me still. Then is Filon begin to curse and cry.

"You, Raoul! I make you pay for this!"

He work with his feet and beat the water with his hands. But me, I can see the pool rising to his breast. After a little Filon see that also, then he leave off to struggle and make as if he laugh, but not with his eyes—never any more with his eyes while he live.

"Well, Raoul," he says, "you will have your fun, but man, do not make it too long."

"It will not be long, Filon," say I.

After that he is still until the water is come to his shoulders, then he speak softly: "Raoul, my friend, there is in the bank of Sacramento eight hundred dollars. It shall be his who saves me from this pool. Eight hundred dollars. Think, Raoul!"

"Eight hundred dollars?"

"It is a good sum," say he.

"But you will not need it now, Filon."

By that I see the water is rising fast. Then he burst out:

"Is it that you mean to kill me, Raoul. Mother of God, is it so?"

"It is so, Filon."

After that I do not know how it is. The water is rising fast, the water is very swift in the pool and curl back against his throat. I think he is pray to God and to me; then he fight in the water—he choke—he cry. But me, I have run away into that pine wood for a little while. Then I think I will go and get that rope quick—but when I come again there is Filon under the pool. I can see that clearly, but a little way under the dark water. His body is bent down stream and flows with its flowing like the bent grass that grows by the water border, like the long grass that is covered and rots under flood water. It is shaken with the shaking of Crèvecœur. His eyes are open, and his mouth, like a fish, and the water goes over them. It is as if he laugh down there under the pool; I see his body shake. His arms stream out from him like the blades of wet grass; his hand come up to the top and whirl about and go down with the running water. But never they grasp nor go forward. He is fast there in the quick-sands of Crèvecœur.

Yes, M'siu, it is so what you have said. M'siu the Sheriff has also told me. If I had taken my flock and gone my way, telling never any man, then I should have missed this trouble and the talk of hanging. But consider! M'siu is perhaps accustomed to think what is best to be done in an evil case; but me, I have never before need to hide what I have done. How shall I begin then? Also, I am a shepherd. Another might leave the sheep of Filon in the pine wood by the ford of Crèvecœur, but a shepherd—no. It is so that the sheep are the most silly of all beasts. They know not to cross the water—but if they are led, they make no fright. They have no cry when a cry is most of need. If a bear or coyote come upon the flock to torment them, they huddle, they run foolishly in twos and threes, making no sound. If there be a rain or untimely snow, the lambs sicken and die plentifully. Ah, non! That man have no heart who will leave sheep to the hills with no shepherding. Me, M'siu, I cannot.

So I take my flocks across the ford, since Filon is in the water, and take all those silly ones toward La Crevasse, and after I think about that business. Three days after, I meet P'tee Pete. I tell him I find the sheep of Filon in the pine wood below Sentinel Rock. Pete, he say that therefore Filon is come to some hurt, and that he look for him. That make me scare lest he should look by the ford of Crèvecœur. So after that, five or six days, when Narcisse Duplin is come up with me, I tell him Filon is gone to Sacramento where his money is; therefore I keep care of his sheep. That is a better tale—eh, M'siu,—for I have to say something. Every shepherd in that range is know those sheep of Filon. All this time I think me to take the sheep to Pierre Jullien in the meadow of Black Mountain. He is not much, that Pierre. If I tell him it is one gift from *Le bon Dieu,* that is explain enough for Pierre Jullien. Then I will be quit of the trouble of Filon Geraud.

So, M'siu, would it have been, but for that dog Helène. That is Filon's she-dog that he raise from a pup. She is—she is *une femme,* that dog! All that first night when we come away from the ford, she cry, cry in her throat all through the dark, and in the light she look at me with her eyes, so to say:

"I know, Raoul! I know what is under the water of Crèvecœur." M'siu, is a man to stand that from a dog? So the next night I beat her, and in the morning she is gone. I think me the good luck to get rid of her. That Helène! M'siu, what you think she do? She have gone back to look in the water for Filon. There she stay, and all sheepmen when they pass that way see that she is a good sheepdog, and that she is much hungry; so they wonder that she will not leave off to look and go with them. After while all people in those parts is been talkin' about that dog of Filon's that look so keen in the water of Crèvecœur. Mebbe four, five weeks after that I have killed Filon, one goes riding by that place and sees Helène make mourn by the water-side over something that stick in the sand. It is Filon. Yes. That quick-sand have spit him out again. So you say; but me, I think it is the devil.

For the rest the sheriff has told you. Here they have brought me, and there is much talk. Of that I am weary, but for this I tell you all how it is about Filon; M'siu, I would not hang. Look you, so long as I stay in this life I am quit of that man, but if I die—there is Filon. So will he do unto me all that I did at the ford of Crèvecœur, and more; for he is a bad one, Filon. Therefore it is as I tell you, M'siu, I, Raoul. By the help of God. Yes.

A CALIFORNIAN

BY

GERALDINE BONNER

A CALIFORNIAN

T WAS nearly ten o'clock when Jack Faraday ascended the steps of Madame Delmonti's bow-windowed mansion and pressed the electric bell. He was a little out of breath and nervous, for, being young and a stranger to San Francisco, and almost a stranger to Madame Delmonti, he did not exactly know at what hour his hostess's *conversazione* might begin, and had upon him the young man's violent dread of being conspicuously early or conspicuously late.

It did not seem that he was either. As he stood in the doorway and surveyed the field, he felt, with a little rising breath of relief, that no one appeared to take especial notice of him. Madame Delmonti's rooms were lit with a great blaze of gas, which, thrown back from many long mirrors and the gold mountings of a quantity of furniture and picture frames, made an effect of dazzling yellow brightness, as brilliantly glittering as the transformation scene of a pantomime.

In the middle of the glare Madame Delmonti's company had disposed themselves in a circle, which had some difficulty in accommodating itself to the long narrow shape of the drawing-room. Now and then an obstinate sofa or extra large plush-covered arm-chair broke the harmonious curve of the circle, and its occupant looked furtively ill at ease, as if she felt the embarrassment of her position in not conforming to the general harmony of the curving line.

The eyes of the circle were fixed on a figure at the piano, near the end of the room—a tall dark Jewess in a brown dress and wide hat, who was singing with that peculiar vibrant richness of tone that is so often heard in the voices of the Californian Jewesses. She was perfectly self-possessed, and her velvet eyes, as her impassioned voice rose a little, rested on Jack Faraday with a cheerful but not very lively interest. Then they swept past him to where, on a sofa, quite out of the circle, two women sat listening.

One was a young girl, large, well-dressed, and exceedingly handsome; the other a peaked lady, passée and thin, with her hair bleached to a canary yellow. The Jewess, still singing, smiled at them, and the girl gave back a lazy smile in return. Then as the song came to a deep and mellow close, Madame Delmonti, with a delicate rustling of silk brushing against silk, swept across the room and greeted her guest.

Madame Delmonti was an American, very rich, a good deal made up, but still pretty, and extremely well preserved. Signor Delmonti, an Italian baritone, whom she had married, and supported ever since, was useful about the house, as he now proved by standing at a little table and ladling punch into small glasses, which were distributed among the guests by the two little Delmonti girls in green silk frocks. Madame Delmonti, with her rouged cheeks and merry grey eyes, as full of sparkle as they had been twenty years ago, was very cordial to her guest, asking him, as they stood in the doorway, whom he would like best to meet.

"Maud Levy, who has been singing," she said, "is one of the belles in Hebrew society. She has a fine voice. You have no objection, Mr. Faraday, to knowing Jews?"

Faraday hastily disclaimed all race prejudices, and she continued, discreetly designating the ladies on the sofa:

"There are two delightful girls. Mrs. Peck, the blonde, is the society writer for the *Morning Trumpet*. She is an elegant woman of a very fine Southern family, but she has had misfortunes. Her marriage was unhappy. She and Peck are separated now, and she supports herself and her two children. There was no hope of getting alimony out of that man."

"And that is Genevieve Ryan beside her," Madame Delmonti went on. "I think you'd like Genevieve. She's a grand girl. Her father, you know, is Barney Ryan, one of our millionaires. He made his money in a quick turn in Con. Virginia, but before that he used to drive the Marysville coach, and he was once a miner. He's crazy about Genevieve and gives her five hundred a month to dress on. I'm sure you'll get on very well together. She's such a refined, pleasant girl"—— and Madame Delmonti, chattering her praises of Barney Ryan's handsome daughter, conducted the stranger to the shrine.

Miss Genevieve smiled upon him, much as she

had upon the singer, and brushing aside her skirts of changeable green and heliotrope silk, showed him a little golden-legged chair beside her. Mrs. Peck and Madame Delmonti conversed with unusual insight and knowledge on the singing of Maud Levy, and Faraday was left to conduct the conversation with the heiress of Barney Ryan.

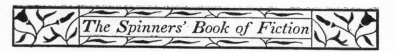

She was a large, splendid-looking girl, very much corseted, with an ivory-tinted skin, eyes as clear as a young child's and smooth freshly red lips. She was a good deal powdered on the bridge of her nose, and her rich hair was slightly tinted with some reddish dye. She was a picture of health and material well being. Her perfectly fitting clothes sat with wrinkleless exactitude over a figure which in its generous breadth and finely curved outline might have compared with that of the Venus of Milo. She let her eyes, shadowed slightly by the white lace edge of her large hat, whereon two pink roses trembled on large stalks, dwell upon Faraday with a curious and frank interest entirely devoid of coquetry. Her manner, almost boyish in its simple directness, showed the same absence of this feminine trait. While she looked like a goddess dressed by Worth, she seemed merely a good-natured, phlegmatic girl just emerging from her teens.

Faraday had made the first commonplaces of conversation, when she asked, eyeing him closely, "Do you like it out here?"

"Oh, immensely," he responded, politely. "It's such a fine climate."

"It is a good climate," admitted Miss Ryan, with unenthusiastic acquiescence; "but we are not so proud of that as we are of the good looks of the Californian women. Don't you think the women are handsome?"

Faraday looked into her clear and earnest eyes. "Oh, splendid," he answered, "especially their eyes."

Miss Ryan appeared to demur to this commendation. "It's generally said by strangers that their figures are unusually handsome. Do you think they are?"

Faraday agreed to this too.

"The girls in the East," said Miss Ryan, sitting upright with a creaking sound, and drawing her gloves through one satin-smooth, bejeweled hand, "are very thin, aren't they? Here, I sometimes think"—she raised her eyes to his in deep and somewhat anxious query—"that they are too fat?"

Faraday gallantly scouted the idea. He said the California woman was a goddess. For the first time in the interview Miss Ryan gave a little laugh.

"That's what all you Eastern men say," she said. "They're always telling me I'm a goddess. Even the Englishmen say that."

"Well," answered Faraday, surprised at his own boldness, "what they say is true."

Miss Ryan silently eyed him for a speculating moment; then, averting her glance, said, pensively: "Perhaps so; but I don't think it's so stylish to be a goddess as it is to be very slim. And then, you know——" Here she suddenly broke off, her eyes fixed upon the crowd of ladies that blocked an opposite doorway in exeunt. "There's mommer. I guess she must be going home, and I suppose I'd better go too, and not keep her waiting."

She rose as she spoke, and with a pat of her hand adjusted her glimmering skirts.

"Oh, Mr. Faraday," she said, as she peered down at them, "I hope you'll give yourself the pleasure of calling on me. I'm at home almost any afternoon after five, and Tuesday is my day. Come whenever you please. I'll be real glad to see you, and I guess popper'd like to talk to you about things in the East. He's been in Massachusetts too."

She held out her large white hand and gave Faraday a vigorous hand-shake.

"I'm glad I came here tonight," she said, smiling. "I wasn't quite decided, but I thought I'd better, as I had some things to tell Mrs. Peck for next Sunday's *Trumpet*. If I hadn't come, I wouldn't have met you. You needn't escort me to Madame Delmonti. I'd rather go by myself. I'm not a bit a ceremonious person. Good-by. Be sure and come and see me."

She rustled away, exchanged farewells with Madame Delmonti, and, by a movement of her head in his direction, appeared to be speaking of Faraday; then joining a fur-muffled female figure near the doorway, swept like a princess out of the room.

For a week after Faraday's meeting with Miss Genevieve Ryan, he had no time to think of giving himself the pleasure of calling upon that fair and flattering young lady. The position which he had come out from Boston to fill was not an unusually exacting one, but Faraday, who was troubled with a New England conscience, and a certain slowness in adapting himself to new conditions of life, was too engrossed in mastering the duties of his clerkship to think of loitering about the chariot wheels of beauty.

By the second week, however, he had shaken down into the new rut, and a favorable opportunity presenting itself in a sunny Sunday afternoon, he donned his black coat and high hat and repaired to the mansion of Barney Ryan, on California Street.

When Faraday approached the house, he felt quite timid, so imposingly did this great structure loom up from the simpler dwellings which surrounded it. Barney Ryan had built himself a palace, and ever since the day he had first moved into it he had been anxious to move out. The ladies of his family would not allow this, and so Barney endured his grandeur as best he might. It was a great wooden house, with immense bay windows thrown out on every side, and veiled within by long curtains of heavy lace. The sweep of steps that spread so proudly from the portico was flanked by two sleeping lions in stone, both appearing, by the savage expressions which distorted their visages, to be suffering from terrifying dreams. In the garden the spiked foliage of the dark, slender dracænas and the fringed fans of giant filamentosas grew luxuriantly with tropical effect.

The large drawing-room, long, and looking longer with its wide mirrors, was even more golden than Mrs. Delmonti's. There were gold moldings about the mirrors and gold mountings to the chairs. In deserts of gold frames appeared small oases of oil-painting. Faraday, hat in hand, stood some time in wavering indecision, wondering in which of the brocaded and gilded chairs he would look least like a king in an historical play. He was about to decide in favor of a pale blue satin settee, when a rustle behind him made him turn and behold Miss Genevieve, magnificent in a trailing robe of the faintest rose-pink and pearls, with diamond ear-rings in her ears, and the powder that she had hastily rubbed on her face still lying white on her long lashes. She smiled her rare smile as she greeted him, and sitting down in one of the golden chairs, leaned her head against the back, and said, looking at him from under lowered lids:

"Well, I thought you were never coming!"

Faraday, greatly encouraged by this friendly reception, made his excuses, and set the conversation going. After the weather had been exhausted, the topic of the Californian in his social aspect came up. Faraday, with some timidity, ventured a question on the fashionable life in San Francisco. A shade passed over Miss Ryan's open countenance.

"You know, Mr. Faraday," she said, explanatorily, "I'm not exactly in society."

"No?" murmured Faraday, mightily surprised, and wondering what she was going to say next.

"Not exactly," continued Miss Ryan, moistening her red under lip in a pondering moment—"not exactly in fash'nable society. Of course we have our friends. But gentlemen from the East that I've met have always been so surprised when I told them that I didn't go out in the most fash'nable circles. They always thought any one with money could get right in it here."

"Yes?" said Faraday, whose part of the conversation appeared to be deteriorating into monosyllables.

"Well, you know, that's not the case at all. With all popper's money, we've never been able to get a real good footing. It seems funny to outsiders, especially as popper and mommer have never been divorced or anything. We've just lived quietly right here in the city always. But," she said, looking tentatively at Faraday to see how he was going to take the statement, "my father's a Northerner. He went back and fought in the war."

"You must be very proud of that," said Faraday, feeling that he could now hazard a remark with safety.

This simple comment, however, appeared to surprise the enigmatic Miss Ryan.

"Proud of it?" she queried, looking in suspended doubt at Faraday. "Oh, of course I'm proud that he was brave, and didn't run away or get wounded; but if he'd been a Southerner we would have been in society now." She looked pensively at Faraday. "All the fashionable people are Southerners, you know. We would have been, too, if we'd have been Southerners. It's being Northerners that really has been such a drawback."

"But your sympathies," urged Faraday, "aren't they with the North?"

Miss Ryan ran the pearl fringe of her tea-gown through her large, handsome hands. "I guess so," she said, indifferently, as if she was considering the subject for the first time; "but you can't expect me to have any very violent sympathies about a war that was dead and buried before I was born."

"I don't believe you're a genuine Northerner, or Southerner either," said Faraday, laughing.

"I guess not," said the young lady, with the same placid indifference. "An English gentleman whom

I knew real well last year said the sympathy of the English was all with the Southerners. He said they were the most refined people in this country. He said they were thought a great deal of in England?" She again looked at Faraday with her air of deprecating query, as if she half expected him to contradict her.

"Who was this extraordinarily enlightened being?" asked Faraday.

"Mr. Harold Courtney, an elegant Englishman. They said his grandfather was a Lord—Lord Hastings—but you never can be sure about those things. I saw quite a good deal of him, and I sort of liked him, but he was rather quiet. I think if he'd been an American we would have thought him dull. Here they just said it was reserve. We all thought——"

A footstep in the hall outside arrested her recital. The door of the room was opened, and a handsome bonneted head appeared in the aperture.

"Oh, Gen," said this apparition, hastily—"excuse me; I didn't know you had your company in there?"

"Come in, mommer," said Miss Ryan, politely; "I want to make you acquainted with Mr. Faraday. He's the gentleman I met at Madame Delmonti's the other evening."

Mrs. Ryan, accompanied by a rich rustling of silk, pushed open the door, revealing herself to Faraday's admiring eyes as a fine-looking woman, fresh in tint, still young, of a stately figure and imposing presence. She was admirably dressed in a walking costume of dark green, and wore a little black jet bonnet on her slightly waved bright brown hair. She met the visitor with an extended hand and a frank smile of open pleasure.

"Genevieve spoke to me of you, Mr. Faraday," she said, settling down into a chair and removing her gloves. "I'm very glad you managed to get around here."

Faraday expressed his joy at having been able to accomplish the visit.

"We don't have so many agreeable gentlemen callers," said Mrs. Ryan, "that we can afford to overlook a new one. If you've been in society, you've perhaps noticed, Mr. Faraday, that gentlemen are somewhat scarce."

Faraday said he had not been in society, therefore had not observed the deficiency. Mrs. Ryan, barely allowing him time to complete his sentence, continued, vivaciously:

"Well, Mr. Faraday, you'll see it later. We entertainers don't know what we are going to do for the lack of gentlemen. When we give parties we ask the young gentlemen, and they all come; but they won't dance, they won't talk, they won't do anything but eat and drink and they never think of paying their party calls. It's disgraceful, Mr. Faraday," said Mrs. Ryan, smiling brightly—"disgraceful!"

Faraday said he had heard that in the East the hostess made the same complaint. Mrs. Ryan, with brilliant fixed eyes, gave him a breathing-space to reply in, and then started off again, with a confirmatory nod of her head:

"Precisely, Mr. Faraday—just the case here. At Genevieve's début party—an elegant affair—Mrs. Peck said she'd never seen a finer entertainment in this city—canvas floors, four musicians, champagne flowing like water. My husband, Mr. Faraday, believes in giving the best at his entertainments; there's not a mean bone in Barney Ryan's body. Why, the men all got into the smoking-room, lit their cigars, and smoked there, and in the ballroom were the girls sitting around the walls, and not more than half a dozen partners for them. I tell you, Mr. Ryan was mad. He just went up there, and told them to get up and dance or get up and go home—he didn't much care which. There's no fooling with Mr. Ryan when he's roused. You remember how mad popper was that night, Gen?"

Miss Ryan nodded an assent, her eyes full of smiling reminiscence. She had listened to her mother's story with unmoved attention and evident appreciation. "Next time we have a party," she said, looking smilingly at Faraday, "Mr. Faraday can come and see for himself."

"I guess it'll be a long time before we have another like that," said Mrs. Ryan, somewhat grimly, rising as Faraday rose to take his leave. "Not but what," she added, hastily, fearing her remark had seemed ungracious, "we'll hope Mr. Faraday will come without waiting for parties."

"But we've had one since then," said Miss Ryan, as she placed her hand in his in the pressure of farewell, "that laid all over that first one."

Having been pressed to call by both mother and daughter, and having told himself that Genevieve Ryan was "an interesting study," Faraday, after some hesitation, paid a second visit to the Ryan mansion. Upon this occasion the Chinese servant, murmuring unintelligibly, showed a rooted aversion to his entering. Faraday, greatly at sea, wondering vaguely if the terrible Barney Ryan had issued a mandate to his hireling to refuse him admittance, was about to turn and depart, when the voice of Mrs. Ryan in the hall beyond arrested him. Bidden to open the door, the Mongolian reluctantly did so and Faraday was admitted.

"Sing didn't want to let you in," said Mrs. Ryan when they had gained the long gold drawing-room, "because Genevieve was out. He never lets any gentlemen in when she's not at home. He thinks I'm too old to have them come to see me."

Then they sat down, and after a little preliminary chat on the Chinese character and the Californian climate, Mrs. Ryan launched forth into her favorite theme of discourse.

"Genevieve will be so sorry to miss you," she said; "she's always so taken by Eastern gentlemen. They admire her, too, immensely. I can't tell you of the compliments we've heard directly and indirectly that they've paid her. Of course I can see that she's an unusually fine-looking girl, and very accomplished. Mr. Ryan and I have spared nothing in her education—nothing. At Madame de Vivier's academy for young ladies—one of the most select in the State—Madame's husband's one of the French nobility, and she always had to support him—Genevieve took every extra—music, languages, and drawing. Professor Rodriguez, who taught her the guitar, said that never outside of Spain had he heard such a touch. 'Señora,' he says to me—that's his way of expressing himself, and it sounds real cute the way he says it—'Señora, is there not some Spanish blood in this child? No one without Spanish blood could touch the strings that way.' Afterwards when Demaroni taught her the mandolin, it was just the same. He could not believe she had not had teaching before. Then Madame Mezzenott gave her a term's lessons on the bandurria, and she said there never was such talent; she might have made a fortune on the concert stage."

"Yes, undoubtedly," Faraday squeezed in, as Mrs. Ryan drew a breath.

"Indeed, Mr. Faraday, everybody has remarked her talents. It isn't you alone. All the Eastern gentlemen we have met have said that the musical talents of the Californian young ladies were astonishing. They all agree that Genevieve's musical genius is remarkable. Everybody declares that there is no one—not among the Spaniards themselves—who sings *La Paloma* as Gen does. Professor Spighetti instructed her in that. He was a wonderful teacher. I never saw such a method. But we had to give him up because he fell in love with Gen. That's the worst of it—the teachers are always falling in love with her; and with her prospects and position we naturally expect something better. Of course it's been very hard to keep her. I say to Mr. Ryan, as each winter comes to an end, 'Well, popper, another season's over and we've still got our Gen.' We feel that we can't be selfish and hope to keep her always, and, with so many admirers, we realize that we must soon lose her, and try to get accustomed to the idea."

"Of course, of course," murmured Faraday, sympathetically, mentally picturing Mrs. Ryan keeping away the suitors as Rizpah kept the eagles and vultures off her dead sons.

"There was a Mr. Courtney who was very attentive last year. His grandfather was an English lord. We had to buy a *Peerage* to find out if he was genuine, and, as he was, we had him quite often to the house. He paid Genevieve a good deal of attention, but toward the end of the season he said he had to go back to England and see his grandfather—his father was dead—and left without saying anything definite. He told me though, that he was coming back. I fully expect he will, though Mr. Ryan doesn't seem to think so. Genevieve felt rather put out about it for a time. She thought he hadn't been upright to see her so constantly and not say anything definite. But she doesn't understand the subserviency of Englishmen to their elders. You know, we have none of that in this country. If my son Eddie wanted to marry a typewriter, Mr. Ryan could never prevent it. I fully expect to see Mr. Courtney again. I'd like you to meet him, Mr. Faraday. I think you'd agree very well. He's just such a quiet, reserved young man as you."

When, after this interview, Faraday descended the broad steps between the sleeping lions, he did not feel so good-tempered as he had done after his first visit. He recalled to mind having heard that Mrs. Ryan, before her marriage, had been a school-teacher, and he said to himself that if she had no more sense then than she had now, her pupils must have received a fearful and wonderful education.

At Madame Delmonti's *conversazione*, given a few evenings later, Faraday again saw Miss Ryan. On the first of these occasions this independent young lady was dressed simply in a high-necked gown and a hat. This evening with her habitual disregard of custom and convention, some whim had caused her to array herself in full gala attire, and, habited in a gorgeous costume of white silk and yellow velvet, with a glimmer of diamonds round the low neck, she was startling in her large magnificence.

Jack Faraday approached her somewhat awe-stricken, but her gravely boyish manner immediately put him at his ease. Talking with her over commonplaces, he wondered what she would say if she knew of her mother's conversation with him. As if in answer to the unspoken thought, she suddenly said, fixing him with intent eyes:

"Mommer said she told you of Mr. Courtney. Do you think he'll come back?"

Faraday, his breath taken away by the suddenness of the attack, felt the blood run to his hair, and stammered a reply.

"Well, you know," she said, leaning toward him confidentially, "I *don't*. Mommer is possessed with the idea that he will. But neither popper nor I think so. I got sort of annoyed with the way he acted—hanging about for a whole winter, and then running away to see his grandfather, like a little boy ten years old! I like men that are their own masters. But I suppose I would have married him. You see, he would have been a lord when his grandfather died. It was genuine—we saw it in the *Peerage*.

She looked into Faraday's eyes. Her own were as clear and deep as mountain springs. Was Miss Genevieve Ryan the most absolutely honest and outspoken young woman that had ever lived, or was she some subtle and unusual form of Pacific Slope coquette?

"Popper was quite mad about it," she continued. "He thought Mr. Courtney was an ordinary sort of person, anyway. I didn't. I just thought him dull, and I suppose he couldn't help that. Mommer wanted to go over to England last summer. She thought we might stumble on him over there. But popper wouldn't let her do it. He sent us to Alaska instead." She paused, and gave a smiling bow to an acquaintance. "Doesn't Mrs. Peck look sweet tonight?" She designated the society editress of the *Morning Trumpet,* whose fragile figure was encased in a pale blue Empire costume. "And that lady over by the door, with the gold crown in her hair, the stout one in red, is Mrs. Wheatley, a professional Delsarte teacher. She's a great friend of mine and gives me Delsarte twice a week."

And Miss Genevieve Ryan nodded to the dispenser of "Delsarte," a large and florid woman, who, taking her stand under a spreading palm tree, began to declaim "The Portrait" of Owen Meredith, and in the recital of the dead lady's iniquitous conduct the conversation was brought to a close.

From its auspicious opening, Faraday's acquaintance with the Ryans ripened and developed with a speed which characterizes the growth of friendship and of fruit in the genial Californian atmosphere. Almost before he felt that he had emerged from the position of a stranger he had slipped into that of an intimate. He fell into the habit of visiting the Ryan mansion on California Street on Sunday afternoons. It became a custom for him to dine there *en famille* at least once a week. The simplicity and light-hearted good-nature of these open-handed and kindly people touched and charmed him. There was not a trace of the snob in Faraday. He accepted the lavish and careless hospitality of Barney Ryan's "palatial residence," as the newspapers delighted to call it, with a spirit as frankly pleased as that in which it was offered.

He came of an older civilization than that which had given Barney Ryan's daughter her frankness and her force, and it did not cross his mind that the heiress of millions might cast tender eyes upon the penniless sons of New England farmers. He said to himself with impatient recklessness that he ought not to and would not fall in love with her. There was too great a distance between them. It would be King Cophetua and the beggar-maid reversed. Clerks at one hundred and fifty dollars a month were not supposed to aspire to only daughters of bonanza kings in the circle from which Faraday had come. So he visited the Ryans, assuring himself that he was a friend of the family, who would dance at Miss Genevieve's wedding with the lightest of hearts.

The Chinese butler had grown familiar with Faraday's attractive countenance and his unabbreviated English, when late one warm and sunny afternoon the young man pulled the bell of the great oaken door of the Ryans' lion-guarded home. In answer to his queries for the ladies, he learned that they were out; but the Mongolian functionary, after surveying him charily through the crack of the door, admitted that Mr. Ryan was within, and conducted the visitor into his presence.

Barney Ryan, suffering from a slight sprain in his ankle, sat at ease in a little sitting-room in the back of the house. Mr. Ryan, being irritable and in some pain, the women-folk had relaxed the severity of their dominion, and allowed him to sit unchecked in his favorite costume for the home circle—shirt sleeves and a tall beaver hat. Beside him on the table stood a bare and undecorated array of bottles, a glass, and a silver water-pitcher.

Mr. Ryan was now some years beyond sixty, but had that tremendous vigor of frame and constitution that distinguished the pioneers—an attribute strangely lacking in their puny and degenerate sons. This short and chunky old man, with his round, thick head, bristling hair and beard, and huge red neck, had still a fiber as tough as oak. He looked coarse, uncouth, and stupid, but in his small gray eyes shone the alert and unconquerable spirit which marked the pioneers as the giants of the West, and which had carried him forward over every obstacle to the summit of his ambitions. Barney Ryan was restless in his confinement; for, despite his age and the completeness of his success, his life was still with the world of men where the bull-necked old miner was a king. At home the women rather domineered over him, and unconsciously made him feel his social deficiencies. At home, too, the sorrow and the pride of his life were always before him—his son, a weak and dissipated boy; and his daughter, who had inherited his vigor and his spirit with a beauty that had descended to her from some forgotten peasant girl of the Irish bogs.

Faraday, with his power of listening interminably, and his intelligent comments, was a favorite of old Ryan's. He greeted him with a growling welcome;

and then, civilities being interchanged, called to the Chinaman for another glass. This menial, rubbing off the long mirrors that decorated the walls, would not obey the mandate till it had been roared at him by the wounded lion in a tone which made the chandelier rattle.

"I never can make those infernal idiots understand me," said old Ryan, plaintively. "They won't do a thing I tell them. It takes the old lady to manage 'em. She makes them skip."

Then after some minutes of discourse on more or less uninteresting matters, the weary old man, glad of a listener, launched forth into domestic topics.

"Gen and the old lady are out buying new togs. I got a letter here that'll astonish them when they get back. It's from that English cuss, Courtney. D'ye ever hear about him? He was hanging about Genevieve all last winter. And this letter says he's coming back, that his grandfather's dead, and he's a lord now, and he's coming back. Do you mind that now, Faraday?" he said, looking with eyes full of humor at the young man.

Faraday expressed a sharp surprise.

"You know, Jack," continued the old man, "we're trained up to having these high-priced Englishmen come out here and eat our dinners, and sleep in our spare rooms, and drink our wines and go home, and when they meet us there forget they've ever seen us before; but we ain't trained up to havin' 'em come back this way, and it's hard to get accustomed to it."

"It's not surprising," said Faraday, coldly.

"I'm not so dead sure of that. But I can tell you the old lady'll be wild about this."

"Does Mrs. Ryan like him so much?" said the visitor, still coldly.

"All women like a lord, and Mrs. Ryan ain't different from the rest of her sex. She's dead stuck on Gen marrying him. I'm not myself, Jack. I'm no Anglomaniac; an American's good enough for me. I'm not spoiling to see my money going to patch up the roof of the ancestral castle of the Courtneys, or pay their ancestral debts—not by a long chalk."

"Do you think he's coming back to borrow money from you to pay off the ancestral debts?" asked Faraday.

"Not to borrow, Jack. Oh no, not to borrow—to get it for keeps—it, and Genevieve with it. And I don't just see how I'm to prevent it. Gen don't seem to care much, but the old lady's got it on her mind that she'd like to have a lord in the family, no matter how high they come; and she can work on Gen. Last summer she wanted to go after him—wanted to track him to his lair; but I thought she might's well stop there, and put m' foot down. Gen don't seem to care about him one way or the other, but then 'Lady Genevieve' sounds pretty nice——"

Here a rustle of millinery, approaching through the drawing-room beyond, cut short old Ryan's confidences. Faraday stood up to receive the ladies, who entered jubilant and unwearied from an afternoon's shopping. Genevieve, a magnificent princess, with the air of fashion given by perfectly setting clothes, much brown fur and velvet, a touch of yellow lace, and a quantity of fresh violets pinned to her corsage, looked as if she would make a very fine Lady Genevieve.

As soon as she heard the news she demanded the letter, and perused it intently, Faraday covertly watching her. Raising her eyes, she met his and said, with a little mocking air, "Well, Mr. Faraday, and what do you think of that?"

"That your mother seems to have been right," said Faraday, steadily eyeing her. An expression of chagrin and disappointment, rapid but unmistakable, crossed her face, dimming its radiance like a breath on a mirror. She gave a little toss to her head, and turning away toward an adjacent looking-glass, took off her veil and settled her hat.

Mrs. Ryan watched her with glowing pride, already seeing her in fancy a member of the British aristocracy; but old Ryan looked rather downcast, as he generally did when confronted by the triumphant gorgeousness of the feminine members of his household. Faraday, too, experienced a sudden depression of spirits so violent and so uncalled for that if he had had room for any other feeling he would have been intensely surprised. Barney Ryan, at the prospect of having to repair the breaches in the Courtney exchequer and ancestral roof-tree, may have experienced a pardonable dejection. But why should Faraday, who assured himself a dozen times a day that he merely admired Miss Genevieve, as any man might admire a charming and handsome girl, feel so desperate a despondency?

To prove to himself that his gloom did not rise from the cause that he knew it did rise from, Faraday continued to be a constant guest at the Ryan mansion, continued to see Miss Genevieve at Madame Delmonti's and at the other small social gatherings, where the presentable young New Englander found himself quite a lion. When Mrs. Ryan saw him alone she flattered his superior intelligence and experience of the world by asking his opinion of the approaching Lord Hastings's matrimonial plans. This frank and outspoken lady was on the thorns of uncertainty, Lord Hastings's flight on his former visit having shaken her faith in him. Quite unconsciously she impressed upon Faraday how completely both she and Genevieve had come to trust him as a tried friend.

With the exaltation of a knight of old, Faraday felt that their trust would never be misplaced. He answered Mrs. Ryan's anxious queries with all the honesty of the calmest friendship. Alone in the great gold drawing-room, he talked to Genevieve on books, on music, on fashion, on society—on all subjects but that of love. And all the while he felt like the nightingale who sings its sweetest music while pressing its breast against a thorn.

Lord Hastings seemed to have lost no time in repairing to the side of the fair lady who was supposed to be the object of his fondest devotions, and whom destiny appeared to have selected as the renovator of Courtney Manor. Four weeks from the day Faraday had heard of his intended visit, the Bostonian received a letter from Mrs. Ryan bidding him to dinner to meet the illustrious guest. It seemed to Faraday that to go to see the newcomer in converse with Genevieve, beautiful in her costliest robes, to view the approving smiles of Mrs. Ryan, and perhaps the happy blushes of Miss Ryan, was the manly and upright course for one who could never be more than the avowed friend and silent worshipper of Barney Ryan's only daughter.

Arriving ten minutes late, he found the party already at the table. It was an inflexible rule of Barney Ryan's to sit down to dinner at the stroke of half-past six, whether his guests were assembled or not—a rule which even his wife's cajoleries and commands were powerless to combat.

Tonight the iron old man might well regard with pride the luxury and splendor that crowned a turbulent career begun in nipping poverty. The round table, glowing beneath the lights of the long crystal chandeliers, sparkled with cut-glass, and shone with antique silverware, while in the center a mass of pale purple orchids spread their fragile crêpe-like petals from a fringe of fern. Opposite him, still unfaded, superbly dressed, and admirably self-possessed, was his smiling consort, toward whom, whatever his pride in her might have been, his feelings this evening were somewhat hostile, as the ambitious and determined lady had forced him to don regulation evening dress, arrayed in which Barney's peace of mind and body both fled.

On either side of the table sat his son and daughter, the latter handsomer than Faraday had ever seen her, her heavy dress of ivory-tinted silk no whiter than her neck, a diamond aigret trembling like spray in her hair. Her brother Eddie, a year and a half her senior, looked as if none of the blood of this vigorous strong-thewed, sturdy stock could run in his veins. He was a pale and sickly looking lad, with a weak, vulgar face, thin hair and red eyelids. Faraday had only seen him once or twice before, and judged from remarks made to him by acquaintances of the family that Eddie did not often honor the parental roof with his presence. Eddie's irregular career appeared to be the one subject on which the family maintained an immovable and melancholy reserve. The disappointment in his only son was the bitter drop in Barney Ryan's cup.

There were other guests at the table. Faraday received a coy bow from Mrs. Peck, who had given her hair an extra bleaching for this occasion, till her pinched and powdered little face looked out from under an orange-colored thatch; Mrs. Wheatley was there too, with a suggestion of large white shoulders shining through veilings of black gauze; and with an air of stately pride, Mrs. Ryan presented him to Lord Hastings. This young man, sitting next Genevieve, was a tall, fair, straight-featured Englishman of gravely unresponsive manners. In the severe perfection of his immaculate evening dress he looked a handsome, well-bred young fellow of twenty-five or six.

As the late guest dropped into his seat, the interrupted conversation regathered and flowed again. Barney Ryan said nothing. He never spoke while eating, and rarely talked when women were present. Genevieve too was quiet, responding with a gently absent smile, when her cavalier, turning upon her his cold and expressionless steely-blue eyes, addressed to her some short regulation remark on the weather, or the boredom of his journey across the plains. The phlegmatic calm of his demeanor remained intact, even under the coquettish onslaughts of Mrs. Peck and Mrs. Wheatley, who extracted from him with wheedling perseverance his opinions on the State, the climate, and the country. Lord Hastings replied with iron-bound and unsmiling brevity, his wide cold glance resting with motionless attention upon the painted physiognomy of Mrs. Peck and the broad and buxom one of Mrs. Wheatley, and his head turning with dignified difficulty in his exceedingly high and tight collar, as one and the other assailed him with queries. Meanwhile the object of his journey, slowly moving her great fan of white ostrich feathers, looked across the table at Faraday and made a little surreptitious *moue*.

The conversation soon became absorbed by the two married ladies, Faraday, and Lord Hastings. Only the Ryans were silent, Genevieve now and then throwing a lazy sentence into the vortex of talk, and Mrs. Ryan being occupied in lending a proud ear to the coruscations of wit that sparkled around the board, or in making covert gestures to the soft-footed Mongols, who moved with deft noiselessness about the table. Eddie Ryan, like his father, rarely spoke in society. In the glare of the chandelier he sat like a strange uncomfortable guest, taking no notice of any one. Toward the end of the feast he conversed in urgent whispers with his mother—a conversation which ended in her surreptitiously giving him her keys under the edge of the table. Before coffee, Eddie left, on the plea of an important engagement, retiring through the drawing-room, softly jingling the keys.

After this dinner, when Lord Hastings's presence had banished all his doubts, when the young Englishman's attractive appearance had impressed itself upon his jealous eye, and Genevieve's gentle indifference had seemed to him but a modest form of encouragement, Faraday found but little time to pay visits to the hospitable home of Barney Ryan.

The family friend that they had all so warmly welcomed and taken to their hearts withdrew himself quietly but firmly from their cheerful circle. When, at rare intervals, he did drop in upon them, he pleaded important business engagements as the reason of his inability to accept their numerous invitations to dinners and theater parties. After these mendacious statements he would wend a gloomy way homeward to his Pine Street boarding-house, and there spend the evening pretending to read, and cursing the fate which had ever brought him within the light of Genevieve's *beaux yeux*. The fable of being the family friend was quite shattered. Faraday had capitulated.

Nearly two months after the dinner, when rumors of Genevieve Ryan's engagement to Lord Hastings were in lively circulation, Faraday called at the lion-guarded mansion on California Street, and, in answering to his regulation request for the ladies, received the usual unintelligible Chinese rejoinder, and was shown into the gold drawing-room. There, standing in front of a long mirror, looking at her skirts with an eye of pondering criticism, was Miss Genevieve, dressed to go out. She caught sight of him in the glass, turned abruptly, and came forward, a color in her face.

"Is that you?" she said, holding out her hand. "I am so glad. I thought it was somebody else." Having thus, with her customary candor, signified to Faraday that she was expecting Lord Hastings, she sat down facing him, and said, abruptly, "Why haven't you been here for so long?"

Faraday made the usual excuses, and did not quail before her cold and steady eyes.

"That's rather funny," she said, as he concluded, "for now you're used to your new position, and it must go more easily, and yet you have less time to see your friends than you did at first."

Faraday made more excuses, and wondered that she should take a cruel pleasure in such small teasing.

"I thought p'r'aps," she said, still regarding him with an unflinching scrutiny, her face grave and almost hard, "that you'd begun to find us too Western, that the novelty had worn off, that our ways were too—too—what shall I say?—too wild and woolly."

A flush of anger ran over Faraday's face. "Your suppositions were neither just nor true," he said, coldly.

"Oh, I don't know," she continued, with a careless movement of her head, and speaking in the high, indifferent tone that a woman adopts when she wishes to be exasperating; "you needn't get mad. Lots of Eastern people feel that way. They come out here and see us constantly, and make friends with us, and then go back and laugh at us, and tell their friends what barbarians we are. It's customary, and nothing to be ashamed of."

"Do you suppose that I am that sort of an Eastern person?" asked Faraday, quietly.

"I don't know," she said, doubtfully. "I didn't think you were at first, but now——"

"But now you do. Why?"

"Because you don't come here any more," she said, with a little air of triumph. "You're tired of us. The novelty is over and so are the visits."

Faraday arose, too bitterly annoyed for speech. Genevieve, rising too, and touching her skirts with an arranging hand, continued, apparently unconscious of the storm she was rousing:

"And yet it seems odd that you should find such a difference. Lord Hastings, now, who's English, and much more conventional, thinks the people here just as refined and particular as any other Americans."

"It's evident," said Faraday, in a voice roughened with anger, "that Lord Hastings's appreciation of the refinement of the Americans is only equaled by your admiration for the talents of the English."

"I do like them," said Genevieve, dubiously, shaking her head, as if she was admitting a not entirely creditable taste, and looking away from him.

There was a moment's silence. Faraday fastened his eyes upon her in a look of passionate confession that in its powerful pleading drew her own back to his.

"You're as honest as you are cruel," he said, almost in a whisper.

She made no reply, but turned her head sharply away, as if in sudden embarrassment. Then, in answer to his conventionally murmured good-byes, she looked back, and he saw her face radiant, alight, with the most beautiful smile trembling on the lips. The splendor of this look seemed to him a mute expression of her happiness—of love reciprocated, ambition realized—and in it he read his own doom. He turned blindly round to pick up his hat; the door behind him was opened, and there, handsome, debonair, fresh as a May morning, stood Lord Hastings, hat in hand.

"I hope you're not vexed, Miss Ryan," said this young man, "but I'm very much afraid I'm just a bit late."

After this Faraday thought it quite unnecessary to visit Barney Ryan's "palatial mansion" for some time. Genevieve's engagement would soon be announced, and then he would have to go and offer his congratulations. As to whether he would dance at her wedding with a light heart—that was another matter. He assured himself that she was making a splendid and eminently suitable marriage. With her beauty and money and true simple heart she would deck the fine position which the Englishman could give her. He wished her every happiness, but that he should stand by and watch the progress of the courtship seemed to him an unnecessary twisting of the knife in the wound. Even the endurance of New England human nature has its limits, and Faraday could stand no more. So he refused an invitation to a tea from Mrs. Ryan, and one to a dinner and another to a small musical from Miss Ryan, and alone in his Pine Street lodgings, for the first time in his life, read the "social columns" with a throbbing heart.

One Saturday afternoon, two weeks from the day that he had last seen Genevieve, he sat in his room trying to read. He had left the office early, and though it was still some hours before dark, a heavy unremitting rain had enveloped the afternoon in a

premature twilight. The perpetual run of water from a break in the gutter near his window sounded drearily through the depressing history of the woes and disappointments of David Grieve. The gloom of the book and the afternoon was settling upon Faraday with the creeping stealthiness of a chill, when a knock sounded upon his door, and one of the servants without acquainted him with the surprising piece of intelligence that a lady was waiting to see him in the sitting-room below.

As he entered the room, dim with the heavy somberness of the leaden atmosphere, he saw his visitor standing looking out of the window—a tall, broad-shouldered, small-waisted striking figure, with a neat black turban crowning her closely braided hair. At his step she turned, and revealed the gravely handsome face of Genevieve Ryan. He made no attempt to take her hand, but murmured a regulation sentence of greeting; then, looking into her eyes, saw for the first time that handsome face marked with strong emotion. Miss Ryan was shaken from her phlegmatic calm; her hand trembled on the back of the chair before her; the little knot of violets in her dress vibrated to the beating of her heart.

"This is not a very conventional thing to do," she said, with her usual ignoring of all preamble, "but I can't help that. I had something to talk to you about, Mr. Faraday, and as you would not come to see me, I had to come to see you."

"What is it that you wanted to see me about?" asked Faraday, standing motionless, and feeling in the sense of oppression and embarrassment that seemed to weigh upon them both the premonition of an approaching crisis.

She made no answer for a moment, but stood looking down, as if in an effort to choose her words or collect her thoughts, the violets in her dress rising and falling with her quickened breathing.

"It's rather hard to know how to say—anything," she said at length.

"If I can do anything for you," said the young man, "you know it would always be a happiness to me to serve you."

"Oh, it's not a message or a favor," she said, hastily. "I only wanted to say something"—she paused in great embarrassment—"but it's even more queer, more unusual, than my coming here."

Faraday made no response, and for a space both were silent. Then she said, speaking with a peculiar low distinctness:

"The last time I saw you I seemed very disagreeable. I wanted to make sure of something. I wanted to make sure that you were fond of me—to surprise it out of you. Well—I did it. You are fond of me. I made you show it to me." She raised her eyes, brilliant and dark, and looked into his. "If you were to swear to me now that I was wrong I would know you were not telling the truth," she said, with proud defiance. "You love me."

"Yes," said Faraday, slowly, "I do. What then?"

"What then?" she repeated. "Why do you go away—go away from me?"

"Because," he answered, "I am too much of a man to live within sight of the woman I love and can never hope for."

"Can never hope for?" she exclaimed, aghast. "Are you—are you married?"

The sudden horror on her face was a strange thing for Faraday to see.

"No," he said, "I am not married."

"Then, did she tell you that you never could hope for her?" said Miss Genevieve Ryan, in a tremulous voice.

"No. It was not necessary. I knew myself."

"You did yourself a wrong, and her too," she broke out, passionately. "You should have told her, and given her a chance to say—to say what she has a right to say, without making her come to you, with her love in her hand, to offer it to you as if she was afraid you were going to throw it back in her face. It's bad enough being a woman anyway, but to have the feelings of a woman, and then have to say a thing like this—it's—it's—ghastly."

"Genevieve!" breathed Faraday.

"Why don't you understand?" she continued, desperately. "You won't see it. You make me come here and tell it to you this way. I may be badly mannered and unconventional, but I have feelings and pride like other women. But what else could I do?"

Her voice suddenly broke into soft appeal, and she held out her hands toward him with a gesture as spontaneous in its pleading tenderness as though made by a child. Faraday was human. He dashed away the chair that stood between them and clasped the trembling hands in his.

"Why is it," she asked, looking into his face with shining troubled eyes—"why is it you acted this way?

Was it Lord Hastings? I refused him two weeks ago. I thought I'd marry him once, but that was before I knew you. Then I waited for you, and you didn't come, and I wrote to you, and you wouldn't come. And so I had to come and tell you myself, and it's been something dreadful."

Faraday made no response, but feeling the smooth hands curled warm inside his, he stood listening to those soft accents that issued with the sweetness that love alone lends to women's voices from lips he had thought as far beyond his reach as the key of the rainbow.

"Do you think it was awful for me to do it?" she queried, in whispering anxiety.

He shook his head.

"Well," she said, laughing a littte and turning her head half away, as her former embarrassment began to reassert itself over her subsiding nervousness, "I've often wished I was a man, but if it's always as awful as that to propose to a person, I'm quite content to be a woman."

GIDEON'S KNOCK

BY

MARY HALLECK FOOTE

GIDEON'S KNOCK

Y A curious coincidence, whenever George Fleming was translated to a wider berth, it was my luck to succeed him in the job he had just quitted. This had happened more than once, in the chances and changes that befall the younger men in the mining profession, before we began to jolly each other about it—always at long range.

When I heard he had resigned from the Consolidated Resumption, to everybody's surprise, at a time of great prosperity to the mine, I hailed my chance and congratulated myself that I should speedily be asked to fill his place: and I was!

I wrote him on the spot a playful letter, alluding to my long, stern chase and begging him to hold on this time till I could shake him by the hand; I had come to have a personal sentiment toward him apart from the natural desire to meet face to face the author of my continued advancement. But to this letter I received no word of reply.

His silence haunted me, rather—I thought about him a good deal while I was closing up my affairs in other directions before taking over the Consolidated Resumption. Meanwhile the company's cashier,

Joshua Dean, a man of trust but small initiative, was filling the interregnum.

I found him living alone in the manager's house with the Flemings' Chinese cook as man of all work. The Resumption has never tolerated a boarding-house or a village or compound within sight of its official windows. Its first manager was a son of the chief owner, who built his house in the style of a gentleman's country-seat, small but exclusive and quite apart from the work. I liked the somber seclusion of the place, planted deep with trees of about twenty years' growth, showing their delicate, changing greens against the darker belt of pines. But its aspect increased, if anything, that uneasy sensation, like a cold wind in my back, which I still had in thinking of Fleming.

I had driven out to dine with Dean on the evening of my arrival. It was the last week in January; there had been much rain already for the foothills. Wet sprays from the untrimmed rose hedges disputed my passage through the inner gate. Discolored pine-needles lay in sodden drifts on the neglected grass. The hydrant leaked frozen puddles down the brick-paved walk. Mounting the veranda steps I laid my hand on the knocker, when an old Chinese servant popped his head out at a side-door and violently beckoned me in that way.

Dean, as I knew, had made his home with the Flemings for some time before their departure. After a few talks with him and a survey of the house I decided we might venture to continue the arrangement without getting in each other's way. It was a house peculiarly adapted to a *solitude à deux*. There was no telephone nearer than the office. I argued that Fleming was a man who could protect himself from frivolous intrusions, and his wife could have had but little in common with her neighbors in the village.

He had resigned on account of her health, I was told. It must have been a hasty flitting or an inconclusive one. The odd, attractive rooms were full of their belongings still. We two casual bachelors with our circumspect habits could make no impression on the all but speaking silence of those empty rooms. They filled me at times with a curious emotion of sadness and unrest.

Joshua seldom talked of the Flemings, though I knew he received letters from them. That he was deeply attached to their memory, hoarded it and brooded over it, I could not doubt. I even suspected some jealous sentiment on his part which made it hard for him to see me using their chairs, planting myself amongst their cushions and investigating their book-shelves. I thought it strange they had left so many things behind them of a personal nature. They seemed to have ceased to care for what most of us rolling stones are wont to cling to. Their departure had something unspeakable in it—akin to sudden death, or a sickness of the heart that made life indifferent to them.

"They must have loved this room!" I said to him one evening. It was during the black rains of February—Dean and I with our chairs to the fire, waiting for the Eastern mail. The night watchman's orders were to stop for it if the trains were anywhere near on time. At this storm season the Westbound

"*He* no lock!" Jim planted himself in front of me; his voice quavered nervously. "All time I *un*-lock! Fi' 'tlock whistle blow—I go quick! Nobody wait. I all time run."

"Why should you run? What is the knocker for?" I repeated. At this I stepped past him, startling him somewhat, and hurled open the front door. I had heard our coy watchman going down the path.

"Tomorrow night, Fahey," I shouted, "you bring the bag in this way. Knock, man! There's the knocker—see?"

Jim looked at me with eyes aghast. He gathered himself for speech, breathing deeply.

"Mis' Oth' (my name is Othet), I tell you: Long time—*long* time, no man knock flon' do'. In this house, no good. No good knock. Sometime some—come—you no man see!" He lowered his voice to a rapid whisper, spreading his yellow palms tremulously. "You tell man come knock flon' do'—I go 'way. Too much bad thing!"

Muttering to himself he retreated. "Now what has he got on his mind do you suppose? Could you make out what he was driving at?"

Dean smiled, a non-committal smile. "It would be rather awkward for us, wouldn't it, if Jim should leave? We are too far from the coast for city servants in winter. I doubt if any of the natives could be persuaded to stay in this house alone."

"You think Jim would leave if I made Fahey knock at that door every night?"

Joshua answered me obliquely. "If I could ever quote anything straight, I would remind you of a saying in one of George Eliot's novels that 'we've

all got to take a little trouble to keep sane and call things by the same names as other people.' Perhaps Jim doesn't take quite trouble enough. I have difficulty sometimes myself to find names for things. I should like to hear you classify a certain occurrence I have in mind, not unconnected, I think, with Jim's behavior tonight. I've never discussed it, of course. In fact, I've never spoken of it before." He smiled queerly. "It's very astonishing how they know things."

"The menials?"

He nodded. "Jim was in the house at the time. No one knows that he heard it,—no one ever told him. But he is thinking of it tonight just as I am. He's never forgotten it for a moment, and never will."

Joshua dragged the charred logs forward and stooped amid their sparks to lay a fresh one with its back to the chimney. Then he rose and looked out; as he stood in the door, I could hear the hissing of fine snow turning to rain and the drenched bamboo whipping the piazza posts; over all, the larger lament of the pines, and, from the long rows of lights in the gulch, the diapason of the stamp-heads thundering on through the night.

"'Identities of sensation,' said Joshua, quoting again as he shut the door, "are strong with persons who live in lonely places! Jim and I have lived here too long."

"Well, I hope you won't live here another moment till you have told me that story," I urged, and we drew again to the fire.

"There was a watchman here before Fahey," he

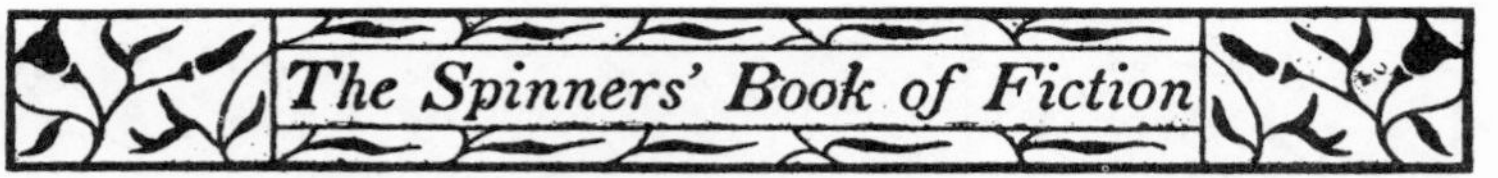

began, "an old plainsman, with a Bible name, Gideon. He looked like the pictures of old Ossawattamie Brown, and he had for the Flemings a most unusual regard. It was as strong as his love for his family. It was because of what Fleming did for his son, young Gid, when they caught him stealing specimens with a gang of old offenders. Gid was nineteen, and a pretty good boy, we thought. Such things happen between men of the right sort every day, I suppose,—Fleming would say so. But it was his opportunity to do it for a man who could feel and remember, and he made a friend for life right there. It is too long a story to tell, but young Gid's all right—working in the city, married and happy,—trusted like any other man. It wasn't in the blood, you see.

"Before his boy got into trouble, Fleming used to call the old man 'Gideon,' talked to him any old way; but after his pride fell down it was always 'Mr. Gideon,' and a few words when he brought the mail, about the weather or the conduct of the trains. The old man appeared to stand taller in those moments at the door, when he brought to the house the very food of its existence. They lived upon their letters, for both the children were away. The army boy in the Philippines; it was during the Mindanao campaign; and Constance (Joshua, I noticed, took a deep breath before the name), the daughter, was at school in the East. Gideon could gauge the spirits of the two, waiting here for what he brought them. He kept tally of the soldier's letters, the thin blue ones that came strolling in by the transport lines. But hers—her letters were his pride.

"'It's there all right,' he would say—'she never

misses a Monday mail, the little one!' or, as the winter months wore on—'you'll be counting the weeks now, madam. Six more letters and then the telegram from Ogden, and I hope it's my privilege to bring it, madam.' For as Fleming gave him his title, the old man passed it back with a glow of emphasis, putting devotion into the 'madam' and life service into the 'Mr. Fleming, sir.'

"Then she came home—Constance—she was no longer the little one. Taller than her mother, and rather silent, but her looks were a language, and her motions about the house—I suppose no words could measure their pride in her, or their shrinking when they thought of her in contact with the world. People laughed a little, looking at her, when her mother talked of the years they were going to have together. And she would rebuke the laugh and say, 'We do not marry early in my family, nor the Flemings either.' When the August heat came on, they thought she was too pale—they spared her for a visit to some friends who had a houseboat off Belvedere, or some such place. It was an ambush of fate. She came home, thin, brown, from living on the water,—happy! too happy for safety. She brought her fate with her, the last man you'd suppose could ever cross her path. He was from Hawaii, an Englishman—not all English, some of us thought. Handsome as a snake; a face that kept no marks. Eyes all black—nothing of the pupil showing. They say such eyes are not to be trusted. I never liked him. I'd better not try to describe him.

"It seemed madness to me, but I suppose they were no more helpless than other fathers and mothers.

He had plenty to say for himself, and introductions—all sorts of credentials, except a pair of eyes. They had to let it go on; and he took her away from them six months after she saw him first. That's happiness, if you call it so!"

Again I added, "It is life."

"There was not much left of it in this house after she went," Joshua mused. "It was then they asked me to come up and stay with them. A silence of three does not press quite so close as a silence of two. And we talked sometimes. The mine had taken a great jump; it was almost a mockery the way things boomed. The letters, I noticed, were not what the schoolgirl letters had been to her mother. They came all right, they were punctual, but something I felt sure was wrong. Mrs. Fleming would not have missed a mail for anything in the world—every hour's delay wore upon her. She would play her game of solitaire, long after bed-time, at that desk by the drop-light. It seemed she could not read; nothing held her. She was irritable with Fleming, and then she would pet him piteously to make up. He was always gentle. He would watch her over his book as she walked up and down in the back room in the light between the dining-room curtains. If he saw I noticed, he'd look away and begin to talk.

"I have gone a little ahead of my story, for this was after the dark weather came on and the mails were behind; we knew there was some new strain on her spirits. You could see her face grow small and her flesh waste away.

"One night we sat here, Fleming and I, and she

was pacing in her soft, weary way in the back of the room. There came a knock. It was Gideon's, yet none of us had heard the gate click nor any step outside. She stood back, for she never showed any impatience—she tried to pretend that she expected nothing. Fleming opened the door; he stood there an instant looking out.

"'Didn't you hear a knock?' he asked me. Before I could answer he went outside, closing the door, and we heard him go down the steps slowly.

"When he came in he merely said, 'A jar of wind.'

"'A jar of wind!' Mrs. Fleming mocked him. The knock came again as she spoke. Once, twice, then the light tap: I have described Gideon's knock. We did not pretend again it was the wind.

"'You go this time;' Fleming tried to laugh. 'See if there is anything doing.'

"There was nothing doing whatever, and nothing to be seen. I turned on the electrics outside, and Fleming, seeing the light, came out to join me. I asked him if those were his tracks—a man's footsteps could be seen printed in the fresh, light snow as far as the lowest step and back. All beyond, where the light streamed down the path to the gate, was sky-fresh snow softly laid without wind. 'Those are my tracks,' he said. 'There were no others before—sure,' he repeated, 'and there is no one down at the gate. You need not go down there. Say nothing to her,' he continued as we re-opened the door.

"She was expecting us. She was very pale but half smiling, braving it out. She fixed her eyes on

Fleming and then on me. 'Did you not *both* hear that knock?' As she spoke it came again. I stood nearest the door; I hurled it open. Absolutely nothing. The lights, burning in a silly way, made shadows on the steps. Not a mark, not even a leaf-track on the path we could see below.

"I went over to the telephone and called up the post-office. What happened at the house in my absence I do not know. I found the drawing-room empty; Fleming joined me coming from his wife's room.

"'She is fearfully upset by that knocking,' he said. 'Can't we think up some explanation?'

"I feared he would have less courage for inventing explanations after what I had to tell him.

"I had followed the track of a horse and cart to the stable and found Gideon's old mare at her hitching-post; the cart was empty, the muddy lap-robe dragging over the wheel. At the post-office they told me Gideon had started for the mine an hour and a half ago. 'Hasn't he got out there with that telegram yet?' they added. From the telegraph office, where they knew Gideon's hours, they had sent a message across to the post-office to be carried out by him with the mail. The voice on the telephone remarked, 'I guess they ought to get that wire pretty soon. It was marked *Important.*'

"Fleming was cold and shaking as he listened. 'Drive back along the road through the woods, Joshua'—he seldom called me by that name. 'I think something has happened to the old man. His knock is on duty tonight, but where is he?'

"It came again, and following it a low cry from

the passage behind closed doors. 'She heard it too,' said Fleming. And he went to his wife.

"I called up the landing-man to help me—Tommy Briscoe; I knew he wouldn't spread any talk about. The search was not long. A lantern burning by itself in the woods showed us where he had stopped the cart and half turned and tramped around in the snow. He'd dropped the bag out, probably, missed it and looked for it on foot, setting his lantern down. He'd gone back quite a bit along the road, and, coming back with it, the light in his eyes, he had made a misstep, and the shaft—the old Granite Hill shaft, you know—it's close to the road. We found him in the sump at the bottom. There had been too much rain, but it is a deep shaft anyway. He kept his hold on the bag, and he kept his senses long enough to hook it onto a poor little stray pine-root above the water, where he died. It was a cruel death, but his face was good to look at."

"And the telegram?" I asked.

"It was safe. He'd saved everything, except himself. They were driven over to Colfax that night, with not a moment to spare——"

"But you haven't told me what it was."

"The message? Yes, it was from her, Constance—sent from an address in the city. It said—I suppose I may repeat it. It is part of the night's work.

"'Come to me, mother,' it said. 'I am here. I need you.'"

"And they were in time?"

"To bid her good-by," said Joshua. "There was no hope for her but in death. Of course, they never explained. She simply fled from—we don't know what. As long as she could she bore it without complaint, and then she came home. She had them both with her and she knew them.

"I believe they were willing to give her up. It was the only solution left. They were very fixed in their ideas about divorce, and what comes after. They believed in staking all or nothing and abiding the result. The logic of her choice was death. They saw her free, without a stain, without an obligation in this life, even to her child, for it lay dead beside her. They did grieve for that. They wanted it to live. It would have been something—yet, I believe, even that was best.

"They lived on here for a while, if you call it living; but the silence in these rooms was more than she could endure. And I need not tell you that the watchman, who was put on after Gideon, had orders to leave that knocker alone."

"And you think," I asked, "that while Gideon lay dead at the bottom of the shaft, his knock was 'marching on'?" I regretted instantly the turn of my last sentence. Joshua stiffened as he replied:

"No; I cannot assert that he was dead, but I am convinced that what was left of him, of his mortal—or immortal—consciousness, was not concerned with himself. What may happen to us at that last boundary post is one of the mysteries no man can solve till he gets there."

"Joshua," I said, "the drift of your conclusion is a tribute to Gideon's faithfulness—well deserved I have no doubt. But if you'll allow me to say so, it is not a tribute to the healthy state of your mind. I regret to say it, but I fear that I agree with you: I think you have lived in this house too long."

"If I have lived here too long for any other reason," he answered gently, "enough has been said. It is better we should understand each other. But, as to my mind—I prefer to keep it unhealthy, if by that you mean the tendency to project it a little farther than reason, founded on such laws of the universe as we know, can help us. Healthy minds are such as accept things—endeavor to forget what gives immeasurable pain. I prefer the pain."

A YELLOW MAN AND A WHITE

BY

ELEANOR GATES

Reprinted from *Scribner's Magazine* of June, 1905
by permission

A YELLOW MAN AND A WHITE

FONG WU sat on the porch of his little square-fronted house, chanting into the twilight. Across his padded blouse of purple silk lay his *sam-yen* banjo. And as, from time to time, his hymn to the Three Pure Ones was prolonged in high, fine quavers, like the uneven, squeaky notes of a woman's voice, he ran his left hand up the slender neck of the instrument, rested a long nail of his right on its taut, snake's-skin head, and lightly touched the strings; then, in quick, thin tones, they followed the song to Sang-Ching.

The warm shadows of a California summer night were settling down over the wooded hills and rocky gulches about Fong Wu's, and there was little but his music to break the silence. Long since, the chickens had sleepily sought perches in the hen yard, with its high wall of rooty stumps and shakes, and on the branches of the Digger pine that towered beside it. Up the dry creek bed, a mile away, twinkled the lights of Whiskeytown; but no sounds from the homes of the white people came down to the lonely Chinese. If his clear treble was interrupted, it was by the cracking of a dry branch as a cottontail sped past on its way to a stagnant pool, or it was by a dark-emboldened coyote, howling, dog-like, at the moon which, white as the snow that eternally coifs the Sierras, was just rising above their distant, cobalt line.

One year before, Fong Wu, heavily laden with his effects, had slipped out of the stage from Redding and found his way to a forsaken, ramshackle building below Whiskeytown. His coming had proved of small interest. When the news finally got about that "a monkey" was living in "Sam Kennedy's old place," it was thought, for a while, that laundering, thereafter, would be cheaply done. This hope, however, was soon dispelled. For, shortly after his arrival, as Fong Wu asked at the grocery store for mail, he met Radigan's inquiry of "You do my washee, John ?" with a grave shake of the head. Similar questions from others were met, later, in a similar way. Soon it became generally known that the "monkey at Sam Kennedy's" did not do washing; so he was troubled no further.

Yet if Fong Wu did not work for the people of Whiskeytown, he was not, therefore, idle. Many a sunrise found him wandering through the chaparral thickets back of his house, digging here and there in the red soil for roots and herbs. These he took home, washed, tasted, and, perhaps, dried. His mornings were mainly spent in cooking for his abundantly supplied table, in tending his fowls and house, and in making spotless and ironing smooth various undergarments—generous of sleeve and leg.

But of an afternoon, all petty duties were laid aside, and he sorted carefully into place upon his shelves numerous little bunches and boxes of dried

herbs and numerous tiny phials of pungent liquid that had come to him by post; he filled wide sheets of foolscap with vertical lines of queer characters and consigned them to big, plainly addressed, well-stamped envelopes; he scanned closely the last newspapers from San Francisco, and read from volumes in divers tongues, and he pored over the treasured Taoist book, "The Road to Virtue."

Sunday was his one break in the week's routine. Then, the coolies who panned or cradled for gold in the tailings of near-by abandoned mines, gathered at Fong Wu's. On such occasions, there was endless, lively chatter, a steady exchange of barbering—one man scraping another clean, to be, in turn, made hairless in a broad band about the poll and on cheek and chin—and much consuming of tasty chicken, dried fish, pork, rice, and melon seeds. To supplement all this, Fong Wu recounted the news: the arrival of a consul in San Francisco, the raid on a slave- or gambling-den, the progress of a tong war under the very noses of the baffled police, and the growth of Coast feeling against the continued, quiet immigration of Chinese. But of the social or political affairs of the Flowery Kingdom—of his own land beyond the sea—Fong Wu was consistently silent.

Added to his Sunday responsibilities as host and purveyor of news, Fong Wu had others. An ailing countryman, whether seized with malaria or suffering from an injury, found ready and efficient attention. The bark of dogwood, properly cooked, gave a liquid that killed the ague; and oil from a diminutive bottle, or a red powder whetted upon the skin with a silver piece, brought out the soreness of a bruise.

Thus, keeping his house, herb-hunting, writing, studying, entertaining, doctoring, Fong Wu lived on at Whiskeytown.

Each evening, daintily manipulating ivory chopsticks, he ate his supper of rice out of a dragon-bordered bowl. Then, when he had poured tea from a pot all gold-encrusted—a cluster of blossoms nodding in a vase at his shoulder the while—he went out upon the porch of the square-fronted house.

And there, as now, a scarlet-buttoned cap on his head, his black eyes soft with dreaming, his richly wrought sandals tapping the floor in time, his long queue—a smooth, shining serpent—in thick coils about his tawny neck, Fong Wu thrummed gently upon the three-stringed banjo, and, in peace, chanted into the twilight.

* * * * * * * *

Flying hoofs scattered the gravel on the strip of road before Fong Wu's. He looked through the gloom and saw a horse flash past, carrying a skirted rider toward Whiskeytown. His song died out. He let his banjo slip down until its round head rested between his feet. Then he turned his face up the gulch.

Despite the dusk, he knew the traveler: Mrs. Anthony Barrett, who, with her husband, had recently come to live in a house near Stillwater. Every evening, when the heat was over, she went by, bound for the day's mail at the post-office. Every evening, in the cool, Fong Wu saw her go, and sometimes she gave him a friendly nod.

Her mount was a spirited, mouse-dun mustang, with crop-ears, a roached mane, and the back markings of a mule. She always rode at a run, sitting with easy erectness. A wide army hat rested snugly on her fair hair, and shaded a white forehead and level-looking eyes. But notwithstanding the sheltering brim, on her girlish face were set the glowing, scarlet seals of wind and sun.

As he peered townward after her, Fong Wu heard the hurrying hoof-beats grow gradually fainter and fainter—and cease. Presently the moon topped the pines on the foot-hills behind him, bathing the gulch in light. The road down which she would come sprang into view. He watched its farthest open point. In a few moments the hoof-beats began again. Soon the glint of a light waist showed through the trees. Next, horse and rider rounded a curve at hand. Fong Wu leaned far forward.

And then, just as the mustang gained the strip of road before the square-fronted house, it gave a sudden, unlooked-for, outward leap, reared with a wild snort, and, whirling, dashed past the porch—riderless.

With an exclamation, Fong Wu flung his banjo aside and ran to the road. There under a manzanita bush, huddled and still, lay a figure. He caught it up, bore it to the porch, and put it gently down.

A brief examination, made with the deftness practise gives, showed him that no bones were broken. Squatting beside the unconscious woman, he next played slowly with his long-nailed fingers upon her pulse. Its beat reassured him. He lighted a lamp and held it above her. The scarlet of her cheeks was returning.

The sight of her, who was so strong and active,

stretched weak and fainting, compelled Fong Wu into spoken comment. "The petal of a plum blossom," he said compassionately, in his own tongue.

She stirred a little. He moved back. As, reviving, she opened her eyes, they fell upon him. But he was half turned away, his face as blank and lifeless as a mask.

She gave a startled cry and sat up. "Me hurtee?" she asked him, adopting pidgin-English. "Me fallee off?"

Fong Wu rose. "You were thrown," he answered gravely.

She colored in confusion. "Pardon me," she said, "for speaking to you as if you were a coolie." Then, as she got feebly to her feet—"I believe my right arm is broken."

"I have some knowledge of healing," he declared; "let me look at it." Before she could answer, he had ripped the sleeve away. "It is only a sprain," he said. "Wait." He went inside for an amber liquid and bandages. When he had laved the injured muscles, he bound them round.

"How did it happen?" she asked, as he worked. He was so courteous and professional that her alarm was gone.

"Your horse was frightened by a rattler in the road. I heard it whir."

She shuddered. "I ought to be thankful that I didn't come my cropper on it," she said, laughing nervously.

He went inside again, this time to prepare a cupful of herbs. When he offered her the draught, she screwed up her face over its nauseating fumes.

"If that acts as strongly as it tastes," she said, after she had drunk it, "I'll be well soon."

"It is to keep away inflammation."

"Oh! Can I go now?"

"Yes. But tomorrow return, and I will look at the arm." He took the lamp away and replaced his red-buttoned cap with a black felt hat. Then he silently preceded her down the steps to the road. Only when the light of her home shone plainly ahead of them, did he leave her.

They had not spoken on the way. But as he bowed a good night, she addressed him. "I thank you," she said. "And may I ask your name?"

"Kwa"—he began, and stopped. Emotion for an instant softened his impassive countenance. He turned away. "Fong Wu," he added, and was gone.

The following afternoon the crunch of cart wheels before the square-fronted house announced her coming. Fong Wu closed "The Book of Virtue," and stepped out upon the porch.

A white man was seated beside her in the vehicle. As she sprang from it, light-footed and smiling, and mounted the steps, she indicated him politely to the Chinese.

"This is my husband," she said. "I have told him how kind you were to me last night."

Fong Wu nodded.

Barrett hastened to voice his gratitude. "I certainly am very much obliged to you," he said. "My wife might have been bitten by the rattler, or she might have lain all night in pain if you hadn't found her. And I want to say that your treatment was splendid. Why, her arm hasn't swollen or hurt her.

I'll be hanged if I can see—you're such a good doctor—why you stay in this——"

Fong Wu interrupted him. "I will wet the bandage with medicine," he said, and entered the house.

They watched him with some curiosity as he treated the sprain and studied the pulse. When he brought out her second cup of steaming herbs, Mrs. Barrett looked up at him brightly.

"You know we're up here for Mr. Barrett's health," she said. "A year or so after we were married, he was hurt in a railway collision. Since then, though his wounds healed nicely, he has never been quite well. Dr. Lord, our family physician, prescribed plenty of rough work, and a quiet place, far from the excitement of a town or city. Now, all this morning, when I realized how wonderful it was that my arm wasn't aching, I've been urging my husband—what do you suppose?—to come and be examined by you!"

Fong Wu, for the first time, looked fully at the white man, marking the sallow, clayey face, with its dry, lined skin, its lusterless eyes and drooping lids.

Barrett scowled at his wife. "Nonsense, dear," he said crossly; "you know very well that Lord would never forgive me."

"But Fong Wu might help you," she declared.

Fong Wu's black eyes were still fixed searchingly upon the white man. Before their scrutiny, soul-deep, the other's faltered and fell.

"You might help him, mightn't you, Fong Wu?" Mrs. Barrett repeated.

An expression, curious, keen, and full of meaning, was the answer. Then, "I might if he——" Fong Wu said, and paused.

Past Mrs. Barrett, whose back was toward her husband, the latter had shot a warning glance. "Come, come, Edith," he cried irritably; "let's get home."

Mrs. Barrett emptied her cup bravely. "When shall we call again?" she asked.

"You need not come again," Fong Wu replied. "Each day you have only to dampen the bandages from these." He handed her a green-flowered box containing twelve tiny compartments; in each was a phial.

"And I sha'n't have to take any more of this—this awful stuff?" she demanded gaily, giving back the cup.

"No."

"Ah! And now, I want to thank you again, with all my heart. Here,"—she reached into the pocket of her walking-skirt,—"here is something for your trouble." Two double-eagles lay on her open palm.

Fong Wu frowned at them. "I take no money," he said, a trifle gruffly. And as she got into the cart, he closed the door of his home behind him.

It was a week before Mrs. Barrett again took up her rides for the mail. When she did, Fong Wu did not fail to be on his porch as she passed. For each evening, as she cantered up the road, spurring the mustang to its best paces, she reined to speak to him. And he met her greetings with unaccustomed good humor.

Then she went by one morning before sunrise, riding like the wind. A little later she repassed, whipping her horse at every gallop. Fong Wu, called to his door by the clatter, saw that her face was white and drawn. At noon, going up to the post-office, he heard a bit of gossip that seemed to bear upon her unwonted trip. Radigan was rehearsing it excitedly to his wife, and the Chinese busied himself with his mail and listened—apparently unconcerned.

"I c'n tell you she ain't afraid of anythin', that Mrs. Barrett," the post-master was saying; "neither th' cayuse she rides or a critter on two legs. An' that fancy little drug-clerk from 'Frisco got it straight from th' shoulder."

"S-s-sh!" admonished his wife, from the back of the office. "Isn't there some one outside?"

"Naw, just th' chink from Kennedy's. Well, as I remarked, she did jus' light into that dude. 'It was criminal!' she says, an' her eyes snapped like a whip; 'it was criminal! an' if I find out for sure that you are guilty, I'll put you where you'll never do it again.' Th' young gent smirked at her an' squirmed like a worm. 'You're wrong, Mrs. Barrett,' he says, lookin' like th' meek puppy he is, 'an' you'll have t' look some place else for th' person that done it.' But she wouldn't talk no longer—jus' walked out, as mad as a hornet."

"Well, well," mused Mrs. Radigan. "I wonder what 'twas all about. 'Criminal,' she said, eh? That's funny!" She walked to the front of the office and peeked through the wicket. But no one was loitering near except Fong Wu, and his face was the picture of dull indifference.

That night, long after the hour for Mrs. Barrett's regular trip, and long past the time for his supper-song, Fong Wu heard slow, shuffling steps approach the house. A moment afterward, the knob of his door was rattled. He put out his light and slipped a knife into his loose sleeve.

After some fumbling and moving about on the porch, a man called out to him. He recognized the voice.

"Fong Wu! Fong Wu!" it begged. "Let me in. I want to see you; I want to ask you for help—for something I need. Let me in; let me in."

Fong Wu, without answering, relit his lamp, and, with the air of one who is at the same time both relieved and a witness of the expected, flung the door wide.

Then into the room, writhing as if in fearful agony, his hands palsied, his face a-drip and, except for dark blotches about the mouth, green-hued, his eyes wild and sunken, fell, rather than tottered, Anthony Barrett.

"Fong Wu," he pleaded, from the floor at the other's feet, "you helped my wife when she was sick, now help me. I'm dying! I'm dying! Give it to me, for God's sake! give it to me." He caught at the skirt of Fong Wu's blouse.

The Chinese retreated a little, scowling. "What do you want?" he asked.

A paroxysm of pain seized Barrett. He half rose and stumbled forward. "You know," he panted, "you know. And if I don't have some, I'll die. I can't get it anywhere else. She's found me out, and scared the drug-clerk. Oh, just a little, old man, just a little!" He sank to the floor again.

"I can give you nothing," said Fong Wu bluntly. "I do not keep—what you want."

With a curse, Barrett was up again. "Oh, you don't," he screamed, leering frenziedly. "You yellow devil! You almond-eyed pigtail! But I know you do! And I must have it. Quick! quick!" He hung, clutching, on the edge of Fong Wu's wide ironing-table, an ashen wreck.

Fong Wu shook his head.

With a cry, Barrett came at him and seized his lean throat. "You damned highbinder!" he gasped. "You saddle-nosed monkey! You'll get me what I want or I'll give you away. Don't I know why you're up here in these woods, with your pretty clothes and your English talk? A-*ha!* You bet I do! You're hiding, and you're wanted,"—he dropped his voice to a whisper,—"the tongs would pay head-money for you. If you don't give it to me, I'll put every fiend in 'Frisco on your trail."

Fong Wu had caught Barrett's wrists. Now he cast him to one side. "Tongs!" he said with a shrug, as if they were beneath his notice. And "Fiends!" he repeated contemptuously, a taunt in his voice.

The white man had fallen prone and was grovelling weakly. "Oh, I won't tell on you," he wailed imploringly. "I won't, I won't, Fong Wu; I swear it on my honor."

Fong Wu grunted and reached to a handy shelf. "I will make a bargain with you," he said craftily; "first, you are to drink what I wish."

"Anything! anything!" Barrett cried.

From a box of dry herbs, long untouched, the Chinese drew out a handful. There was no time for brewing. Outraged nature demanded instant relief.

He dropped them into a bowl, covered them with water, and stirred swiftly. When the stems and leaves were broken up and well mixed, he strained a brown liquid from them and put it to the other's lips.

"Drink," he commanded, steadying the shaking head.

Barrett drank, unquestioningly.

Instantly the potion worked. Calmed as if by a miracle, made drowsy to a point where speech was impossible, the white man, tortured but a moment before, tipped sleepily into Fong Wu's arms. The Chinese waited until a full effect was secured, when he lifted his limp patient to the blanket-covered ironing-table. Then he went out for fuel, built a fire, and, humming softly—with no fear of waking the other—sat down to watch the steeping of more herbs.

* * * * * * * *

What happened next at the square-fronted house was the unexpected. Again there was a sound of approaching footsteps, again some one gained the porch. But this time there was no pausing to ask for admission, there were no weak requests for aid. A swift hand felt for the knob and found it; a strong arm pushed at the unlocked door. And through it, bareheaded, with burning eyes and blanched cheeks, her heavy riding-whip dangling by a thong from her wrist, came the wife of Anthony Barrett.

Just across the sill she halted and swept the dim room. A moment, and the burning eyes fell upon the freighted ironing-table. She gave a piercing cry.

Fong Wu neither spoke nor moved.

After the first outburst, she was quiet—the quiet that is deliberative, threatening. Then she slowly closed her fingers about the whip butt. Fixing her gaze in passionate anger upon him, she advanced a few steps.

"*So it was you*," she said, and her voice was hollow.

To that he made no sign, and even his colorless face told nothing.

She came forward a little farther, and sucked in a long, deep breath. "You *dog* of a Chinaman!" she said at last, and struck her riding-skirt.

Fong Wu answered silently. With an imperative gesture, he pointed out the figure on the ironing-table.

She sprang to her husband's side and bent over him. Presently she began to murmur to herself. When, finally, she turned, there were tears on her lashes, she was trembling visibly, and she spoke in whispers.

"Was I wrong?" she demanded brokenly. "I *must* have been. He's not had it; I can tell by his quick, easy breathing. And his ear has a faint color. You are trying to help him! I know! I know!"

A gleaming white line showed between the yellow of Fong Wu's lips. He picked up a rude stool and set it by the table. She sank weakly upon it, letting the whip fall.

"Thank God! thank God!" she sobbed prayerfully, and buried her face in her arms.

Throughout the long hours that followed, Fong Wu, from the room's shadowy rear, sat watching. He knew sleep did not come to her. For now and then he saw her shake from head to heel convulsively, as he had seen men in his own country quiver

"The petal of a plum blossom."

From a Painting by Albertine Randall Wheelan.

beneath the scourge of bamboos. Now and then, too, he heard her give a stifled moan, like the protest of a dumb creature. But in no other ways did she bare her suffering. Quietly, lest she wake her husband, she fought out the night.

Only once did Fong Wu look away from her. Then, in anger and disgust his eyes shifted to the figure on the table. "The petal of a plum blossom"—he muttered in Chinese—"the petal of a plum blossom beneath the hoofs of a pig!" And again his eyes dwelt upon the grief-bowed wife.

But when the dawn came stealing up from behind the purple Sierras, and Mrs. Barrett raised her wan face, he was studiously reviewing his rows of bottles, outwardly unaware of her presence.

"Fong Wu," she said, in a low voice, "when will he wake?"

"When he is rested; at sunrise, maybe, or at noon."

"And then?"

"He will be feeble. I shall give him more medicine, and he will sleep again."

He rose and busied himself at the fire. Soon he approached her, bringing the gold-encrusted teapot and a small, handleless cup.

She drank thirstily, filling and emptying the cup many times. When she was done, she made as if to go. "I shall see that everything is all right at home," she told him. "After that, I shall come back." She stooped and kissed her husband tenderly.

Fong Wu opened the door for her, and she passed out. In the road, unhitched, but waiting, stood the mustang. She mounted and rode away.

When she returned, not long afterward, she was a new woman. She had bathed her face and donned a fresh waist. Her eyes were alight, and the scarlet was again flaming in her cheeks. Almost cheerfully, and altogether hopefully, she resumed her post at the ironing-table.

It was late in the afternoon before Barrett woke. But he made no attempt to get up, and would not eat. Fong Wu administered another dose of herbs, and without heeding his patient's expostulations. The latter, after seeking his wife's hand, once more sank into sleep.

Just before sunset, Fong Wu, who scorned to rest, prepared supper. Gratefully Mrs. Barrett partook of some tender chicken and rice cakes. When darkness shut down, they took up their second long vigil.

But it was not the vigil of the previous night. She was able to think of other things than her husband's condition and the doom that, of a sudden, had menaced her happiness. Her spirits having risen, she was correspondingly impatient of a protracted, oppressive stillness, and looked about for an interruption, and for diversion. Across from her, a celestial patrician in his blouse of purple silk and his red-buttoned cap, sat Fong Wu. Consumed with curiosity—now that she had time to observe him closely—she longed to lift the yellow, expressionless mask from his face—a face which might have patterned that of an oriental sphinx. At midnight, when he approached the table to satisfy himself of Barrett's progress, and to assure her of it, she essayed a conversation.

Glancing up at his laden shelves, she said, "I

have been noticing your medicines, and how many kinds there seem to be."

"For each ailment that is visited upon man, earth offers a cure," he answered. "Life would be a mock could Death, unchallenged, take it."

"True. Have you found in the earth, then, the cure for each ailment of man?"

"For most, yes. They seek yet, where I learned the art of healing, an antidote for the cobra's bite. I know of no other they lack."

"Where you were taught they must know more than we of this country know."

Fong Wu gave his shoulders a characteristic shrug.

"But," she continued, "you speak English so perfectly. Perhaps you were taught that in this country."

"No—in England. But the other, I was not."

"In England! Well!"

"I went there as a young man."

"But these herbs, these medicines you have—they did not come from England, did they?"

He smiled. "Some came from the hills at our back." Then, crossing to his shelves and reaching up, "This"—he touched a silk-covered package—"is from Sumbawa in the Indian Sea; and this"—his finger was upon the cork of a phial—"is from Feng-shan, Formosa; and other roots are taken in winter from the lake of Ting-ting-hu, which is then dry; and still others come from the far mountains of Chamur."

"Do you know," Mrs. Barrett said tentatively, "I have always heard that Chinese doctors give horrid things for medicine—sharks' teeth, frogs' feet, lizards' tails, and—and all sorts of dreadful things."

Fong Wu proffered no enlightenment.

"I am glad," she went on, "that I have learned better."

After a while she began again: "Doubtless there is other wonderful knowledge, besides that about doctoring, which Chinese gentlemen possess."

Fong Wu gave her a swift glance. "The followers of Laou-Tsze know many things," he replied, and moved into the shadows as if to close their talk.

Toward morning, when he again gave her some tea, she spoke of something that she had been turning over in her mind for hours.

"You would not take money for helping me when I was hurt," she said, "and I presume you will refuse to take it for what you are doing now. But I should like you to know that Mr. Barrett and I will always, always be your friends. If"—she looked across at him, no more a part of his rude surroundings than was she—"if ever there comes a time when we could be of use to you, you have only to tell us. Please remember that."

"I will remember."

"I cannot help but feel," she went on, and with a sincere desire to prove her gratitude, rather than to pry out any secret of his, "that you do not belong here—that you are in more trouble than I am. For what can a man of your rank have to do in a little town like this!"

He was not displeased with her. "The ancient sage," he said slowly, "mounted himself upon a black ox and disappeared into the western wilderness of

Thibet. Doubtless others, too, seek seclusion for much thinking."

"But you are not the hermit kind," she declared boldly. "You belong to those who stay and fight. Yet here you are, separated from your people and your people's graves—alone and sorrowful."

"As for my living people, they are best without me; as for my people dead, I neither worship their dust nor propitiate devils. The wise one said, 'Why talk forever on of men who are long gone?'"

"Yet——" she persisted.

He left the stove and came near her. "You are a woman, but you know much. You are right. My heart is heavy for a thing I cannot do—for the shattered dreams of the men of Hukwang." He beat his palms together noiselessly, and moved to and fro on soft sandals. "Those dreams were of a young China that was to take the place of the old—but that died unborn."

She followed his words with growing interest. "I have heard of those dreams," she answered; "they were called 'reform.'"

"Yes. And now all the dreamers are gone. They had voyaged to glean at Harvard, Yale, Cornell, and in the halls of Oxford. There were 'five loyal and six learned,' and they shed their blood at the Chen Chih Gate. One there was who died the death that is meted a slave at the court of the Son of Heaven. And one there was"—his face shrank up, as if swiftly aging; his eyes became dark, upturning slits; as one who fears pursuit, he cast a look behind him—"and one there was who escaped beyond the blood-bathed walls of the Hidden City and gained the Sumatra

Coast. Then, leaving Perak, in the Straits Settlements, he finally set foot upon a shore where men, without terror, may reach toward higher things."

"And was he followed?" she whispered, comprehending.

"He fled quietly. For long are the claws of the she-panther crouched on the throne of the Mings."

Both fell silent. The Chinese went back to the stove, where the fire was dying. The white woman, wide awake, and lost in the myriad of scenes his tale had conjured, sat by the table, for once almost forgetful of her charge.

The dragging hours of darkness past, Anthony Barrett found sane consciousness. He was pale, yet strengthened by his long sleep, and he was hungry. Relieved and overjoyed, Mrs. Barrett ministered to him. When he had eaten and drunk, she helped him from the table to the stool, and thence to his feet. Her arm about him, she led him to the door. Fong Wu had felt his pulse and it had ticked back the desired message, so he was going home.

"Each night you are to come," Fong Wu said, as he bade them good-by. "And soon, very soon, you may go from here to the place from which you came."

Mrs. Barrett turned at the door. A plea for pardon in misjudging him, thankfulness for his help, sympathy for his exile—all these shone from her eyes. But words failed her. She held out her hand.

He seemed not to see it; he kept his arms at his sides. A "dog of a Chinaman" had best not take a woman's hand.

She went out, guiding her husband's footsteps, and helped him climb upon the mustang from the height

of the narrow porch. Then, taking the horse by the bridle, she moved away down the slope to the road.

Fong Wu did not follow, but closed the door gently and went back to the ironing-table. A handkerchief lay beside it—a dainty linen square that she had left. He picked it up and held it before him by two corners. From it there wafted a faint, sweet breath.

Fong Wu let it flutter to the floor. "The perfume of a plum petal," he said softly, in English; "the perfume of a plum petal."

THE JUDGMENT OF MAN

BY

JAMES HOPPER

THE JUDGMENT OF MAN

WE WERE sitting around the big center table in the *sala* of the "House of Guests" in Ilo-Ilo. We were teachers from Occidental Negros. It was near Christmas; we had left our stations for the holidays—the cholera had just swept them and the aftermath was not pleasant to contemplate—and so we were leaning over the polished *narra* table, sipping a sweet, false Spanish wine from which we drew, not a convivial spirit, but rather a quiet, reflective gloom. All the shell shutters were drawn back; we could see the tin-roofed city gleam and crackle with the heat, and beyond the lithe line of cocoanuts, the iridescent sea, tugging the heart with offer of coolness. But, all of us, we knew the promise to be Fake, monumental Fake, knew the alluring depths to be hot as corruption, and full of sharks.

Somebody in a monotonous voice was cataloguing the dead, enumerating those of us who had been conquered by the climate, by the work, or through their own inward flaws. He mentioned Miller with some sort of disparaging gesture, and then Carter of Balangilang, who had been very silent, suddenly burst into speech with singular fury.

"Who are you, to judge him?" he shouted. "Who are you, eh? Who are we, anyway, to judge him?"

Headlong outbursts from Carter were nothing new to us, so we took no offense. Finally some one said, "Well, he's dead," with that tone that signifies final judgment, the last, best, most charitable thing which can be said of the man being weighed.

But Carter did not stop there. "You didn't know him, did you?" he asked. "You didn't know him; tell me now, *did* you know him?" He was still extraordinarily angry.

We did not answer. Really, we knew little of the dead man—excepting that he was mean and small, and not worth knowing. He was mean, and he was a coward; and to us in our uncompromising youth these were just the unpardonable sins. Because of that we had left him alone; yes, come to think of it, very much alone. And we knew little about him.

"Here, I'll tell you what I know," Carter began again, in a more conciliatory tone; "I'll tell you everything I know of him." He lit a cheroot.

"I first met him right here in Ilo-Ilo. I had crossed over for supplies; he was fresh from Manila and wanted to get over to Bacolod to report to the Sup. and be assigned to his station. When I saw him he was on the *muelle*, surrounded by an army of bluffing *cargadores*. About twelve of them had managed to get a finger upon his lone carpet-bag while it was being carried down the gang-plank, and each and all of them wanted to get paid for the job. He was in a horrible pickle; couldn't speak a word of Spanish or Visayan. And the first thing he said when I had extricated him, thanks to my vituperative knowledge of these sweet tongues, was: 'If them niggahs, seh, think Ah'm a-goin' to learn their cussed lingo, they're mahtily mistaken, seh!'

"After that remark, coming straight from the heart, I hardly needed to be told that he was from the South. He was from Mississippi. He was gaunt, yellow, malarial, and slovenly. He had 'teached' for twenty years, he said, but in spite of this there was about him something indescribably rural, something of the sod—not the dignity, the sturdiness of it, but rather of the pettiness, the sordidness of it. It showed in his dirty, flapping garments, his unlaced shoes, his stubble beard, in his indecent carelessness in expectorating the tobacco he was ceaselessly chewing. But these, after all, were some of his minor traits. I was soon to get an inkling of one of his major ones—his prodigious meanness. For when I rushed about and finally found a lorcha that was to sail for Bacolod and asked him to chip in with me on provisions, he demurred.

"'Ah'd like to git my own, seh,' he said in that decisive drawl of his.

"'All right,' I said cheerfully, and went off and stocked up for two. My instinct served me well. When, that evening, Miller walked up the gang-plank, he carried only his carpet-bag, and that was flat and hungry-looking as before. The next morning he shared my provisions calmly and resolutely, with an air, almost, of conscious duty. Well, let that go; before another day I was face to face with his other flaming characteristic.

"Out of Ilo-Ilo we had contrary winds at first; all night the lorcha—an old grandmother of a craft, full of dry-rot spots as big as woodpeckers' nests—flapped heavily about on impotent tacks, and when the sun rose we found ourselves on the same spot from which we had watched its setting. Toward ten o'clock, however, the monsoon veered, and, wing-and-wing, the old boat, creaking in every joint as if she had the dengue, grunted her way over flashing combers with a speed that seemed almost indecent. Then, just as we were getting near enough to catch the heated glitter of the Bacolod church-dome, to see the golden thread of beach at the foot of the waving cocoanuts, the wind fell, slap-bang, as suddenly as if God had said hush—and we stuck there, motionless, upon a petrified sea.

"I didn't stamp about and foam at the mouth; I'd been in these climes too long. As for Miller, he was from Mississippi. We picked out a comparatively clean spot on the deck, near the bow; we lay down on our backs and relaxed our beings into infinite patience. We had been thus for perhaps an hour; I was looking up at a little white cloud that seemed receding, receding into the blue immensity behind it. Suddenly a noise like thunder roared in my ears. The little cloud gave a great leap back into its place; the roar dwindled into the voice of Miller, in plaintive, disturbed drawl. 'What the deuce are the niggahs doing?' he was saying.

"And certainly the behavior of that Visayan crew was worthy of question. Huddled quietly at the stern, one after another they were springing over the rail into the small boat that was dragging behind, and even as I looked the last man disappeared with the painter in his hand. At the same moment I became aware of a strange noise. Down in the bowels of the lorcha a weird, gentle commotion was going on, a multitudinous 'gluck-gluck' as of many bottles being emptied. A breath of hot, musty air was sighing out of the hatch. Then the sea about the poop began to rise,—to rise slowly, calmly, steadily, like milk in a heated pot.

"'By the powers,' I shouted, 'the old tub is going down!'

"It was true. There, upon the sunlit sea, beneath the serene sky, silently, weirdly, unprovoked, the old boat, as if weary, was sinking in one long sigh of lassitude. And we, of course, were going with it. A few yards away from the stern-post was the jolly-boat with the crew. I looked at them, and in my heart I could not condemn them for their sly departure; they were all there, *arraiz*, wife, children, and crew, so heaped together that they seemed only a meaningless tangle of arms and legs and heads; the water was half an inch from the gunwale, and the one man at the oars, hampered, paralyzed on all sides, was splashing helplessly while the craft pivoted like a top. There was no anger in my heart, yet I was not absolutely reconciled to the situation. I searched the deck with my eyes, then from the jolly-boat the *arraiz* obligingly yelled, '*El biroto, el biroto!*'

"And I remembered the rotten little canoe lashed amidships. It didn't take us long to get it into the water (the water by that time was very close at hand). I went carefully into it first so as to steady it for Miller, and then, both of us at once, we saw that it would hold only one. The bottom, a hollowed log, was stanch enough, but the sides, made of pitched bamboo lattice, were sagging and torn. It would hold only one.

"'Well, who is it?' I asked. In my heart there was no craven panic, but neither was there sacrifice. Some vague idea was in my mind, of deciding who should get the place by some game of chance, tossing up a coin, for instance.

"But Miller said, 'Ah cain't affawd to take chances, seh; you must git out.'

"He spoke calmly, with great seriousness, but without undue emphasis—as one enunciating an uncontrovertible natural law. I glanced up into his face, and it was in harmony with his voice. He didn't seem particularly scared; he was serious, that's all; his eyes were set in that peculiar, wide-pupiled stare of the man contemplating his own fixed idea.

"'No, seh; Ah cain't affawd it,' he repeated.

"The absurdity of the thing suddenly tingled in me like wine. 'All right!' I shouted, in a contagion of insanity; 'all right, take the darned thing!'

"And I got out. I got out and let him step stiffly into the boat, which I obligingly sent spinning from the lorcha with one long, strong kick. Then I was alone on the deck, which suddenly looked immense, stretched on all sides, limitless as loneliness itself. A heavy torpor fell from the skies and amid this general silence, this immobility, the cabin door alone seemed to live, live in weird manifestation. It had been left open, and now it was swinging and slamming to and fro jerkily, and shuddering from top to bottom. Half in plan, half in mere irritation at this senseless, incessant jigging, I sprang toward it and with one nervous pull tore it, hinge and all, from the rotten woodwork. I heaved it over the side, went in head first after it, took a few strokes and lay, belly down, upon it. Just then the lorcha began to rise by the head; the bowsprit went up slowly like a finger pointing solemnly to heaven; then, without a sound, almost instantaneously, the whole fabric disappeared. Across the now unoccupied space Miller and I rushed smoothly toward each other, as if drawn by some gigantic magnet; our crafts bumped gently, like two savages caressingly rubbing noses; they swung apart a little and lay side by side, undulating slightly.

"And we remained there, little black specks upon the flashing sea. Two hundred yards away was the lorcha's boat; they had reshuffled themselves more advantageously and were pulling slowly toward land. Not twenty feet from me Miller sat upright in his canoe as if petrified. I was not so badly off. The door floated me half out of water, and that was lukewarm, so I knew that I could stand it a long time. What bothered me, though, was that the blamed raft was not long enough; that is, the upper part of my body being heavier, it took more door to support it, so that my feet were projecting beyond the lower edge, and every second or so the nibbling of some imaginary shark sent them flying up into the air in undignified gymnastics. The consoling part of it was that Miller was paying no notice. He still sat up, rigid, in his canoe, clutching the sides stiffly and looking neither to right nor left. From where I lay I could see the cords of his neck drawn taut, and his knuckles showing white.

"'Why the deuce don't you paddle to shore?' I

shouted at length, taking a sudden disgust of the situation.

"He did not turn his head as he answered, 'Ah—Ah,' he stammered, the words coming hard as hiccoughs out of his throat, 'Ah don't know haow.'

"'Drop the sides of your boat and try,' I suggested.

"He seemed to ponder carefully over this for a while. 'Ah think it's safer to stay this-a-way,' he decided finally.

"'But, good Lord, man,' I cried, angry at this calm stupidity, 'if that's what you're going to do, you'd better get on this door here and let me take the boat. I'll paddle ashore and come back for you.'

"He turned his head slowly. He contemplated my raft long, carefully, critically.

"'Ah think Ah'll be safer heyah, seh,' he decided. 'It's a little bit o' old door, and Ah reckon they's a heap of sharks around.'

"After that I had little to say. Given the premises of the man, his conclusions were unquestionable. And the premises were a selfishness so tranquil, so ingenuous, so fresh, I might say, that I couldn't work up the proper indignation. It was something so perfect as to challenge admiration. On the whole, however, it afforded a poor subject for conversation; so we remained there, taciturn, I on my door, half-submerged in the tepid water, my heels flung up over my back, he in his dugout, rigid, his hands clutching the sides as if he were trying to hold up the craft out of the liquid abyss beneath.

"And thus we were still when, just as the sun was setting somberly, a velos full of chattering natives

"NOT TWENTY FEET FROM ME MILLER SAT UPRIGHT IN HIS CANOE AS IF PETRIFIED."

═

FROM A PAINTING BY MERLE JOHNSON.

picked us up. They landed us at Bacolod, and Miller left me to report to the Sup. I departed before sun-up the next morning for my station. I didn't want to see Miller again.

"But I did. One night he came floundering through my pueblo. It was in the middle of the rainy season. He wasn't exactly caked with mud; rather, he seemed to ooze it out of every pore. He had been assigned to Binalbagan, ten miles further down. I stared when he told me this. Binalbagan was the worst post on the island, a musty, pestilential hole with a sullenly hostile population, and he—well, inefficiency was branded all over him in six-foot letters. I tried to stop him overnight, but he would not do it, and I saw him splash off in the darkness, gaunt, yellow, mournful.

"I saw little of him after that. I was busy establishing new barrio-schools, which were to give me excuses for long horseback rides of inspection. I felt his presence down there in that vague way by which you are aware of a person behind your back without turning around. Rumors of his doings reached me. He was having a horrible time. On the night of his arrival he had been invited to dinner by the Presidente, a kind old primitive soul, but when he found that he was expected to sit at the table with the family, he had stamped off, indignant, saying that he didn't eat with no niggers. As I've said before, the town was hostile, and this attitude did not help matters much. He couldn't get the school moneys out of the Tesorero—an unmitigated rascal—but that did not make much difference, for he had no pupils anyhow. He couldn't speak a word of

"With him, I must say, the *camisa* did not mean all that I have suggested, not the sort of degradation of which it is the symbol in other men. The most extravagant imagination could not have linked him with anything that smacked of romance, romance however sordid. His vices, I had sized it, would come rather from an excess of calculation than from a lack of it. No, that *camisa* was just a sign of his meanness, his prodigious meanness. And of that I was soon given an extraordinary example.

"I had with me a young fellow named Ledesma, whom I was training to be assistant *maestro*. He was very bright, thirsty to learn, and extremely curious of us white men. I don't believe that the actions of one of them, for fifty miles around, ever escaped him, and every day he came to me with some talk, some rumor, some gossip about my fellow-exiles which he would relate to me with those strange interrogative inflections that he had brought from his native dialect into English—as if perpetually he were seeking explanation, confirmation. One morning he said to me: 'The *maestro* Miller, he does not eat.'

"'No?' I answered, absent-mindedly.

"'No, he never eats,' he reiterated authoritatively, although that peculiar Visayan inflection of which I have spoken gave him the air of asking a question.

"'Oh, I suppose he does,' I said, carelessly.

"'He does not eat,' he repeated. 'Every one in Binalbagan say so. Since he there, he has not bought anything at the store.'

"'His *muchachos* bring him chicken,' I suggested.

"'No, señor; he very funny; he has no *muchachos;* not one *muchacho* has he.'

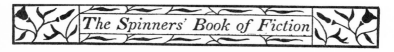

Spanish; no one in the town, of course, knew any English—he must have been horribly lonely. He began to wear *camisas*, like the natives. That's always a bad sign. It shows that the man has discovered that there is no one to care how he dresses—that is, that there is no longer any public opinion. It indicates something subtly worse—that the man has ceased looking at himself, that the *I* has ceased criticising, judging, stiffening up the *me*,—in other words, that there is no longer any conscience. That white suit, I tell you, is a wonderful moral force; the white suit, put on fresh every morning, heavily starched, buttoned up to the chin, is like an armor, ironcladding you against the germ of decay buzzing about you, ceaselessly vigilant for the little vulnerable spot. Miller wore *camisas*, and then he began to go without shoes. I saw that myself. I was riding through his pueblo on my way to Dent's, and I passed his school. I looked into the open door as my head bobbed by at the height of the stilt-raised floor. He was in his *camisa* and barefooted; his long neck stretched out of the collarless garment with a mournful, stork-like expression. Squatting on the floor were three trouserless, dirt-incrusted boys; he was pointing at a chart standing before their eyes, and all together they were shouting some word that exploded away down in their throats in tremendous effort and never seemed to reach their lips. I called out and waved my hand as I went by, and when I looked back, a hundred yards farther, I saw that he had come out upon the bamboo platform outside of the door, gaping after me with his chin thrown forward in that mournful, stork-like way—I should have gone back.

"'Well, he probably has canned provisions sent him.'

"'No, señor; the *cargadores* they say that never, never have they carried anything for him. He does not eat.'

"'Very well,' I concluded, somewhat amused; 'he does not eat.'

"The boy was silent for a minute, then, 'Señor Maestro,' he asked with suspicious ingenuousness, 'can Americans live without eating?'

"So that I was not able to drop the subject as easily as I wished. And coming to a forced consideration of it, I found that my anxiety to do so was not very beautiful after all. A picture came to me—that of Miller on his bamboo platform before his door, gazing mournfully after me, his chin thrown forward. It did not leave me the day long, and at sundown I saddled up and trotted off toward Binalbagan.

"I didn't reach the pueblo that night, however. Only a mile from it I plunged out of the moonlight into the pitch darkness of a hollow lane cutting through Don Jaime's hacienda. Banana palms were growing thick to right and left; the way was narrow and deep—it was a fine place for cutthroats, but that avocation had lost much of its romantic charm from the fact that, not three weeks before, an actual cutthroating had taken place, a Chinese merchant having been boloed by *tusilanes*. Well, I was trotting through, my right hand somewhat close to my holster, when from the right, close, there came a soft, reiterated chopping noise. I pulled up my pony. The sound kept up—a discreet, persistent chopping; then I saw, up above, the moonlit top of a palm shuddering, though all about it the others remained motionless, petrified as if of solid silver. It was a very simple thing after all: some one in there was cutting down a palm to get bananas, an occupation very common in the Philippines, and very pacific, in spite of the ominous air given to it by the gigantic bolo used. However, something prompted me to draw the midnight harvester out.

"'Heh, *ladron*, what are you doing there?' I shouted in dialect.

"'There was a most sudden silence. The chopping ceased, the palm stopped vibrating. A vague form bounded down the lane, right up against my horse's nose, rolled over, straightened up again, and vanished into the darkness ahead. Unconsciously I spurred on after it. For a hundred yards I galloped with nothing in sight. Then I caught a rapid view of the thing as it burst through a shaft of moonlight piercing the glade, and it showed as a man, a grotesque figure of a man in loose white pantaloons. He was frightened, horribly frightened, all hunched up with the frenzy to escape. An indistinct bundle was on his right shoulder. Like a curtain the dark snapped shut behind him again, but I urged on with a wild hallo, my blood all a-tingle with the exultation of the chase. I gained—he must have been a lamentable runner, for my poor little pony was staggering under my tumultuous weight. I could hear him pant and sob a few yards in advance; then he came into sight, a dim, loping whiteness ahead. Suddenly the bundle left his shoulder; something rolled along the ground under my horse's hoofs—

and I was standing on my head in a soft, oozy place. I was mad, furiously mad. I picked myself up, went back a few yards, and taking my pony by the nose picked *him* up. A touch of his throbbing flanks, however, warned me as I was putting my foot into the stirrup. I left him there and thundered on foot down the lane. I have said I was mad. 'Yip-yip-yah-ah, yip-yip-yah-ah!' I yelled as I dashed on—a yell I had heard among California cattlemen. It must have paralyzed that flying personage, for I gained upon him shockingly. I could hear him pant, a queer, patient panting, a sigh rather, a gentle, lamenting sighing, and the white *camisa* flapped ghostily in the darkness. Suddenly he burst out of obscurity, past the plantation, into the glaring moonlight. And I—I stopped short, went down on my hands and knees, and crouched back into the shadow. For the man running was Miller; Miller, wild, sobbing, disheveled, his shoulders drawn up to his ears in terrible weariness, his whole body taut with fear, and scudding, scudding away, low along the ground, his chin forward, mournful as a stork. Soon he was across the luminous space, and then he disappeared into the darkness on the other side, flopped head first into it as if hiding his face in a pillow.

"I returned slowly to my horse. He was standing where I had left him, his four legs far apart in a wide base. Between them was the thing cast off by Miller which had thrown us. I examined it by the light of a box of matches. It was a bunch of bananas, one of those gigantic clusters which can be cut from the palms. I got on my horse and rode back home.

"I didn't go to see him any more. A man who will

steal bananas in a country where they can be bought a dozen for one cent is too mean to be worth visiting. I had another reason, too. It had dawned on me that Miller probably did not care to see any of us, that he had come down to a mode of life which would not leave him appreciative of confrontations with past standards. It was almost charity to leave him to himself.

"So I left him to himself, and he lived on in his pestilential little hole, alone—lived a life more squalid every day. It wasn't at all a healthy life, you can understand, no healthier physically than morally. After a while I heard that he was looking bad, yellow as a lemon, and the dengue cracking at his bones. I began to think of going to him after all, of jerking him out of his rut by force, if necessary, making him respect the traditions of his race. But just then came that Nichols affair, and flaring, his other bad side—his abject cowardice—reappeared to me. You remember the Nichols thing—boloed in the dark between my town and Himamaylan. His *muchacho* had jumped into the ditch. Afterward he got out and ran back the whole way, fifteen miles, to my place. I started down there. My idea was to pick up Miller as I passed, then Dent a little further down, find the body, and perhaps indications for White of the constabulary, to whom I had sent a messenger and who could not reach the place till morning. Well, Miller refused to go. He had caught hold of some rumor of the happening; he was barricaded in his hut and was sitting on his bed, a big Colt's revolver across his knees. He would not go, he said it plainly. 'No, seh; Ah cain't take chances; Ah cain't affawd it.' He said this without much fire, almost tranquilly, exactly as he had, you remember, at the time of our shipwreck. It was not so amusing now, however. Here, on land, amid this swarming, mysterious hostility, at this crisis, it seemed a shocking betrayal of the solidarity that bound all us white men. A red rage took possession of me. I stood there above him and poured out vituperation for five good minutes. I found the most extraordinary epithets; I lowered my voice and pierced him with venomous thrusts. He took it all. He remained seated on his bed, his revolver across his knees, looking straight at some spot on the floor; whenever I'd become particularly effective he'd merely look harder at the spot, as if for him it contained something of higher significance—a command, a rule, a precept—I don't know what, and then he'd say, 'No, Ah cain't; Ah cain't affawd it.'

"I burst out of there, a-roar like a bombshell. I rode down to Dent; we rode down to the place and did—what there was to be done. Miller I never wanted to see again.

"But I did. Some three weeks later a carrier came to me with a note—a penciled scrawl upon a torn piece of paper. It read:

" 'I think I am dying. Can you come see me?

'MILLER.'

"I went down right away. He was dead. He had died there, alone, in his filthy little hut, in that God-forsaken pueblo, ten miles from the nearest white man, ten thousand miles from his home.

"I'll always remember our coming in. It was night. It had been raining for thirty-six hours, and as we stepped into the unlighted hut, my *muchacho* and I, right away the floor grew sticky and slimy with the mud on our feet, and as we groped about blindly, we seemed ankle-deep in something greasy and abominable like gore. After a while the boy got a torch outside, and as he flared it I caught sight of Miller on his cot, backed up into one corner. He was sitting upright, staring straight ahead and a little down, as if in careful consideration. As I stepped toward him the pliable bamboo floor undulated; the movement was carried to him and he began to nod, very gently and gravely. He seemed to be saying: 'No, Ah cain't affawd it.' It was atrocious. Finally I was by his side and he was again motionless, staring thoughtfully. Then I saw he was considering. In his hands, which lay twined on his knees, were a lot of little metallic oblongs. I disengaged them. The *muchacho* drew nearer, and with the torch over my shoulder I examined them. They were photographs, cheap tintypes. The first was of a woman, a poor being, sagging with overwork, a lamentable baby in her arms. The other pictures were of children—six of them, boys and girls, of all ages from twelve to three, and under each, in painful chirography, a name was written—Lee Miller, Amy Miller, Geraldine Miller, and so on.

"You don't understand, do you? For a moment I didn't. I stared stupidly at those tintypes, shuffled and reshuffled them; the torch roaredin my ear. Then, suddenly, understanding came to me, sharp as a pang. He had a wife and seven children.

"A simple fact, wasn't it, a commonplace one, almost vulgar, you might say. And yet what a change of view produced by it, what a dislocation of judgment! I was like a man riding through a strange country, in a storm, at night. It is dark, he cannot see, he has never seen the country, yet as he rides on he begins to picture to himself the surroundings, his imagination builds for him a landscape—a mountain there, a river here, wind-streaming trees over there—and right away it exists, it *is*, it has solidity, mass, life. Then suddenly comes a flash of lightning, a second of light, and he is astounded, absolutely astounded to see the real landscape different from that indestructible thing that his mind had built. Thus it was with me. I had judged, oh, I had judged him thoroughly, sized him up to a certainty, and bang, came the flare of this new fact, this extremely commonplace fact, and I was all off. I must begin to judge again, only it would never do that man any good.

"A hundred memories came back to me, glared at me in the illumination of that new fact. I remember the *camisa*, the bare feet. I saw him running down the lane with his bunch of stolen bananas. I recalled that absurd scene on the waters; I heard him say: 'No, seh; Ah cain't affawd to take chances; Ah cain't affawd it.'

"Of course he couldn't afford it. Think—a wife and seven children!

"That night I went through his papers, putting things in order, and from every leaf, every scrap, came corroboration of the new fact. He was one of those pitiful pedagogues of the rural South, shiftless, half-educated, inefficient. He had never been able to earn much, and his family had always gently starved. Then had come the chance—the golden chance—the Philippines and a thousand a year. He had taken the bait, had come ten thousand miles to the spot of his maximum value. Only, things had not gone quite right. Thanks to the beautiful red-tape of the department, three months had gone before he had received his first month's pay. Then it had come in Mex., and when he had succeeded in changing it into gold it had dwindled to sixty dollars. Of course, he had sent it all back, for even then it would take it six more weeks to reach its destination, and sixty dollars is hardly too much to tide over five months for a family of eight. These five months had to be caught up in some way, so every month his salary, depreciated ten per cent by the change, had gone across the waters. He wore *camisas* and no shoes, he stole bananas. And his value, shoeless, *camisa*-clothed, was sixty dollars a month. He was just so much capital. He had to be careful of that capital.

"'Ah cain't affawd to take chances; Ah cain't affawd it.' Of course he couldn't.

"And so he had fought on blindly, stubbornly, and, at last, with that pitiful faculty we have, all of us, of defeating our own plans, he had killed himself, he had killed the capital, the golden goose.

"Yes, I found confirmation, but, after all, I did not need it. I had learned it all; understanding had come to me, swift, sharp, vital as a pang, when in the roaring light of the torch I had looked upon the pale little tintypes, the tintypes of Lee and Amy and Jackson aud Geraldine."

THE LEAGUE OF THE OLD MEN

BY

JACK LONDON

THE LEAGUE OF THE OLD MEN

T THE Barracks a man was being tried for his life. He was an old man, a native from the Whitefish River, which empties into the Yukon below Lake Le Barge. All Dawson was wrought up over the affair, and likewise the Yukon-dwellers for a thousand miles up and down. It has been the custom of the land-robbing and sea-robbing Anglo-Saxon to give the law to conquered peoples, and ofttimes this law is harsh. But in the case of Imber the law for once seemed inadequate and weak. In the mathematical nature of things, equity did not reside in the punishment to be accorded him. The punishment was a foregone conclusion, there could be no doubt of that; and though it was capital, Imber had but one life, while the tale against him was one of scores.

In fact, the blood of so many was upon his hands that the killings attributed to him did not permit of precise enumeration. Smoking a pipe by the trail-side or lounging around the stove, men made rough estimates of the numbers that had perished at his hand. They had been whites, all of them, these poor murdered people, and they had been slain singly, in pairs, and in parties. And so purposeless and wanton had been these killings, that they had long been a mystery to the mounted police, even in the time of the captains, and later, when the creeks realized, and a governor came from the Dominion to make the land pay for its prosperity.

But more mysterious still was the coming of Imber to Dawson to give himself up. It was in the late spring, when the Yukon was growling and writhing under its ice, that the old Indian climbed painfully up the bank from the river trail and stood blinking on the main street. Men who had witnessed his advent, noted that he was weak and tottery, and that he staggered over to a heap of cabin-logs and sat down. He sat there a full day, staring straight before him at the unceasing tide of white men that flooded past. Many a head jerked curiously to the side to meet his stare, and more than one remark was dropped anent the old Siwash with so strange a look upon his face. No end of men remembered afterward that they had been struck by his extraordinary figure, and forever afterward prided themselves upon their swift discernment of the unusual.

But it remained for Dickensen, Little Dickensen, to be the hero of the occasion. Little Dickensen had come into the land with great dreams and a pocketful of cash; but with the cash the dreams vanished, and to earn his passage back to the States he had accepted a clerical position with the brokerage firm of Holbrook and Mason. Across the street from the office of Holbrook and Mason was the heap of cabin-logs upon which Imber sat. Dickensen looked out of the window at him before he went to lunch; and when he came back from lunch he looked out of the window, and the old Siwash was still there.

Dickensen continued to look out of the window, and he, too, forever afterward prided himself upon his swiftness of discernment. He was a romantic little chap, and he likened the immobile old heathen to the genius of the Siwash race, gazing calm-eyed upon the hosts of the invading Saxon. The hours swept along, but Imber did not vary his posture, did not by a hair's-breadth move a muscle; and Dickensen remembered the man who once sat upright on a sled in the main street where men passed to and fro. They thought the man was resting, but later, when they touched him, they found him stiff and cold, frozen to death in the midst of the busy street. To undouble him, that he might fit into a coffin, they had been forced to lug him to a fire and thaw him out a bit. Dickensen shivered at the recollection.

Later on, Dickensen went out on the sidewalk to smoke a cigar and cool off; and a little later Emily Travis happened along. Emily Travis was dainty and delicate and rare, and whether in London or Klondike, she gowned herself as befitted the daughter of a millionaire mining engineer. Little Dickensen deposited his cigar on an outside window ledge where he could find it again, and lifted his hat.

They chatted for ten minutes or so, when Emily Travis, glancing past Dickensen's shoulder, gave a startled little scream. Dickensen turned about to see, and was startled, too. Imber had crossed the street and was standing there, a gaunt and hungry-looking shadow, his gaze riveted upon the girl.

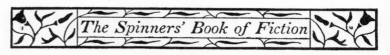

"What do you want?" Little Dickensen demanded, tremulously plucky.

Imber grunted and stalked up to Emily Travis. He looked her over, keenly and carefully, every square inch of her. Especially did he appear interested in her silky brown hair, and in the color of her cheek, faintly sprayed and soft, like the downy bloom of a butterfly wing. He walked around her, surveying her with the calculating eye of a man who studies the lines upon which a horse or a boat is builded. In the course of his circuit the pink shell of her ear came between his eye and the westering sun, and he stopped to contemplate its rosy transparency. Then he returned to her face and looked long and intently into her blue eyes. He grunted and laid a hand on her arm midway between the shoulder and elbow. With his other hand he lifted her forearm and doubled it back. Disgust and wonder showed in his face, and he dropped her arm with a contemptuous grunt. Then he muttered a few guttural syllables, turned his back upon her, and addressed himself to Dickensen.

Dickensen could not understand his speech, and Emily Travis laughed. Imber turned from one to the other, frowning, but both shook their heads. He was about to go away, when she called out:

"Oh, Jimmy! Come here!"

Jimmy came from the other side of the street. He was a big, hulking Indian clad in approved white-man style, with an Eldorado king's sombrero on his head. He talked with Imber, haltingly, with throaty spasms. Jimmy was a Sitkan, possessed of no more than a passing knowledge of the interior dialects.

"Him Whitefish man," he said to Emily Travis. "Me savve um talk no very much. Him want to look see chief white man."

"The Governor," suggested Dickensen.

Jimmy talked some more with the Whitefish man, and his face went grave and puzzled.

"I t'ink um want Cap'n Alexander," he explained. "Him say um kill white man, white woman, white boy, plenty kill um white people. Him want to die."

"Insane, I guess," said Dickensen.

"What you call dat?" queried Jimmy.

Dickensen thrust a finger figuratively inside his head and imparted a rotary motion thereto.

"Mebbe so, mebbe so," said Jimmy, returning to Imber, who still demanded the chief man of the white men.

A mounted policeman (unmounted for Klondike service) joined the group and heard Imber's wish repeated. He was a stalwart young fellow, broad-shouldered, deep-chested, legs cleanly built and stretched wide apart, and tall though Imber was, he towered above him by half a head. His eyes were cool, and gray, and steady, and he carried himself with the peculiar confidence of power that is bred of blood and tradition. His splendid masculinity was emphasized by his excessive boyishness,—he was a mere lad,—and his smooth cheek promised a blush as willingly as the cheek of a maid.

Imber was drawn to him at once. The fire leaped into his eyes at sight of a sabre slash that scarred his cheek. He ran a withered hand down the young fellow's leg and caressed the swelling thew. He smote the broad chest with his knuckles, and pressed and prodded the thick muscle-pads that covered the shoulders like a cuirass. The group had been added to by curious passers-by—husky miners, mountaineers, and frontiersmen, sons of the long-legged and broad-shouldered generations. Imber glanced from one to another, then he spoke aloud in the Whitefish tongue.

"What did he say?" asked Dickensen.

"Him say um all the same one man, dat p'liceman," Jimmy interpreted.

Little Dickensen was little, and what of Miss Travis, he felt sorry for having asked the question.

The policeman was sorry for him and stepped into the breach. "I fancy there may be something in his story. I'll take him up to the captain for examination. Tell him to come along with me, Jimmy."

Jimmy indulged in more throaty spasms, and Imber grunted and looked satisfied.

"But ask him what he said, Jimmy, and what he meant when he took hold of my arm."

So spoke Emily Travis, and Jimmy put the question and received the answer.

"Him say you no afraid," said Jimmy.

Emily Travis looked pleased.

"Him say you no *skookum*, no strong, all the same very soft like little baby. Him break you, in um two hands, to little pieces. Him t'ink much funny, very strange, how you can be mother of men so big, so strong, like dat p'liceman."

Emily Travers kept her eyes up and unfaltering, but her cheeks were sprayed with scarlet. Little Dickensen blushed and was quite embarrassed. The policeman's face blazed with his boy's blood.

"Come along, you," he said gruffly, setting his shoulder to the crowd and forcing a way.

Thus it was that Imber found his way to the Barracks, where he made full and voluntary confession, and from the precincts of which he never emerged.

Imber looked very tired. The fatigue of hopelessness and age was in his face. His shoulders drooped depressingly, and his eyes were lack-luster. His mop of hair should have been white, but sun- and weather-beat had burned and bitten it so that it hung limp and lifeless and colorless. He took no interest in what went on around him. The court-room was jammed with the men of the creeks and trails, and there was an ominous note in the rumble and grumble of their low-pitched voices, which came to his ears like the growl of the sea from deep caverns.

He sat close by a window, and his apathetic eyes rested now and again on the dreary scene without. The sky was overcast, and a gray drizzle was falling. It was flood-time on the Yukon. The ice was gone, and the river was up in the town. Back and forth on the main street, in canoes and poling-boats, passed the people that never rested. Often he saw these boats turn aside from the street and enter the flooded square that marked the Barracks' parade-ground. Sometimes they disappeared beneath him, and he heard them jar against the house-logs and their occupants scramble in through the window. After that came the slush of water against men's legs as they waded across the lower room and mounted the stairs. Then they appeared in the doorway, with doffed hats and dripping sea-boots, and added themselves to the waiting crowd.

And while they centered their looks on him, and in grim anticipation enjoyed the penalty he was to pay, Imber looked at them, and mused on their ways, and on their Law that never slept, but went on unceasing, in good times and bad, in flood and famine, through trouble and terror and death, and which would go on unceasing, it seemed to him, to the end of time.

A man rapped sharply on a table, and the conversation droned away into silence. Imber looked at the man. He seemed one in authority, yet Imber divined the square-browed man who sat by a desk farther back to be the one chief over them all and over the man who had rapped. Another man by the same table uprose and began to read aloud from many fine sheets of paper. At the top of each sheet he cleared his throat, at the bottom moistened his fingers. Imber did not understand his speech, but the others did, and he knew that it made them angry. Sometimes it made them very angry, and once a man cursed him, in single syllables, stinging and tense, till a man at the table rapped him to silence.

For an interminable period the man read. His monotonous, sing-song utterance lured Imber to dreaming, and he was dreaming deeply when the man ceased. A voice spoke to him in his own Whitefish tongue, and he roused up, without surprise, to look upon the face of his sister's son, a young man who had wandered away years agone to make his dwelling with the whites.

"Thou dost not remember me," he said by way of greeting.

"Nay," Imber answered. "Thou art Howkan who went away. Thy mother be dead."

"She was an old woman," said Howkan.

But Imber did not hear, and Howkan, with hand upon his shoulder, roused him again.

"I shall speak to thee what the man has spoken, which is the tale of the troubles thou hast done and which thou hast told, O fool, to the Captain Alexander. And thou shalt understand and say if it be true talk or talk not true. It is so commanded."

Howkan had fallen among the mission folk and been taught by them to read and write. In his hands he held the many fine sheets from which the man had read aloud and which had been taken down by a clerk when Imber first made confession, through the mouth of Jimmy, to Captain Alexander. Howkan began to read. Imber listened for a space, when a wonderment rose up in his face and he broke in abruptly.

"That be my talk, Howkan. Yet from thy lips it comes when thy ears have not heard."

Howkan smirked with self-appreciation. His hair was parted in the middle. "Nay, from the paper it comes, O Imber. Never have my ears heard. From the paper it comes, through my eyes, into my head, and out of my mouth to thee. Thus it comes."

"Thus it comes? It be there in the paper?" Imber's voice sank in whisperful awe as he crackled the sheets 'twixt thumb and finger and stared at the charactery scrawled thereon. "It be a great medicine, Howkan, and thou art a worker of wonders."

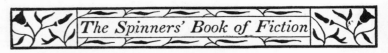

"It be nothing, it be nothing," the young man responded carelessly and pridefully. He read at hazard from the document: "*In that year, before the break of the ice, came an old man, and a boy who was lame of one foot. These also did I kill, and the old man made much noise——*"

"It be true," Imber interrupted breathlessly. "He made much noise and would not die for a long time. But how dost thou know, Howkan? The chief man of the white men told thee, mayhap? No one beheld me, and him alone have I told."

Howkan shook his head with impatience. "Have I not told thee it be there in the paper, O fool?"

Imber stared hard at the ink-scrawled surface. "As the hunter looks upon the snow and says, Here but yesterday there passed a rabbit; and here by the willow scrub it stood and listened, and heard, and was afraid; and here it turned upon its trail; and here it went with great swiftness, leaping wide; and here, with greater swiftness and wider leapings, came a lynx; and here, where the claws cut deep into the snow, the lynx made a very great leap; and here it struck, with the rabbit under and rolling belly up; and here leads off the trail of the lynx alone, and there is no more rabbit,—as the hunter looks upon the markings of the snow and says thus and so and here, dost thou, too, look upon the paper and say thus and so and here be the things old Imber hath done?"

"Even so," said Howkan. "And now do thou listen, and keep thy woman's tongue between thy teeth till thou art called upon for speech."

Thereafter, and for a long time, Howkan read

to him the confession, and Imber remained musing and silent. At the end, he said:

"It be my talk, and true talk, but I am grown old, Howkan, and forgotten things come back to me which were well for the head man there to know. First, there was the man who came over the Ice Mountains, with cunning traps made of iron, who sought the beaver of the Whitefish. Him I slew. And there were three men seeking gold on the Whitefish long ago. Them also I slew, and left them to the wolverines. And at the Five Fingers there was a man with a raft and much meat."

At the moments when Imber paused to remember, Howkan translated and a clerk reduced to writing. The court-room listened stolidly to each unadorned little tragedy, till Imber told of a red-haired man whose eyes were crossed and whom he had killed with a remarkably long shot.

"Hell," said a man in the forefront of the onlookers. He said it soulfully and sorrowfully. He was red-haired. "Hell," he repeated. "That was my brother Bill." And at regular intervals throughout the session, his solemn "Hell" was heard in the court-room; nor did his comrades check him, nor did the man at the table rap him to order.

Imber's head drooped once more, and his eyes went dull, as though a film rose up and covered them from the world. And he dreamed as only age can dream upon the colossal futility of youth.

Later, Howkan roused him again, saying: "Stand up, O Imber. It be commanded that thou tellest why you did these troubles, and slew these people, and at the end journeyed here seeking the Law."

Imber rose feebly to his feet and swayed back and forth. He began to speak in a low and faintly rumbling voice, but Howkan interrupted him.

"This old man, he is damn crazy," he said in English to the square-browed man. "His talk is foolish and like that of a child."

"We will hear his talk which is like that of a child," said the square-browed man. "And we will hear it, word for word, as he speaks it. Do you understand?"

Howkan understood, and Imber's eyes flashed, for he had witnessed the play between his sister's son and the man in authority. And then began the story, the epic of a bronze patriot which might well itself be wrought into bronze for the generations unborn. The crowd fell strangely silent, and the square-browed judge leaned head on hand and pondered his soul and the soul of his race. Only was heard the deep tones of Imber, rhythmically alternating with the shrill voice of the interpreter, and now and again, like the bell of the Lord, the wondering and meditative "Hell" of the red-haired man.

"I am Imber of the Whitefish people." So ran the interpretation of Howkan, whose inherent barbarism gripped hold of him, and who lost his mission culture and veneered civilization as he caught the savage ring and rhythm of old Imber's tale. "My father was Otsbaok, a strong man. The land was warm with sunshine and gladness when I was a boy. The people did not hunger after strange things, nor hearken to new voices, and the ways of their fathers were their ways. The women found favor in the eyes of the young men, and the young men looked upon them with content. Babes hung at the breasts of the women, and they were heavy-hipped with increase of the tribe. Men were men in those days. In peace and plenty, and in war and famine, they were men.

"At that time there was more fish in the water than now, and more meat in the forest. Our dogs were wolves, warm with thick hides and hard to the frost and storm. And as with our dogs, so with us, for we were likewise hard to the frost and storm. And when the Pellys came into our land we slew them and were slain. For we were men, we Whitefish, and our fathers and our fathers' fathers had fought against the Pellys and determined the bounds of the land.

"As I say, with our dogs, so with us. And one day came the first white man. He dragged himself, so, on hand and knee, in the snow. And his skin was stretched tight, and his bones were sharp beneath. Never was such a man, we thought, and we wondered of what strange tribe he was, and of its land. And he was weak, most weak, like a little child, so that we gave him a place by the fire, and warm furs to lie upon, and we gave him food as little children are given food.

"And with him was a dog, large as three of our dogs, and very weak. The hair of this dog was short, and not warm, and the tail was frozen so that the end fell off. And this strange dog we fed, and bedded by the fire, and fought from it our dogs, which else would have killed him. And what of the moose meat and the sun-dried salmon, the man and dog took strength to themselves; and what of the strength, they became big and unafraid. And the man spoke loud words and laughed at the old men and young men, and looked boldly upon the maidens. And the dog fought with our dogs, and for all of his short hair and softness slew three of them in one day.

"When we asked the man concerning his people, he said, 'I have many brothers,' and laughed in a way that was not good. And when he was in his full strength he went away, and with him went Noda, daughter to the chief. First, after that, was one of our bitches brought to pup. And never was there such a breed of dogs,—big-headed, thick-jawed, and short-haired, and helpless. Well do I remember my father, Otsbaok, a strong man. His face was black with anger at such helplessness, and he took a stone, so, and so, and there was no more helplessness. And two summers after that came Noda back to us with a man-child in the hollow of her arm.

"And that was the beginning. Came a second white man, with short-haired dogs, which he left behind him when he went. And with him went six of our strongest dogs, for which, in trade, he had given Koo-So-Tee, my mother's brother, a wonderful pistol that fired with great swiftness six times. And Koo-So-Tee was very big, what of the pistol, and laughed at our bows and arrows. 'Woman's things,' he called them, and went forth against the bald-face grizzly, with the pistol in his hand. Now it be known that it is not good to hunt the bald-face with a pistol, but how were we to know?

and how was Koo-So-Tee to know? So he went against the bald-face, very brave, and fired the pistol with great swiftness six times; and the bald-face but grunted and broke in his breast like it were an egg, and like honey from a bee's nest dripped the brains of Koo-So-Tee upon the ground. He was a good hunter, and there was no one to bring meat to his squaw and children. And we were bitter, and we said, 'That which for the white men is well, is for us not well.' And this be true. There be many white men and fat, but their ways have made us few and lean.

"Came the third white man, with great wealth of all manner of wonderful foods and things. And twenty of our strongest dogs he took from us in trade. Also, what of presents and great promises, ten of our young hunters did he take with him on a journey which fared no man knew where. It is said they died in the snow of the Ice Mountains where man has never been, or in the Hills of Silence which are beyond the edge of the earth. Be that as it may, dogs and young hunters were seen never again by the Whitefish people.

"And more white men came with the years, and ever, with pay and presents, they led the young men away with them. And sometimes the young men came back with strange tales of dangers and toils in the lands beyond the Pellys, and sometimes they did not come back. And we said: 'If they be unafraid of life, these white men, it is because they have many lives; but we be few by the Whitefish, and the young men shall go away no more.' But the young men did go away; and the young women went also; and we were very wroth.

"It be true, we ate flour, and salt pork, and drank tea which was a great delight; only, when we could not get tea, it was very bad and we became short of speech and quick of anger. So we grew to hunger for the things the white men brought in trade. Trade! trade! all the time was it trade! One winter we sold our meat for clocks that would not go, and watches with broken guts, and files worn smooth, and pistols without cartridges and worthless. And then came famine, and we were without meat, and two-score died ere the break of spring.

"'Now are we grown weak,' we said; 'and the Pellys will fall upon us, and our bounds be overthrown.' But as it fared with us, so had it fared with the Pellys, and they were too weak to come against us.

"My father, Otsbaok, a strong man, was now old and very wise. And he spoke to the chief, saying: 'Behold, our dogs be worthless. No longer are they thick-furred and strong, and they die in the frost and harness. Let us go into the village and kill them, saving only the wolf ones, and these let us tie out in the night that they may mate with the wild wolves of the forest. Thus shall we have dogs warm and strong again.'

"And his word was harkened to, and we Whitefish became known for our dogs, which were the best in the land. But known we were not for ourselves. The best of our young men and women had gone away with the white men to wander on trail and river to far places. And the young women came back old and broken, as Noda had come, or they came not at all. And the young men came back to sit by our fires for a time, full of ill speech and rough ways, drinking evil drinks and gambling through long nights and days, with a great unrest always in their hearts, till the call of the white men came to them and they went away again to the unknown places. And they were without honor and respect, jeering the old-time customs and laughing in the faces of chief and shamans.

"As I say, we were become a weak breed, we Whitefish. We sold our warm skins and furs for tobacco and whiskey and thin cotton things that left us shivering in the cold. And the coughing sickness came upon us, and men and women coughed and sweated through the long nights, and the hunters on trail spat blood upon the snow. And now one, and now another, bled swiftly from the mouth and died. And the women bore few children, and those they bore were weak and given to sickness. And other sicknesses came to us from the white men, the like of which we had never known and could not understand. Smallpox, likewise measles, have I heard these sicknesses named, and we died of them as die the salmon in the still eddies when in the fall their eggs are spawned and there is no longer need for them to live.

"And yet, and here be the strangeness of it, the white men come as the breath of death; all their ways lead to death, their nostrils are filled with it; and yet they do not die. Theirs the whiskey, and tobacco, and short-haired dogs; theirs the many sicknesses, the smallpox and measles, the coughing and mouth-bleeding; theirs the white skin, and softness to the frost and storm; and theirs the pistols that shoot six times very swift and are worthless. And yet they grow fat on their many ills, and prosper, and lay a heavy hand over all the world and tread mightily upon its peoples. And their women, too, are soft as little babes, most breakable and never broken, the mothers of men. And out of all this softness, and sickness, and weakness, come strength, and power, and authority. They be gods, or devils, as the case may be. I do not know. What do I know, I, old Imber of the Whitefish? Only do I know that they are past understanding, these white men, far-wanderers and fighters over the earth that they be.

"As I say, the meat in the forest became less and less. It be true, the white man's gun is most excellent and kills a long way off; but of what worth the gun, when there is no meat to kill? When I was a boy on the Whitefish there was moose on every hill, and each year came the caribou uncountable. But now the hunter may take the trail ten days and not one moose gladden his eyes, while the caribou uncountable come no more at all. Small worth the gun, I say, killing a long way off, when there be nothing to kill.

"And I, Imber, pondered upon these things, watching the while the Whitefish, and the Pellys, and all the tribes of the land, perishing as perished the meat of the forest. Long I pondered. I talked with the shamans and the old men who were wise. I went apart that the sounds of the village might not disturb me, and I ate no meat, so that my belly should not press upon me and make me slow of eye and ear. I sat long and sleepless in the forest, wide-eyed for the sign, my ears patient and keen for the word that

"All their ways lead to death."

═

From a Painting by Maynard Dixon.

MAYNARD DIXON
'07

was to come. And I wandered alone in the blackness of night to the river bank, where was wind-moaning and sobbing of water, and where I sought wisdom from the ghosts of old shamans in the trees and dead and gone.

"And in the end, as in a vision, came to me the short-haired and detestable dogs, and the way seemed plain. By the wisdom of Otsbaok, my father and a strong man, had the blood of our own wolf-dogs been kept clean, wherefore had they remained warm of hide and strong in the harness. So I returned to my village and made oration to the men. 'This be a tribe, these white men,' I said. 'A very large tribe, and doubtless there is no longer meat in their land, and they are come among us to make a new land for themselves. But they weaken us, and we die. They are a very hungry folk. Already has our meat gone from us, and it were well, if we would live, that we deal by them as we have dealt by their dogs.'

"And further oration I made, counseling fight. And the men of the Whitefish listened, and some said one thing, and some another, and some spoke of other and worthless things, and no man made brave talk of deeds and war. But while the young men were weak as water and afraid, I watched that the old men sat silent, and that in their eyes fires came and went. And later, when the village slept and no one knew, I drew the old men away into the forest and made more talk. And now we were agreed, and we remembered the good young days, and the free land, and the times of plenty, and the gladness and sunshine; and we called ourselves brothers, and swore great secrecy, and a mighty oath to cleanse the land of the evil breed that had come upon it. It be plain we were fools, but how were we to know, we old men of the Whitefish?

"And to hearten the others, I did the first deed. I kept guard upon the Yukon till the first canoe came down. In it were two white men, and when I stood upright upon the bank and raised my hand they changed their course and drove in to me. And as the man in the bow lifted his head, so, that he might know wherefore I wanted him, my arrow sang through the air straight to his throat, and he knew. The second man, who held paddle in the stern, had his rifle half to his shoulder when the first of my three spear-casts smote him.

"'These be the first,' I said, when the old men had gathered to me. 'Later we will bind together all the old men of all the tribes, and after that the young men who remain strong, and the work will become easy.'

"And then the two dead white men we cast into the river. And of the canoe, which was a very good canoe, we made a fire, and a fire, also, of the things within the canoe. But first we looked at the things, and they were pouches of leather which we cut open with our knives. And inside these pouches were many papers, like that from which thou hast read, O Howkan, with markings on them which we marveled at and could not understand. Now, I am become wise, and I know them for the speech of men as thou hast told me."

A whisper and buzz went around the court-room when Howkan finished interpreting the affair of the canoe, and one man's voice spoke up: "That was the lost '91 mail, Peter James and Delaney bringing it in and last spoken at Le Barge by Matthews going out." The clerk scratched steadily away, and another paragraph was added to the history of the North.

"There be little more," Imber went on slowly. "It be there on the paper, the things we did. We were old men, and we did not understand. Even I, Imber, do not now understand. Secretly we slew, and continued to slay, for with our years we were crafty and we had learned the swiftness of going without haste. When white men came among us with black looks and rough words, and took away six of the young men with irons binding them helpless, we knew we must slay wider and farther. And one by one we old men departed up river and down to the unknown lands. It was a brave thing. Old we were, and unafraid, but the fear of far places is a terrible fear to men who are old.

"So we slew, without haste, and craftily. On the Chilkoot and in the Delta we slew, from the passes to the sea, wherever the white men camped or broke their trails. It be true, they died, but it was without worth. Ever did they come over the mountains, ever did they grow and grow, while we, being old, became less and less. I remember, by the Caribou Crossing, the camp of a white man. He was a very little white man, and three of the old men came upon him in his sleep. And the next day I came upon the four of them. The white man alone still breathed, and there was breath in him to curse me once and well before he died.

"And so it went, now one old man, and now another. Sometimes the word reached us long after of how they died, and sometimes it did not reach us. And the old men of the other tribes were weak and afraid, and would not join with us. As I say, one by one, till I alone was left. I am Imber, of the Whitefish people. My father was Otsbaok, a strong man. There are no Whitefish now. Of the old men I am the last. The young men and young women are gone away, some to live with the Pellys, some with the Salmons, and more with the white men. I am very old, and very tired, and it being vain fighting the Law, as thou sayest, Howkan, I am come seeking the Law."

"O Imber, thou art indeed a fool," said Howkan.

But Imber was dreaming. The square-browed judge likewise dreamed, and all his race rose up before him in a mighty phantasmagoria—his steel-shod, mail-clad race, the law-giver and world-maker among the families of men. He saw it dawn red-flickering across the dark forests and sullen seas; he saw it blaze, bloody and red, to full and triumphant noon; and down the shaded slope he saw the blood-red sands dropping into night. And through it all he observed the Law, pitiless and potent, ever unswerving and ever ordaining, greater than the motes of men who fulfilled it or were crushed by it, even as it was greater than he, his heart speaking for softness.

DOWN THE FLUME WITH THE SNEATH PIANO

BY

BAILEY MILLARD

Reprinted from *The Century Magazine*
by permission

DOWN THE FLUME WITH THE SNEATH PIANO

HAD halted at Camp Five to catch my breath. This flying down a Sierran lumber-flume, scurrying through the heady air like another Phaeton, was too full of thrills to be taken all in one gasp. I dropped limply into the rawhide-bottomed chair under the awning in front of the big board shanty which was on stilts beside the airy flume, and gazed on down the long, gleaming, tragic, watery way to the next steep slide. Then I looked at the frail little flume-boat which had borne Oram Sheets and me thus far on our hazardous journey to the valley. Perhaps I shivered a bit at the prospect of more of this hair-raising adventure. At any rate, Oram, the intrepid flume-herder, laughed, dug his picaroon into a log, and asked:

"Sorry yeh come? Wal, it does git onto a man's nerve the first trip. Strange so many brash ones like you wanter try, but few on 'em ever dast git in ag'in. But I've be'n down so often." Then he peered about the cabin. "Looks like none o' the boys was to home. Wish they was; they might git us up a little dinner. It's jest twelve."

He went inside the open door, and I heard him

foraging about, the shanty echoing hollowly to the clumping of his big boots. By and by his nasal note was resumed:

"Come in, pardner! Here's a great find: a big can o' green gages an' a hunk o' jerk an' a lot o' cold biscuits."

Inside, with my legs under the greasy, coverless table, I chewed the jerk like one who was determined to give his jaws the benefit of strenuous physical culture, and listened while Oram rattled on, with his mouth full of the sodden, half-baked biscuits.

"You might n't think it," said he, "but three years ago this here was the most scrumptious camp on the hull flume. Ol' man Hemenway lived here then with his daughter Jess. She kep' house fer him. Jess was a great gal. Every man along the flume, from Skyland to Mill Flat, was in love with her. Shape? You couldn't beat that there gal for figger if yeh was to round up every actress in the country. She had a pair o' big round baby-blue eyes, an' was as pretty as any o' them there cigarette picters. A little on the strawbary-blonde, but not too much red in her hair, an' yet spunky as a badger when yeh teased her.

"The boys down this way didn't have much show. It looked like Jess had hit it off with Jud Brusie, a big, husky, clean-lookin' chap up to the h'ist. Jud used ter send her down notes stuck in sticks wedged inter the clamps, an' he used ter sneak down this way on Sundays when he'd git a chanst. She'd meet him up to the Riffles there by that big bunch o' yaller pines we passed. He didn't dast come down here nary time till ol' man Hemenway he got laid up with a busted laig from slippin' off the trestle in the snow. That there was Jud's show ter git in his fine work. Used ter bring down deer-meat for the ol' man, an' sody-water from that there spoutin' spring up ter Crazy Cañon; an' it begun to look like Hemenway'd give in an' let him have her. But he seemed to hold off.

"The boys used ter nearly josh the life out o' Jud. One fellow—his name was Phil Pettis—was skunkin' mean enough to read a note Jud sent down oncet an' tell about it roun' Skyland; but that was the only time any of 'em ever done anything like that, fer Jud jest laid fer Phil an' went through him like a buzz-saw an' chucked him inter the flume.

"No, it didn't kill Phil, but he got tol'able well used up. His clothes was nearly all tore off, an' his hands got some bruised where he caught on to the aidges before he got a holt an' lifted himself out in a still place. He'd be'n all right only he got mixed up with a string o' lumber that was a-comin' down, an' so he had to go to the hospital.

"One thing about Jess—she was a singer all right. I ain't never heer'd ary one o' them there the-*ay*-ter gals that could beat her singin'. She warbled like a lark with his belly full o' grubworms. It was wuth ridin' a clamp from here to Mill Flat to hear her sing. She had a couple o' hymn-books an' a stack o' them coon songs the newspapers gives away, an' I tell yeh, she'd sing them there songs like she'd knowed 'em all her life. Picked out the tunes some ways on a little string-thing like a sawed-off guitar. Sounds like muskeeters hummin' aroun'. Yes, a mandy-linn—that's it. But that there mandy-linn didn't soot her a little bit. She was crazy ter have a pianner. I heer'd her tell her paw, who was aroun' ag'in workin' after his busted laig got well, she'd give ten years o' her life for any ol' cheap pianner he could skeer up fer her.

"'Wal,' says he, 'how in tunket am I a-goin' ter git anything like that—thirty miles off'n the road, an' nary way o' freightin' it up or down the cañon to this camp?'

"'Couldn't yeh have it brung up to Skyland by the stage road,' asts she, 'an' then have it rafted down the flume? Jest a little one?' she asts very earnest-like.

"'Gee whittaker!' says he, laughin' all over. 'You'll be a-wantin' 'em to send yeh down a parlor-keer nex'.'

"Then she gits hot in the collar an' cries an' takes on, an' Jud, who was a-hangin' aroun', has to walk her up to the Riffles; an' he must 'a' comforted her a heap, fer she comes back alone, singin,' 'Nearer, my God, to Thee,' like a angel.

"The' was a big spill up to the Devil's Gate,—one o' them places back there where the flume hangs onto the side o' the cliff, about half a mile above the bottom o' the gulch,—an' Jud Brusie an' all hands has to work there three days an' nights ter git things straightened out. Jud worked so derned hard, up all night an' hangin' on ter the ropes he was let up an' down by till yeh'd think he was ready to drop, that the soop'rintendent said he'd make Jud flume boss when he got back from Noo York, where he was a-goin' fer a few months. The soop'rintendent—that's Mr. Sneath—went over the hull flume with

Jud a little while before he lit out for the East, p'intin' things out ter him that he wanted did when he got back. I was down here flume-herdin' at Five when him an' Jud come along in a dude-lookin' flume-boat, rigged out in great style. I stopped 'em back there a ways with my picaroon, when they sung out, an' they walked down here on the side planks. Jest as they got near the camp the soop'rintendent he stopped like he'd struck a rotten plank an' stared at the house.

"'Who's that singin'?' says he.

"'Miss Hemenway,' says Jud, proud-like.

"'She's got an awful sweet voice,' says the ol' man. 'It oughter be trained. She ought to go to a hot-house'—or something like that. 'Conservatory?' Yes, that's it.

"'She's mighty anxious to l'arn,' says Jud. 'She wants a pianner awful bad.'

"'Does she?' says the soop'rintendent. 'She oughter have one.'

"When he come along to the house he says to Jess, who stuck her head outer the door an' looked kinder skeer'd-like, says he, 'I wish yeh'd sing a few songs fer me.'

"Wal, yeh could see wal enough that Jess's knees was a-knockin' together, but she tunes up her mandy-linn, scratches at the strings with a little chip, an' gits started all right on 'Rock o' Ages,' an' gits to goin' along kinder quavery-like fer a while, an' then she busts right inter, 'He'r dem Bells,' so strong an' high an' wild that it takes the ol' man right out o' his boots.

"He claps his hands an' yells, 'Hooray! Give us another!'

"Then she saws along on, 'Gather at the River,' an' chops inter, 'All Coons Looks Alike ter Me,' in a way to stop the mill.

"Her paw stan's aroun' all the while, tickled t' death an' smilin' all over.

"'Wal,' says the soop'rintendent, when Jess she stops ter git her wind, 'yer all right, Miss Hemenway. Yer as full o' music as a wind-harp in a tornado.' Then he says to her paw on the Q. T., 'If yeh was ter let that gal go ter the city an' l'arn some o' them high-toned op'ry songs, yeh wouldn't have to be picaroonin' lumber strings much longer.'

"'Yes,' says Hemenway, bloated up like a gobbler an' lookin' at Jess where she stan's with her face red an' still a-puffin' for breath; 'an' she thinks she could l'arn right here if she only had a pianner.'

"'She'd oughter have one,' says Mr. Sneath. 'I wish——' he says, an' then he breaks off like a busted log-chain. 'But we couldn't git it down here.'

"'What's that?' asts Hemenway.

"'We got a pianner up to our place, an' Mrs. Sneath won't be a-fingerin' on it fer five months. She's a-goin' East with me. If we could only git it down here an' back all right. If the' 's only a road from Skyland down here or from Mill Flat up, but the' ain't, so the' 's no use talkin'. Couldn't ship it down to the Flat an' up on mule-back, or nothin', either; so I guess it can't be did.'

"'Why not send it down the flume?' asts Jess, timid-like. I could see she was jest crazy about gittin' it.

"'Oh, the flume is old, an' it's rotten in places, an' such a heavy load might go through.'

"'Why, it holds up the grub-boat all right,' says Jess. 'Oh, if I could only have that pianner down here! I can play a little already, an' I'd l'arn a lot. I'd practise eight hours a day.'

"'How about gittin' the meals?' asts Hemenway.

"'Wal, I'd set up, then, an' practise all night,' says she.

"'I'm afeard that 'u'd be pretty hard on yer paw,' says Mr. Sneath, smilin'. 'Wal, Jud, we got ter be goin'.'

"So they gits inter their dude boat, an' Jess she skips along after 'em, an' jest as they's about to ontie, she yells out to the soop'rintendent:

"'Cain't I have it? Cain't I have it? Cain't yeh send it down the flume? Please say yeh will. I'll take the best kind o' keer of it. It sha'n't git a single scratch.'

"Mr. Sneath he looks at her a minute kinder tender-like, an' I knowed them big eyes o' hern was a-doin' their work. Them big soft baby eyes would 'a' drawed sap outer a dead log.

"'Wal,' says he, 'we'll see. If Mrs. Sneath's willin' I guess it'll be all right.'

"'Thank you, thank you, thank you!' she yells as the boat flies down the flume.

"I seed Jud blow a kiss to her, an' I knowed she was happy as a bird. She was a-singin' aroun' the shanty all day, an' at supper she done nothin' but talk, talk, talk about that there pianner.

"'Don't be so awful gay, Miss Hemenway,' says I, for I was afeard she might be disapp'inted. 'Yeh ain't got it yet. Yeh know, Mr. Sneath's a' awful busy man, an' he may fergit it.'

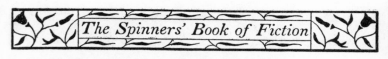

"'Oh, he won't fergit! Jud'll poke him up on it,' says she. 'An' I think I'll have it put right over there in that corner. No, that's on the flume side, an' it might draw dampness there. Over there by the winder's the place, an' plenty o' light, too. Wonder if they'll think to send down a stool.'

"I had to skin up to Skyland nex' day. Jud says the soop'rintendent has to light out quicker'n he'd thought, but he didn't fergit about the pianner. Mis' Sneath was as easy as greased skids, but Mr. Sneath he didn't know exactly. He sends the pianner over to the warehouse there 'longside the flume an' has the men slap together a stout boat to run her down in; but at the las' minute he backs out. He was a-lookin' at the pianner standin' there in the warehouse, an' he says to Jud, says he:

"'That there pianner has be'n in our family ever sence we was married. Marthy allus sot a heap o' store by that pianner. It was my first present to her, an' I know she thinks a hull lot of it, even if she don't seem ter keer. Trouble is, she don't know what sendin' it down the flume means. Yeh see, it ain't like a long string o' lumber—weight's all in one place, an' she might break through. This flume ain't what it was thirteen years ago, yeh know.'

"Jud he argies with him, 'cos he knows Jess's heart'll be broke if she don't git the pianner; an' after a while he thinks he's got it all fixed; but jest afore Sneath an' his wife takes the stage he telaphones down to the warehouse to let the pianner stay there till he comes back. Then he goes away, an' Jud is as down in the mouth as if he'd run his fist ag'in' a band-saw. He mopes aroun' all day, an' he's afeard to tell Jess; but as I was a-goin' back to Five that night, he tells me to break it to her gentle-like an' say he'd done his best. Which I did. Wal, that gal jest howls when I tells her, an' sobs an' sobs an' takes on like a baby coyote with the croup. But her dad he quiets her at last.

"Jud he hardly dasts to show up on Sunday, but when he does, she won't look at him fer quite a while. Then some o' that strawbary-blonde in her comes out in some o' the dernedest scoldin' yeh ever heer'd.

"'It's too bad, Jessie,' says he, 'but it ain't my fault. I done my best. He backed out at the las' minute; he backed out, an' I couldn't do no more than if a tree dropped on me. He backed out.'

"After a while he takes her off up the flume a piece, an' they stays there a long time, but she don't seem satisfied much when she comes back. There is hell a-poppin' there for about three days over that there pianner, an' the ol' man he gits so sick of it he gives her warnin' he'll light out if she don't quit. Wal, she quiets down some after that, but she makes Jud as mis'able as a treed coon fer over a week. She keeps a-tryin' an' a-tryin' to git him to send the pianner down anyway. She tells him she'll send it back afore the Sneaths gits home.

"'He told me I could have it; he promised me,' says she, 'he promised me, an' I'll never marry you unless you send it down. You can do it; you're goin' to be boss, an' you know it will be all right. I'll see that they ain't a scratch on it; an' you can put it in the warehouse, an' they'll never know it's be'n away.'

"An' so she keeps a-teasin' an' a-teasin', till finally Jud he gits desperate.

"'Oram,' says he to me one day, 'Oram, you're a ol' flume man. What do you think o' runnin' that pianner down to Five?'

"I shakes my head. I likes the boy, an' I don't want ter see him take sech big chances o' gittin' inter trouble. Somebody might tell Sneath, an' then it might be all off about his bein' flume boss. Besides, nobody had never run no pianner down no flume before, an' yeh couldn't tell what might happen.

"'D' yeh think, honest, Oram,' says he, 'the ol' flume's likely ter give way anywheres?'

"'No,' says I; 'she's strong as a railroad-track.'

"'Wal, then,' says he, 'I'm a-goin' to do it. You come down Sunday an' we'll take her out afore anybody's out o' the bunk-house.'

"I tries to argy him out of it, but he won't listen. So Sunday, about five in the mornin', I goes up to Skyland, an' we slides the big boat inter the flume an' gits the pianner onto the rollers, an' 't ain't much trouble to load her all right; fer, yer know, them big boats has flat tops like decks, an' things sets up on top of 'em. But while we was a-doin' that an' the boat is hitched tight to a stanchion 'longside o' the flume, the water backs up behind so high that it looks as though the pianner is a-goin' ter git wet. This skeers Jud, an' he seems to lose his head someways.

"'Hustle up, Oram!' says he, very nervous-like. 'The boat's crowdin' down so it won't let any water past. Ontie that rope.'

"I takes a good notice o' the pianner, an' I don't like her looks, sittin' up there so high on that little deck.

"'We oughter tie her on good an' tight,' says I.

"She's a upright, yeh see, an' she's as top-heavy as a pile-driver. I was afeard she'd strike a low limb or somethin' an' git smashed. So I goes to settle her a bit an' lay her down on her back an' tie her on; but he says he don't know about that layin'-down business, an' declares she'll ride all right. He speaks pretty sharp, too. So I gits a little huffy an' onties the rope, an' we starts.

"Wal, she don't go very fast at first, 'cos she's heavy an' they ain't none too much water in front; but after a while we comes to the Devil's Slide,—you remember the place,—an' we scoots down there like the mill-tails o' hell.

"'Gee-whiz!' says Jud. 'She's a-rockin' like a teeter. I hope she'll stay on all right.' He was settin' back with me, behind the pianner, an' we both tries to holt on to her an' keep her stiddy, but we cain't do much more'n set down an' cuss haff the time, we're so afeard we'll git throwed out. Wal, after we come to the foot of the slide, we breathes easy-like, an' Jud he says it's all right, for that there was the wust place. For about three miles the pianner set on that boat as stiddy as a church, an' from there on down to Four it was pretty good sailin'. Of course we went a good deal faster in the steep places than any other boat ever sent down the flume, because the heft o' the thing, when she got started, was bound to make her fly, water or no water. In a good many places we run ahead o' the stream, an' then in the quiet spots the water would catch up to us an' back up behind us an' shove us along.

"Between Four an' Five there's a place we used ter call Cape Horn. The flume is bracketed onto a cliff, yeh know, fer about a mile, an' it's a skeery place any way yeh shoot it; yeh scoot aroun' them there sharp curves so lively, an' yeh look down there four or five hundred feet inter the bottom o' the cañon. That's where yeh shut yer eyes. Yeh remember? Wal, when I sees Cape Horn ahead I gits a little skeer'd when I thinks how she might rock. We run onto a place where I could look away ahead, an' there, wavin' her apron or somethin', is a gal, an' I knows it's Jess, out from Five to see the pianner come down. Jud he knows, too, an' waves back.

"We runs out onto the brackets, turns a sharp curve, an' she begins to wabble an' stagger like a drunken man, floppin' back an' forth, an' the strings an' things inside is a-hummin' an' a-drummin'.

"'Slow her down!' yells Jud. 'Slow her down, or we'll never git past the Horn!'

"I claps on the brake, but she's so heavy she don't pay no 'tention to it, though I makes smoke 'long them planks, I tell yer. She scoots ahead faster'n ever, an' bows to the scenery, this way an' that, like she was crazy, an' a-hummin' harder than ever.

"'Slow her down! Ease her down!' hollers Jud, grittin' his teeth an' holdin' onto her with all his hundred an' eighty pounds weight. But 't ain't no good. I gits a holt oncet, but the water backs up behind us an' we goes a-scootin' down on a big wave that sloshes out o' the flume on both sides an' sends us flyin' toward that Horn fer further orders.

"When we gits to the sharpest curve we knows we're there all right. She wabbles on one side an' then on the other, so I can see chunks o' sky ahead right under her. An' then, all of a sudden, she gives a whoopin' big jump right off the top o' the boat, an' over the side o' the flume she goes, her strings all a-singin' like mad, an' sailin' down four hundred feet. Jud had a holt of her before she dropped, an' if I hadn't 'a' grabbed him he'd 'a' gone over, too.

"You might not believe it, pardner, but we run a quarter of a mile down that there flume before we hears her strike. Jeroosalem! What a crash! I never heer'd one o' them big redwoods that made half so much noise when she dropped. How she did roar! An' I tell yeh what was strange about that there noise: it seemed like all the music that everybody had ever expected to play on that pianner for the nex' hundred years come a-boomin' out all to oncet in one great big whoop-hurray that echered up an' down that cañon fer half an hour.

"'We've lost somethin',' says I, cheerful-like, fer I thinks the' 's no use cryin' over spilt pianners.

"But Jud he never says nothin',—jest sets there like he was froze plumb stiff an' couldn't stir a eyelid—sets there, starin' straight ahead down the flume. Looks like his face is caught in the air and held that way.

"Of course, now our load's gone, the brake works all right, an' I hooks a-holt onto the side about a hundred feet from where Jess stands like a marble statute, lookin' down inter the gulch.

"'Come on, Jud,' says I, layin' my hand onto his arm soft-like; 'we gits out here.'

"He don't say nothin', but tries to shake me off. I gits him out at last, an' we goes over to where poor Jess stands, stiff an' starin' down inter the gulch. When she hears our feet on the side planks, she starts up an' begins to beller like a week-old calf; an' that fetches Jud outer his trance for a while, an' he puts his arm aroun' her an' he helps her back along the walk till we comes to a place where we gits down an' goes over to view the wreck.

"Great snakes, pardner, but it was a sight! The pianner had flew down an' lit onto a big, flat rock, an' the' wasn't a piece of her left as big as that there plate. There was all kinds o' wires a-wrigglin' aroun' on the ground an' a-shinin' in the sun, an' the' was white keys an' black keys an' the greatest lot o' them little woolly things that strikes the strings all mixed up with little bits o' mahogany an' nuts an' bolts an' little scraps o' red flannel an' leather, an' pegs an' bits o' iron that didn't look as if it had ever been any part o' the machine. It was the dernedest mess! I picked up somethin' Jess said was a pedal,—a little piece o' shiny iron about as long as that,—'n' that was the only thing that seemed to have any shape left to it. The litter didn't make any pile at all—jest a lot o' siftin' sawdust-stuff scattered aroun' on the rocks.

"'She struck tol'able hard,' says I, lookin' at Jud. But he don't say nothin'; jest stan's over there on the side o' the rock an' looks as if he'd like to jump off another fifty feet the' was there.

"'Don't take it like that, Jud,' says Jess, grabbin' holt o' him an' not payin' any 'tention to my bein' there. 'Cry, cuss, swear—anything, but don't be so solemn-like. It's my fault, Juddie dear—all my fault. Can yeh ever, ever fergive me? Yeh said yeh didn't think it was safe, an' I kep' a-goadin' yeh to it; an' now——' She broke out a-blubberin' an' a-bellerin' again, an' he puts his arm aroun' her an' smiles, an' says soft-like:

"'It don't matter much. I can raise the money an' buy a new one fer Mis' Sneath. How much do they cost?' says he.

"'Oh, I dunno! Five hundred dollars, I think. It's an awful lot o' money!'

"'Wal, I got three-fifty saved up,—you know what fer,—an' I can raise the rest an' put a new pianner in the place o' that one,' says he.

"He looks at the wreck, an' fer the first time I sees his eyes is jest a little damp.

"They didn't either of 'em seem to take any notice o' me, an' I didn't feel that I counted, nohow.

"'An' we cain't git married,' says Jud, sorrowful-like, 'fer ever so long. There'll be nothin' to house-keep on till I can save up some more.'

"'Yes, we can, too,' says she. 'I don't keer if yeh ain't got so much as a piece o' bale-rope.'

"'But yer paw?'

"'I don't keer,' says she, very hard-like, a-stampin' her foot. 'He can like it or lump it.'

"Wal, I sneaks away an' leaves 'em there, an' by an' by they comes up to where I sets on top o' the boat, an' Jud isn't so plumb gloomy as I thinks he'd be.

"Him an' her goes down ter Fresno nex' day an' buys one o' that same identical make o' pianners an' has it shipped up on the first freight-wagon to Sky-land. An' they puts it inter the warehouse, an' there she stands till Mr. Sneath comes home with his wife.

"When Mis' Sneath she sees the pianner brung inter her house she don't notice any difference fer a while; but one day she sets down ter play, an' she pounds out a few music, an' then she gives a jump an' looks all over the machine an' she says, 'Good Lord!' An' Sneath he comes in, an' they has a great time over how the' 's be'n sech a change in that pianner. She finally makes up her mind it's a bran'-new one, an' sends fer Jud an' asts him what he knows about it. An' he cain't lie a little bit, so he up an' tells her that her pianner is all inter sawdust an' scrap-iron down on the rocks, an' that this is a new one that he owes a hundred an' fifty dollars on down ter Fresno.

"Then she busts out a-laughin', an' says:

"'Why, that old tin-pan! I'm glad it flew the flume. It wasn't wuth twenty dollars. I got a noo grand pianner on the way here that I ordered in Noo York. I'll make this here one a weddin' present to you an' Jess.'

"And the soop'rintendent he writes out his check an' sends it down to Fresno to pay off the hundred an' fifty, an' when the weddin' it comes off he gives 'em a set o' chiny dishes besides.

"Jud's flume boss now, an' Jess she plays that pianner an' sings like a bird. When we gits down ter Mill Flat I'll show yeh their house. It's a white one up on the side o' the hill, jest across the gulch from the mill.

"Wal, yeh had all the grub yeh want, pardner? Say, ain't them green gages sour? They sets yer teeth on aidge all right. An' I couldn't find the boys' sugar-can. If yer full up, I guess we'd better git inter the boat."

I took my seat behind Oram and a particularly

offensive pipe he had just lighted. Looking down the long, swift-running, threatening flume, I shuddered; for since Oram's recital the native hue of my resolution had been "sicklied o'er with the pale cast of thought." I remarked that if he saw any of those Cape Horn curves ahead to let me know and I would get out and walk.

"Don't yeh be skeer'd by what I told yeh," said he. "Yeh got a pretty fair-sized head, but yeh ain't quite so top-heavy as Mis' Sneath's big upright. An', besides, the' ain't no more Cape Horn on this flume; they calls that place Pianner P'int now."

THE CONTUMACY OF SARAH L. WALKER

BY

MIRIAM MICHELSON

Reprinted from *Munsey's Magazine* of April, 1904
by permission

THE CONTUMACY OF SARAH L. WALKER

HE BOARD will now pass to consideration of the case of Mrs.—Mrs. Walker."

The president looked from the report in front of her to the superintendent sitting opposite.

The Rev. Alexander McCaleb rose slowly to his feet.

"I regret exceedingly," he said, "to have to report this case to the board. I need not say that if it had been possible to convince Mrs. Walker of the error of her ways, no pains or time would have been spared. But I have done all that I could. Mrs. Walker persists. She—ah!—she flouts all authority, and—ah!—sets such an example of rebellious conduct that I fear the discipline of the home may be gravely compromised."

The president knitted her pretty, dark brows. Her hair was white, with a soft, youthful whiteness that haloed her head as if it was a joke of old Time's. She was new to her office, and was conscious of a critical atmosphere that subtly underlined the formality of the proceedings—an official formality that made the meeting of the lady managers of this Old People's Home a formidable affair.

"I see no record of any case of disciplining heretofore," she said, troubled. "There is no precedent by which the chair can be——"

"But there are the by-laws," suggested the superintendent. He reached over to his own desk, and read from a pamphlet that had lain open there: "If any inmate of the home shall persistently and willfully disobey the rules, the superintendent shall report such case to the board of managers. If, after full and complete investigation, and a notice to that effect having been duly served, said inmate shall continue to persist in contumacy, the board is by a majority vote empowered to expel."

A little hush fell upon the assemblage at this invocation of its dread powers.

"It seems rather hard on the old bodies, doesn't it?" the president was encouraged to remark.

"But it is plainly stated in the by-laws," said the recording secretary, a bright-eyed, business-like matron.

"And dear Mr. McCaleb is so patient and tactful that it is seldom necessary," remarked the single member of this week's visiting committee.

"I thank you, Mrs. Davis." The superintendent bowed in his stateliest manner. "I do my best—I try always to do my best. Old people are trying, we all know."

The president looked up from her perusal of the by-laws.

"Suppose we have the old lady in," she said. "Mr. McCaleb, will you send for Mrs. Walker?"

The old lady held her head haughtily as she walked into the handsomely furnished office. The president, mindful of her official capacity, looked severely upon Mrs. Walker—Sarah Lucinda Walker, according to the cramped signature of the home's register, widow, a native of Maine, aged sixty-seven on her entrance into the home five years ago. And Mrs. Walker—a miracle of aged neatness, trim, straight, little, in her sober black and immaculate cap—looked severely back.

"Be seated, Mrs. Walker," said the president.

"Thank you." Mrs. Walker crossed with a formal "Good morning, ladies," and took the chair indicated.

"Now, Mr. McCaleb, if you please——" said the president.

The superintendent rose.

"Ladies," he began with a solemnity that made the offender quake within, though outwardly she was calm as the president herself, "it is with positive pain that I have to report to you the case of Mrs. Sarah Lucinda Walker. It is now fully three months since I began to labor with her—three months since I warned her of this very thing that has come to pass, an investigation by your honorable board. On the 9th of January"—he glanced methodically at a notebook—"I sent her a copy of the by-laws, with the section referring to insubordination underscored in red ink. On the 23d I made a personal call upon her, and sought to convince her how impossible it was that such conduct could be tolerated. On February 7th I publicly reprimanded her. On the 13th—five days ago—I informed her that, after considering it prayerfully, I had laid the matter before your honorable body, and that she should hold herself in readiness to be summoned before you to meet the following charges:

"First, insubordination; second, breaking Rule VIII of the house regulations; third, taking food from the table; fourth, disturbing neighbors in early morning; and fifth, defacing the building."

Mr. McCaleb took his seat. The shocked gaze of the board bent itself upon the criminal. The bad little old lady's far-sighted eyes swept insolently past them all and met the president's—twenty years younger than her own.

"Do you like birds, ma'am?" she asked, herself in an eager, bird-like way. And then, without waiting for an answer, she went on: "I love 'em—anything that's got wings. Old Cap'n Walker used to say, 'Sary Lucindy, they was a moughty fine ornithologist spiled when God A'mighty made you a woman 'stead of a man.' He was a free-spoken man, Cap'n Walker, not so pious-mouthed as some, but he had charity in his soul, which is more than some others has."

She swept a superbly disdainful look toward the Rev. McCaleb. The recording secretary tapped reprovingly with her pencil, but the president only listened.

"Now, ma'am, we ain't paupers, we old folks. Every one of us, as you know, has paid our thousand dollars in. An' we ain't bad children as needs disciplinin'; an' they's no use treatin' grandmothers an' great-grandmothers as though they was. It's in me to love birds, an' no 'mount of rules and regulations is goin' to change me. My canary bird died the same year Cap'n Walker saved every other soul on board his ship and went down alone to the bottom with her. Since then I've sort o' adopted the sparrers. Why, haven't I spent every afternoon through the summer out in the park a-feedin' them my lunch? An' now that winter's come, d'ye think I'd have the face to desert them?

"'Not one of them is forgotten before God'—do you remember, ma'am? One of 'em seemed to be in the early winter. It was before my rheumatism got so bad. I was out in the park the afternoon the first snow fell, an' this poor little crittur with a wing broke kep' a trailin' an' chirpin' an' scuttlin' in front o' me. It'd fell out o' the nest; hardly covered with feathers, it was. I picked it up an' carried it to my room in my apron. Poor little mite—how it fluttered an' struggled! I kep' it overnight in my spool-box. In the mornin' I fed it; by noon the sun come out, an' I let it out on the window-sill, where I keep my house plants; just a bit o' musk—the cap'n liked musk—an' a pot o' bergamot. Do you know, ma'am, that little thing was that contented by the end of the week that I could leave the windows open an' nary a wing's stroke away would it go? That was in December, 'fore it got to be known that I kep' a bird in my room. That mild spell we had 'fore Christmas it did fly away one morning, but at sundown there it was back again; an' when it came on to snow that night I felt same's I used to 'tween voyages, when I could hear how the ocean'd get lashed to a fury, an' Cap'n Walker'd be fast asleep safe beside me.

"Of course it was a pity that when the bird came back it showed others the way—but wasn't it cute of it, ma'am? An' wasn't it just like a lot o' children hangin' 'round at maple-syrup time? They did make a clatter an' a racket in the early mornin' when I wouldn't be up an' they'd be ready for breakfast. But wasn't it for all the world like children with empty little stummicks an' chatterin' tongues? When Mis' Pearson complained of me an' the noise, I didn't take it kind of her. Take food from the table? Course I did. But it was my own lunch, that I'd a right to go hungry for ef I wanted to, an' nobody's affair.

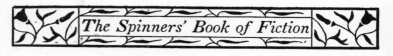

"But I tell you, ma'am, one day—it was that day Mr. McCaleb sent me that printed notice, an' everybody on my floor see it comin' an' knew it was something shameful an' legal—that evening I tried honestly to keep 'em out. I pulled down the shade—it was a bitter cold day, a regular blizzard blowing—an' I sat with my back to the window an' tried to read my Bible while them birds jest shrieked themselves hoarse outside. Well, guess where that Bible opened to! 'Yea, the sparrow hath found a house and the swallow a nest for herself where she may lay her young.' That was a message, ma'am, a straight, sure message. I opened the window an' scattered their bread-crumbs out on the sill, which I had made jest the least bit wider for them—that's what he calls 'defacin' the buildin'.' After that, I told Mr. McCaleb flat-footed that if he had the heart to starve them innocent critturs in the dead o' winter, it was more than I had. I told him if he'd wait till spring, I'd promise never to open the window that faces south after that; but till they could shift for themselves, I'd shift for them. That's all. Thank *you*, ma'am, for letting me have my say."

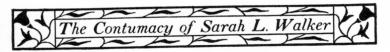

She smiled into the president's soft eyes, and rose, looking like a trim, saucy, gray-haired sparrow about to take flight. The president's smile started back to her, but on the way it had to pass the recording secretary, the visiting committee, and the Rev. Alexander McCaleb. By the time it had made the journey it was shorn of half its sympathetic understanding.

"You admit then, Mrs. Walker, that you have broken the rule against having pets in the room?" the president asked with gravity. "It is a necessary rule. Fancy what would be the condition of the place if a lady in No. 117 had a tame sparrow, a gentleman in No. 120 a monkey, his neighbor a spaniel, the lady across the way a cat, and so on! I appreciate—we all do, and Mr. McCaleb more than all of us—how tender and charitable a nature yours is, but"—she looked at the recording secretary to gain courage—"but we simply must enforce the rules. I know so good a housekeeper as you must have been will understand this, and agree with me when I say that such a disciplinarian as Captain Walker no doubt was—unfortunately, I never had the pleasure of his acquaintance—would have been the first to counsel you to obey the rules. Won't you think it over from our point of view, Mrs. Walker, when you go back to your room? Do! Good afternoon."

It was a very dejected Sarah Lucinda Walker that returned to her room. Her depression was noted and audibly commented upon by Mrs. Pearson, her next-door neighbor and arch-enemy. In fact, the whole corridor was alive with the news of her defeat.

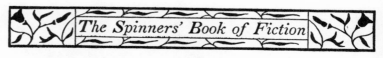

At the lunch-table it was the sole topic of conversation, and in the library old Colonel Rockwell—in the pauses of a quavering rendition of "Rocked in the Cradle of the Deep"—bet Mr. Patterson three of the cigars his nephew always sent him on Fridays that Mrs. Walker, being a woman of spirit, would not yield even though the ultimatum were expulsion.

Mrs. Walker heard of the wager, of course, that afternoon. They were a hundred or more antiquated and unseaworthy vessels, all anchored in a semi-genteel haven; and from morning till night, till sun should cease for them to shine and water to flow, they had nothing to do but to listen to the whispering tide that told of the great ocean of life beyond, or to gossip among themselves of their own voyages dead and done.

The incorrigible Mrs. Walker's spotless little room, with its bag of dried crusts on the window-sill, saved for her pet, became the storm center that afternoon. Every old lady who could possibly claim acquaintance called to inquire her intentions; every old gentleman leaned hard upon his cane as he lifted his hat to her in the halls with the deference due a gallant rebel. They loved a rebel, these old children, at the end of their lives fallen again into the domain of "you must" and "you must not."

Sarah Lucinda Walker's world rocked beneath her. She intended, she believed, to obey the rules, to cast off the one creature on earth to which she could still play Lady Bountiful; to shut her hospitable window and her loving old heart on all these fluttering, visiting strangers who had heard of her generosity, and with every hour carried the news of it further.

She intended all this, but when the time came she did simply as old Colonel Rockwell had wagered she would. She opened wide her windows and fed the hungry throng that whirred about her, scattering crumbs and floating feathers over the immaculate marble of Mr. McCaleb's front door-step.

A knock at the door brought her to her senses. She put a withered little old hand, very like a sparrow's claw, upon the window-sash to shut it hastily, and then, too proud to deceive, turned boldly to meet her fate.

Mrs. Pearson, on the lookout at her half-open door, saw the official-looking document handed to her.

"It's her notice to leave," she said in an awed whisper to herself.

In the face of so great a calamity she felt, not triumph, but a shocked sense of loss, of self-reproach. Five minutes after she was in her enemy's room.

"You mustn't—you mustn't cry, dear Mrs. Walker," she sobbed, putting her arms about the slender old shoulders.

"Am I crying?" the little old lady answered. "I can't help it—I'm so happy!"

"Happy!" Mrs. Pearson's dazed old eyes turned bewildered from the envelope with the home's letter-head on it to the bird-like creature in her arms. "And you've got your notice to leave?"

"Did you think it was that? So did I for a minute, an' it 'most killed me. But I opened it, an' found a note from the president—that dear, dear president! She wants to know if I'll take care of her summer cottage till the spring comes. An', Marthy Pearson,

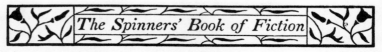

they's chickens up there—fancy breeds—a whole yard of 'em—an' I'm to have the feedin' of 'em! Ain't it enough to make a body cry for joy? Say, Marthy, would you—would you mind feedin' the sparrers?—only on the very stormiest days—McCaleb would never suspect you, an' spring's near!"

BREAKING THROUGH

BY

W. C. MORROW

Reprinted from *Success Magazine* of September, 1906
by permission

BREAKING THROUGH

RAY," SAID his mother, whom he shyly and secretly worshipped, without her ever suspecting the least of it beneath his cautious reserve and occasional outbursts of temper, "my son, I hope you will remember, tonight. You are nearly a man."

She was a wise woman, and said it kindly and meant it well; but his face flamed, his eyes hardened, and he sullenly walked away. Mrs. Gilbert sighed, and went about the preparations for the young people's party which her daughters, aged sixteen and eighteen, were to give that evening. She could not foresee what her son would do. Would her gentle warning, filled with the tender pride of a mother's love for her one man-child, drive him with his dog to the woods, whither many a time before this day a word less pointed had sent him, there to live for a week or longer at a time, in a manner that he had never disclosed?—or would the disjointed thing within him which harried his somber, lonely life force him in a blind moment to make a disgraceful scene at the gathering? She prayed that neither would happen, and that the sunshine fighting for egress through his darkness would come forth soft and genial and very fine and sweet, as it did sometimes, and always unaccountably. . . .

The worst had happened at the party. No doubt it was intolerable,—but not so bad as when (he was then only four) he had tried to kill a boy for lying about him and was whipped mercilessly by his father,—for here, in the library, he was sitting before Mr. Gilbert, who was pale and whose eyes had a deep, inscrutable look. He was a large and powerful man, and had a genial nature, with force and sternness. The lad had never seen him looking thus, and so evidently guarding a prisoner, and the boy felt a strange weight within.

Whatever had happened must have left a shadow on the assemblage, for, though faint sounds came through the closed doors, they were somewhat lacking in the robustness of youth. Ray did not deign an effort to remember. More than that, he hoped that it never would come back, for it might be disturbing to his solitudes. Of his attempts to remember the attack on the boy ten years ago, there had never come any result but the recollection of a wholly disconnected event,—when he was enveloped in a swirl of flame and smoke from a fierce grass fire, and had to fight his way through to life. He did not try to think what his father's purpose was in holding him a prisoner tonight. Was it to give him a lecture? Pshaw! The beautiful, peaceful woods would make him forget that child's-play, and he would steal away to them with Cap this very night, as soon as all were asleep.

Thus, motionless and in silence, sat he and his father, seemingly through an endless, aching time.

After a while the guests quietly left. His sisters omitted their customary good night to their father. All sounds from the servants ended. Then entered his mother, uncommonly pale, and in silence looked from her son to her husband. She was small and dainty, and very, very pretty, the boy reflected. It was a pity that her bright eyes should be dim tonight and her sweet mouth drawn. She looked worn and as though she dreaded something.

"Are you ready?" Mr. Gilbert asked, regarding her fixedly.

Her lip trembled, but there came a flash from her eyes. "Do you really mean it?" she asked.

"Certainly. It must be done."

"My dear, dear, he's too large for——"

"He'll never be too large for it so long as he is a boor and coward, insults our guests, scandalizes us all, shames his sisters, and treats his parents with open scorn. He won't try to be like other people and accept his world as he finds it. His inordinate conceit is a disease. It is eating up his own life and making our lives miserable. We will cure it."

He had spoken calmly, but with a low vibration of tone; and as he came to his feet he looked very tall and terrible. Ray's blood began to rise, and as he looked about for something undefined he felt the heat and smelled the smoke of the grass fire of ten years ago.

He knew he was a coward. That was the shame and the curse of his life. He did not think it had always been so, but believed it had come about gradually. At first he had not minded the whippings that other boys gave him because of his temper and his physical inadequacy, for he had invited the punishment; but when they all learned that his fighting spirit had weakened, that they could whip him easily, that they need not wait for provocation, and that he would never tell, they bullied and hounded and beat him until he had come to know a craven, sordid fear, which spread from the boys to the whole terrible world in which the masculine entity must fight for a place.

"I am ready," said Mrs. Gilbert, trying to hide a sigh.

"Come," Mr. Gilbert ordered the boy, looking at him for the first time in two hours.

The boy quailed before that look, the most dreadful thing he had ever seen. It made him numb and sick, and when he rose he staggered; for, though tall, he was slender and had little strength. The weight on his chest became a pain and fixed on his throat, to choke and torment him.

His mother had gone out. He followed his father, and the three went out into the back yard, the boy bareheaded. The night was sharp and the moon very bright. All the boy's power of thought was suspended.

In silence they walked down the terraces of the park-like yard in the rear. Cap, Ray's dog, his only intimate, came bounding forward for his young master's unfailing good night, but Mr. Gilbert angrily ordered him away. The animal, astonished and hurt, slunk away, keeping a watchful view of the group, and sat down at a distance and gazed in wonder. They passed through a gate into an orchard, and shut the dog out.

Mr. Gilbert selected an apple tree, because the wood was tougher than that of a peach. From it he cut two switches a yard long, and carefully pared the knots, his wife observing without a word or a movement, and the boy looking away into the distance. When Mr. Gilbert had done, he ordered his son to prepare.

The lad numbly, dumbly removed his coat and waistcoat, slipped his suspenders down, tightened the strap at the back of his trousers, clasped his hands in front, and bowed his head. The dog, which had crept to the fence and was peering through the pickets, whined anxiously and was quivering. When roughly ordered away by Mr. Gilbert, he went upon a terrace that overlooked the fence, and trembled as he watched. The boy did not once look toward him. He was struggling with the pain in his throat.

Mr. Gilbert offered one of the switches to his wife.

"Oh, how can you!" she pleaded.

"You must," he firmly said. "I'll relieve you when you are tired."

The boy's mind suddenly cleared, and he comprehended. A whipping from his father would be frightful enough,—not for the blows; they were nothing. The plan was not alone to humiliate him beyond all measure, but to scourge his soul, ravage the sanctuary of his mother there, rend him asunder, and cast him into an unthinkable hell of isolation; for she was the bond that held him to the world, she was the human comfort and sweetness of his life.

Since his tenth year his discipline had been solely in her hands, his father having given him up as worthless, hopeless. She had whipped him many a time, but not for two years; and he had felt no pain, no shame, no outrage, no resentment. The case of the teacher was different. Ray had solemnly sworn, renewing the oath every day, that when he came to manhood he would beat his teacher to death for whipping him so often and severely because of his dulness, his apathy, or his rebellion; the whippings from his mother had only increased his tenderness for her, and, in some way that he could not understand, his pity also. Perhaps it was because he vaguely felt that she was impairing something in herself that was precious to him. Never had she conquered him; never had he cried out in pain, never pleaded for mercy, never confessed penitence nor promised reform.

Mrs. Gilbert shut her teeth hard, and, deathly white in the moonlight, raised the switch. It was poised a moment, and then her arm fell limp to her side; but the look that her son had seen in his father's eyes held her and steeled her with a sort of desperate madness, and her arm again rose.

A long cry, an anguished wail, almost superhuman in its power to shatter the silence of the night, and more startling than any human cry could be, struck disorganizingly through the drama. It may have hastened the catastrophe. Mr. Gilbert was unnerved for a moment, and in exasperation picked up a clod and threw it at the offending dog trembling on the terrace. When he turned again, his son was kneeling beside his unconscious mother, peering anxiously into her pallid face, and calling her softly.

In a stride Mr. Gilbert was upon him. A hand armed with strength and fury caught up the shirt on the lad's shoulder, raised him, and flung him away with so great violence that the slender body struck the ground as a log. Mr. Gilbert tenderly picked up his wife and bore her into the house.

The fall had half stunned the boy. As he slowly struggled to a sitting posture the moon danced fantastically, and some black trees crowning a near hill bowed and rose, and walked sidewise to and fro. A whine, low, cautious, packed with sympathy and solicitude, pleaded at the pickets, but the boy gave it no attention. He sat for a time, rose giddily, swayed as he dressed himself, and with deliberation walked to the gate. The dog, whining, trembling, crawled to meet him; but the boy, instead of caressing him, ordered him quietly but firmly to the kennel. Obedience was slow, and the animal looked up incredulous, wondering. The order had to be repeated. Finally the dog obeyed, frequently pausing to look back, but his master stood inflexible.

Passing round the house, and without thinking or caring about hat and overcoat, he noiselessly passed out the front gate, for a moment studied the big house that had cradled him, bred much of his anguish, and held all of his love, and firmly stepped out into the road. There was a gnawing ache somewhere. Assuredly that one blow,—and from *her*,—could not have caused it. After finding it in his throat, he was much relieved, and struck out on secure legs.

It did not occur to him that he was an outlaw and outcast. He did not think at all. Hence there was no plan in his going. He did not even understand that something deeper within him than had ever operated before had assumed, in the disqualifica-

tion of his ordinary ruling powers, an imperious regency, and that it was infinitely greater or infinitely less than his usual intelligence. He simply went on, thinking nothing, remembering nothing. The beautiful highway, arched by great trees, above which rode the moon in keeping pace with him, was a tunnel under a luminous sea; he half walked, half floated, in the crystal water, and had no wonder that he breathed it. The houses along the way were the palaces of lordly gnomes that inhabited the deep.

Whatever was leading him turned him out of the avenue at last and drifted him along a winding road that was as beautiful in its less conventional way. He did not reflect that all of this was familiar, shamefully familiar. It was the road to his grandmother's, but he had not visited her for a year.

Her great wisdom and tact had gone to a study of the strange, unhappy child; she had been kind to him in every cautious, delicate fashion that she could devise; but he had ceased coming, and avoided her when she visited his home, and she had never known why. She was a patient woman and good; she knew prayer, and in her peaceful twilight she walked with God; yet no revelation had come at her appeals, for the times were not ready; and the boy went his way alone and silent, forever alone and silent, and unhappy, unhappy!

A white picket fence was presently marching with him alongside the shining road. He did not consciously recognize it, and it brought no rekindling of an old terror, an old shame; but soon, on the other side of it, a distance away, there broke on the stillness a challenge that he remembered, and its tone was contempt. He understood it, and woke with a start, because of a sudden fluff of flame and a whiff of smoke from the grass fire of ten years ago, and the ache in his throat gave him a strangling wrench. His head rolled; the moon swung through an arc of alarming length. That call beyond the fence struck the dominant note of his life, and it was Fear. Yet it came from a mere animal,—his grandmother's old buckskin horse, the most docile of creatures.

Ray had never feared the wild things of the woods. The cry of the panther in the dead of night is dreadful, but it had no terrors for the boy in the forest solitude. Other fierce pad-footed members of the cat tribe had come and sniffed him as he lay under the stars, and experience had taught him to feign sleep, for a suspicion of his wakefulness would send them bounding away, and he was lonely, always lonely. One night, roused from slumber, he sleepily put his hand on the shaggy head of a bear that was curiously rummaging him, and he was sorry that the beast took alarm and trotted away,—he would have been comfortable to hug. That was before the dog had come into his life. He could never understand why he was not afraid of anything whatever—not even of the terrific lightning and thunder that sometimes flamed and crashed and bellowed all about him,—except human beings and the forces that they controlled; and at times he wondered why Cap loved him and the buckskin horse would kill him from hate if he could.

Here, then, beyond the picket fence, was the proclamation of his shame,—coming from a gentle, superannuated horse with no more spirit than a snail's.

By some means, perhaps instinctive,—for all the world, when it finds out, will hunt down and destroy whatsoever fears it (although the boy had not reasoned it out thus),—the beast had learned that the boy was afraid, and had then found an interest in life. Let him but have a glimpse of Ray, and, ears back, lips drawn from hideous yellow teeth, and head thrust horribly forward, he would snort, charge,—and the boy would run abjectly. The horse had never thus treated another living thing. So the boy had stayed away from his grandmother's, and she had never suspected, and her love and prayers had brought no revelation.

As the fence intervened, the horse knew that a charge would be useless; but when, with a neat leap, the boy nimbly caught his feet on the ground within the pasture, the buckskin advanced in his minatory way. Ray did not know why he had leaped the fence, unless the wrench in his throat had hurled him over or the flame and smoke of the grass fire had driven him; nor did he know why he went steadily to meet the horse, nor why his nostrils stretched and his arms strained and his hands clenched, nor why there was a fierce eagerness in him; a rasping thirst for something dried his tongue. The horse came on, and the boy, perfectly calm, as fatally went to meet him. There was no calculation of results, yet the lad knew that a horse's teeth and hoofs may be deadly. He knew only that he was not going forward to end all his wretchedness, as, last year, the shoemaker who drank had done with a shotgun, and young Corson, the thieving clerk, with poison. It occurred to the boy that he cared nothing about the teeth and hoofs of any horse, and nothing about what they might do.

So ridiculous was the *fiasco* that he would have laughed had he not been sorry for the beast; for to see any rampant thing so suddenly stricken with fear, when there was not the least danger nor any intent of harm, was pitiful to see. He wished to assure the buckskin that he was only a boy, a frail boy at that, and not what the animal had apparently taken him to be,—a spawn of Darkness and Terror. He followed up the trembling beast, trying to reassure him and to get near and pet him; but the creature fled wildly at every advance, and when not pursued stood with head aloft, ears cocked, and nostrils vibrant, quivering in fear.

Seeing the uselessness of further pacific effort, the boy sprang over the fence, went back to the main highway, and by the unseen Hand was led into the short cut past Mr. Elderby's house, where the greatest terror of his life—human excepted—had months ago driven him to use the long way round. He did not know, nor for a moment consider, why he chose the short cut tonight. He turned into it, walking free and strong.

Girls had meant nothing in the boy's life. That was because they did not seem members of his species, but something fragile, mysterious, and ranking somewhere between flowers and angels. Thus his feeling for them was composed of a little awe, more reverence, and a sense of great remoteness. Never had he observed them thoughtfully without reflecting that they were, in a general way, much like his mother, or at least of her species; therefore they must be sweet and dainty and gentle and kind. His only large swellings of the heart had come from his thinking about them, particularly Grace Elderby, now twelve years old. Nothing could have been so grand, for instance, as an opportunity to rescue her, single-handed, from wild savages that had her tied to a tree and were piling fagots about her; then to dance in fiendish glee about her as the flames rose. He would dash up on a splendid charger, his sword flashing in the sun; savage heads would roll in the dust, or fall open, cleaved in twain; there would be wild yells of fright and a wilder flight for life; he would leap from his horse, speak reassuring words while he severed her bonds, mount with her in his arms, and fly away, away, away.

Twice had Grace seen his shame. She had seen him pale, and run when her father's big, noisy dog had made a flamboyant show of rage, and she had seen him stand mute and white when Andy Carmichael, older and larger and much stronger than Ray, grossly insulted him in her presence. The Elderby dog was the terror that had closed the short cut,—closed it to Ray alone.

Thus into the short cut swung Ray, walking strong and free, the ache in his throat not so painful as before. The dog would be on guard, and the boy was empty-handed.

The shadows were deep under the trees, or possibly the dog's hate and rage blinded him to what the buckskin had seen, or perhaps he was of a different metal. Near the rear of the premises the big brute came in so great a fury that he broke through the palings. The ensuing collision,—for the boy stood his ground,—was so violent that Ray went down underneath, and an ecstasy thrilled him when the flame swished and the smoke stung, and he felt something sink into his shoulder and a stifle of hot, foamy breath in his face.

It seemed to have been easily and quickly done. True, when he came erect he was weak and tired, and swayed dizzily, and wondered why. As, without the least exultation, or even triumph, or even gratification, he looked down at his work, and saw with surprise how deeply the ground had been torn up, two men with sticks came running out,—evidently there had been some noise, despite all his care for silence. One was Mr. Elderby, the other his coachman. The gentleman stood in astonishment as the boy, controlling his heavy breathing, stepped into the moonlight and calmly faced him.

"Ray Gilbert! What are you doing here, at this time of night?"

"I was walking in the path. Your dog attacked me."

"What did you kill him with?"

"My hands."

Mr. Elderby stood in wonder as he studied the lad. "I'm thankful to God that you are alive. It's a miracle." He noticed that Ray's clothing was torn nearly to rags. In compassion he laid a hand on Ray's shoulder, quickly withdrew it, and examined it in the moonlight. "You are hurt, my son. Come into the house. I'll put you to bed and send for the doctor and your parents."

"Thank you, sir; I have something to do."

"But you must have attention.—Jake, hitch up the bay to the light buggy,—quick,—and drive him home."

"No, sir; but I'm much obliged. I have something to do. Good night." The shadows enveloped him.

The short cut led him over a sharp hill and into the road again, and there he sat on the bank till his strength came back. Then he went on till he arrived at a gate leading into a private avenue. The ache in his throat was nearly gone. Passing quietly up the driveway and round to the rear of the house, he came to a window, which was open at the top, and sharply tapped on the glass.

"Who's that?" came a voice.

"Dress and come out, Andy Carmichael. I'm Ray Gilbert."

The sash was thrown up and the boy glowered in the opening. "Ray Gilbert!—you cowardly, sneaking puppy! What do you want?"

"I want to see you. Dress and come out. Don't wake anybody."

He spoke quietly, trying to appear his usual self lest this monster, this overshadowing terror of his life, should see whatever it was that had frightened the horse and slain the dog. This was the boy who had beaten him so often and with such merciless, sodden, gluttonous enjoyment; the boy who, when he did not care to give the beatings himself—no provocation was ever needed,—would stand threateningly by and let the smaller boys, even to the little ones with soft, puny fists, beat the coward as long as they wished, merely for the love of beating what did not resist; the boy whose lies had brought undeserved whippings from the teacher; the boy who openly insulted him whenever he pleased, and, worst of all, had humiliated him before Grace Elderby. It was the presence of this boy at the party that evening, and the looks that he gave Ray, and the sly tortures he inflicted, that had sent up the curtain on the night's drama.

In wondering surprise Andy studied the bare-headed, ragged, dirty figure standing in the moon-light; and as crimson looks a muddy brown in such a light, he mistook the smears on the other's face and the dark splotches on his clothing. What could the creature want of him at this time of night and with that extraordinary appearance? Likely Ray had been set upon and was seeking any refuge. It would be joyous to complete the work that the others had begun. Andy soon emerged from the house.

"Come this way," said his mysterious visitant, and perplexed Andy followed him to the rear of the fowl-house, where the light was clear. The flame and smoke of the old grass fire were strong in the air.

Ray halted, and faced him.

"Take off your coat," he quietly said, removing his own tattered garment.

"What for?" with a slight quaver composed of anger—and something else; for there was a touch of the uncanny here.

"We are going to fight."

"Fight, eh! What put that into your fool head?" Under the initial impulse from the challenge, Andy was all heat and eagerness, and he bristled and swelled; but though, in some vital ways, human sense is less acute than brute sense, Andy did feel some-thing of what the buckskin had felt, something of what had slain the dog, and his heart thumped with a strange heaviness. "What do you want to fight for? I'd beat the life out of you."

It failed of the effect intended, and Andy found his head suddenly twisted to one side by a slap on the cheek. He stepped back, white with fury, tossed his coat aside, and hurled himself upon the slender figure waiting with such unearthly composure.

* * * * * * * *

Dawn was flooding the east, and still the boy lurched and floundered on and on, keeping to the road that led into the wilderness. Occasionally he would stop for a minute's rest and to listen for the baying of Frazier's bloodhound; and he wondered, in a purely detached and scientific way, whether he had sufficient strength and acuteness left for another such grapple. It was merely an engaging speculation, and was complicated with his determination to perform another task before his work was done. It would nearly break his heart to be stopped now. Likely the dog would not attack him, but merely hold him at bay until the pursuers came to his summons; but if the dog would not attack, then the boy must. Would strength or even life be left for the last and most important of all the tasks to which the Hand was leading him?—for there was a good distance yet to be covered, and work to be done at the end of it. He was thankful that the ache had entirely left his throat and that a strange warmth had kindled in his breast.

Perhaps they had not really meant what they said about setting Frazier's bloodhound to run him down. The remark had come from the yardman, not Mr.

"Dawn was flooding the east, and still the boy lurched and floundered on and on."

From a Painting by Gordon Ross.

ROSS

Carmichael himself, who had appeared too stunned to think of anything but his son. If they had wished to kill the outlaw, or take him and send him to jail, why had they not seized and bound him instead of staring at him so queerly, and then the yardman foolishly saying, as Ray staggered away and they picked up the limp figure, that they would get Frazier's bloodhound and set him on the trail? They were two strong men against a mere boy, who was so exhausted that only with a mighty effort could he stand. It was Andy's final despairing cry that had waked them.

Without either triumph or regret the boy struggled on. The broadening of day made him partly aware of the savage presence that he made and of the likelihood that traffic might open on the road at any time. Some of his clothing was gone, and he had bound the remaining strips and rags about him as best he could. He did not know about the aspect of his face and hair, but he realized that should any one encounter him in the road he might be forced to do something distasteful, and that the urgent task ahead might be interrupted.

A horseman and two market wagons passed at intervals, but the boy was hidden at the roadside. So he reeled on and on, and so he came at last to the great pine. There he turned out and crawled as much as walked through the trees and undergrowth to the summit of a low ridge, where he felt the sunshine fall on his half-naked back. It was so luxurious that he paused in the full glare of it, and slowly turned, as one very cold before a warming fire, and reveled in it. With every moment he felt it pouring into him, tingling softly as it ran. It was odd with what cheerful industry it hunted out the coldest places in him and kindled snug little fires under them. Most of all, it gave attention to the warm place that had already started in the center, and that one woke to a wonderful glow. Thus refreshed, he descended the slope on the farther side and came to a morass threaded by a friendly stream. At the edge of the bog he halted and looked keenly about. It had been two years since his last visit to this spot, and, though his memory of the woods was excellent, he now found himself dull and his vision bad. Ordinarily he would have found at once what he was seeking. Up and down along the margin he stumbled, straining his dim eyes, crawling sometimes and using groping hands in the search. Surely no one else could have come upon this remote spot, found the treasure, and taken it away!

At last! It had seemed to him a very long time; but all else was submerged in the joy of the first triumph, the first elation, that the lad had felt in many, many a day. Every shadow that had lain on his conscience vanished, every shame that had cursed his years was swept away, all bitterness took flight, and something fine and sweet raced through him deliciously.

There was no waste of precious time in hunting for something with which to dig. Then, too, the glorious sun had mounted, and was pouring its flood of light and warmth on his work and him. Like the tines of a digging-fork, his fingers sank into the ground.

The precious treasure, hugged gently, reverently, with a fierce sense of protection, was balm to every hurt. With it thus clasped, the boy laboriously made the ascent of the ridge on his return, and paused on the summit. There was something strange in the distance with which the descending slope to the road stretched so far, so bewilderingly far. He contemplated it, and wondered if he could compass it in a lifetime. The impulse to go on—for this last task was only half done—overcame the check from the illusion, and he started down. His knees developed a foolish way of suddenly flexing and seating him hard on the ground. At first it was annoying, but when it happened the second time the absurdity of it, and the ridiculous suddenness of the surprise that it caused, made the boy laugh aloud. It astonished him to hear himself laugh, for that was very unusual, and he wondered. But he rose, staggered on, and found himself chuckling inside,—a most astonishing thing! He could not imagine why he was doing it. When he dropped the third time his voice rang in so loud and merry a laugh that two blue jays came and scolded him terrifically, and he laughed at them till his tears ran. He was so absurdly happy that he feared he would hug his treasure too hard.

If only his mother were with him, that she might see how funny it all was, and laugh and be happy with him, and then walk with him hand in hand through the beautiful woods, while he showed her all the wonderful things that he knew! But no; his sisters and his father must be with them,—and Grace, and Andy, too, and the teacher and dear old grandmother. What a glorious time they would have!

The boy started, for a sweet, coaxing smother had suddenly fallen on him. He fought it away and rose with great difficulty and in some alarm lest he should not reach the road. On he lurched, clinging to the bushes as he swayed, trying not to laugh, for he had an idea that he was very crass and silly. He saw the road, only a rod away, and suddenly reflected that he was not presentable. Though staying till night would delay the completion of his task, there was no help for it, and he was content, and laughed because he was. And he knew that he really needed rest; for suppose his legs should practise those grotesque eccentricities in the road, and somebody should see! He sat down, carefully guarding his treasure, to wait in happy patience. He would not sleep, and so lose something of his conscious peace, something of thinking about what was going to happen at the end. No, he *must* not sleep.

The frantically joyous barking of a dog standing over him—not at all like the deep baying of Frazier's bloodhound,—woke the boy, and he tried to raise his head, but it fell back like lead. He laughed drowsily in quiet happiness, as he feebly patted the devoted head.

"Dear old Cap," he said. "You came, didn't you?"

Messengers from Elderby's and Carmichael's had brought strange news to the boy's parents. In alarm they had started out in the surrey, taking Cap, in the sure faith that he would find their son. They had seen that Andy was recovering,—he had been much more frightened than hurt. It was they whose crashing through the bushes the boy heard after Cap had announced his find. They halted and paled when they saw the torn, bruised, helpless figure smiling at them from the ground, and so full of loving gladness merely tc see them that there was no room for surprise at their being there. The mother was quicker than the father; she ran forward and fell on her knees beside her son.

"My boy!" she cried in a choke.

He took her hand and smiled into her face. In all her life she had never seen a smile so sweet, so happy. With his free hand he lifted his treasure.

"Mother," radiantly, "here it is!"

"What, my poor dear?"

"Don't you remember? I told you two years ago that I'd found it, and you said you'd be very glad if I'd bring it to you when I came this way again."

She opened the parcel, wrapped with so fond care in leaves and damp moss.

"Why, it's the rare and beautiful fern, and you were taking it to me! Bless your dear heart!" and, much to his surprise, she began to cry.

A LOST STORY

BY

FRANK NORRIS

Reprinted from *The Century Magazine* of July, 1903
by permission

A LOST STORY

T NINE o'clock that morning Rosella arrived in her little office on the third floor of the great publishing house of Conant & Company, and putting up her veil without removing her hat, addressed herself to her day's work. She went through her meager and unimportant mail, wrote a few replies, and then turned to the pile of volunteer manuscripts which it was her duty to read and report upon.

For Rosella was Conant's "reader," and so well was she acquainted with the needs of the house, so thorough was she in her work, and so great was the reliance upon her judgment, that she was the only one employed. Manuscripts that she "passed up" went direct to Conant himself, while the great army of the "declined" had no second chance. For the "unavailables" her word was final.

From the first—which was when her initial literary venture, a little book of short tales of Sicily and the Sicilians, was published by the house—her relations with the Conants had been intimate. Conant believed in her, and for the sake of the time when her books could be considered safe investments, was willing to lose a few dollars during the time of her apprenticeship. For the tales had enjoyed only a fleeting *succès d'estime*. Her style was, like her temperament, delicately constructed and of extreme refinement, not the style to appeal to the masses. It was "searched," a little *précieuse*, and the tales themselves were diaphanous enough, polished little *contes*, the points subtle, the action turning upon minute psychological distinctions.

Yet she had worked desperately hard upon their composition. She was of those very few who sincerely cannot write unless the mood be propitious; and her state of mind, the condition of her emotions, was very apt to influence her work for good or ill, as the case might be.

But a *succès d'estime* fills no purses, and favorable reviews in the literary periodicals are not "negotiable paper." Rosella could not yet live wholly by her pen, and thought herself fortunate when the house offered her the position of reader.

This arrival of hers was no doubt to be hastened, if not actually assured, by the publication of her first novel, "Patroclus," upon which she was at this time at work. The evening before, she had read the draft of the story to Trevor, and even now, as she cut the string of the first manuscript of the pile, she was thinking over what Trevor had said of it, and smiling as she thought.

It was through Conant that Rosella had met the great novelist and critic, and it was because of Conant that Trevor had read Rosella's first little book. He had taken an interest at once, and had found occasion to say to her that she had it in her to make a niche for herself in American letters.

He was a man old enough to be her grandfather, and Rosella often came to see him in his study, to advise with him as to doubtful points in her stories or as to ideas for those as yet unwritten. To her his opinion was absolutely final. This old gentleman, this elderly man of letters, who had seen the rise and fall of a dozen schools, was above the influence of fads, and he whose books were among the classics even before his death was infallible in his judgments of the work of the younger writers. All the stages of their evolution were known to him—all their mistakes, all their successes. He understood; and a story by one of them, a poem, a novel, that bore the stamp of his approval, was "sterling." Work that he declared a failure was such in very earnest, and might as well be consigned as speedily as possible to the grate or the waste-basket.

When, therefore, he had permitted himself to be even enthusiastic over "Patroclus," Rosella had been elated beyond the power of expression, and had returned home with blazing cheeks and shining eyes, to lie awake half the night thinking of her story, planning, perfecting, considering and reconsidering.

Like her short stories, the tale was of extreme delicacy in both sentiment and design. It was a little fanciful, a little elaborate, but of an ephemeral poetry. It was all "atmosphere," and its success depended upon the minutest precision of phrasing and the nicest harmony between idea and word. There was much in mere effect of words; and more important than mere plot was the feeling produced by the balancing of phrases and the cadence of sentence and paragraph.

Only a young woman of Rosella's complexity, of her extreme sensitiveness, could have conceived "Patroclus," nor could she herself hope to complete it successfully at any other period of her life. Any earlier she would have been too immature to adapt herself to its demands; any later she would have lost the spontaneity, the *jeunesse*, and the freshness which were to contribute to its greatest charm.

The tale itself was simple. Instead of a plot, a complication, it built itself around a central idea, and it was the originality of this idea, this motif, that had impressed Trevor so strongly. Indeed, Rosella's draft could convey no more than that. Her treatment was all to follow. But here she was sure of herself. The style would come naturally as she worked.

She was ambitious, and in her craving to succeed, to be recognized and accepted, was all that passionate eagerness that only the artist knows. So far success had been denied her; but now at last she seemed to see light. Her "Patroclus" would make her claims good. Everything depended upon that.

She had thought over this whole situation while she removed the wrappings from the first manuscript of the pile upon her desk. Even then her fingers itched for the pen, and the sentences and phrases of the opening defined themselves clearly in her mind. But that was not to be the immediate work. The unlovely bread-and-butter business pressed upon her. With a long breath she put the vision from her and turned her attention to the task at hand.

After her custom, she went through the pile,

glancing at the titles and first lines of each manuscript, and putting it aside in the desk corner to be considered in detail later on.

She almost knew in advance that of the thirty-odd volunteers of that day's batch not one would prove available. The manuscripts were tagged and numbered in the business office before they came to her, and the number of the first she picked up that morning was 1120, and this since the first of the year. Of the eleven hundred she had accepted only three. Of these three, two had failed entirely after publication; the third had barely paid expenses. What a record! How hopeless it seemed! Yet the strugglers persisted. Did it not seem as if No. 1120, Mrs. Allen Bowen of Bentonville, South Dakota—did it not seem as if she could know that the great American public has no interest in, no use for, "Thoughts on the Higher Life," a series of articles written for the county paper—foolish little articles revamped from Ruskin and Matthew Arnold?

And 1121—what was this? The initial lines ran: "'Oh, damn everything!' exclaimed Percival Holcombe, as he dropped languidly into a deep-seated leather chair by the club window which commanded a view of the noisy street crowded with fashion and frivolity, wherein the afternoon's sun, freed from its enthralling mists, which all day long had jealously obscured his beams, was gloating o'er the panels of the carriages of noblemen who were returning from race-track and park, and the towhead of the little sweeper who plied his humble trade which earned his scanty supper that he ate miles away from that gay quarter wherein Percival Holcombe, who——"

Rosella paused for sheer breath. This sort did not need to be read. It was declined already. She picked up the next. It was in an underwear-box of green pasteboard.

"The staid old town of Salem," it read, "was all astir one bright and sunny morning in the year 1604." Rosella groaned. "Another!" she said. "Now," she continued, speaking to herself and shutting her eyes—"now about the next page the 'portly burgess' will address the heroine as 'Mistress,' and will say, 'An' whither away so early?'" She turned over to verify. She was wrong. The portly burgess had said: "Good morrow, Mistress Priscilla. An' where away so gaily bedizened?" She sighed as she put the manuscript away. "Why, and, oh, why *will* they do it!" she murmured.

The next one, 1123, was a story "Compiled from the Memoirs of One Perkin Althorpe, Esq., Sometime Field-Coronet in His Majesty's Troop of Horse," and was sown thick with objurgation—"Odswounds!" "Body o' me!" "A murrain on thee!" "By my halidom!" and all the rest of the sweepings and tailings of Scott and the third-rate romanticists.

"Declined," said Rosella, firmly, tossing it aside. She turned to 1124:

"About three o'clock of a roseate day in early spring two fashionables of the softer sex, elegantly arrayed, might have been observed sauntering languidly down Fifth Avenue.

"'Are you going to Mrs. Van Billion's musicale tonight?' inquired the older of the two, a tall and striking demi-brunette, turning to her companion.

"'No, indeed,' replied the person thus addressed,

a blonde of exquisite coloring. 'No, indeed. The only music one hears there is the chink of silver dollars. Ha! ha! ha! ha!'"

Rosella winced as if in actual physical anguish. "And the author calls it a 'social satire'!" she exclaimed. "How can she! How can she!"

She turned to the next. It was written in script that was a model of neatness, margined, correctly punctuated, and addressed, "Harold Vickers," with the town and State. Its title was "The Last Dryad," and the poetry of the phrase stuck in her mind. She read the first lines, then the first page, then two.

"Come," said Rosella, "there is something in this." At once she was in a little valley in Bœotia in the Arcadian day. It was evening. There was no wind. Somewhere a temple, opalescent in the sunset, suggested rather than defined itself. A landscape developed such as Turner in a quiet mood might have evolved, and with it a feeling of fantasy, of remoteness, of pure, true classicism. A note of pipes was in the air, sheep bleated, and Daphne, knee-deep in the grass, surging an answer to the pipes, went down to meet her shepherd.

Rosella breathed a great sigh of relief. Here at last was a possibility—a new writer with a new, sane view of his world and his work. A new poet, in fine. She consulted the name and address given—Harold Vickers, Ash Fork, Arizona. There was something in that Harold; perhaps education and good people. But the Vickers told her nothing. And where was Ash Fork, Arizona; and why and how had "The Last Dryad" been written there, of all places the green world round? How came the inspiration for that classic *paysage*, such as Ingres would have loved, from the sage-brush, and cactus? "Well," she told herself, "Moore wrote 'Lalla Rookh' in a back room in London, among the chimney-pots and soot. Maybe the proportion is inverse. But, Mr. Harold Vickers of Ash Fork, Arizona, your little book is, to say the least, well worth its ink."

She went through the other manuscripts as quickly as was consistent with fairness, and declined them all. Then settling herself comfortably in her chair, she plunged, with the delight of an explorer venturing upon new ground, into the pages of "The Last Dryad."

* * * * * * * *

Four hours later she came, as it were, to herself, to find that she sat lax in her place, with open, upturned palms, and eyes vacantly fixed upon the opposite wall. "The Last Dryad," read to the final word, was tumbled in a heap upon the floor. It was past her luncheon hour. Her cheeks flamed; her hands were cold and moist; and her heart beat thick and slow, clogged, as it were, by its own heaviness.

But the lapse of time was naught to her, nor the fever that throbbed in her head. Her world, like a temple of glass, had come down dashing about her. The future, which had beckoned her onward,—a fairy in the path wherein her feet were set,—was gone, and at the goal of her ambition and striving she saw suddenly a stranger stand, plucking down the golden apples that she so long and passionately had desired.

For "The Last Dryad" was her own, her very, very own and cherished "Patroclus."

That the other author had taken the story from a different view-point, that his treatment varied, that the approach was his own, that the wording was his own, produced not the least change upon the final result. The idea, the motif, was identical in each; identical in every particular, identical in effect, in suggestion. The two tales were one. That was the fact, the unshakable fact, the block of granite that a malicious fortune had flung athwart her little pavilion of glass.

At first she jumped to the conclusion of chicanery. At first there seemed no other explanation. "He stole it," she cried, rousing vehemently from her inertia—"mine—mine. He stole my story."

But common sense prevailed in the end. No, there was no possible chance for theft. She had not spoken of "Patroclus" to any one but Trevor. Her manuscript draft had not once left her hands. No; it was a coincidence, nothing more—one of those fateful coincidences with which the scientific and literary worlds are crowded. And he, this unknown Vickers, this haphazard genius of Ash Fork, Arizona, had the prior claim. Her "Patroclus" must remain unwritten. The sob caught and clutched at her throat at last.

"Oh," she cried in a half-whisper—"oh, my chance, my hopes, my foolish little hopes! And now *this!* To have it all come to nothing—when I was so proud, so buoyant—and Mr. Trevor and all! Oh, could anything be more cruel!"

And then, of all moments, *ex machina*, Harold Vickers's card was handed in.

She stared at it an instant, through tears, amazed

and incredulous. Surely some one was playing a monstrous joke upon her today. Soon she would come upon the strings and false bottoms and wigs and masks of the game. But the office boy's contemplation of her distress was real. Something must be done. The whole machine of things could not indefinitely hang thus suspended, inert, waiting her pleasure.

"Yes," she exclaimed all at once. "Very well; show him in;" and she had no more than gathered up the manuscript of "The Last Dryad" from the floor when its author entered the room.

He was very young,—certainly not more than twenty-three,—tall, rather poorly dressed, an invalid, beyond doubt, and the cough and the flush on the high cheek-bone spelled the name of the disease. The pepper-and-salt suit, the shoe-string cravat, and the broad felt hat were frankly Arizona. And he was diffident, constrained, sitting uncomfortably on the chair as a mark of respect, smiling continually, and, as he talked, throwing in her name at almost every phrase:

"No, Miss Beltis; yes, Miss Beltis; quite right, Miss Beltis."

His embarrassment helped her to her own composure, and by the time she came to question him as to his book and the reasons that brought him from Ash Fork to New York, she had herself in hand.

"I have received an unimportant government appointment in the Fisheries Department," he explained, "and as I was in New York for the week I thought I might—not that I wished to seem to hurry you, Miss Beltis—but I thought I might ask if you had come to—to my little book yet."

In five minutes of time Rosella knew just where Harold Vickers was to be placed, to what type he belonged. He was the young man of great talent who, so far from being discovered by the outside world, had not even discovered himself. He would be in two minds as yet about his calling in life, whether it was to be the hatching of fish or the writing of "Last Dryads." No one had yet taken him in hand, had so much as spoken a word to him. If she told him now that his book was a ridiculous failure, he would no doubt say—and believe—that she was quite right, that he had felt as much himself. If she told him his book was a little masterpiece, he would be just as certain to tell himself, and with equal sincerity, that he had known it from the first.

He had offered his manuscript nowhere else as yet. He was as new as an overnight daisy, and as destructible in Rosella's hands.

"Yes," she said at length, "I have read your manuscript." She paused a moment, then: "But I am not quite ready to pass upon it yet."

He was voluble in his protestations.

"Oh, that is all right," she interrupted. "I can come to the second reading in a day or two. I could send you word by the end of the week."

"Thank you, Miss Beltis." He paused awkwardly, smiling in deprecatory fashion. "Do you—from what you have seen of it—read of it—do you—how does it strike you? As good enough to publish—or fit for the waste-basket?"

Ah, why had this situation leaped upon her thus unawares, and all unprepared! Why had she not been allowed time, opportunity, to fortify herself!

What she said now would mean so much. Best err, then, on the safe side; and which side was that? Her words seemed to come of themselves, and she almost physically felt herself withdraw from the responsibility of what this other material Rosella Beltis was saying.

"I don't know," said the other Rosella. "I should not care to say—so soon. You see—there are so many manuscripts. I generally trust to the first impression on the second reading." She did not even hear his answer, but she said, when he had done speaking, that even in case of an unfavorable report there were, of course, other publishers.

But he answered that the judgment of such a house as the Conants would suffice for him. Somehow he could not peddle his story about New York. If the Conants would not take his work, nobody would.

And that was the last remark of importance he made. During the few remaining moments of his visit they spoke of unessentials, and before she was aware, he had gone away, leaving with her a memorandum of his address at the time.

* * * * * * * *

She did not sleep that night. When she left the office she brought "The Last Dryad" home with her, and till far into the night she read it and re-read it, comparing it and contrasting it with "Patroclus," searching diligently if perhaps there were not some minute loophole of evasion, some devious passage through which she might escape. But amid the shattered panes of her glass pavilion the block of stone persisted, inert, immovable. The stone could not be raised, the little edifice could not be rebuilt.

Then at last, inevitably, the temptation came—came and grew and shut about her and gripped her close. She began to temporize, to advance excuses. Was not her story the better one? Granted that the idea was the same, was not the treatment, the presentation, more effective? Should not the fittest survive? Was it not right that the public should have the better version? Suppose "Patroclus" had been written by a third person, and she had been called upon to choose between it and "The Last Dryad," would she not have taken "Patroclus" and rejected the other? Ah, but "Patroclus" was not yet written! Well, that was true. But the draft of it was; the idea of it had been conceived eight months ago. Perhaps she had thought of her story before Vickers had thought of his. Perhaps? No; it was very probable; there was no doubt of it, in fact. That was the important thing: the conception of the idea, not the execution. And if this was true, her claim was prior.

But what would Conant say of such reasoning, and Trevor—would they approve? Would they agree?

"Yes, they would," she cried the instant the thought occurred to her. "Yes, they would, they would, they would; I know they would. I am sure of it; sure of it."

But she knew they would not. The idea of right persisted and persisted. Rosella was on the rack, and slowly, inevitably, resistlessly the temptation grew and gathered, and snared her feet and her hands, and, fold on fold, lapped around her like a veil.

A great and feminine desire to shift the responsibility began to possess her mind.

"I cannot help it," she cried. "I am not to blame. It is all very well to preach, but how would—any one do in my case? It is not my fault."

And all at once, without knowing how or why, she found that she had written, sealed, stamped, and addressed a note to Harold Vickers declining his story.

But this was a long way from actually rejecting "The Last Dryad"—rejecting it in favor of "Patroclus." She had only written the note, so she told herself, just to see how the words would look. It was merely an impulse; would come to nothing, of course. Let us put it aside, that note, and seriously consider this trying situation.

Somehow it seemed less trying now; somehow the fact of her distress seemed less poignant. There was a way out of it—stop. No; do not look at the note there on the table. There was a way out, no doubt, but not that one; no, of course not that one. Rosella laughed a little. How easily some one else, less scrupulous, would solve this problem! Well, she could solve it, too, and keep her scruples as well; but not tonight. Now she was worn out. Tomorrow it would look different to her.

She went to bed and tossed wide-eyed and wakeful till morning, then rose, and after breakfast prepared to go to the office as usual. The manuscript of "The Last Dryad" lay on her table, and while she was wrapping it up her eye fell upon the note to Harold Vickers.

"Why," she murmured, with a little grimace of astonishment—"why, how is this? I thought I burned that last night. How *could* I have forgotten!"

She could have burned it then. The fire was crackling in the grate; she had but to toss it in. But she preferred to delay.

"I will drop it in some ash-can or down some sewer on the way to the office," she said to herself. She slipped it into her muff and hurried away. But on the way to the cable-car no ash-can presented itself. True, she discovered the opening of a sewer on the corner where she took her car. But a milkman and a police officer stood near at hand in conversation, occasionally glancing at her, and no doubt they would have thought it strange to see this well-dressed young woman furtively dropping a sealed letter into a sewer-vent.

She held it awkwardly in her hand all of her way down-town, and still carried it there when she had descended from her car and took her way up the cross-street toward Conant's.

She suddenly remembered that she had other letters to mail that morning. For two days the weekly epistles that she wrote home to her mother and younger sister had been overlooked in her pocket. She found a mail-box on the corner by the Conant building and crossed over to it, holding her mother's and sister's letters in one hand and the note to Vickers in the other.

Carefully scanning the addresses, to make sure she did not confuse the letters, she dropped in her home correspondence, then stood there a moment irresolute.

Irresolute as to what, she could not say. Her decision had been taken in the matter of "The Last Dryad." She would accept it, as it deserved. Whether she was still to write "Patroclus" was a matter to be considered later. Well, she was glad she had settled it all. If she had not come to this conclusion she might have been, at that very instant, dropping the letter to Harold Vickers into the box. She would have stood, thus, facing the box, have raised the cast-iron flap,—this with one hand,—and with the other have thrust the note into the slide—thus.

Her fingers closed hard upon the letter at the very last instant—ah, not too late. But suppose she had, but for one second, opened her thumb and forefinger and—what? What would come of it?

And there, with the letter yet on the edge of the drop she called up again the entire situation, the identity of the stories, the jeopardizing—no, the wrecking—of her future career by this chance-thrown barrier in the way. Why hesitate, why procrastinate? Her thoughts came to her in a whirl. If she acted quickly now,—took the leap with shut eyes, reckless of result,—she could truly be sorry then, truly acknowledge what was right, believe that Vickers had the prior claim without the hard necessity of acting up to her convictions. At least, this harrowing indecision would be over with.

"Indecision?" What was this she was saying? Had she not this moment told herself that she was resolved—resolved to accept "The Last Dryad"? Resolved to accept it? Was that true? Had she done so? Had she not made up her mind long ago to decline it—decline it with full knowledge that its author would destroy it once the manuscript should be returned?

These thoughts had whisked through her mind

with immeasurable rapidity. The letter still rested half in, half out of the drop. She still held it there.

By now Rosella knew if she let it fall she would do so deliberately, with full knowledge of what she was about. She could not afterward excuse herself by saying that she had been confused, excited, acting upon an unreasoned impulse. No; it would be deliberate, deliberate, deliberate. She would have to live up to that decision, whatever it was, for many months to come, perhaps for years. Perhaps,—who could say?—perhaps it might affect her character permanently. In a crisis little forces are important, disproportionately so. And then it was, and thus it was, that Rosella took her resolve. She raised the iron flap once more, and saying aloud and with a ring of defiance in her voice: "Deliberately, deliberately; I don't care," loosed her hold upon the letter. She heard it fall with a soft rustling impact upon the accumulated mail-matter in the bottom of the box.

A week later she received her letter back with a stamped legend across its face informing her with dreadful terseness that the party to whom the letter was addressed was deceased. She divined a blunder, but for all that, and with conflicting emotions, sought confirmation in the daily press. There, at the very end of the column, stood the notice:

VICKERS. At New York, on Sunday, November 12, Harold Anderson Vickers, in the twenty-third year of his age. Arizona papers please copy. Notice of funeral hereafter.

Three days later she began to write "Patroclus."

* * * * *

Rosella stood upon the door-step of Trevor's house, closing her umbrella and shaking the water from the folds of her mackintosh. It was between eight and nine in the evening, and since morning a fine rain had fallen steadily. But no stress of weather could have kept Rosella at home that evening. A week previous she had sent to Trevor the type-written copy of the completed "Patroclus," and tonight she was to call for the manuscript and listen to his suggestions and advice.

She had triumphed in the end—triumphed over what, she had not always cared to inquire. But once the pen in her hand, once "Patroclus" begun, and the absorption of her mind, her imagination, her every faculty, in the composition of the story, had not permitted her to think of or to remember anything else.

And she saw that her work was good. She had tested it by every method, held it up to her judgment in all positions and from all sides, and in her mind, so far as she could see, and she was a harsh critic for her own work, it stood the tests. Not the least of her joys was the pleasure that she knew Trevor would take in her success. She could foresee just the expression of his face when he would speak, could forecast just the tones of the voice, the twinkle of the kindly eyes behind the glasses.

When she entered the study, she found Trevor himself, as she had expected, waiting for her in slippers and worn velvet jacket, pipe in hand, and silk skullcap awry upon the silver-white hair. He extended an inky hand, and still holding it and talking, led her to an easy-chair near the hearth.

Even through the perturbation of her mind Rosella could not but wonder—for the hundredth time—

at the apparent discrepancy between the great novelist and the nature of his books. These latter were, each and all of them, wonders of artistic composition, compared with the hordes of latter-day pictures. They were the aristocrats of their kind, full of reserved force, unimpeachable in dignity, stately even, at times veritably austere.

And Trevor himself was a short, rotund man, rubicund as to face, bourgeois as to clothes and surroundings (the bisque statuette of a fisher-boy obtruded the vulgarity of its gilding and tinting from the mantelpiece), jovial in manner, indulging even in slang. One might easily have set him down as a retired groceryman—wholesale perhaps, but none the less a groceryman. Yet touch him upon the subject of his profession, and the bonhomie lapsed away from him at once. Then he became serious. Literature was not a thing to be trifled with.

Thus it was tonight. For five minutes Trevor filled the room with the roaring of his own laughter and the echoes of his own vociferous voice. He was telling a story—a funny story, about what Rosella, with her thoughts on "Patroclus," could not for the life of her have said, and she must needs listen in patience and with perfunctory merriment while the narrative was conducted to its close with all the accompaniment of stamped feet and slapped knees.

"'Why, becoth, mithtah,' said that nigger. 'Dat dawg ain' good fo' nothin' ailse; so I jes rickon he 'th boun' to be a coon dawg;'" and the author of "Snow in April" pounded the arm of his chair and roared till the gas-fixtures vibrated.

Then at last, taking advantage of a lull in the talk,

Rosella, unable to contain her patience longer, found breath to remark:

"And 'Patroclus'—my—my little book?"

"Ah—hum, yes. 'Patroclus,' your story. I've read it."

At once another man was before her, or rather the writer—the novelist—*in* the man. Something of the dignity of his literary style immediately seemed to invest him with a new character. He fell quiet, grave, not a little abstracted, and Rosella felt her heart sink. Her little book (never had it seemed so insignificant, so presumptuous as now) had been on trial before a relentless tribunal, had indeed undergone the ordeal of fire. But the verdict, the verdict! Quietly, but with cold hands clasped tight together, she listened while the greatest novelist of America passed judgment upon her effort.

"Yes; I've read it," continued Trevor. "Read it carefully—carefully. You have worked hard upon it. I can see that. You have put your whole soul into it, put all of yourself into it. The narrative is all there, and I have nothing but good words to say to you about the construction, the mere mechanics of it. But——"

Would he never go on? What was this? What did that "But" mean? What else but disaster could it mean? Rosella shut her teeth.

"But, to speak frankly, my dear girl, there is something lacking. Oh, the idea, the motif—that——" he held up a hand. "That is as intact as when you read me the draft. The central theme, the approach, the grouping of the characters, the dialogue—all good—all good. The thing that is lacking I find very hard to define. But the *mood* of the story, shall we say?—the mood of the story is——" he stopped, frowning in perplexity, hesitating. The great master of words for once found himself at a loss for expression. "The mood is somehow truculent, when it should be as suave, as quiet, as the very river you describe. Don't you see? Can't you understand what I mean? In this 'Patroclus' the atmosphere, the little, delicate, subtle sentiment, is everything—everything. What was the mere story? Nothing without the proper treatment. And it was just in this fine, intimate relationship between theme and treatment that the success of the book was to be looked for. I thought I could be sure of you there. I thought that you of all people could work out that motif adequately. But"— he waved a hand over the manuscript that lay at her elbow—"this—it is not the thing. This is a poor criticism, you will say, merely a marshaling of empty phrases, abstractions. Well, that may be; I repeat, it is very hard for me to define just what there is of failure in your 'Patroclus.' But it is empty, dry, hard, barren. Am I cruel to speak so frankly? If I were less frank, my dear girl, I would be less just, less kind. You have told merely the story, have narrated episodes in their sequence of time, and where the episodes have stopped there you have ended the book. The whole animus that should have put the life into it is gone, or, if it is not gone, it is so perverted that it is incorrigible. To *my* mind the book is a failure."

Rosella did not answer when Trevor ceased speaking, and there was a long silence. Trevor looked at her anxiously. He had hated to hurt her. Rosella gazed vaguely at the fire. Then at last the tears filled her eyes.

'I am sorry, very, very sorry," said Trevor, kindly. "But to have told you anything but the truth would have done you a wrong—and, then, no earnest work is altogether wasted. Even though 'Patroclus' is—not what we expected of it, your effort over it will help you in something else. You did work hard at it. I saw that. You must have put your whole soul into it."

"That," said Rosella, speaking half to herself—"that was just the trouble."

But Trevor did not understand.

HANTU

BY

HENRY MILNER RIDEOUT

Reprinted from *The Atlantic Monthly* of May, 1906
by permission

HANTU

THE SCHOONER *Fulmar* lay in a cove on the coast of Banda. Her sails, half hoisted, dripped still from an equatorial shower, but, aloft, were already steaming in the afternoon glare. Dr. Forsythe, captain and owner, lay curled round his teacup on the cabin roof, watching the horizon thoughtfully, with eyes like points of glass set in the puckered bronze of his face. The "Seventh Officer," his only white companion, watched him respectfully. All the Malays were asleep, stretched prone or supine under the forward awning. Only Wing Kat stirred in the smother of his galley below, rattling tin dishes, and repeating, in endless falsetto singsong, the Hankow ditty which begins,—

"'Yaou-yaou!' remarked the grasshoppers."

Ashore, the coolies on the nutmeg plantations had already brought out their mace to dry, and the baskets lay in vermilion patches on the sun-smitten green, like gouts of arterial blood. White vapors round the mountain peaks rose tortuously toward the blue; while seaward, rain still filled the air as with black sand drifting down aslant, through gaps in which we could descry far off a steel-bright strip of fair weather that joined sea and sky, cutting under a fairy island so that it seemed suspended in the air.

"That's a pretty bit of land," said the doctor lazily. "'*Jam medio apparet fluctu nemorosa Zacynthos.*' It might be, eh?—Humph!—Virgil and Shakespeare are the only ones who sometimes make poetry endurable. All the others are just little swollen Egos."

This was an unusual excursion, and he quickly returned to practical matters.

"There's a better anchorage over there," he drawled, waving the milk-tin toward Zacynthos. "And less danger of our being caught than here. But no use; we've got to humor the crew, of course. When they say '*pulo burrantu,*' that settles it. Haunted islands—ghosts—fatal to discipline. I used to have cruises spoiled by that sort of thing. We must stay here and chance being found."

He shot a stream of Java sugar into the tea, and, staring at the sleepers, rubbed his shaven head thoughtfully.

"Oh, yes, 'superstition,' all very easy to say," he muttered, half to himself. "But who *knows*, eh? Must be something in it, at times."

His mood this afternoon was new and surprising. Nor was it likely to occur often in such a man. He had brought the *Fulmar* round the south of Celebes, making for Ceram; but as the Dutch had forbidden him to travel in the interior, saying that the natives were too dangerous just then; and as Sidin, the mate, had sighted the Dutch tricolor flying above drab hulls that came nosing southward from Amboina way,

we had dodged behind the Bandas till nightfall. The crew laughed at the *babi blanda*—Dutch pigs; but every man of them would have fled ashore had they known that among the hampers and bundled spears in our hold lay the dried head of a little girl, a human sacrifice from Engano. If we got into Ceram (and got out again), the doctor would reduce the whole affair to a few tables of anthropological measurements, a few more hampers of birds, beasts, and native rubbish in the hold, and a score of paragraphs couched in the evaporated, millimetric terms of science. There would be a few duplicates for Raffles, some tin-lined cases, including the clotted head of the little girl, for the British Museum; the total upshot would attract much less public notice than the invention of a new "part" for a motor car; and the august structure of science, like a coral tree, would increase by another atom. In the meantime, we lay anchored, avoiding ironclads and ghosts.

Dinner we ate below, with seaward port-holes blinded, and sweat dripping from our chins. Then we lay on the cabin roof again, in breech-clouts, waiting for a breeze, and showing no light except the red coals of two Burmah cheroots.

For long spaces we said nothing. Trilling of crickets ashore, sleepy cooing of nutmeg-pigeons, chatter of monkeys, hiccough of tree lizards, were as nothing in the immense, starlit silence of the night, heavily sweet with cassia and mace. Forward, the Malays murmured now and then, in sentences of monotonous cadence.

"No, you can't blame them," said the captain abruptly, with decision. "Considering the unholy strangeness of the world we live in——" He puffed twice, the palm of his hand glowing. "Things you can't explain," he continued vaguely. "Now this,—I thought of it today, speaking of *hantu*. Perhaps you can explain it, being a youngster without theories. The point is, of what follows, how much, if any, was a dream? Where were the partition lines between sleep and waking,—between what we call Certainty, and—the other thing? Or else, by a freak of nature, might a man live so long—Nonsense!—Never mind; here are the facts."

Eleven years ago, I had the *Fulmar* a ten months' cruise out of Singapore, and was finally coming down along Celebes, intending to go over to Batavia. We anchored on just such a day as this has been, off a little old river-mouth, so badly silted that she had to lie well out. A chief in a *campong* half a day inland had promised to send some specimens down that evening,—armor, harps, stone Priapuses, and birds of paradise. The men were to come overland, and would have no boats. So I went ashore with three or four Malays, and the Old Boy's time we had poking in and out over the silt to find fairway, even for the gig. At last we could make round toward a little clearing in the bamboos, with a big canary tree in the middle. All was going well, when suddenly the mate grunted, pointing dead ahead. That man Sidin has the most magnificent eyes: we were steering straight into a dazzling glare. I couldn't see anything, neither could the crew, for some time.

"*Tuggur!*" cried the mate. He was getting nervous. Then all of a sudden—"*Brenti!*"

The crew stopped like a shot. Then they saw, too, and began to back water and turn, all pulling different ways and yelling: "*Prau hantu! . . . sampar! . . . Sakit lepra! Kolera! . . . hantu!*"

As we swung, I saw what it was,—a little carved prau like a child's toy boat, perhaps four feet long, with red fiber sails and red and gilt flags from stem to stern. It was rocking there in our swell, innocently, but the crew were pulling for the schooner like crazy men.

I was griffin enough at the time, but I knew what it meant, of course,—it was an enchanted boat, that the priests in some village—perhaps clear over in New Guinea—had charmed the cholera or the plague on board of. Same idea as the Hebrew scapegoat.

"*Brenti!*" I shouted. The Malays stopped rowing, but let her run. Nothing would have tempted them within oar's-length of that prau.

"See here, Sidin," I protested, "I go ashore to meet the *kapala's* men."

"We do not go," the fellow said. "If you go, Tuan, you die: the priest has laid the cholera on board that prau. It has come to this shore. Do not go, Tuan."

"She hasn't touched the land yet," I said.

This seemed to have effect.

"Row me round to that point and land me," I ordered. "*Hantu* does not come to white men. You go out to the ship; when I have met the soldier-messengers, row back, and take me on board with the gifts."

The mate persuaded them, and they landed me on the point, half a mile away, with a box of cheroots, and a roll of matting to take my nap on. I walked round to the clearing, and spread my mat under the canary tree, close to the shore. All that blessed afternoon I waited, and smoked, and killed a snake, and made notes in a pocket Virgil, and slept, and smoked again; but no sign of the bearers from the *campong*. I made signals to the schooner,—she was too far out to hail,—but the crew took no notice. It was plain they meant to wait and see whether the *hantu* prau went out with the ebb or not; and as it was then flood, and dusk, they couldn't see before morning. So I picked some bananas and chicos, and made a dinner of them; then I lighted a fire under the tree, to smoke and read Virgil by,—in fact, spent the evening over my notes. That editor was a *pukkah* ass! It must have been pretty late before I stretched out on my matting.

I was a long time going to sleep,—if I went to sleep at all. I lay and watched the firelight and shadows in the *lianas*, the bats fluttering in and out across my patch of stars, and an ape that stole down from time to time and peered at me, sticking his blue face out from among the creepers. At one time a shower fell in the clearing, but only pattered on my ceiling of broad leaves.

After a period of drowsiness, something moved and glittered on the water, close to the bank; and there bobbed the ghost prau, the gilt and vermilion flags shining in the firelight. She had come clear in on the flood,—a piece of luck. I got up, cut a withe of bamboo, and made her fast to a root. Then I fed the fire, lay down again, and watched her back and fill on her tether,—all clear and ruddy in the flame, even the carvings, and the little wooden figures of wizards on her deck. And while I looked, I grew drowsier and drowsier; my eyes would close, then half open, and there would be the *hantu* sails and the fire for company, growing more and more indistinct.

So much for Certainty; now begins the Other. Did I fall asleep at all? If so, was my first waking a dream-waking, and the real one only when the thing was gone? I'm not an imaginative man; my mind, at home, usually worked with some precision; but this,—there seems to be, you might say, a blur, a—film over my mental retina. You see, I'm not a psychologist, and therefore can't use the big, foggy terms of man's conceit to explain what he never can explain,—himself, and Life.

The captain tossed his cheroot overboard, and was silent for a space.

"The psychologists forget Æsop's frog story," he said at last. "Little swollen Egos, again."

Then his voice flowed on, slowly, in the dark.

I ask you just to believe this much: that I for my part feel sure (except sometimes by daylight) that I was not more than half asleep when a footfall seemed to come in the path, and waked me entirely. It didn't sound,—only seemed to come. I believe, then, that I woke, roused up on my elbow, and stared over at the opening among the bamboos where the path came into the clearing. Some one moved down the bank, and drew slowly forward to the edge of the firelight. A strange, whispering, uncertain kind of voice said something,—something in Dutch.

I didn't catch the words, and it spoke again:—

"What night of the month is this night?"

If awake, I was just enough so to think this a natural question to be asked first off, out here in the wilds.

"It's the 6th," I answered in Dutch. "Come down to the fire, Mynheer."

You know how bleary and sightless your eyes are for a moment, waking, after the glare of these days. The figure seemed to come a little nearer, but I could only see that it was a man dressed in black. Even that didn't seem odd.

"Of what month?" the stranger said. The voice was what the French call "veiled."

"June," I answered.

"And what year?" he asked.

I told him—or It.

"He is very late," said the voice, like a sigh. "He should have sent long ago."

Only at this point did the whole thing begin to seem queer. As evidence that I must have been awake, I recalled afterwards that my arm had been made numb by the pressure of my head upon it while lying down, and now began to tingle.

"It is very late," the voice repeated. "Perhaps too late——"

The fire settled, flared up fresh, and lighted the man's face dimly,—a long, pale face with gray mustache and pointed beard. He was all in black, so that his outline was lost in darkness; but I saw that round his neck was a short white ruff, and that heavy leather boots hung in folds, cavalier-fashion, from his knees. He wavered there in the dark, against the flicker of the bamboo shadows, like a picture by that Dutch fellow—What's-his-name-again—a very dim, shaky, misty Rembrandt.

"And you, Mynheer," he went on, in the same toneless voice, "from where do you come to this shore?"

"From Singapore," I managed to reply.

"From Singapura," he murmured. "And so white men live there now?—*Ja, ja,* time has passed."

Up till now I may have only been startled, but this set me in a blue funk. It struck me all at once that this shaky old whisper of a voice was not speaking the Dutch of nowadays. I never before knew the depths, the essence, of that uncertainty which we call fear In the silence, I thought a drum was beating,—it was the pulse in my ears. The fire close by was suddenly cold.

"And now you go whither?" it said.

"To Batavia," I must have answered, for it went on:—

"Then you may do a great service to me and to another. Go to Jacatra in Batavia, and ask for Pieter Erberveld. Hendrik van der Have tells him to cease—before it is too late, before the thing becomes accursed. Tell him this. You will have done well, and I—shall sleep again. Give him the message——"

The voice did not stop, so much as fade away unfinished. And the man, the appearance, the eyes, moved away further into the dark, dissolving, retreating. A shock like waking came over me—a rush of clear consciousness——

Humph! Yes, been too long away from home;

for I know (mind you, *know*) that I saw the white of that ruff, the shadowy sweep of a cloak, as something turned its back and moved up the path under the pointed arch of bamboos, and was gone slowly in the blackness. I'm as sure of this as I am that the fire gave no heat. But whether the time of it all had been seconds or hours, I can't tell you.

What? Yes, naturally. I jumped and ran up the path after it. Nothing there but starlight. I must have gone on for half a mile. Nothing: only ahead of me, along the path, the monkeys would chatter and break into an uproar, and then stop short—every treetop silent, as they do when a python comes along. I went back to the clearing, sat down on the mat, stayed there by clinching my will power, so to speak,—and watched myself for other symptoms, till morning. None came. The fire, when I heaped it, was as hot as any could be. By dawn I had persuaded myself that it was a dream. No footprints in the path, though I mentioned a shower before.

At sunrise, the *kapala's* men came down the path, little chaps in black mediæval armor made of petroleum tins, and coolies carrying piculs of stuff that I wanted. So I was busy,—but managed to dismast the *hantu* prau and wrap it up in matting, so that it went aboard with the plunder.

Yet this other thing bothered me so that I held the schooner over, and made pretexts to stay ashore two more nights. Nothing happened. Then I called myself a grandmother, and sailed for Batavia.

Two nights later, a very singular thing happened. The mate—this one with the sharp eyes—is a quiet chap; seldom speaks to me except on business. He was standing aft that evening, and suddenly, without any preliminaries, said:

"Tuan was not alone the other night."

"What's that, Sidin?" I spoke sharply, for it made me feel quite angry and upset, of a sudden. He laughed a little, softly.

"I saw that the fire was a cold fire," he said. That was all he would say, and we've never referred to it again.

You may guess the rest, if you know your history of Java. I didn't then, and didn't even know Batavia,—had been ashore often, but only for a *toelatingskaart* and some good Dutch chow. Well, one afternoon, I was loafing down a street, and suddenly noticed that the sign-board said, "Jacatra-weg." The word made me jump, and brought the whole affair on Celebes back like a shot,—and not as a dream. It became a live question; I determined to treat it as one, and settle it.

I stopped a fat Dutchman who was paddling down the middle of the street in his pyjamas, smoking a cigar.

"Pardon, Mynheer," I said. "Does a man live here in Jacatra-weg named Erberveld?"

"*Nej*," he shook his big shaved head. "*Nej*, Mynheer, I do not know."

"Pieter Erberveld," I suggested.

The man broke into a horse-laugh.

"*Ja, ja*," he said, and laughed still. "I did not think of him. *Ja*, on this way, opposite the timber yard, you will find his house." And he went off, bowing and grinning hugely.

The nature of the joke appeared later, but I wasn't inclined to laugh. You've seen the place. No? Right opposite a timber yard in a cocoanut grove: it was a heavy, whitewashed wall, as high as a man, and perhaps two perches long. Where the gate should have been, a big tablet was set in, and over that, on a spike, a skull, grinning through a coat of cement. The tablet ran in eighteenth-century Dutch, about like this:—

> By Reason of the Detestable Memory of the Convicted Traitor, Pieter Erberveld, No One Shall Be Permitted to Build in Wood or Stone or to Plant Anything upon This Ground, from Now till Judgment Day. Batavia, April 14, Anno 1772.

You'll find the story in any book: the chap was a half-caste Guy Fawkes who conspired to deliver Batavia to the King of Bantam, was caught, tried, and torn asunder by horses. I nosed about and went through a hole in a side wall: nothing in the compound but green mould, dried stalks, dead leaves, and blighted banana trees. The inside of the gate was blocked with five to eight feet of cement. The Dutch hate solidly.

But Hendrik van der Have? No, I never found the name in any of the books. So there you are. Well? Can a man dream of a thing before he knows that thing, or——

The captain's voice, which had flowed on in slow and dispassionate soliloquy, became half audible, and ceased. As we gave ear to the silence, we became aware that a cool stir in the darkness was growing into a breeze. After a time, the thin crowing of

game-cocks in distant villages, the first twitter of birds among the highest branches, told us that night had turned to morning. A soft patter of bare feet came along the deck, a shadow stood above us, and the low voice of the mate said:

"*Ada kapal api disitu, Tuan—saiah kirah—ada kapal prrang.*"

"Gunboat, eh?" Captain Forsythe was on his feet, and speaking briskly. "*Bai, tarek jangcar.* Breeze comes just in time."

We peered seaward from the rail; far out, two pale lights, between a red coal and a green, shone against the long, glimmering strip of dawn.

"Heading this way, but there's plenty of time," the captain said cheerfully. "Take the wheel a minute, youngster—that's it,—keep her in,—they can't see us against shore where it's still night."

As the schooner swung slowly under way, his voice rose, gay as a boy's:—

"Come on, you rice-fed admirals!" He made an improper gesture, his profile and outspread fingers showing in the glow-worm light of the binnacle. "If they follow us through by the Verdronken Rozengain, we'll show them one piecee navigation. Can do, eh? These old iron-clad junks are something a man knows how to deal with."

MISS JUNO

BY

CHARLES WARREN STODDARD

MISS JUNO

I

HERE was an episode in the life of Paul Clitheroe that may possibly throw some little light upon the mystery of his taking off; and in connection with this matter it is perhaps worth detailing.

One morning Paul found a drop-letter in the mail which greeted him daily. It ran as follows:

> DEAR OLD BOY:
>
> Don't forget the reception tomorrow. Some one will be here whom I wish you to know.
>
> Most affectionately,
>
> HARRY ENGLISH.

The "tomorrow" referred to was the very day on which Paul received the sweet reminder. The reception of the message somewhat disturbed his customary routine. To be sure, he glanced through the morning journal as usual; repaired to the Greek chop-house with the dingy green walls, the smoked ceiling, the glass partition that separated the guests from a kitchen lined with shining copper pans, where a cook in a white paper cap wafted himself about in clouds of vapor, lit by occasional flashes of light and ever curling flames, like a soul expiating its sins in a prescribed but savory purgatory. He sat in his chosen seat, ignored his neighbors with his customary nonchalance, and returned to his room, as if nothing were about to happen. But he accomplished little, for he felt that the day was not wholly his; so slight a cause seemed to change the whole current of his life from hour to hour.

In due season Paul entered a street car which ran to the extreme limit of San Francisco. Harry English lived not far from the terminus, and to the cozy home of this most genial and hospitable gentleman the youth wended his way. The house stood upon the steep slope of a hill; the parlor was upon a level with the street,—a basement dining-room below it,—but the rear of the house was quite in the air and all of the rear windows commanded a magnificent view of the North Bay with its islands and the opposite mountainous shore.

"Infinite riches in a little room," was the expression which came involuntarily to Paul's lips the first time he crossed the threshold of Thespian Lodge. He might have said it of the Lodge any day in the week; the atmosphere was always balmy and soothing; one could sit there without talking or caring to talk; even without realizing that one was not talking and not being talked to; the silence was never ominous; it was a wholesome and restful home, where Paul was ever welcome and whither he often fled for refreshment.

The walls of the whole house were crowded with pictures, framed photographs and autographs, chiefly of theatrical celebrities; both "Harry," as the world familiarly called him, and his wife, were members of the dramatic profession and in their time had played many parts in almost as many lands and latitudes.

There was one chamber in this delightful home devoted exclusively to the pleasures of entomology, and there the head of the house passed most of the hours which he was free to spend apart from the duties of his profession. He was a man of inexhaustible resources, consummate energy, and unflagging industry, yet one who was never in the least hurried or flurried; and he was Paul's truest and most judicious friend.

The small parlor at the Englishes was nearly filled with guests when Paul Clitheroe arrived upon the scene. These guests were not sitting against the wall talking at each other; the room looked as if it were set for a scene in a modern society comedy. In the bay window, a bower of verdure, an extremely slender and diminutive lady was discoursing eloquently with the superabundant gesticulation of the successful society amateur; she was dilating upon the latest production of a minor poet whose bubble reputation was at that moment resplendent with local rainbows. Her chief listener was a languid beauty of literary aspirations, who, in a striking pose, was fit audience for the little lady as she frothed over with delightful, if not contagious, enthusiasm.

Mrs. English, who had been a famous belle—no one who knew her now would for a moment question the fact—devoted herself to the entertainment of a group of silent people, people of the sort that are not only colorless, but seem to dissipate the color in their immediate vicinity. The world is full of such; they spring up, unaccountably, in locations where they appear to the least advantage. Many a clever person who would delight to adorn a circle he longs to enter, and where he would be hailed with joy, through modesty, hesitates to enter it; while others, who are of no avail in any wise whatever, walk bravely in and find themselves secure through a quiet system of polite insistence. Among the latter, the kind of people to be merely tolerated, we find, also, the large majority.

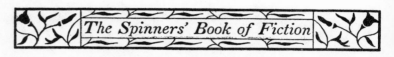

Two children remarkably self-possessed seized upon Paul the moment he entered the room: a beautiful lad as gentle and as graceful as a girl, and his tiny sister, who bore herself with the dignity of a little lady of Lilliput. He was happy with them, quite as happy as if they were as old and experienced as their elders and as well entertained by them, likewise. He never in his life made the mistake that is, alas, made by most parents and guardians, of treating children as if they were little simpletons who can be easily deceived. How often they look with scorn upon their elders who are playing the hypocrite to eyes which are, for the most part, singularly critical! Having paid his respects to those present—he was known to all—Paul was led a willing captive into the chamber where Harry English and a brother professional, an eccentric comedian, who apparently never uttered a line which he had not learned out of a playbook, were examining with genuine enthusiasm certain cases of brilliantly tinted butterflies.

The children were quite at their ease in this house, and no wonder; California children are born philosophers; to them the marvels of the somewhat celebrated entomological collection were quite familiar; again and again they had studied the peculiarities of the most rare and beautiful specimens of insect life under the loving tutelage of their friend, who had spent his life and a small fortune in gathering together his treasures, and they were even able to explain in the prettiest fashion the origin and use of the many curious objects that were distributed about the rooms.

Meanwhile Mme. Lillian, the dramatic one, had left her bower in the bay window and was flitting to and fro in nervous delight; she had much to say and it was always worth listening to. With available opportunities she would have long since become famous and probably a leader of her sex; but it was her fate to coach those of meaner capacities who were ultimately to win fame and fortune while she toiled on, in genteel poverty, to the end of her weary days.

No two women could be more unlike than this many-summered butterfly, as she hovered among her friends, and a certain comedy queen who was posing and making a picture of herself; the latter was regarded by the society-privates, who haunted with fearful delight the receptions at Thespian Lodge, with the awe that inspired so many inexperienced people who look upon members of the dramatic profession as creatures of another and not a better world, and considerably lower than the angels.

Two hours passed swiftly by; nothing ever jarred upon the guests in this house; the perfect suavity of the host and hostess forbade anything like antagonism among their friends; and though such dissimilar elements might never again harmonize, they were tranquil for the time at least.

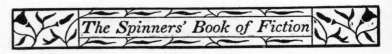

The adieus were being said in the chamber of entomology, which was somewhat overcrowded and faintly impregnated with the odor of *corrosive sublimate*. From the windows overlooking the bay there was visible the expanse of purple water and the tawny, sunburnt hills beyond, while pale-blue misty mountains marked the horizon with an undulating outline. A ship under full sail—a glorious and inspiring sight—was bearing down before the stiff, westerly breeze.

Mme. Lillian made an apt quotation which terminated with a Delsartean gesture and a rising inflection that seemed to exact something from somebody; the comedienne struck one of her property attitudes, so irresistibly comic that every one applauded, and Mme. Lillian laughed herself to tears; then they all drifted toward the door. As mankind in general has much of the sheep in him, one guest having got as far as the threshold, the others followed; Paul was left alone with the Englishes and those clever youngsters, whose coachman, accustomed to waiting indefinitely at the Lodge, was dutifully dozing on the box seat. The children began to romp immediately upon the departure of the last guest, and during the riotous half-hour that succeeded, there was a fresh arrival. The door-bell rang; Mrs. English, who was close at hand, turned to answer it and at once bubbled over with unaffected delight. Harry, still having his defunct legions in solemn review, recognized a cheery, un-American voice, and cried, "There she is at last!" as he hastened to meet the newcomer.

Paul was called to the parlor where a young lady of the ultra-blonde type stood with a faultlessly gloved hand in the hand of each of her friends; she was radiant with life and health. Of all the young ladies Paul could at that moment remember having seen, she was the most exquisitely clad; the folds of her gown fell about her form like the drapery of a statue; he was fascinated from the first moment of their meeting. He noticed that nothing about her was ever disarranged; neither was there anything superfluous or artificial, in manner or dress. She was in his opinion an entirely artistic creation. She met him with a perfectly frank smile, as if she were an old friend suddenly discovering herself to him, and when Harry English had placed the hand of this delightful person in one of Paul's she at once withdrew the other, which Mrs. English fondly held, and struck it in a hearty half-boyish manner upon their clasped hands, saying, "Awfully glad to see you, Paul!" and she evidently meant it.

This was Miss Juno, an American girl bred in Europe, now, after years of absence, passing a season in her native land. Her parents, who had taken a country home in one of the California valleys, found in their only child all that was desirable in life. This was not to be wondered at; it may be said of her in the theatrical parlance that she "filled the stage." When Miss Juno dawned upon the scene the children grew grave, and, after a little delay, having taken formal leave of the company, they entered their carriage and were rapidly driven homeward.

If Paul and Miss Juno had been formed for one another and were now, at the right moment and under the most favorable auspices, brought together for the first time, they could not have mated more naturally. If Miss Juno had been a young man, instead of a very charming woman, she would of course have been Paul's chum. If Paul had been a young woman—some of his friends thought he had narrowly escaped it and did not hesitate to say so—he would instinctively have become her confidante. As it was, they promptly entered into a sympathetic friendship which seemed to have been without beginning and was apparently to be without end.

They began to talk of the same things at the same moment, often uttering the very same words, and then turned to one another with little shouts of unembarrassed laughter. They agreed upon all points, and aroused each other to a ridiculous pitch of enthusiasm over nothing in particular.

Harry English beamed; there was evidently nothing wanted to complete his happiness. Mrs. English, her eyes fairly dancing with delight, could only exclaim at intervals, "Bless the boy!" or, "What a pair of children!" then fondly pass her arm about the waist of Miss Juno—which was not waspish in girth—or rest her hand upon Paul's shoulder with a show of maternal affection peculiarly grateful to him. It was with difficulty the half-dazed young fellow could keep apart from Miss Juno. If he found she had wandered into the next room, while he was engaged for a moment, he followed at his earliest convenience, and when their eyes met they smiled responsively without knowing why, and indeed not caring in the least to know.

They were as ingenuous as two children in their

liking for one another; their trust in each other would have done credit to the Babes in the Wood. What Paul realized, without any preliminary analysis of his mind or heart, was that he wanted to be near her, very near her; and that he was miserable when this was not the case. If she was out of his sight for a moment the virtue seemed to have gone from him and he fell into the pathetic melancholy which he enjoyed in the days when he wrote a great deal of indifferent verse, and was burdened with the conviction that his mission in life was to make rhymes without end.

In those days, he had acquired the habit of pitying himself. The emotional middle-aged woman is apt to encourage the romantic young man in pitying himself; it is a grewsome habit, and stands sturdily in the way of all manly effort. Paul had outgrown it to a degree, but there is nothing easier in life than a relapse—perhaps nothing so natural, yet often so unexpected.

Too soon the friends who had driven Miss Juno to Thespian Lodge and passed on—being unacquainted with the Englishes—called to carry her away with them. She was shortly—in a day or two in fact—to rejoin her parents, and she did not hesitate to invite Paul to pay them a visit. This he assured her he would do with pleasure, and secretly vowed that nothing on earth should prevent him. They shook hands cordially at parting, and were still smiling their baby smiles in each other's faces when they did it. Paul leaned against the door-jamb, while the genial Harry and his wife followed his new-found friend to the carriage, where they were duly presented to its occupants—said occupants promising to place Thespian Lodge upon their list. As the carriage whirled away, Miss Juno waved that exquisitely gloved hand from the window and Paul's heart beat high; somehow he felt as if he had never been quite so happy. And this going away struck him as being a rather cruel piece of business. To tell the whole truth, he couldn't understand why she should go at all.

He felt it more and more, as he sat at dinner with his old friends, the Englishes, and ate with less relish than common the delicious Yorkshire pudding and drank the musty ale. He felt it as he accompanied his friends to the theater, where he sat with Mrs. English, while she watched with pride the husband whose impersonations she was never weary of witnessing; but Paul seemed to see him without recognizing him, and even the familiar voice sounded unfamiliar, or like a voice in a dream. He felt it more and more when good Mrs. English gave him a nudge toward the end of the evening and called him "a stupid," half in sport and half in earnest; and when he had delivered that excellent woman into the care of her liege lord and had seen them securely packed into the horse-car that was to drag them tediously homeward in company with a great multitude of suffocating fellow-sufferers, he felt it; and all the way out the dark street and up the hill that ran, or seemed to run, into outer darkness—where his home was—he felt as if he had never been the man he was until now, and that it was all for *her* sake and through *her* influence that this sudden and unexpected transformation had come to pass. And it seemed to him that if he were not to see her again, very soon, his life would be rendered valueless; and that only to see her were worth all the honor and glory that he had ever aspired to in his wildest dreams; and that to be near her always and to feel that he were much—nay, everything—to her, as before God he felt that at that moment she was to him, would make his life one long Elysium, and to death would add a thousand stings.

II

Saadi had no hand in it, yet all Persia could not outdo it. The whole valley ran to roses. They covered the earth; they fell from lofty trellises in fragrant cataracts; they played over the rustic arbors like fountains of color and perfume; they clambered to the cottage roof and scattered their bright petals in showers upon the grass. They were of every tint and texture; of high and low degree, modest or haughty as the case might be—but roses all of them, and such roses as California alone can boast. And some were fat or *passé*, and more's the pity, but all were fragrant, and the name of that sweet vale was Santa Rosa.

Paul was in the garden with Miss Juno. He had followed her thither with what speed he dared. She had expected him; there was not breathing-space for conventionality between these two. In one part of the garden sat an artist at his easel; by his side a lady somewhat his senior, but of the type of face and figure that never really grows old, or looks it. She was embroidering flowers from nature, tinting them to the life, and rivaling her companion in artistic effects. These were the parents of Miss Juno—or rather not quite that. Her mother had been twice married; first, a marriage of convenience darkened the earlier years of her life; Miss Juno was the only reward for an age of domestic misery. A clergyman joined these parties—God had nothing to do with the compact; it would seem that he seldom has. A separation very naturally and very properly followed in the course of time; a young child was the only possible excuse for the delay of the divorce. Thus are the sins of the fathers visited upon the grandchildren. Then came a marriage of love. The artist who having found his ideal had never known a moment's weariness, save when he was parted from her side. Their union was perfect; God had joined them. The stepfather to Miss Juno had always been like a big brother to her—even as her mother had always seemed like an elder sister.

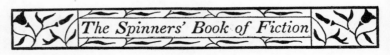

Oh, what a trio was that, my countrymen, where liberty, fraternity and equality joined hands without howling about it and making themselves a nuisance in the nostrils of their neighbors!

Miss Juno stood in a rose-arbor and pointed to the artists at their work.

"Did you ever see anything like that, Paul?"

"Like what?"

"Like those sweet simpletons yonder. They have for years been quite oblivious of the world about them. Thrones might topple, empires rise and fall, it would matter nothing to them so long as their garden bloomed, and the birds nested and sung, and he sold a picture once in an age that the larder might not go bare."

"I've seen something like it, Miss Juno. I've seen fellows who never bothered themselves about the affairs of others,—who, in short, minded their own business strictly—and they got credit for being selfish."

"Were they happy?"

"Yes, in their way. Probably their way wasn't my way, and their kind of happiness would bore me to death. You know happiness really can't be passed around, like bon-bons or sherbet, for every one to taste. I hate bon-bons: do you like them?"

"That depends upon the quality and flavor—and—perhaps somewhat upon who offers them. I never buy bon-bons for my private and personal pleasure. Do any of you fellows really care for bon-bons?"

"That depends upon the kind of happiness we are in quest of; I mean the quality and flavor of the girl we are going to give them to."

"Have girls a flavor?"

"Some of them have—perhaps most of them haven't; neither have they form nor feature, nor tint nor texture, nor anything that appeals to a fellow of taste and sentiment."

"I'm sorry for these girls of yours——"

"You needn't be sorry for the girls; they are not my girls, and not one of them ever will be mine if I can help it——"

"Oh, indeed!"

"They are nothing to me, and I'm nothing to them; but they are just—they are just the formless sort of thing that a formless sort of fellow always marries; they help to fill up the world, you know."

"Yes, they help to fill a world that is overfull

already. Poor Mama and Eugene don't know how full it is. When Gene wants to sell a picture and can't, he thinks it's a desert island."

"Probably they could live on a desert island and be perfectly happy and content," said Paul.

"Of course they could; the only trouble would be that unless some one called them at the proper hours they'd forget to eat—and some day they'd be found dead locked in their last embrace."

"How jolly!"

"Oh, very jolly for very young lovers; they are usually such fools!"

"And yet, I believe I'd like to be a fool for love's sake, Miss Juno."

"Oh, Paul, you are one for your own,—at least I'll think so, if you work yourself into this silly vein!"

Paul was silent and thoughtful. After a pause she continued.

"The trouble with you is, you fancy yourself in love with every new girl you meet—at least with the latest one, if she is at all out of the ordinary line."

"The trouble with me is that I don't keep on loving the same girl long enough to come to the happy climax—if the climax *is* to be a happy one; of course it doesn't follow that it is to be anything of the sort. I've been brought up in the bosom of too many families to believe in the lasting quality of love. Yet they are happy, you say, those two gentle people perpetuating spring on canvas and cambric. See, there is a small cloud of butterflies hovering about them—one of them is panting in fairy-like ecstasy on the poppy that decorates your Mama's hat!"

Paul rolled a cigarette and offered it to Miss Juno, in a mild spirit of bravado. To his delight she accepted it, as if it were the most natural thing in the world for a girl to do. He rolled another and they sat down together in the arbor full of contentment.

"Have you never been in love?" asked Paul suddenly.

"Yes, I suppose so. I was engaged once; you know girls instinctively engage themselves to some one whom they fancy; they imagine themselves in love, and it is a pleasant fallacy. My engagement might have gone on forever, if he had contented himself with a mere engagement. He was a young army officer stationed miles and miles away. We wrote volumes of letters to each other—and they were clever letters; it was rather like a seaside novelette, our love affair. He was lonely, or restless, or something, and pressed his case. Then Mama and Gene—those ideal lovers—put their feet down and would none of it."

"And you——?"

"Of course I felt perfectly wretched for a whole week, and imagined myself cruelly abused. You see he was a foreigner, without money; he was heir to a title, but that would have brought him no advantages in the household."

"You recovered. What became of him?"

"I never learned. He seemed to fade away into thin air. I fear I was not very much in love."

"I wonder if all girls are like you—if they forget so easily?"

"You have yourself declared that the majority have neither form nor feature; perhaps they have no feeling. How do men feel about a broken engagement?"

"I can only speak for myself. There was a time when I felt that marriage was the inevitable fate of all respectable people. Some one wanted me to marry a certain some one else. I didn't seem to care much about it; but my friend was one of those natural-born match-makers; she talked the young lady up to me in such a shape that I almost fancied myself in love and actually began to feel that I'd be doing her an injustice if I permitted her to go on loving and longing for the rest of her days. So one day I wrote her a proposal; it was the kind of proposal one might decline without injuring a fellow's feelings in the least—and she did it!" After a thoughtful pause he continued:

"By Jove! But wasn't I immensely relieved when her letter came; such a nice, dear, good letter it was, too, in which she assured me there had evidently been a mistake somewhere, and nothing had been further from her thoughts than the hope of marrying me. So she let me down most beautifully——"

"And offered to be a sister to you?"

"Perhaps; I don't remember now; I always felt embarrassed after that when her name was mentioned. I couldn't help thinking what an infernal ass I'd made of myself."

"It was all the fault of your friend."

"Of course it was; I'd never have dreamed of proposing to her if I hadn't been put up to it by the match-maker. Oh, what a lot of miserable marriages are brought on in just this way! You see when I like a girl ever so much, I seem to like her too well to marry her. I think it would be mean of me to marry her."

"Why?"

"Because—because I'd get tired after a while; everybody does, sooner or later,—everybody save your Mama and Eugene,—and then I'd say something or do something I ought not to say or do, and I'd hate myself for it; or she'd say something or do something that would make me hate her. We might, of course, get over it and be very nice to one another; but we could never be quite the same again. Wounds leave scars, and you can't forget a scar—can you?"

"You may scar too easily!"

"I suppose I do, and that is the very best reason why I should avoid the occasion of one."

"So you have resolved never to marry?"

"Oh, I've resolved it a thousand times, and yet, somehow, I'm forever meeting some one a little out of the common; some one who takes me by storm, as it were; some one who seems to me a kind of revelation, and then I feel as if I must marry her whether or no; sometimes I fear I shall wake up and find myself married in spite of myself—wouldn't that be frightful?"

"Frightful indeed—and then you'd have to get used to it, just as most married people get used to it in the course of time. You know it's a very matter-of-fact world we live in, and it takes very matter-of-fact people to keep it in good running order."

"Yes. But for these drudges, these hewers of wood and drawers of water, that ideal pair yonder could not go on painting and embroidering things of beauty with nothing but the butterflies to bother them."

"Butterflies don't bother; they open new vistas of beauty, and they set examples that it would do the world good to follow; the butterfly says, 'my mission is to be brilliant and jolly and to take no thought of the morrow.'"

"It's the thought of the morrow, Miss Juno, that spoils today for me,—that morrow—who is going to pay the rent of it? Who is going to keep it in food and clothes?"

"Paul, you have already lived and loved, where there is no rent to pay and where the clothing worn is not worth mentioning; as for the food and the drink in that delectable land, nature provides them both. I don't see why you need to take thought of the morrow; all you have to do is to take passage for some South Sea Island, and let the world go by."

"But the price of the ticket, my friend; where is that to come from? To be sure I'm only a bachelor, and have none but myself to consider. What would I do if I had a wife and family to provide for?"

"You'd do as most other fellows in the same predicament do; you'd provide for them as well as you could; and if that wasn't sufficient, you'd desert them, or blow your brains out and leave them to provide for themselves."

"An old bachelor is a rather comfortable old party. I'm satisfied with my manifest destiny; but I'm rather sorry for old maids—aren't you?"

"That depends; of course everything in life depends; some of the most beautiful, the most blessed, the most bountifully happy women I have ever known were old maids; I propose to be one myself—if I live long enough!"

After an interlude, during which the bees boomed among the honey-blossoms, the birds caroled on the boughs, and the two artists laughed softly as they chatted at their delightful work, Paul resumed:

"Do you know, Miss Juno, this anti-climax strikes me as being exceedingly funny? When I met you the other day, I felt as if I'd met my fate. I know well enough that I'd felt that way often before, and promptly recovered from the attack. I certainly never felt it in the same degree until I came face to face with you. I was never quite so fairly and squarely face to face with any one before. I came here because I could not help myself. I simply had to come, and to come at once. I was resolved to propose to you and to marry you without a cent, if you'd let me. I didn't expect that you'd let me, but I felt it my duty to find out. I'm dead sure that I was very much in love with you—and I am now; but somehow it isn't that spoony sort of love that makes a man unwholesome and sometimes drives him to drink or to suicide. I suppose I love you too well to want to marry you; but God knows how glad I am that we have met, and I hope that we shall never really part again."

"Paul!"—Miss Juno's rather too pallid cheeks were slightly tinged with rose; she seemed more than ever to belong to that fair garden, to have become a part of it, in fact;—"Paul," said she, earnestly enough, "you're an awfully good fellow, and I like you *so* much; I shall always like you; but if you had been fool enough to propose to me I should have despised you. Shake!" And she extended a most shapely hand that clasped his warmly and firmly. While he still held it without restraint, he added:

"Why I like you so much is because you are unlike other girls; that is to say, you're perfectly natural."

"Most people who think me unlike other girls, think me unnatural for that reason. It is hard to be natural, isn't it?"

"Why, no, I think it is the easiest thing in the world to be natural. I'm as natural as I can be, or as anybody can be."

"And yet I've heard you pronounced a bundle of affectations."

"I know that—it's been said in my hearing, but I don't care in the least; it is natural for the perfectly natural person *not* to care in the least."

"I think, perhaps, it is easier for boys to be natural, than for girls," said Miss Juno.

"Yes, boys are naturally more natural," replied Paul with much confidence.

Miss Juno smiled an amused smile.

Paul resumed—"I hardly ever knew a girl who didn't wish herself a boy. Did you ever see a boy who wanted to be a girl?"

"I've seen some who ought to have been girls—and who would have made very droll girls. I know an old gentleman who used to bewail the degeneracy of the age and exclaim in despair, 'Boys will be girls!'" laughed Miss Juno.

"Horrible thought! But why is it that girlish boys are so unpleasant while tom-boys are delightful?"

"I don't know," replied she, "unless the girlish boy has lost the charm of his sex, that is manliness; and the tom-boy has lost the defect of hers—a kind of selfish dependence."

"I'm sure the girls like you, don't they?" he added.

"Not always; and there are lots of girls I can't endure!"

"I've noticed that women who are most admired by women are seldom popular with men; and that the women the men go wild over are little appreciated by their own sex," said Paul.

"Yes, I've noticed that; as for myself my best friends are masculine; but when I was away at boarding-school my chum, who was immensely popular, used to call me Jack!"

"How awfully jolly; may I call you 'Jack' and will you be my chum?"

"Of course I will; but what idiots the world would think us."

"Who cares?" cried he defiantly. "There are millions of fellows this very moment who would give their all for such a pal as you are—Jack!"

There was a fluttering among the butterflies; the artists had risen and were standing waist-deep in the garden of gracious things; they were coming to Paul and Miss Juno, and in amusing pantomime announcing that pangs of hunger were compelling their return to the cottage; the truth is, it was long past the lunch hour—and a large music-box which had been set in motion when the light repast was laid had failed to catch the ear with its tinkling aria.

All four of the occupants of the garden turned leisurely toward the cottage. Miss Juno had rested her hand on Paul's shoulder and said in a delightfully confidential way: "Let it be a secret that we are chums, dear boy—the world is such an idiot."

"All right, Jack," whispered Paul, trying to hug himself in delight, 'Little secrets are cozy.'"

And in the scent of the roses it was duly embalmed.

III

Happy is the man who is without encumbrances—that is if he knows how to be happy. Whenever Paul Clitheroe found the burden of the day becoming oppressive he cast it off, and sought solace in a change of scene. He could always, or almost always, do this at a moment's notice. It chanced, upon a certain occasion, when a little community of artists were celebrating the sale of a great picture—the masterpiece of one of their number—that word was sent to Paul to join their feast. He found the large studio where several of them worked intermittently, highly decorated; a table was spread in a manner to have awakened an appetite even upon the palate of the surfeited; there were music and dancing, and bacchanalian revels that went on and on from night to day and on to night again. It was a veritable feast of lanterns, and not until the last one had burned to the socket and the wine-vats were empty and the studio strewn with unrecognizable debris and permeated with odors stale, flat and unprofitable, did the revels cease. Paul came to dine; he remained three days; he had not yet worn out his welcome, but he had resolved, as was his wont at intervals, to withdraw from the world, and so he returned to the Eyrie,—which was ever his initial step toward the accomplishment of the longed-for end.

Not very many days later Paul received the breeziest of letters; it was one of a series of racy rhapsodies

that came to him bearing the Santa Rosa postmark. They were such letters as a fellow might write to a college chum, but with no line that could have brought a blush to the cheek of modesty—not that the college chum is necessarily given to the inditing of such epistles. These letters were signed "Jack."

"Jack" wrote to say how the world was all in bloom and the rose-garden one bewildering maze of blossoms; how Mama was still embroidering from nature in the midst thereof, crowned with a wreath of butterflies and with one uncommonly large one perched upon her Psyche shoulder and fanning her cheek with its brilliantly dyed wing; how Eugene was reveling in his art, painting lovely pictures of the old Spanish Missions with shadowy outlines of the ghostly fathers, long since departed, haunting the dismantled cloisters; how the air was like the breath of heaven, and the twilight unspeakably pathetic, and they were all three constantly reminded of Italy and forever talking of Rome and the Campagna, and Venice, and imagining themselves at home again and Paul with them, for they had resolved that he was quite out of his element in California; they had sworn he must be rescued; he must return with them to Italy and that right early. He must wind up his affairs and set his house in order at once and forever; he should never go back to it again, but live a new life and a gentler life in that oldest and most gentle of lands; they simply *must* take him with them and seat him by the shore of the Venetian Sea, where he could enjoy his melancholy, if he must be melancholy, and find himself for the first time provided with a suitable background. This letter came to him inlaid with rose petals; they showered upon him in all their fragrance as he read the inspiring pages, and, since "Jack" with quite a martial air had issued a mandate which ran as follows, "Order No. 19—Paul Clitheroe will, upon receipt of this, report immediately at headquarters at Santa Rosa," he placed the key of his outer door in his pocket and straightway departed without more ado.

* * * * * * * *

They swung in individual hammocks, Paul and "Jack," within the rose-screened veranda. The conjugal affinities, Violet and Eugene, were lost to the world in the depths of the rose-garden beyond sight and hearing.

Said Jack, resuming a rambling conversation which had been interrupted by the noisy passage of a bee, "That particular bee reminds me of some people who fret over their work, and who make others who are seeking rest, extremely uncomfortable."

Paul was thoughtful for a few moments and then remarked: "And yet it is a pleasant work he is engaged in, and his days are passed in the fairest fields; he evidently enjoys his trade even if he does seem to bustle about it. I can excuse the buzz and the hum in him, when I can't always in the human tribes."

"If you knew what he was saying just now, perhaps you'd find him as disagreeable as the man who is condemned to earn his bread in the sweat of his brow, and makes more or less of a row about it."

"Very likely, Jack, but these bees are born with business instincts, and they can't enjoy loafing; they don't know how to be idle. Being as busy as a busy bee must be being very busy!"

"There is the hum of the hive in that phrase, old boy! I'm sure you've been working up to it all along. Come now, confess, you've had that in hand for some little time."

"Well, what if I have? That is what writers do, and they have to do it. How else can they make their dialogue in the least attractive? Did you ever write a story, Jack?"

"No, of course not; how perfectly absurd!"

"Not in the least absurd. You've been reading novels ever since you were born. You've the knack of the thing, the telling of a story, the developing of a plot, the final wind-up of the whole concern, right at your tongue's end."

"Paul, you're an idiot."

"Idiot, Jack? I'm nothing of the sort and I can prove what I've just been saying to you about yourself. Now, listen and don't interrupt me until I've said my say."

Paul caught hold of a branch of vine close at hand and set his hammock swinging slowly. Miss Juno settled herself more comfortably in hers, and seemed much interested and amused.

"Now," said Paul, with a comical air of importance—"now, any one who has anything at his tongue's end, has it, or *can*, just as well as not, have it at his finger's end. If you can tell a story well, and you can, Jack, you know you can, you can write it just as well. You have only to tell it with your pen instead of with your lips; and if you will only write it exactly as you speak it, so long as your verbal version is a good one, your pen version is bound to be equally as good; moreover, it seems to me that in this way one is likely to adopt the most natural style, which is, of course, the best of all styles. Now what do you say to that?"

"Oh, nothing," after a little pause—"however, I doubt that any one, male or female, can take up pen for the first time and tell a tale like a practised writer."

"Of course not. The practised writer has a style of his own, a conventional narrative style which may be very far from nature. People in books very seldom talk as they do in real life. When people in books begin to talk like human beings the reader thinks the dialogue either commonplace or mildly realistic, and votes it a bore."

"Then why try to write as one talks? Why not cultivate the conventional style of the practised writer?"

"Why talk commonplaces?" cried Paul a little tartly. "Of course most people must do so if they talk at all, and they are usually the people who talk all the time. But I have known people whose ordinary conversation was extraordinary, and worth-putting down in a book—every word of it."

"In my experience," said Miss Juno, "people who talk like books are a burden."

"They needn't talk like the conventional book, I tell you. Let them have something to say and say it cleverly—that is the kind of conversation to make books of."

"What if all that we've been saying here, under the rose, as it were, were printed just as we've said it?"

"What if it were? It would at least be natural,

and we've been saying something of interest to each other; why should it not interest a third party?"

Miss Juno smiled and rejoined, "I am not a confirmed eavesdropper, but I often find myself so situated that I cannot avoid overhearing what other people are saying to one another; it is seldom that, under such circumstances, I hear anything that interests me."

"Yes, but if you knew the true story of those very people, all that they may be saying in your hearing would no doubt possess an interest, inasmuch as it would serve to develop their history."

"Our conversation is growing a little thin, Paul, don't you think so? We couldn't put all this into a book."

"If it helped to give a clue to our character and our motives, we could. The thing is to be interesting: if we are interesting, in ourselves, by reason of our original charm or our unconventionality, almost anything we might say or do ought to interest others. Conventional people are never interesting."

"Yet the majority of mankind is conventional to a degree; the conventionals help to fill up; their habitual love of conventionality, or their fear of the unconventional, is what keeps them in their place. This is very fortunate. On the other hand, a world full of people too clever to be kept in their proper spheres, would be simply intolerable. But there is no danger of this!"

"Yes, you are right," said Paul after a moment's pause;—"you are interesting, and that is why I like you so well."

"You mean that I am unconventional?"

"Exactly. And, as I said before, that is why I'm so awfully fond of you. By Jove, I'm so glad I'm not in love with you, Jack."

"So am I, old boy; I couldn't put up with that at all; you'd have to go by the next train, you know; you would, really. And yet, if we are to write a novel apiece we shall be obliged to put love into it; love with a very large L."

"No we wouldn't; I'm sure we wouldn't."

Miss Juno shook her golden locks in doubt—Paul went on persistently:—"I'm dead sure we wouldn't; and to prove it, some day I'll write a story without its pair of lovers; everybody shall be more or less spoony—but nobody shall be really in love."

"It wouldn't be a story, Paul."

"It would be a history, or a fragment of a history, a glimpse of a life at any rate, and that is as much as we ever get of the lives of those around us. Why can't I tell you the story of one fellow—of myself for example; how one day I met this person, and the next day I met that person, and next week some one else comes on to the stage, and struts his little hour and departs. I'm not trying to give my audience, my readers, any knowledge of that other fellow. My reader must see for himself how each of those fellows in his own way has influenced me. The story is my story, a study of myself, nothing more or less. If the reader don't like me he may lay me down in my cloth or paper cover, and have nothing more to do with me. If I'm not a hero, perhaps it's not so much my fault as my misfortune. That people are interested in me, and show it in a thousand different ways, assures me that *my* story, not the story of those with whom I'm thrown in contact, is what interests them. It's a narrow-gauge, single-track story, but it runs through a delightful bit of country, and if my reader wants to look out of my windows and see things as I see them and find out how they influence me, he is welcome; if he doesn't, he may get off at the very next station and change cars for Elsewhere."

"I shall have love in my story," said Miss Juno, with an amusing touch of sentiment that on her lips sounded like polite comedy.

"You may have all the love you like, and appeal to the same old novel-reader who has been reading the same sort of love story for the last hundred years, and when you've finished your work and your reader has stood by you to the sweet or bitter end, no one will be any the wiser or better. You've taught nothing, you've untaught nothing—and there you are!"

"Oh! A young man with a mission! Do you propose to revolutionize?"

"No; revolutions only roil the water. You might as well try to make water flow up-hill as to really revolutionize anything. I'd beautify the banks of the stream, and round the sharp turns in it, and weed it out, and sow water-lilies, and set the white swan with her snow-flecked breast afloat. That's what I'd do!"

"That's the art of the landscape gardener; I don't clearly see how it is of benefit to the novelist, Paul! Now, honestly, is it?"

"You don't catch my meaning, Jack; girls are deuced dull, you know,—I mean obtuse." Miss Juno flushed. "I wasn't referring to the novel; I was saying that instead of writing my all in a vain effort to revolutionize anything in particular, I'd try to get all the good I could out of the existing evil, and make the best of it. But let's not talk in this vein any longer; I hate argument. Argument is nothing but a logical or illogical set-to; begin it as politely as you please, it is not long before both parties throw aside their gloves and go in with naked and bloody fists; one of the two gets knocked out, but he hasn't been convinced of anything in particular; he was not in condition, that is all; better luck next time."

"Have you the tobacco, Paul?" asked Miss Juno, extending her hand. The tobacco was silently passed from one hammock to the other; each rolled a cigarette, and lit it. Paul blew a great smoke ring into the air; his companion blew a lesser one that shot rapidly after the larger halo, and the two were speedily blended in a pretty vapor wraith.

"That's the ghost of an argument, Jack," said Paul, glancing above. He resumed: "What I was about to say when I was interrupted"—this was his pet joke; he knew well enough that he had been monopolizing the conversation of the morning—"what I was about to say was this: my novel shall be full of love, but you won't know that it is love—I mean the every-day love of the every-day people. In my book everybody is going to love everybody else—or almost everybody else; if there is any sort of a misunderstanding it sha'n't matter much. I hate rows; I believe in the truest and the fondest fellowship. What is true love? It is bosom friendship; that is the purest passion of love. It is the only love that lasts."

There was a silence for the space of some minutes; Paul and Miss Juno were quietly, dreamily smoking. Without, among the roses, there was the boom of bees; the carol of birds, the flutter of balancing butterflies. Nature was very soothing, she was in one of her sweetest moods. The two friends were growing drowsy. Miss Juno, if she at times betrayed a feminine fondness for argument, was certainly in no haste to provoke Paul to a further discussion of the quality of love or friendship; presently she began rather languidly:

"You were saying I ought to write, and that you believe I can, if I will only try. I'm going to try; I've been thinking of something that happened within my knowledge; perhaps I can make a magazine sketch of it."

"Oh, please write it, Jack! Write it, and send the manuscript to me, that I may place it for you; will you? Promise me you will!" The boy was quite enthusiastic, and his undisguised pleasure in the prospect of seeing something from the pen of his pal—as he loved to call Miss Juno—seemed to awaken a responsive echo in her heart.

"I will, Paul; I promise you!"—and the two struck hands on it.

IV

When Paul returned to the Eyrie, it had been decided that Miss Juno was to at once begin her first contribution to periodic literature. She had found her plot; she had only to tell her story in her own way, just as if she were recounting it to Paul. Indeed, at his suggestion, she had promised to sit with pen in hand and address him as if he were actually present. In this way he hoped she would drop into the narrative style natural to her, and so attractive to her listeners.

As for Paul Clitheroe, he was to make inquiry among his editorial friends in the Misty City, and see if he might not effect some satisfactory arrangement with one or another of them, whereby he would be placed in a position enabling him to go abroad in the course of a few weeks, and remain abroad indefinitely. He would make Venice his headquarters; he would have the constant society of his friends; the fellowship of Jack; together, after the joint literary labors of the day, they would stem the sluggish tide of the darksome canals and exchange sentiment and cigarette smoke in mutual delight. Paul was to write a weekly or a semi-monthly letter to the journal employing him as a special correspondent. At intervals, in the company of his friends, or alone, he would set forth upon one of those charming excursions so fruitful of picturesque experience, and return to his lodgings on the Schiavoni, to work them up into magazine articles; these would later, of course, get into book form; from the book would come increased reputation, a larger source of revenue, and the contentment of success which he so longed for, so often thought he had found, and so seldom enjoyed for any length of time.

All this was to be arranged,—or rather the means to which all this was the delightful end—was to be settled as soon as possible. Miss Juno, having finished her story, was to send word to Paul and he was to hie him to the Rose Garden; thereafter at an ideal dinner, elaborated in honor of the occasion, Eugene was to read the maiden effort, while the author, sustained by the sympathetic presence of her admiring Mama and her devoted Paul, awaited the verdict.

This was to be the test—a trying one for Miss Juno. As for Paul, he felt quite patriarchal, and yet, so genuine and so deep was his interest in the future of his protégée, that he was already showing symptoms of anxiety.

The article having been sent to the editor of the first magazine in the land, the family would be ready to fold its æsthetic tent and depart; Paul, of course, accompanying them.

It was a happy thought; visions of Venice; the moonlit lagoon; the reflected lamps plunging their tongues of flame into the sea; the humid air, the almost breathless silence, broken at intervals by the baying of deep-mouthed bells; the splash of oars; the soft tripping measure of human voices and the refrain of the gondoliers; Jack by his side—Jack now in her element, with the maroon fez of the distinguished howadji tilted upon the back of her handsome head, her shapely finger-nails stained with henna, her wrists weighed down with their scores of tinkling bangles! Could anything be jollier?

Paul gave himself up to the full enjoyment of this dream. Already he seemed to have overcome every obstacle, and to be reveling in the subdued but sensuous joys of the Adriatic queen. Sometimes he had fled in spirit to the sweet seclusion of the cloistral life at San Lazaro. Byron did it before him;—the plump, the soft-voiced, mild-visaged little Arminians will tell you all about that, and take immense pleasure in the telling of it. Paul had also known a fellow-writer who had emulated Byron, and had even distanced the Byron record in one respect at least—he had outstayed his lordship at San Lazaro!

Sometimes Paul turned hermit, in imagination, and dwelt alone upon the long sands of the melancholy Lido; not seeing Jack, or anybody, save the waiter at the neighboring restaurant, for days and days together. It was immensely diverting, this dream-life that Paul led in far distant Venice. It was just the life he loved, the ideal life, and it wasn't costing him a cent—no, not a *soldo*, to speak more in the Venetian manner.

While he was looking forward to the life to come, he had hardly time to perfect his arrangements for a realization of it. He was to pack everything and store it in a bonded warehouse, where it should remain until he had taken root abroad. Then he would send for it and settle in the spot he loved best of all, and there write and dream and drink the wine of the country, while the Angelus bells ringing thrice a day awoke him to a realizing sense of the fairy-like flight of time just as they have been doing for ages past, and, let us hope, as they will continue to do forever and forever.

One day he stopped dreaming of Italy, and resolved to secure his engagement as a correspondent. Miss Juno had written him that her sketch was nearly finished; that he must hold himself in readiness to answer her summons at a moment's notice. The season was advancing; no time was to be lost, etc. Paul started at once for the office of his favorite journal; his interview was not entirely satisfactory. Editors, one and all, as he called upon them in succession, didn't seem especially anxious to send the young man abroad for an indefinite period; the salary requested seemed exorbitant. They each made a proposition; all said: "This is the best I can do at present; go to the other offices, and if you receive a better offer we advise you to take it." This seemed reasonable enough, but as their best rate was fifteen dollars for one letter a week he feared that even the highly respectable second-class accommodations of all sorts to which he must confine himself would be beyond his means.

Was he losing interest in the scheme which had afforded him so many hours of sweet, if not solid, satisfaction? No, not exactly. Poverty was more picturesque abroad than in his prosaic native land. His song was not quite so joyous, that was all; he would go to Italy; he would take a smaller room; he would eat at the Trattoria of the people; he would make studies of the peasant, the *contadini*. Jack had written, "There is pie in Venice when we are there; Mama knows how to make pie; pie cannot be purchased elsewhere. Love is the price thereof!" And pie is very filling. Yes, he would go to Europe on fifteen dollars per week and find paradise in the bright particular Venetian Pie!

V

After many days a great change came to pass. Everybody knew that Paul Clitheroe had disappeared without so much as a "good-by" to his most intimate friends. Curiosity was excited for a little while, but for a little while only. Soon he was forgotten, or remembered by no one save those who had known and loved him and who at intervals regretted him.

And Miss Juno? Ah, Miss Juno, the joy of Paul's young dreams! Having been launched successfully at his hands, and hoping in her brave, off-hand way to be of service to him, she continued to write as much for his sake as for her own; she knew it would please him beyond compare were she to achieve a pronounced literary success. He had urged her to write a novel. She had lightly laughed him to scorn—and had kept turning in her mind the possible plot for a tale. One day it suddenly took shape; the whole thing seemed to her perfectly plain sailing; if Clitheroe had launched her upon that venturesome sea, she had suddenly found herself equipped and able to sail without the aid of any one.

She had written to Paul of her joy in this new discovery. Before her loomed the misty outlines of fair far islands; she was about to set forth to people these. Oh, the joy of that! The unspeakable joy of it! She spread all sail on this voyage of discovery—she asked for nothing more save the prayers of her old comrade. She longed to have him near her so that together they might discuss the situations in her story, one after another. If he were only in Venice they would meet daily over their dinner, and after dinner she would read to him what she had written since they last met; then they would go in a gondola for a moonlight cruise; of course it was always moonlight in Venice! Would this not be delightful and just as an all-wise Providence meant it should be? Paul had read something like this in the letters which she used to write him when he was divided against himself; when he began to feel himself sinking, without a hand to help him. Venice was out of the question then; it were vain for him to even dream of it.

So time went on; Miss Juno became a slave of the lamp; her work grew marvelously under her pen. Her little people led her a merry chase; they whispered in her ears night and day; she got no rest of them—but rose again and again to put down the clever things they said, and so, almost before she knew it, her novel had grown into three fine English volumes with inch-broad margins, half-inch spacings, large type and heavy paper. She was amazed to find how important her work had become.

Fortune favored her. She found a publisher who was ready to bring out her book at once; two sets of proofs were forwarded to her; these she corrected with deep delight, returning one to her London publisher and sending one to America, where another publisher was ready to issue the work simultaneously with the English print.

It made its appearance under a pen-name in England—anonymously in America. What curiosity it awakened may be judged by the instantaneous success of the work in both countries: Tauchnitz at once added it to his fascinating list; the French and German translators negotiated for the right to run it as a serial in Paris and Berlin journals. Considerable curiosity was awakened concerning the identity of the authorship, and the personal paragraphers made a thousand conjectures, all of which helped the sale of the novel immensely and amused Miss Juno and her confidants beyond expression.

All this was known to Clitheroe before he had reached the climax that forced him to the wall. He had written to Miss Juno; and he had called her "Jack" as of old, but he felt and she realized that he felt that the conditions were changed. The atmosphere of the rose-garden was gone forever; the hopes and aspirations that were so easy and so airy then, had folded their wings like bruised butterflies, or faded like the flowers. She resolved to wait until he had recovered his senses and then perhaps he would come to Venice and to them—which in her estimation amounted to one and the same thing.

She wrote to him no more; he had not written her for weeks, save only the few lines of congratulation on the success of her novel, and to thank her for the author's copy she had sent him: the three-volume London edition with a fond inscription on the fly-leaf—a line in each volume. This was the end of all that.

Once more she wrote, but not to Clitheroe; she wrote to a friend she had known when she was in the far West, one who knew Paul well and was always eager for news of him.

The letter, or a part of it, ran as follows:

"VENICE, ITALY, June —, 18—.

"Of course such weather as this is not to be shut out-of-doors; we feed on it; we drink it in; we bathe in it, body and soul. Ah, my friend, know a June in Venice before you die! Don't dare to die until you have become saturated with the aerial-aquatic beauty of this Divine Sea-City!

Oh, I was about to tell you something when the charms of this Syren made me half-delirious and of course I forgot all else in life—I always do so. Well, as we leave in a few days for the delectable Dolomites, we are making our rounds of P. P. C.'s,—that is, we are revisiting every nook and corner in the lagoon so dear to us. We invariably do this; it is the most delicious leave-taking imaginable. If I were only Niobe I'd water these shores with tears—I'm sure I would; but you know I never weep; I never did; I don't know how; there is not a drop of brine in my whole composition.

"Dear me! how I do rattle on—but you know my moods and will make due allowance for what might strike the cold, unfeeling world as being garrulity.

"We had resolved to visit that most enchanting of all Italian shrines, San Francisco del Deserto. We had not been there for an age; you know it is rather a long pull over, and one waits for the most perfect hour when one ventures upon the outskirts of the lagoon.

"Oh, the unspeakable loveliness of that perfect day! The mellowing haze that veiled the water; the heavenly blue of the sea, a mirror of the sky, and floating in between the two, so that one could not be quite sure whether it slumbered in the lap of the sea or hung upon the bosom of the sky, that ideal summer island—San Francisco del Deserto.

"You know it is only a few acres in extent—not more than six, I fancy, and four-fifths of it are walled about with walls that stand knee-deep in sea-grasses. Along, and above it, are thrust the tapering tops of those highly decorative cypresses without which Italy would not be herself at all. There is such a monastery there—an ideal one, with cloister, and sundial, and marble-curbed well, and all that; at least so

I am told; we poor feminine creatures are not permitted to cross the thresholds of these Holy Houses. This reminds me of a remark I heard made by a very clever woman who wished to have a glimpse of the interior of that impossible Monte Casino on the mountain top between Rome and Naples. Of course she was refused admission; she turned upon the poor Benedictine, who was only obeying orders—it is a rule of the house, you know—and said, 'Why do you refuse me admission to this shrine? Is it because I am of the same sex as the mother of your God?' But she didn't get in for all that. Neither have I crossed the threshold of San Francisco del Deserto, but I have wandered upon the green in front of the little chapel; and sat under the trees in contemplation of the sea and wished—yes, really and truly wished—that I were a barefooted Franciscan friar with nothing to do but look picturesque in such a terrestrial paradise.

"What do you think happened when we were there the other day? Now at last I am coming to it. We were all upon the Campo in front of the chapel—Violet, Eugene and I; the Angelus had just rung; it was the hour of all hours in one's lifetime; the deepening twilight—we had the moon to light us on our homeward way—the inexpressible loveliness of the atmosphere, the unutterable peace, the unspeakable serenity—the repose in nature—I cannot begin to express myself!

"Out of the chapel came the Father Superior. He knows us very well, for we have often visited the island; he always offers us some refreshment, a cup of mass wine, or a dish of fruit, and so he did on this

occasion. We were in no hurry to leave the shore and so accepted his invitation to be seated under the trees while he ordered the repast.

"Presently he returned and was shortly followed by a young friar whom we had never seen before; there are not many of them there—a dozen perhaps—and their faces are more or less familiar to us, for even we poor women may kneel without the gratings in their little chapel, and so we have learned to know the faces we have seen there in the choir. But this one was quite new to us and so striking; his eyes were never raised; he offered us a dish of bread and olives, while the abbot poured our wine, and the very moment we had served ourselves he quietly withdrew.

"I could think of but one thing—indeed we all thought of it at the same moment—'tis Browning's—

> "'What's become of Waring
> Since he gave us all the slip?'"

"You know the lines well enough. Why did we think of it?—because we were all startled, so startled that the abbot who usually sees us to our gondola, made his abrupt adieus, on some slight pretext, and the door of the monastery was bolted fast.

"Oh, me! How long it takes to tell a little tale—to be sure! We knew that face, the face of the young friar; we knew the hand—it was unmistakable; we have all agreed upon it and are ready to swear to it on our oaths! That novice was none other than Paul Clitheroe!"

A LITTLE SAVAGE GENTLEMAN

BY

ISOBEL STRONG

Reprinted from *Scribner's Magazine*
by permission

A LITTLE SAVAGE GENTLEMAN

F YOU want a child as badly as all that," my brother said, "why not adopt a chief's son, some one who is handsome and well-born, and will be a credit to you, instead of crying your eyes out over a little common brat who is an ungrateful cub, and ugly into the bargain?"

I wasn't particularly fond of the "common brat," but I had grown used to tending him, bandaging his miserable little foot and trying to make his lot easier to bear; and he had been spirited away. One may live long in Samoa without understanding the whys and wherefores. His mother may have been jealous of my care of the child and carried him away in the night; or the clan to which he belonged may have sent for him, though his reputed father was our assistant cook. At any rate, he had gone—departed as completely and entirely as though he had vanished into thin air, and I, sitting on the steps of the veranda, gave way to tears.

Two days later, as I hastened across the courtyard, I turned the corner suddenly, nearly falling over a small Samoan boy, who stood erect in a gallant pose before the house, leaning upon a long stick of sugar-cane, as though it were a spear.

"Who are you?" I asked, in the native language.

"I am your son," was the surprising reply.

"And what is your name?"

"Pola," he said. "Pola, of Tanugamanono, and my mother is the white chief lady, Teuila of Vailima."

He was a beautiful creature, of an even tint of light bronze-brown; his slender body reflected the polish of scented cocoanut oil, the tiny garment he called his *lava-lava* fastened at the waist was coquettishly kilted above one knee. He wore a necklace of scarlet berries across his shoulders, and a bright red hibiscus flower stuck behind his ear. On his round, smooth cheek a single rose-leaf hid the dimple. His large black eyes looked up at me with an expression of terror, overcome by pure physical courage. From the top of his curly head to the soles of his high-arched slender foot he looked *tama'alii*—high-bred. To all my inquiries he answered in purest high-chief Samoan that he was my son.

My brother came to the rescue with explanations. Taking pity on me, he had gone to our village (as we called Tanugamanono) and adopted the chief's second son in my name, and here he was come to present himself in person.

I shook hands with him, a ceremony he performed very gracefully with great dignity. Then he offered me the six feet of sugar-cane, with the remark that it was a small, trifling gift, unworthy of my high-chief notice. I accepted it with a show of great joy and appreciation, though by a turn of the head one could see acres of sugar-cane growing on the other side of the river.

There was an element of embarrassment in the

possession of this charming creature. I could not speak the Samoan language very well at that time, and saw, by his vague but polite smile, that much of my conversation was incomprehensible to him. His language to me was so extremely "high-chief" that I couldn't understand more than three words in a sentence. What made the situation still more poignant was that look of repressed fear glinting in the depths of his black velvety eyes.

I took him by the hand (that trembled slightly in mine, though he walked boldly along with me) and led him about the house, thinking the sight of all the wonders of Vailima might divert his mind. When I threw open the door of the hall, with its pictures and statues, waxed floor and glitter of silver on the sideboard, Pola made the regulation quotation from Scripture, "And behold the half has not been told me."

He went quite close to the tiger-skin, with the glass eyes and big teeth. "It is not living?" he asked, and when I assured him it was dead he remarked that it was a large pussy, and then added, gravely, that he supposed the forests of London were filled with these animals.

He held my hand quite tightly going up the stairs, and I realized then that he could never have mounted a staircase before. Indeed, everything in the house, even chairs and tables, books and pictures, were new and strange to this little savage gentleman.

I took him to my room, where I had a number of letters to write. He sat on the floor at my feet very obediently while I went on with my work. Looking down a few minutes later I saw that he had fallen asleep, lying on a white rug in a childish, graceful attitude, and I realized again his wild beauty and charm.

Late in the day, as it began to grow dark, I asked Pola if he did not want to go home.

"No, Teuila," he answered, bravely.

"But you will be my boy just the same," I explained. "Only you see Tumau (his real mother) will be lonely at first. So you can sleep at the village and come and see me during the day."

His eyes lit up with that and the first smile of the day overspread his face, showing the whitest teeth imaginable.

It was not long before he was perfectly at home in Vailima. He would arrive in the morning early, attended by a serving-man of his family, who walked meekly in the young chief's footsteps, carrying the usual gift for me. Sometimes it was sugar-cane, or a wreath woven by the village girls, or a single fish wrapped in a piece of banana-leaf, or a few fresh water prawns, or even a bunch of wayside flowers; my little son seldom came empty-handed.

It was Pola who really taught me the Samoan language. Ordinarily the natives cannot simplify their remarks for foreigners, but Pola invented a sort of Samoan baby-talk for me; sometimes, if I could not understand, he would shake me with his fierce little brown hands, crying, "Stupid, stupid!" But generally he was extremely patient with me, trying a sentence in half a dozen different ways, with his bright eyes fixed eagerly on my face, and when the sense of what he said dawned upon me and I repeated it to prove that I understood, his own countenance would light up with an expression of absolute pride and triumph. "Good!" he would say, approvingly. "Great is your high-chief wisdom!"

Once we spent a happy afternoon together in the forest picking up queer land-shells, bright berries and curious flowers, while Pola dug up a number of plants by the roots. I asked him the next day what he had done with the beautiful red flowers. His reply was beyond me, so I shook my head. He looked at me anxiously for a moment with that worried expression that so often crossed his face in conversation with me, and, patting the floor, scraped up an imaginary hole, "They sit down in the dusty," he said in baby Samoan. "Where?" I asked. "In front of Tumau." And then I understood that he had planted them in the ground before his mother's house.

Another time he came up all laughter and excitement to tell of an adventure.

"Your brother," he said, "the high-chief Loia, he of the four eyes (eye-glasses), came riding by the village as I was walking up to Vailima. He offered me a ride on his chief-horse and gave me his chief-hand. I put my foot on the stirrup, and just as I jumped the horse shied, and, as I had hold of the high-chief Loia, we both fell off into the road *palasi*."

"Yes," I said, "you both fell off. That was very funny."

"*Palasi!*" he reiterated.

But here I looked doubtful. Pola repeated his word several times as though the very sound ought to convey some idea to my bemuddled brain, and then a bright idea struck him. I heard his bare feet pattering swiftly down the stairs. He came flying back, still laughing, and laid a heavy dictionary in my lap. I hastily turned the leaves, Pola questing in each one like an excited little dog, till I found the definition of his word, "to fall squash like a ripe fruit on the ground."

"*Palasi!*" he cried, triumphantly, when he saw I understood, making a gesture downward with both hands, the while laughing heartily. "We both fell off *palasi!*"

It was through Pola that I learned all the news of Tanugamanono. He would curl up on the floor at my feet as I sat in my room sewing, and pour forth an endless stream of village gossip. How Mata, the native parson, had whipped his daughter for going to a picnic on Sunday and drinking a glass of beer.

"Her father went whack! whack!" Pola illustrated the scene with gusto, "and Maua cried, ah! ah! But the village says Mata is right, for we must not let the white man's evil come near us."

"Evil?" I said; "what evil?"

"Drink," said Pola, solemnly.

Then he told how "the ladies of Tanugamanono" bought a pig of Mr. B., a trader, each contributing a dollar until forty dollars were collected. There was to be a grand feast among the ladies on account of the choosing of a maid or *taupo*, the young girl who represents the village on all state occasions. When the pig came it turned out to be an old boar, so tough and rank it could not be eaten. The ladies were much ashamed before their guests, and asked the white man for another pig, but he only laughed at them. He had their money, so he did not care.

"That was very, very bad of him," I exclaimed, indignantly.

"It is the way of white people," said Pola, philosophically.

It was through my little chief that we learned of a bit of fine hospitality. It seems that pigs were scarce in the village, so each house-chief pledged himself to refrain from killing one of them for six months. Any one breaking this rule agreed to give over his house to be looted by the village.

Pola came up rather late one morning, and told me, hilariously, of the fun they had had looting Tupuola's house.

"But Tupuola is a friend of ours," I said. "I don't like to hear of all his belongings being scattered."

"It is all right," Pola explained. "Tupuola said to the village, 'Come and loot. I have broken the law and I will pay the forfeit.'"

"How did he break the law?" I asked.

"When the high-chief Loia, your brother of the four eyes, stopped the night at Tanugamanono, on his way to the shark fishing, he stayed with Tupuola, so of course it was chiefly to kill a pig in his honor."

"But it was against the law. My brother would not have liked it, and Tupuola must have felt badly to know his house was to be looted."

"He would have felt worse," said Pola, "to have acted unchiefly to a friend."

We never would have known of the famine in Tanugamanono if it had not been for Pola. The hurricane had blown off all the young nuts from the cocoanut palms and the fruit from the breadfruit trees, while the taro was not yet ripe. We passed the village daily. The chief was my brother's dear friend; the girls often came up to decorate the place for a dinner party, but we had no hint of any distress in the village.

One morning I gave Pola two large ship's biscuits from the pantry.

"Be not angry," said Pola, "but I prefer to carry these home."

"Eat them," I said, "and I will give you more."

Before leaving that night he came to remind me of this. I was swinging in a hammock reading a novel when Pola came to kiss my hand and bid me good night.

"*Love*," I said, "*Talofa*."

"*Soifua*," Pola replied, "may you sleep;" and then he added, "Be not angry, but the biscuits——"

"Are you hungry?" I asked. "Didn't you have your dinner?"

"Oh, yes, plenty of pea-soupo" (a general name for anything in tins); "but you said, in your high-chief kindness, that if I ate the two biscuits you would give me more to take home."

"And you ate them?"

He hesitated a perceptible moment, and then said: "Yes, I ate them."

He looked so glowing and sweet, leaning forward to beg a favor, that I suddenly pulled him to me by his bare, brown shoulders for a kiss. He fell against the hammock and two large round ship's biscuits slipped from under his *lava-lava*.

"Oh, Pola!" I cried, reproachfully. It cut me to the heart that he should lie to me.

He picked them up in silence, repressing the tears that stood in his big black eyes, and turned to go. I felt there was something strange in this, one of those mysterious Samoan affairs that had so often baffled me.

"I will give you two more biscuits," I said, quietly, "if you will explain why you told a wicked lie and pained the heart that loved you."

"Teuila," he cried, anxiously, "I love you. I would not pain your heart for all the world. But they are starving in the village. My father, the chief, divides the food, so that each child and old person and all shall share alike, and today there was only green baked bananas, two for each, and tonight when I return there will be again a division of one for each member of the village. It seems hard that I should come here and eat and eat, and my brother and my two little sisters, and the good Tumau also, should have only one banana. So I thought I would say to you, 'Behold, I have eaten the two biscuits,' and then you would give me two more and that would be enough for one each to my two sisters and Tumau and my brother, who is older than I."

That night my brother went down to the village and interviewed the chief. It was all true, as Pola had said, only they had been too proud to mention it. Mr. Stevenson sent bags of rice and kegs of beef to the village, and gave them permission to dig for edible roots in our forest, so they were able to tide over until the taro and yams were ripe.

Pola always spoke of Vailima as "our place," and Mr. Stevenson as "my chief." I had given him a little brown pony that exactly matched his own skin.

A missionary, meeting him in the forest road as he was galloping along like a young centaur, asked, "Who are you?"

"I," answered Pola, reining in his pony with a gallant air, "am one of the Vailima men!"

He proved, however, that he considered himself a true Samoan by a conversation we had together once when we were walking down to Apia. We passed a new house where a number of half-caste carpenters were briskly at work.

"See how clever these men are, Pola," I said, "building the white man's house. When you get older perhaps I will have you taught carpentering, that you may build houses and make money."

"Me?" asked Pola, surprised.

"Yes," I replied. "Don't you think that would be a good idea?"

"I am the son of a chief," said Pola.

"I know," I said, "that your highness is a very great personage, but all the same it is good to know how to make money. Wouldn't you like to be a carpenter?"

"No," said Pola, scornfully, adding, with a wave of his arm that took in acres of breadfruit trees, banana groves, and taro patches, "Why should I work? All this land belongs to me."

Once, when Pola had been particularly adorable, I told him, in a burst of affection, that he could have anything in the world he wanted, only begging him to name it.

He smiled, looked thoughtful for an instant, and then answered, that of all things in the world, he would like ear-rings, like those the sailors wear.

I bought him a pair the next time I went to town. Then, armed with a cork and a needleful of white silk, I called Pola, and asked if he wanted the ear-rings badly enough to endure the necessary operation.

He smiled and walked up to me.

"Now, this is going to hurt, Pola," I said.

He stood perfectly straight when I pushed the needle through his ear and cut off a little piece of silk. I looked anxiously in his face as he turned his head for me to pierce the other one. I was so nervous that my hands trembled.

"Are you *sure* it does not hurt, Pola, my pigeon?" I asked, and I have never forgotten his answer.

"My father is a soldier," he said.

Pola's dress was a simple garment, a square of white muslin hemmed by his adopted mother. Like all Samoans, he was naturally very clean, going with the rest of the "Vailima men" to swim in the waterfall twice a day. He would wash his hair in the juice of wild oranges, clean his teeth with the inside husk of the cocoanut, and, putting on a fresh *lava-lava*, would wash out the discarded one in the river, laying it out in the sunshine to dry. He was always decorated with flowers in some way—a necklace of jessamine buds, pointed red peppers, or the scarlet fruit of the pandanas. Little white boys looked naked without their clothes, but Pola in a strip of muslin, with his wreath of flowers, or sea-shells, some ferns twisted about one ankle, perhaps, or a boar's tusk fastened to his left arm with strands of horse-hair, looked completely, even handsomely, dressed.

He was not too proud to lend a helping hand at

any work going—setting the table, polishing the floor of the hall or the brass handles of the old cabinet, leading the horses to water, carrying pails for the milkmen, helping the cook in the kitchen, the butler in the pantry, or the cowboy in the fields; holding skeins of wool for Mr. Stevenson's mother, or trotting beside the lady of the house, "Tamaitai," as they all called her, carrying seeds or plants for her garden. When my brother went out with a number of natives laden with surveying implements, Pola only stopped long enough to beg for a cane-knife before he was leading the party. If Mr. Stevenson called for his horse and started to town it was always Pola who flew to open the gate for him, waving a "*Talofa!*" and "Good luck to the traveling!"

The Samoans are not reserved, like the Indians, or haughty, like the Arabs. They are a cheerful, lively people, who keenly enjoy a joke, laughing at the slightest provocation. Pola bubbled over with fun, and his voice could be heard chattering and singing gaily at any hour of the day. He made up little verses about me, which he sang to the graceful gestures of the Siva or native dance, showing unaffected delight when commended. He cried out with joy and admiration when he first heard a hand-organ, and was excitedly happy when allowed to turn the handle. I gave him a box of tin soldiers, which he played with for hours in my room. He would arrange them on the floor, talking earnestly to himself in Samoan.

"These are brave brown men," he would mutter. "They are fighting for Mata'afa. Boom! Boom! These are white men. They are fighting the

Samoans. Pouf!" And with a wave of his arm he knocked down a whole battalion, with the scornful remark, "All white men are cowards."

After Mr. Stevenson's death so many of his Samoan friends begged for his photograph that we sent to Sydney for a supply, which was soon exhausted. One afternoon Pola came in and remarked, in a very hurt and aggrieved manner, that he had been neglected in the way of photographs.

"But your father, the chief, has a large fine one."

"True," said Pola. "But that is not mine. I have the box presented to me by your high-chief goodness. It has a little cover, and there I wish to put the sun-shadow of Tusitala, the beloved chief whom we all revere, but I more than the others because he was the head of my clan."

"To be sure," I said, and looked about for a photograph. I found a picture cut from a weekly paper, one I remember that Mr. Stevenson himself had particularly disliked. He would have been pleased had he seen the scornful way Pola threw the picture on the floor.

"I will not have that!" he cried. "It is pig-faced. It is not the shadow of our chief." He leaned against the door and wept.

"I have nothing else, Pola," I protested. "Truly, if I had another picture of Tusitala I would give it to you."

He brightened up at once. "There is the one in the smoking-room," he said, "where he walks back and forth. That pleases me, for it looks like him." He referred to an oil painting of Mr. Stevenson by Sargent. I explained that I could not give him that.

"Then I will take the round one," he said, "of tin." This last was the bronze *bas-relief* by St. Gaudens. I must have laughed involuntarily, for he went out deeply hurt. Hearing a strange noise in the hall an hour or so later, I opened the door, and discovered Pola lying on his face, weeping bitterly.

"What *are* you crying about?" I asked.

"The shadow, the shadow," he sobbed. "I want the sun-shadow of Tusitala."

I knocked at my mother's door across the hall, and at the sight of that tear-stained face her heart melted, and he was given the last photograph we had, which he wrapped in a banana-leaf, tying it carefully with a ribbon of grass.

We left Samoa after Mr. Stevenson's death, staying away for more than a year. Pola wrote me letters by every mail in a large round hand, but they were too conventional to bear any impress of his mind. He referred to our regretted separation, exhorting me to stand fast in the high-chief will of the Lord, and, with his love to each member of the family, mentioned by name and title, he prayed that I might live long, sleep well, and not forget Pola, my unworthy servant.

When we returned to Samoa we were up at dawn, on shipboard, watching the horizon for the first faint cloud that floats above the island of Upulu. Already the familiar perfume came floating over the waters—that sweet blending of many odors, of cocoanut-oil and baking breadfruit, of jessamine and gardenia. It smelt of home to us, leaning over the rail and watching. First a cloud, then a shadow growing more and more distinct until we saw the outline of the island. Then, as we drew nearer, the deep purple of the distant hills, the green of the rich forests, and the silvery ribbons where the waterfalls reflect the sunshine.

Among the fleet of boats skimming out to meet us was one far ahead of the others, a lone canoe propelled by a woman, with a single figure standing in the prow. As the steamer drew near I made out the figure of Pola, dressed in wreaths and flowers in honor of my return. As the anchor went down in the bay of Apia and the custom-house officer started to board, I called out, begging him to let the child come on first. He drew aside. The canoe shot up to the gangway, and Pola, all in his finery of fresh flowers, ran up the gangway and stepped forth on the deck. The passengers drew back before the strange little figure, but he was too intent upon finding me to notice them.

"Teuila!" he cried, joyfully, with the tears rolling down his cheeks. I went forward to meet him, and, kneeling on the deck, caught him in my arms.

LOVE AND ADVERTISING

BY

RICHARD WALTON TULLY

Reprinted from *The Cosmopolitan Magazine* of April, 1906
by permission

LOVE AND ADVERTISING

DO NOT demand," said Mr. Pepper, "I simply suggest a change. If you wish me to resign"—his self-deprecatory manner bespoke an impossible supposition—"very well. But, if you see fit to find me a new assistant——" He paused, with an interrogatory cough.

It was the senior partner who answered, "We shall consider the matter."

The advertising manager's lean face took on an expression of satisfaction. He bowed and disappeared through the door.

Young Kaufmann, the junior partner, smiled covertly. But the elder man's face bespoke keen disappointment. For it must be explained that Mr. Pepper's simple announcement bore vitally upon the only dissension that had ever visited the firm of Kaufmann & Houghton during the thirty years of its existence.

In 1875, when John Houghton, fresh from college, had come to New York to find his fortune, the elder Kaufmann had been a candy manufacturer with a modest trade on the East Side. Young Houghton had taken the agency of a glucose firm. The disposal of this product had brought the two together, with the result that a partnership had been formed to carry on a wholesale confectionery business. Success in this venture had led to new and more profitable fields—the chewing-gum trade.

The rise to wealth of these two was the result of the careful plodding of the German workman, who kept the "K. & H." products up to an unvarying standard, joined with the other's energy and acumen in marketing the output. And this mutual relation had been disturbed by but one difference. When Houghton was disposed to consider a college man for a vacancy, Kaufmann had always been ready with his "practical man dot has vorked hiss vay." And each time, in respect to his wishes, Houghton had given in, reflecting that perhaps (as Kaufmann said) it had been that he, himself, was a good business man in spite of his college training, not because of it; and, after all, college ideals had sunk since *his* time. And the college applicant had been sent away.

Young Johann Kaufmann graduated from grammar school. Houghton suggested high school and college.

"Vat? Nein!" said the elder Kaufmann. "I show him how better the gum to make."

And he did. He put on an apron as of yore and started his son under his personal supervision in the washing-room. He took off his apron when Johann knew all about handling chicle products, from importing-bag to tin-foil wrapper. Then he died.

And this year troublesome conditions had come on. The Consolidated Pepsin people were cutting in severely. Orders for the great specialty of K. & H.—"Old Tulu"—had fallen. Something had to be done.

Houghton, now senior partner, had proposed, and young Kaufmann agreed, that an advertising expert be secured. But the agreement ended there. For the first words of the junior partner showed Houghton that the spirit of the father was still sitting at that desk opposite, and smiling the same fat, phlegmatic smile at his supposed weakness for "dose college bitzness."

They had compromised upon Mr. Pepper, secured from Simpkins' Practical Advertising School. But at the end of six months, Pepper's so-called "follow-up campaign" had failed to meet materially the steady inroads of the western men. He had explained that it was the result of his need of an assistant. It was determined to give him one.

Then, one night as he sat in his library, John Houghton had looked into a pair of blue eyes and promised to "give Tom Brainard the chance." In consequence he had had his hair tousled, been given a resounding kiss and a crushing hug from the young lady on his knees. For Dorothy Houghton, despite her nineteen years, still claimed that privilege from her father.

In that way, for the first time, a college man had come into the employ of K. & H., and been made the assistant of Mr. Pepper at the salary he demanded—"any old thing to start the ball rolling."

And now had come the information that the senior partner's long-desired experiment had ended in failure.

Young Kaufmann turned to his work with the air of one who has given a child its own way and seen it come to grief.

"I—I suppose," Houghton said slowly, "we'll have to let Brainard go."

And then a peculiar thing happened. Through the open window, floating in the summer air, he seemed to see a familiar figure. It was dressed in fluffy white, and carried a parasol over its shoulders. It fluttered calmly in, seated itself on the sill, and gazed at him with blue eyes that were serious, reproachful.

"Daddy!" it said, and it brushed away a wisp of hair by its ear—just as another one, long ago, had used to. "Daddy!" it faltered. "Why did I ask you to give him the place, if it wasn't because—because——"

The spell was broken by Kaufmann's voice. "Whatefer you do, I am sooted," he was saying. It might have been his father. "But if w'at Pepper says about Brainard——"

The senior partner straightened up and pushed a button. "Yes. But we haven't heard what Brainard says about Pepper."

Several moments later, Tom Brainard entered. Medium-sized and muscular, he was dressed in a loose-fitting suit that by its very cut told his training. He stood between them as Mr. Pepper had done, but there was nothing of the other's ingratiating deference in his level look.

"Sit down, Brainard," said Houghton. The newcomer did so, and the senior partner marked an attitude of laziness and indifference.

Houghton became stern. "Brainard," he began, "I gave you a chance with us because——" He paused.

The other colored. "I had hoped to make good without that."

"But this morning Mr. Pepper——"

"Said we couldn't get along together. That's true."

"Ah! You admit!" It was Kaufmann.

"Yes."

There was a pause. Then Houghton spoke. "I can't tell you how much this disappoints me, Brainard. The fact is, for years I have tried to shut my eyes to the development of college training. In my time there was not the call for practicality that there is today. Yet it seems to me that the training in our colleges has grown less and less practical. Why do the colleges turn out men who spend their time in personal gossip over sport or trivialities?"

"You remember that the King of Spain—or was it Cambodia—puzzled his wise men for a year as to why a fish, when dropped into a full pail of water, didn't make it overflow."

"What's that got to do with it?"

"Because I must answer as the king did: It's not so—the pail *does* overflow. They hadn't thought to try it."

"You mean that I am wrong."

"Yes. Are you sure your gossips were 'college men'?"

"Ah!" Houghton made a gesture to his partner, who was about to speak. "Then let us commence at the root of the matter. Mr. Kaufmann and I have often discussed the subject. In this case you are the one who has 'tried it.' Suppose you explain our mistake."

"I'd be glad to do that," said Brainard, "because I've heard a lot of that talk."

"Well?"

"Well—of course when I say 'college man' I mean college graduate."

"Why?"

"If a kitten crawls into an oven, is it a biscuit?"

There was an earnestness that robbed the question of any flippancy.

Houghton laughed. "No!"

"If a dub goes into college and gets flunked out in a month, is he a college man?"

"Hardly."

"Oh, but he calls himself one. He goes to Podunk all decorated up in geraniums and the rest of his life is a 'college man.' I'm not talking about him or the man who comes to college to learn to mix cocktails—inside. He may last to the junior year. I'm talking about the graduate—they're only about a tenth of the college. But they're the finished product. Mr. Kaufmann, you wouldn't try to sell gum that had only gone as far as the rolling-room, would you?"

"W'at—me?"

"Would you?"

"No." The junior partner was puzzled.

"That's because you want it to go through all the processes. Well, let's talk only about the boy who has gone all the way through the man factory."

Houghton nodded. "That's fair."

"The trouble is, people don't do that. They persist in butting into the college world, jerking out some sophomore celebration, and saying, 'What use is this silly thing in the real world?'"

"Well, aren't they right?"

"No. That's just the point. The college world is a mimic world—and your lifetime is just four years. The sophomore celebration is a practical thing there; perhaps it's teaching loyalty—that generally comes first. That's your college rolling-room. But the graduate—he's learned to do *something* well. I never knew a college man who wasn't at least responsible."

"But——"

"But here's the trouble: after selecting say two hundred fellows out of an entering bunch of six hundred, and developing the thing each is best fitted for, *father* steps in and the boy who would have made a first-class professor is put into business and blamed for being impractical. The fellow who has been handling thousands of dollars in college management and running twenty assistants—the man who could have taken the place—has no father to give him the boost necessary, and the other man's failure has queered his chances. He has to go to work as a mere clerk under a man—excuse me, I don't want to do any knocking."

"You think the whole trouble is caused by misdirected nepotism."

"Yes."

"Ah——" It was young Kaufmann again. "But you said that you were trained in advertising on your college paper."

"Yes—and I was going to tell you today, if Mr. Pepper hadn't, that the money you're paying for me is utterly wasted."

"Ah!"

"Yes. I can't look in the face of a hungry designer and beat him down to within a dollar of the cost of materials. And—and—my suggestions upon broader lines don't seem to cause much hooray."

"Well—" the junior partner sat up—"since you admit——" He paused for his partner to speak the words of discharge.

But Houghton was looking quizzically at the college man. "What was your idea as to broader lines?"

Brainard hesitated. "Well, it seemed to me that Pepper is trying to do two things that are antagonistic: be '*élite*' and sell chewing-gum. The fact is that *élite* people don't chew gum. I'd like to know how the statement, 'Old Tulu—Best by Test,' will make a kid on the corner with a cent in his fist have an attack of mouth-watering."

Kaufmann roused himself. "It is true. Our gum *is* the best."

"I'm not disputing that, but still it's *gum*. If you're trying to increase the vulgar habit of gum-chewing—well—you can't do it by advertising the firm's financial standing, its age, or the purity of its output. That would do for an insurance company or a bank—but *gum!* Who cares for purity! All they want to know is if it *schmeckt gut*." This last with a humorous glance at Kaufmann.

The latter was scowling. Brainard was touching a tender spot.

"Well, what would you do?"

Brainard flushed. He felt the tone of sarcasm in the elder man's voice. He tightened his lips. "At least, I'd change the name of the gum!"

"Change the name!" Kaufmann was horrified.

"Well, nobody wants 'Old Tulu.' They want 'New Tulu' or 'Fresh Tasty Tulu.' At least, something to appeal to the imagination of Sadie-at-the-ribbon-counter."

"Oh!" observed Houghton. "And the name you suggest?"

"Well,—say something like 'Lulu Tulu.'"

"Gott!" Kaufmann struck the desk a blow with his fist. It was an insult to his father's memory.

Brainard rose. "I'm sorry," he said, "if I have offended. To save you any further bother, I'll just cut it out after Saturday. I—thank you for the chance"— he smiled a little ruefully—"the chance you have given me. Good day, gentlemen."

He turned on his heel and left the office.

As John Houghton was driven home that night, he became suddenly conscious that he would soon meet the apparition of the afternoon in the flesh. And though, of course, there was no need, he found himself rehearsing the justification of his position. "Lulu Tulu" indeed! Imagine the smile that would have illumined the faces at the club on such an announcement. The impudence of the boy to have suggested it to him—him who had so often held forth upon the value of conservatism in business! And he remembered with pride the speaker who had once said, "It is such solid vertebræ as Mr. Houghton that form the backbone of our business world." That speaker had been Bender, of the New York Dynamo Company. Poor Bender! The Western Electric Construction had got him after all.

This line of thought caused Houghton to reach in his pocket and produce a letter. He went over the significant part again.

"Our Mr. Byrnes reports the clinching of the subway vending-machine contract," it read, "and this, together with our other business, will give us over half of the New York trade. With this statement before us, we feel that we can make a winning fight if you still refuse to consider our terms. In view of recent developments, we cannot repeat our former offer, but if you will consider sixty-seven as a figure——"

Sixty-seven! And a year before he would not have taken one hundred and ten! In the bitterness of the moment, he wondered if he, too, would finally go the way that Bender had.

And then, as the butler swung the door back, he was recalled to the matter of Tom Brainard by the sight of a familiar figure that floated toward him as airily as had its astral self that afternoon.

He kissed her and went to his study. Just before dinner was not a time to discuss such things. But later, as he looked across the candelabra at his daughter, all smiles and happiness in that seat that had been her mother's, he regretted that he had not, for——

"Daddy," Dorothy was saying, "I got such a funny note from Tom this afternoon. He says there has been a change at the office and that you will explain."

"Yes."

"Well——?" She paused eagerly. "It's something awfully good—I know."

Her father frowned and caught her eye. "Later," he said significantly.

The girl read the tone, and the gaiety of the moment before was gone. After that they ate in silence.

One cigar—two cigars had been smoked when she stole into the library. Since coffee (whether from design or chance he never knew), she had rearranged her hair. Now it was low on her neck in a fashion of long ago, with a single curl that strayed over a white shoulder to her bosom. She knelt at his side without a word.

He looked down at her. Somehow he had never seen her like this before—that curious womanly expression.

"Tell me," was all she said.

And, as he told Tom Brainard's failure to fit in, he watched her closely. "I'm sorry," he concluded.

"So am I, daddy," she returned steadily; "because I am going to marry him."

"What?"

"Oh, you knew—you must have," she said, "when I asked you to give him the chance."

The father was silent. In fancy he again heard Dolly Warner promising, against her parents' advice, to wait for her John to "get on in the world."

"Well?" he asked.

"Do you think you've given him a fair chance?"

He was restored to his usual poise. "I suppose he complained that I didn't."

Dorothy's eyes went wide. "No, he said that after I had heard the news from you, he would leave everything to me."

"Oh!"

"But, father, I don't think you *have* been fair. Tom is right. *I* don't chew gum, do I?"

"Well——" He was indignant. Then he stopped thoughtfully. "No."

"But Mary downstairs does. She wouldn't be offended at 'Lulu Tulu.' I dare say she'd think it 'just grand.'"

He returned no answer.

"Come, daddy," she went on. "New York has grown lots—even since I was little. And—and some people get behind the times. They think they're being dignified when it's only that they're antiquated."

He looked shrewdly at her. "I never heard you talk like that before. Where did you——"

"Tom said that a week ago," she admitted. "And he said, too, that he could double the results if he only had full swing. Instead, you admit he's a mere clerk for that horrid Pepper. Oh, daddy, daddy," she pleaded. "Give him a chance." Then her voice went low again. "I'm going to marry him anyway," she said, "and you don't want this between. If he fails, I'll stand the loss from what mother left me. Give him full swing—a real chance, daddy! He's going to be—*your son.*"

John Houghton looked into the earnest girlish face. He wound the curl about his finger. "Kaufmann has always wanted to visit the Fatherland," he said irrelevantly.

She gave a quick, eager look. "And that Pepper could go on a vacation."

Days drag very slowly at a summer resort, especially when one has promised not to write to him. But Dorothy's father had kept his word, so she could but do the same. Behind, in the sweltering city, in full charge for six weeks was Tom Brainard. His authority included permission to invent and use any new labels or trade-marks he saw fit.

The girl at the seashore, however, was also busy—amusing her father that he might not give too much time to thinking. And then, when three of the six weeks had passed, came the accident to the motor car.

She was told that with rest and no worries, her father would recover in a week or two. She cheerfully fitted into the rôle of assistant to the nurse in charge, and, as soon as the doctor allowed, prepared to read his mail to him as he lay, eyes and head bandaged. But as she opened and glanced over the accumulated letters, she suddenly went pale. She read one in particular from end to end, and then, with a scared, furtive look at the bandaged figure, slipped it into a pocket.

Later, when her father had finished dictating to her, she answered the concealed letter herself.

Again the days drifted. The bandages were removed; but still the girl continued to scan the mail. Her vigilance was rewarded. She flushed over a second letter which, with one in a worn envelope, she took to her father.

He saw the careworn expression. "My little girl has been overworking," he said.

She held out the worn letter. "I've had this for some time—but—but I waited for something more, and here it is." She showed the other.

He took the first, and when he had finished, his hand was trembling.

"I regret to report that things are in a chaos," it

ran. "All of the regular advertising has been withdrawn. The usual entertainment money for salesmen (classed under this head) has been stopped. In consequence, our city trade has tumbled fearfully—and you know how bad it was before. The worst news I have to offer is in regard to Mr. Brainard personally. Our detective reports that his time outside is spent in most questionable company. He has been seen drinking at roof-gardens with a certain dissipated pugilist named Little Sullivan, and was traced with this man to the apartment of a song-and-dance woman named Violette. He seems to be spending money extravagantly and visits certain bohemian quarters in the vicinity of Jones Street, where he puts in his time with disreputable-looking men. I beg leave to advise immediate action.—Mowbray."

"My God!" groaned Houghton. This explained that derisive offer of fifty-one from Consolidated Pepsin.

"And you kept this from me?"

"They said not to worry you," she said. "I—I've had enough for two. Besides, I answered it."

"You did! What——?"

"I told them to wait a little longer."

The father groaned again.

"I just *had* to, daddy; and then today this letter came."

He seized it eagerly. It read: "You were right about waiting. Suspend all action."

"What does it mean?" she asked.

"We'll find out tomorrow," he answered grimly.

The 4:30 train gave John Houghton just time to

reach the office before it closed. Dorothy went home. Her father, roused by the evil news of the day before, had impressed her with all that it might mean in a material way. As though that mattered!—as though anything could hurt her more! She would have been willing to go with Tom Brainard in rags before—but now!

She sat by the telephone with clenched fists, her traveling veil still pushed up on her hat, the lines that had come into her face during the past week deepening with the dusk. At last—a long, sharp ring! "Yes—father—not dine at home—meet you at the Yolland—a guest. Yes—but about Tom—what?—7:30—But about Tom, daddy? Good-by?!! But, daddy!!!"

It was no use. He had hung up. She called feverishly for the office, but the reply was, "They do not answer." Mechanically she went up to her room. "The blue mousseline, Susan," she said.

As the maid laid it out, she walked the floor. Through the window the park lay green and inviting. She longed to fly to the cool grass and run—and run——

From below came the loud, rasping notes of a street-piano that, in some incomprehensible fashion, had wandered to the deserted row of houses. The noise, for all that there was a pleasing swing to the air, irritated her. She threw the man a quarter. "Go away," she waved.

At last the maid said her mistress was ready, and Dorothy, without questioning the decision, allowed herself to be put into the brougham.

The drive seemed hours long, and then—her

father's face told her nothing. Without a word, he led her to a reception-room. As they entered, a figure sprang to meet them.

For a moment she hesitated. Then, "Tom!" she cried, and caught his hand.

He saw the whiteness of her face, and all the yearnings of their separation matched it upon his.

"Dorothy!" he faltered.

Her father interrupted. "Tom is to explain how he has quadrupled our business in the last week."

A sudden weakness seized her. She followed them unsteadily. Seated at a table, however, she was able to smile again. At that moment, the orchestra, striking up, suddenly caught her attention. "Tum—tum-tum—tum-tum—tum"—that haunting, swinging melody of the street-piano.

"What tune is that?" she asked.

Brainard smiled. "*That* is a tune that has suddenly become popular. Any night you may see hundreds of East Side children dancing on the asphalt and singing it."

"Yes," she said. "I heard it on a street-piano."

"It's called," he went on, "'My Lulu Tulu Girl.' All the grinders have it. Billy Tompkins, Noughty-three, who lives in the Jones Street social settlement, worked that for me. Those dagoes worship him—saved a kid's life or something."

A light came into John Houghton's eyes.

"That's part of the scheme. Aspwell wrote the song. I found him down in bohemia working on an opera. But, for the sake of old days in the senior extravaganza, he turned off 'My Lulu Tulu Girl.' You know those orders on your desk are for our new brand, 'Lulu Tulu.' The song was introduced two weeks ago at the Metropolitan Roof by Violette, a young lady who married our old football trainer, Little Sullivan. We'll hear her later—I have tickets. Then we'll go to Leith's; there's a turn there by 'Jim Bailey and his Six Lulu Tulu Girls'—rather vulgar (while they dance they chew the gum and perform calisthenics with it) but it seems to go. Then——"

"Tom!"

"After we've dined, I'll show you our regular magazine and newspaper advertising in the reading-room—double space. You see, I couldn't ask you to increase, so I stopped it for a time and saved up. But I hope you'll stand for it regularly. It's mainly pictures of Miss Lulu Tulu in a large Florodora hat, with verses below apostrophizing the poetry of motion of her jaws. Then there's a line of limericks about the adventures of the 'Lulu Tulu Gummies'—small gum-headed tykes—always in trouble until they find Lulu. I got Phillips to do that as a personal favor."

"Also Noughty-something, I suppose," remarked Houghton.

"Yes. But he graduated before my time. I knew his work in the college annual. He's in the magazines now. Then I got Professor Wheaton—'Jimmy the Grind' we used to call him—his folks wanted him to be a poet—imagine Jimmy a poet!—I got Professor Wheaton to give us some readers on 'Tulu as a Salivary Stimulant,' 'The Healthful Effect of Pure Saliva on Food Products' and 'The Degenerative Effect of Artificially Relieving an Organ of its Proper Functions.' That hits the Pepsin people, you see——"

And so it ran—until he had covered his plan fully, and Dorothy's face with happy smiles.

"Tom," said the father, "if I had opened that letter instead of Dolly!"

Dorothy suddenly became demure under their gaze, and sought to change the subject. "Then you admit, daddy, that a college man is of some use?"

"I'll admit that Tom got the business. But that was because he is naturally clever and business-like, not because——"

"Just a moment," said Brainard. "I think I can show that you're mistaken. I found out that Pepper was doing the wrong thing—by the first rule of criticism (freshman English): 'What is the author trying to do? Does he do it? Is it worth doing?' Substitute 'advertising man' for 'author' and you have a business that is worth doing (since you continue it)—and by the other two questions I saw his 'incongruity of subject-matter and expression.' My economics taught me the 'law of supply and demand.' 'Analytical research of original authorities' taught me where the demand was. There was only the problem of a cause to stimulate it. Through 'deductive logic' and 'psychology' I got the cause that would appeal, and the effect worked out in an increased demand which we were ready to supply—just like a problem in math."

The elder man smiled. "I don't understand a word you say, but it seems to have *worked* well. In the future, bring in as many of your Noughty friends as we need. I'll answer for Kaufmann."

The other shook his head. "I'm not sure they would be any too anxious."

Houghton gasped in surprise. "What's that—they wouldn't be anxious to go into *business!* Why not?"

"Why not?" There was equal amazement in the younger man's tone. "Would you be anxious to leave a place where you're surrounded by friends you've tried—friends that won't stab you in the back the next minute and call it a 'business deal'—where you're respected and in control of things, and plunge out to become a freshman in the world-life, to do the sorting and trying all over again?"

"I remember—I remember——"

"And besides, what right has any one to assume that *business* is above art, charity or even mere learning? Billy Tompkins, in the slums helping dagoes, is a failure to his father—so is Aspwell with his opera—so is Williams with his spectacles in his lab. But—who knows—when the Great Business is finally balanced——" He stopped, conscious that he was growing too rhetorical.

"If you loved college ideals so much more than business," observed Houghton, "then why did you come to us?"

A different light stole into the younger man's eyes. "Because"—he answered, "because I loved something else better than either." And he reached his hand under the cloth to one who understood.

That is all—except that the next offer of Consolidated Pepsin was, "Will you please name your own terms?"

THE TEWANA

BY

HERMAN WHITAKER

Reprinted from *The Blue Mule*
A Western Magazine of Stories, of February, 1906
by permission

THE TEWANA

SHE WAS a Tewana of the Tehuantepec Isthmus, a primal woman, round-armed, deep-breasted, shapely as the dream on which Canova modeled Venus. Her skin was of the rich gold hue that marks the blood unmuddied by Spanish strain; to see her, poised on a rich hip by the river's brink, wringing her tresses after the morning bath, it were justifiable to mistake her for some beautiful bronze. Moreover, it were easy to see her, for, in Tehuantepec, innocence is thoughtless as in old Eden. When Paul Steiner passed her one morning, she gave him the curious open-eyed stare of a deer, bade him a pleasant "*Buenos dias, Señor!*" and would have proceeded, undisturbed, with her toilet, but that he spoke. In this he was greatly mistaken. Gringos there are—praise the saints!—who can judge Tehuantepec by the insight of kindred purity, but Paul had to learn by the more uncomfortable method of a stone in the face.

He ought not, however, to be too severely handled for his dulness. Though a mining engineer, nature had endowed him with little beyond the algebraic qualities necessary to the profession; a German-

American, a dull birth and heredity had predestined him for that class which clothes its morality in fusty black and finds safety in following its neighbor in the cut of its clothes and conduct. As then, he was not planned for original thinking, it is not at all surprising that he should—when pitchforked by Opportunity into the depths of tropical jungles—lose his moral bearings, fail to recognize a virtue that went in her own golden skin, and so go down before a temptation that, of old, populated the sexless desert.

That his error continued in the face of Andrea's stone is certainly more remarkable, though this also should be charged rather against her mismarksmanship than to the wearing quality of his electro-plate morality. It is doubtful if even the ancient Jews had found "stoning" as efficacious a "cure for souls" had they thrown wide as she. Anyway, Paul stood "unconvicted," as the revivalists have it, and being moved to chagrin instead of shame, he carried the story of Andrea's surprising modesty to Bachelder.

Here was a man of other parts. An artist, he had traced the spinning meridians over desert and sea, following the fluttering wing of the muse till she rewarded his deathless hope by pausing for him in this small Indian town. Expecting to stay a week, he had remained fifteen years, failing to exhaust in that long time a tithe of its form and color. Screened by tropical jungle, a mask of dark palms laced with twining *bejucas*, it sat like a wonderfully blazoned cup in a wide green saucer that was edged with the purple of low environing hills—a brimming cup of inspiration. Save where some oaken grill supplied an ashen note, its adobe streets burned in smoldering rose, purple and gold—the latter always predominant. It glowed in the molten sunlight, shone in the soft satin of a woman's skin; the very dust rose in auriferous clouds from the wooden-wheeled ox-carts. But for its magenta tiling, the pillared market stood, a huge monochrome, its deep yellows splashed here and there with the crimson of the female hucksters' dresses. This was their every-day wear—a sleeveless bodice, cut low over the matchless amplitudes and so short that the smooth waist showed at each uplift of the round, bronze arms; a skirt that was little more than a cloth wound about the limbs; a shawl, all of deep blood color. Small wonder that he had stayed on, and on, and on, while the weeks merged into months, and months into years.

He lived in the town's great house, an old feudal hacienda with walls two yards thick, recessed windows oaken grilled, and a pleasant patio where the hidalgo could take his ease under cocoanut palms and lemon trees while governments went to smash without. Here Bachelder was always to be found in the heat of the day, and here he listened with huge disgust to Paul's story. Because of their faith, strength and purity—according to their standards—he had always sworn by the Tewana women, setting them above all others, and though a frank sinner against accepted moral codes, he would never have confused nudity with vice.

"Man!" he exclaimed—so loudly that Rosa, his housekeeper, imagined that something was going wrong again with the painting—"Man! all the dollars you will ever earn would buy nothing more than her stone! If you want her, you will have to marry her."

"Oh, don't look so chopfallen!" he went on, scornfully, when Paul blinked. "I mean marriage as she counts it. You will have to court her for a couple of months—flowers, little gifts, small courtesies, that sort of thing; then, if she likes you, she will come and keep your house. When, later, you feel like settling down in the bosom of respectability, there won't be a shred of law to hold you."

Now if Paul lacked wit to analyze and apply to his own government a moral law that has evolved from the painful travail of the generations, it does not follow that he was too stupid to feel irony. Reddening, he put forth the usual declaimer of honorable intention with the glib tongue of passion. He meant well by the girl! Would give her a good home, find her better than she had ever been found in her life! As for marrying? He was not of the marrying kind! Never would! and so on, finishing with a vital question—did Bachelder know where she lived?

His color deepened under the artist's sarcastic glance. "So that's what you're after? I wondered why you picked me for a father confessor. Well, I don't, but you won't have any trouble in finding her. All the women sell something; she's sure to be on the market in the morning. You will get her quite easily. The girls seem to take pride in keeping a Gringo's house—I don't know why, unless it be that they are so dazzled by the things we have that they cannot see us for what we are."

A thousand crimson figures were weaving in and out the market's chrome pillars when Paul entered next morning, but though it was hard to single one person from the red confusion, luck led him almost immediately to where Andrea stood, a basket of tortillas at her feet. Lacking customers, just then, she leaned against a pillar, her scarlet flaming against its chrome, thoughtful, pensive, as Bachelder painted her for "The Enganchada," the girl sold for debt. Her shawl lay beside her basket, so her hair, that had flown loose since the morning bath, fell in a cataract over the polished amplitudes of bosom and shoulders. Save when feeling shot them with tawny flashes—as waving branches filter mottled sunlight on brown waters—her eyes were dark as the pools of Lethe, wherein men plunge and forget the past. They brought forgetfulness to Paul of his moral tradition, racial pride, the carefully conned apology which he did not remember until, an hour later, he fed her entire stock in trade to his dog. It was better so. Black, brown or white women are alike sensitive to the language of flowers, and the lilies he left in her basket served him more sweetly than could his stammering tongue. Next morning, curiosity replaced hostility in her glance, and when he left the market, her brown gaze followed him beyond the portals. Needs not, however, to linger over the courtship. Sufficient that color of skin does not affect the feminine trait that forgiveness comes easier when the offense was provoked by one's own beauty; the story goes on from the time that Andrea moved into his house with a stock of household gear that extorted musical exclamations from all her girl friends.

To their housekeeping Andrea contributed only her handsome body with a contained cargo of unsuspected qualities and virtues that simply dazzled

Paul as they cropped out upon the surface. In public a Tewana bears herself staidly, carrying a certain dignity of expression that of itself reveals how, of old, her forbears came to place limits to the ambition of the conquering Aztec and made even Spanish dominion little more than an uncomfortable name. Though, through courtship, Andrea's stern composure had shown no trace of a thaw, it yet melted like snow under a south wind when she was once ensconced in their little home. Moreover, she unmasked undreamed of batteries, bewildering Paul with infinite variety of feminine complexities. She would be arch, gay, saucy, and in the next breath fall into one of love's warm silences, watching him with eyes of molten bronze. She taught him the love of the tropics without transcending modesty. Also she astonished him, negatively, by the absence of those wide differences of nature and feeling between her and the cultured women of his own land that reading in the primal school of fiction had led him to expect. He learned from her that woman is always woman under any clime or epoch. The greater strength of her physique lessened, perhaps, the vine-like tendency, yet she clung sufficiently to satisfy the needs of his masculinity; and she displayed the feminine unreason, at once so charming and irritating, with sufficient coquetry to freshen her love. Her greatest charm, however, lay in the dominant quality of brooding motherhood, the birthright of primal women and the very essence of femininity. After one of those sweet silences, she would steal on him from behind, and pull his head to her bosom with such a squeeze as a loving mother gives her son.

Yet, under even this mood, her laughter lay close to the surface, and nothing tapped its merry flow quicker than Paul's Spanish. Picking up the language haphazard, he had somehow learned to apply the verb *tumblar* to describe the pouring out of coffee, and he clung to it after correction with a persistence that surely inhered in his dogged German blood. "*Tumbarlo el café!*" he would say, and she would repeat it, faithfully mimicking his accent.

"Tumble out the coffee!" following it with peals of laughter. Or, turning up a saucy face, she would ask, "Shall I tumble out more coffee?" and again the laughter which came as readily at her own misfit attempts at English.

These, few and simple, were learned of Bachelder's woman, and sprung on Paul as surprises on his return from visiting the mining properties, which required his frequent presence. For instance, slipping to his knee on one such occasion, with the great heart of her pulsing against him, she sighed: "I love thee, lovest thou me?"

A lesson from Bachelder pleased him less. Knowing Paul's pride in his German ancestry, and having been present when, in seasons of swollen pride, he had reflected invidiously in Andrea's presence on Mexico and all things Mexican, the artist, in a wicked moment, taught her to lisp "*Hoch der Kaiser!*" *lèse-majesté* that almost caused Paul a fainting-fit.

"You shouldn't have taught her that," he said to Bachelder. But the mischief was done. Whenever, thereafter, through torment of insect or obsession of national pride, he animadverted on her country, she silenced him with the treasonable expression.

She learned other than English from Bachelder's woman, sweating out the dog days in Rosa's kitchen, experimenting with the barbaric dishes Gringos love. She slaved for his comfort, keeping his linen, her house and self so spotlessly clean that as Paul's passion waned, affection grew up in its place—the respectful affection that, at home, would have afforded a permanent basis for a happy marriage. When, a year later, their baby came, no northern benedict could have been more proudly happy.

Watching him playing with the child, Bachelder would wonder if his union also would terminate like all the others of his long experience. In her, for it was a girl baby, Paul's fairness worked out, as she grew, in marvelous delicacies of cream and rose, weaving, moreover, a golden woof through the brown of her hair. From her mother she took a lithe perfection of form. At two she was well started for a raving beauty, and as much through his love for her as for Andrea, Paul had come, like Bachelder, to swear by the Tewana women.

He might have been swearing by them yet, but his company's business suddenly called him north, and no man could have bidden a white wife more affectionate farewell or have been more sure of his own return. "It is a comfort to know that your woman won't go gadding while you are away, and that is more than a fellow can make sure of at home." These were his last words to Bachelder.

He was to be absent two months, but after he had reported adversely on a mine in Sonora, he was ordered to expert a group in far Guerrera, where the mountains turn on edge and earth tosses in horrible tumult. Then came a third order to report in New York for personal conference. Thus the months did sums in simple addition while Andrea waited, serenely confident of his return. Not that she lacked experience of deserted wives, or based hope on her own attractions. Her furious mother love simply could not form, much less harbor, the possibility of Paul's deserting their pretty Lola.

And, barring her loneliness, the year was kind to her, feeding her mother love with small social triumphs. For one, Lola was chosen to sit with three other tots, the most beautiful of Tewana's children, at the feet of the Virgin in the Theophany of the "Black Christ" at the eastern fiesta. From morning to mirk midnight, it was a hard vigil. By day the vaulted church reeked incense; by night a thousand candles guttered under the dark arches, sorely afflicting small, weary eyelids; yet Lola sat it out like a small thoroughbred, earning thereby the priest's kindly pat and her mother's devoted worship.

Then, on her third saint day, the small girl donned her first fiesta costume, a miniature of the heirlooms which descend from mother to daughter, each generation striving to increase the magnificence of the costume just as it strove to add to the gold pieces in the chain which did triple duty as hoard, dowry and necklace. Andrea subtracted several English sovereigns from her own to start Lola's, and, with the American gold eagle, the gift of Bachelder, her *padrino*, godfather, they made an affluent beginning for so small a girl. As for the costume? Its silk, plush, velours, were worked by Andrea's clever fingers curiously and wondrously, even when judged by difficult Tewana standards. Bachelder painted the small thing, kneeling by her mother's side before the great gold altar. Her starched skirt, with its band of red velours, stands of itself leveling her head, so that she looks for all the world like a serious cherub peering out from a wonderfully embroidered bath-cabinet. But ah! the serious devotion of the faces! The muse Bachelder had followed so faithfully was hovering closely when his soul flamed out upon that canvas. It ranks with his "Enganchada." Either would bring him fame, yet they rest, face to face, in a dusty locker, awaiting the day when time or death shall cure the ache that a glimpse of either brings him.

Two months after that canvas was put away, eighteen counting from the day of his departure, Bachelder walked, one day, down to the primitive post-office to see if the mail that was due from the little fishing port of Salina Cruz contained aught for him. *Waded* would better describe his progress, for it was the middle of the rains; water filled the air, dropping in sheets from a livid sky; the streets were rivers running full over the cobble curbs. Such white planters as came in occasionally from the jungle country had been housefast upon their plantations for this month, and, having the town pretty much to himself, the artist's thought turned naturally to Paul, who used to bring doubtful mitigation to his isolation.

He had written the artist twice, but now six months had elapsed since the last letter. "He'll never come back," the artist muttered. "Poor Andrea! But it is better—now."

Warm with the pity the thought inspired, he turned the corner into the street that led to the post-office, and was almost run down by the first mule of a train that came driving through the rain.

"Bachelder!" the rider cried.

It was surely Paul. Pulling up his beast, he thrust a wet hand from under his rain poncha, then, turning in his saddle, he spoke to the woman who rode behind him, "Ethel, this is Mr. Bachelder."

The alternative had happened! As a small hand thrust back the hood of mackintosh, Bachelder found himself staring at a sweet face, while an equally sweet greeting was drowned by echoing questions in his mind. "Good God!" he first thought. "Why did he bring her here?" And upon that immediately followed, "How ever did he get her?"

An evening spent with the pair at the small Mexican hotel increased his wonder. Pleasant, pretty, of a fine sensibility and intellectual without loss of femininity, the girl would have been fitly mated with a man of the finest clay. How could she have married Paul? Bachelder thought, and correctly, that he discerned the reason in a certain warmth of romantic feeling that tinged her speech and manner. Daughter of an Episcopal clergyman in Paul's native town, she had sighed for something different from the humdrum of small teas, dinners, parochial calls, and when Paul came to her with the glamour of tropical travel upon him, she married, mistaking the glamour for him.

"She loved me for the dangers I had passed!" the artist mused, quoting Shakespeare, on his way home. "What a tragedy when she discovers him for a spurious Othello!"

Dropping into the studio next morning, Paul answered the other question. "Why not?" he asked, with a touch of ancestral stolidity. "My work is here. Andrea?" His next words plainly revealed that while his moral plating had cracked and peeled under tropical heat, the iron convention beneath had held without fracture. He began: "It was a beastliness that we committed——"

"That *you* committed," Bachelder sharply corrected. "And what of the child?"

Blinking in the old fashion, Paul went on, "I was coming to that. She cannot be allowed to grow up a little Mexican. I shall adopt her and have her properly educated." Here he looked at Bachelder as though expecting commendation for his honorable intention, and, receiving none, went on, dilating on his plans for the child as if resolved to earn it. Yet, setting aside this patent motive, it was easy to see as he warmed to his subject that Andrea had not erred in counting on Lola to bring him back. With her beauty she would do any man proud! The whole United States would not be able to produce her rival! She should have the best that money could give her!

Wondering at the curious mixture of class egotism, paternal tenderness and twisted morality, Bachelder listened to the end, then said, "Of course, Mrs. Steiner approves of a ready-made family?"

Paul's proud feathers draggled a little, and he reddened. "Well—you see—she thinks Lola is the daughter of a dead mining friend. Some day, of course, I'll tell her. In fact, the knowledge will grow on her. But not now. It wouldn't do. She couldn't understand."

"No?" But the quiet sarcasm was wasted on Paul, and the artist continued, "Aren't you leaving Andrea out of your calculations?"

Paul ruffled like an angry gobbler. His eyes took on an ugly gleam, his jaw stuck out, his expression incarnated Teutonic obstinacy. "Oh, she'll have to be fixed. Luckily it doesn't take much to buy these savage women; their feelings are all on the surface. I'll give her the house, furniture, and a hundred dollars cash. That should make up for the loss of——"

"——a husband?" Bachelder's face darkened. Throughout the conversation he had worn an air of suppression, as though holding, by an effort, something back. Now he straightened with a movement that was analogous to the flexure of a coiled spring. His lips opened, closed again, and he went on with his quiet questioning. "For a husband, yes. They are easy stock to come by. But not for the child of her labor. Supposing she refuses?"

Paul's eyes glinted under his frown. "Then the Jefe-Politico earns the hundred dollars and the law gives her to me."

The spring uncoiled. "Never! She died a month ago of yellow fever."

Under Teuton phlegm lies an hysteria that rivals that of the Latin races. Paul's flame died to ashes and he burst out sobbing, throwing his hands up and out with ungainly gestures. Looking down upon his awkward grief, Bachelder half regretted the just anger that caused him to slip the news like a lightning bolt; he would have felt sorrier but that he perceived Paul's sorrow rooted in the same colossal egotism that would have sacrificed the mother on the altars of its vast conceit. He knew that Paul was grieving for himself, for lost sensations of pride, love and pleasure that he could never experience again. When the ludicrous travesty had partly spent itself, he stemmed the tide with a question.

"If you don't care to see Andrea, I can make the settlements you hinted at."

Paul glanced up, stupidly resentful, through his tears. "The child is dead. That is all off."

"You will do nothing for her?" As much to prop an opinion of human nature that was already too low for comfort as in Andrea's interest, Bachelder asked the question.

"She has the house furnishings," Paul sullenly answered. "That leaves her a sight better off than she was before she knew me."

Rising, the artist walked over to the window. "The river is rising," he said, when he could trust himself to speak. "Another foot, and away goes the bridge. When do you go to the mine?"

"Tomorrow."

"Mrs. Steiner goes with you?"

"No, too wet."

Bachelder hesitated. "I'd offer you my quarters, but—you see I am neither married nor unmarried."

"No!" Paul agreed with ponderous respectability. "It would never do. Besides, I've hired a house of the Jefe-Politico; the one that crowns the Promontory. When the rain slacks we'll move out to the mine."

"There is one thing I should like," he added as he rose to go. "If you would have a stone put over the child's grave—something nice—you're a better judge than me,—I'll——"

"Too late," the artist interrupted. "Andrea broke up her necklace; put savings of eighteen generations into the finest tomb in the cemetery." He looked curiously at Paul, but his was that small order of mind which persistently fixes responsibility for the most inevitable calamity upon some person. To the day of his death he would go on taxing the child's death against Andrea; he did not even comment on this last proof of her devoted love.

After he was gone, Bachelder returned to his window, just in time to see the bridge go. A thin stream in summer, meandering aimlessly between wide banks, the river now ran a full half-mile wide, splitting the town with its yeasty race. An annual occurrence, this was a matter of small moment to the severed halves. Each would pursue the even tenor of its way till the slack of the rains permitted communication by canoe and the rebuilding of the bridge. But it had special significance now in that Andrea lived on the other bank.

He wondered if the news of Paul's return had crossed, muttering: "Poor girl, poor girl!" Adding, a moment later: "But happier than the other. Poor little Desdemona!"

How melancholy is the voice of a flood! Its resurgent dirge will move a new-born babe to frightened wailing, and stirs in strong men a vague uneasiness that roots in the vast and calamitous experience of the race. Call of hungry waters, patter of driving rain, sough of the weird wind, it requires good company and a red-coal fire to offset their moanings of eternity. Yet though the fireless tropics could not supply one, and she lacked the other, the storm voices were hardly responsible for Ethel Steiner's sadness the third morning after her arrival.

Neither was it due to the fact that Paul had failed to come in the preceding night from the mine. Seeming relieved rather than distressed, she had gone quietly to bed. No, it was neither the storm, his absence, nor any of the small miseries that afflict young wives. Poor Desdemona! The curtain was rising early on the tragedy which Bachelder foresaw. Already the glamour was falling from Paul to the tropics, where it rightfully belonged; this morning she was living her bitter hour, fighting down the premonition of a fatal mistake.

What with her thoughtful pauses, she made but a slow toilet, and when the last rebellious curl had been coaxed to its place behind her small ear, she turned, sighing, to the window. One glance, and she started back, pale, clutching her hands. A rocky snout, thrusting far out into the belly of the river's great bow, the Promontory stood high above the ordinary flood level. Once, in far-away Aztec times, a Tewana tradition had it that a cloudburst in the rains had swept it clear of houses, and now Time's slow cycle had brought the same deadly coincidence. Where, last night, a hundred lights had flickered below her windows, a boil of yellow waters spread, cutting off her house, the last and highest, from the mainland. Black storm had drowned the cries of fleeing householders. The flood's mighty voice, bellowing angrily for more victims as it swallowed house after house, had projected but a faint echo into her dreams. Now, however, she remembered that

Carmencita, her new maid, had failed to bring in the morning coffee.

Wringing her hands and loudly lamenting the deadly fear that made her forget her mistress, Carmencita, poor girl, was in the crowd that was helping Paul and Bachelder to launch a freight canoe. When Paul—who had ridden in early from the little village, where he had been storm-stayed—had tried to impress a crew, the peon boatman had sworn volubly that no pole would touch bottom and that one might as well try to paddle the town as a heavy canoe against such a flood. But when Bachelder stepped in and manned the big sweep, a half-dozen followed. Notwithstanding, their river wisdom proved. Paddling desperately, they gained no nearer than fifty yards to the pale face at the window.

"Don't be afraid!" Bachelder shouted, as they swept by. "We'll get you next time!"

If the walls did not melt? Already the flood was licking with hungry tongues the adobe bricks where the plaster had bulged and fallen, and an hour would fly while they made a landing and dragged the canoe back for another cast. The boatmen knew! Their faces expressed, anticipated that which happened as they made the landing half a mile below. Paul saw it first. Through the swift passage he sat, facing astern, helplessly clutching the gunwale, and his cry, raucous as that of a maimed animal, signaled the fall of the house. Sobbing, he collapsed on the bank.

Bachelder looked down upon him. Momentarily stunned, his thought returned along with a feeling of relief that would have framed itself thus in words: "Poor Desdemona! Now she will never know!"

"*Señor! Señor! Mira!*" A boatman touched his shoulder.

Two heads were swirling down the flood, a light and a dark. Bachelder instantly knew Ethel, but, as yet, he could not make out the strong swimmer who was at such infinite pains to hold the fair head above water. Though, time and again, the dark head went under for smotheringly long intervals, Ethel's never once dipped, and, up or down, the swimmer battled fiercely, angling across the flood. She—for long hair stamped her a woman—gained seventy yards shoreward while floating down two hundred. Three hundred gave her another fifty. So, rising and sinking, she drifted with her burden down upon Paul and Bachelder. At fifty yards the artist caught a glimpse of her face, but not till she was almost under their hands did Paul recognize the swimmer.

"Andrea!" he shouted.

Reassured by Bachelder's cheery shout, Ethel had busied herself collecting her watch and other trinkets from the bureau till a smacking of wet feet caused her to turn, startled. A woman stood in the door, a woman of matchless amplitudes, such as of old tempted the gods from heaven. Stark naked, save for the black cloud that dripped below her waist, her bronze beauty was framed by the ponderous arch.

"I don't know who you are," Ethel said, recovering, "but you are very beautiful, and, under the circumstances, welcome. Under ordinary conditions, your advent would have been a trifle embarrassing. I must find you a shawl before the canoes come. Here, take this blanket."

She little imagined how embarrassing the visitation might have proved under very ordinary conditions. Though the news of Paul's return did cross before the bridge was carried away, Andrea did not hear it till that morning, and she would never have had it from a Tewana neighbor. They pitied the bereavement to which widowhood in the most cruel of forms was now added. But among them she unfortunately counted a peon woman of the upper Mexican plateau, one of the class which took from the Conquest only Spanish viciousness to add to Aztec cruelty. Jealous of Andrea's luck—as they had deemed it—in marriage, Pancha had thirsted for the opportunity which came as they drew water together that morning from the brink of the flood.

"'Tis the luck of us all!" she exclaimed, malevolently ornamenting her evil tidings. "They take their pleasure of us, these Gringos, then when the hide wrinkles, ho for a prettier! They say Tewana hath not such another as his new flame, and thy house is a hovel to that he fits up for her on the Promontory."

Here the hag paused, for two good reasons. That the barbed shaft might sink deep and rankle from Andrea's belief that her supplanter was a girl of her tribe, but principally because, just then, she went down under the ruins of her own *olla*. A fighter, after her kind, with many a cutting to her credit, she cowered like a snarling she-wolf among the sharp potsherds cowed by the enormous anger she had provoked; lay and watched while the tall beauty ripped shawl, slip and skirt from her magnificent limbs, then turned and plunged into the flood. Pancha rose and shook her black fist, hurling curses after.

"May the alligators caress thy limbs, the fishes pluck thine eyes, the wolves crack thy bleached bones on the strand."

That was the lightest of them, but, unheeding, Andrea swam on. As her own house stood in the extreme skirt of the town, the Promontory lay more than a mile below, but she could see neither it nor the night's devastation because of the river's bend. Because of the same bend, she had the aid of the current, which set strongly over to the other shore, but apart from this the river was one great danger. Floating logs, huge trees, acres of tangled greenery, the sweepings of a hundred miles of jungle, covered its surface with other and ghastlier trove. Here the saurians of Pancha's curse worried a drowned pig, there they fought over a cow's swollen carcass; yet because of carrion taste or food plethora, they let her by. There an enormous saber, long and thick as a church, turned and tumbled, threshing air and water with enormous spreading branches, creating dangerous swirls and eddies. These she avoided, and, having swum the river at ebb and flood every day of her life from a child, she now easily clove its roar and tumble; swam on, her heat unabated by the water's chill, till, sweeping around the bend, she sighted the lone house on the Promontory.

That gave her pause. Had death, then, robbed her anger? The thought broke the spring of her magnificent energy. Feeling at last the touch of fatigue, she steered straight for the building and climbed in, to rest, at a lower window, without a thought of its being occupied till Ethel moved above.

Who shall divine her thoughts as, standing there

in the door, she gazed upon her rival? Did she not recognize her as such, or was she moved by the touch of sorrow, aftermath of the morning's bitterness, that still lingered on the young wife's face? Events seemed to predicate the former, but, be that as it may, the eyes which grief and despair had heated till they flamed like small crucibles of molten gold, now cooled to their usual soft brown; smiling, she refused the proffered blanket.

"*Ven tu! Ven tu!*" she exclaimed, beckoning. Her urgent accent and gesture carried her meaning, and without question Ethel followed down to a lower window.

"But the canoe?" she objected, when Andrea motioned for her to disrobe. "It will soon be here!"

"*Canoa?*" From the one word Andrea caught her meaning. "*No hay tiempo. Mira!*"

Leaning out, Ethel looked and shrank back, her inexperience convinced by a single glance at the wall. She assisted the strong hands to rip away her encumbering skirts. It took only a short half-minute, and with that afforded time for a small femininity to come into play. Placing her own shapely arm against Ethel's, Andrea murmured soft admiration at the other's marvelous whiteness. But it was done in a breath. Slipping an arm about Ethel's waist, Andrea jumped with her from the window, one minute before the soaked walls collapsed.

If Ethel's head had remained above, she might have retained her presence of mind, and so have made things easier for her saviour, but, not supposing that the whole world contained a mature woman who could not swim, Andrea loosed her as they took the water. A quick dive partially amended the error, retrieving Ethel, but not her composure. Coming up, half-choked, she grappled Andrea, and the two went down together. The Tewana could easily have broken the white girl's grip and—have lost her. Instead, she held her breath and presently brought her senseless burden to the surface.

Of itself, the struggle was but a small thing to her strength, but coming on top of the long swim under the shock and play of emotion, it left her well nigh spent. Yet she struggled shoreward, battling, waging the war of the primal creature that yields not till Death himself reenforces bitter odds.

To this exhaustion, the tales that float in Tehuantepec lay her end, and Bachelder has never taken time to contradict them. But as she floated almost within reach of his hand, she steadied at Paul's shout as under an accession of sudden strength, and looked at her erstwhile husband. Then, if never before, she knew—him, as well as his works! From him her glance flashed to the fair face at her shoulder. What power of divination possessed her? Or was it Bachelder's fancy? He swears to the chosen few, the few who understand, that her face lit with the same glory of tender pity that she held over her sick child. Then, before they could reach her, she shot suddenly up till her bust gleamed wet to the waist, turned, and dived, carrying down the senseless bride.

Shouting, Bachelder also dived—in vain. In vain, the dives of his men. Death, that mighty potentate, loves sweetness full well as a shining mark. Swiftly, silently, a deep current bore them far out on the flooded lands and there scoured a sepulcher safe from saurian teeth, beyond the scope of Pancha's curse. Later, the jungle flowed in after the receding waters and wreathed over the twin grave morning-glories pure as the white wife, glorious orchids rich as Andrea's bronze.

HERE ENDS THE SPINNERS' BOOK OF FICTION
BEING SHORT STORIES BY CALIFORNIA WRITERS
COMPILED BY THE BOOK COMMITTEE OF THE
SPINNERS' CLUB FOR THE SPINNERS' BENEFIT
FUND INA D. COOLBRITH FIRST BENEFICIARY
ILLUSTRATED BY VARIOUS WESTERN ARTISTS
THE DECORATIONS BY SPENCER WRIGHT THE
TYPOGRAPHY DESIGNED BY J. H. NASH PUB
LISHED BY PAUL ELDER AND COMPANY AND
PRINTED FOR THEM AT THE TOMOYE PRESS
NEW YORK NINETEEN HUNDRED AND SEVEN